WILD DOG CITY

Darkeye Volume One

WILD DOG CITY
Darkeye Volume One

Lydia West

Lulu print edition.

First Printing: 2014

ISBN 978-1-312-50029-7

www.koryoswrites.com

Cover art by Aliza Layne.

Dedication

Dedicated to my dog, Asta, who passed away during the completion of this series.

You are loved, and you are missed.

Contents

Acknowledgements

I would like to thank my readers at koryoswrites.com, without whom this series would never have been completed. Your words of encouragement, enthusiasm, art, and especially your critique were all invaluable to me.

I would also like to thank my wonderful cover artist, Aliza Layne, and my good friend Madelaine Morales, who helped me with formatting. Also my parents, who suffered through the nine-month gestation of this series.

Last but most certainly not least, my supporters on Patreon:

Talia Henderson
Not A Lizard
Makinsey
Sparky Lurkdragon
S. W.
Merrick Meyers
Megan Krueger
Emily Aiken

Thank you so much for all of your support!

1
Wild Dogs

It was utterly dark, the cold air sinking in the high concrete tunnel with a dull rushing sound, like the long sigh of an invisible giant. The blackness was really absolute; the platforms and the blandly tiled walls and the trench lined with a metal track were all blanketed in that whispering emptiness. The electric lights that had once lit the subway had long since sputtered out.

But there was a sound, under the humming of air: claws softly scratching concrete.

"Mother!"

The voice was high and strange, the word sharp in the blackness. It came again.

"Mother! Mother, are you here?"

It echoed and faded and the rushing hum continued.

There came a sharp bark, from above.

"Mhumhi!"

"I smell her!" cried the voice. "Oh- I smelled her! Oh, she was here, Sacha, she was here!"

"Mhumhi, come up right away! Hurry!" From far above, where the tunnel sloped, there was a patch of light, arc-shaped, and shadows crossed it.

There was a scrabbling and a scraping, and then a tall, lean dog pushed his way through, squeezing from between a piece of metal siding and a concrete wall, blinking hard in the fierce daylight.

He was not a domestic dog. His coarse coat was patterned brown and black and pale like dappled sunlight. His ears were cupped and round, the expression on his dark face inscrutable, as his skinny tail curled low between his legs.

He was what was called a painted dog: a kind of wild dog.

A little rain was falling, making dark spots on the concrete sidewalk and washing the dust off of the street beyond. The painted dog turned and looked back at the metal siding, sniffing the air. The building he had emerged from was squat and unappealing, all yellow faux-brick with a flat iron roof. There was a door in the wall, a few feet away, but it was heavy, and shut.

A second dog emerged from the hole behind the siding. This one was much smaller, coming barely to Mhumhi's knee, and was solid brown with dark legs. Everything about her was short and squat, even her ears, which were tiny and round, and her eyes were narrow in her small bearlike face.

This dog was called a bush dog, and though she was very small, her expression made it clear that she was just as much a wild dog as her larger companion.

"Don't go down there again, Mhumhi," she said. When she spoke she did not move her lips, but rather opened and closed her mouth, the same harsh sounds that Mhumhi had used emerging somewhere from the back of her throat.

"I think there are dogs that live down there…" she continued, but trailed off, raising a lip slightly in annoyance. Mhumhi was twittering and chirping at her and trying to lick her chin.

"Sacha, I *smelled* her," he whined, between licks- he was mostly bathing her neck, as her chin was so low it was hard for him to get at. "She must be down there- she must have gone down there at some point, sometime…"

"She probably did," Sacha grunted, seeming resigned to the licking. "You don't know how old the scent is."

Mhumhi said nothing to this, but he stopped licking, and trotted a few steps away, looking back at the siding. Sacha eyed him.

"I mean it. Don't go back down there. You'll end up killed, and then what good will that be to us and Kebero?"

"If Mother came back-"

"Don't, Mhumhi."

"But she must be injured, I think, she must be trapped- there were a bunch of rocks that fell down at part of the tunnel, and I was trying to dig at them-"

"She's not injured, Mhumhi," said Sacha, raising her lip a little again, and Mhumhi's tail, which had been wagging, went limp.

"Even if- even if she's dead, I want-"

Sacha's words were hard and flat: "Mother may not be dead."

Mhumhi stiffened. Sacha looked away for a moment.

"Come on, Mhumhi, if you've even got any meat left in you, Kebero is hungry. I've left Kutta with him, but you *know* she'll wander."

Mhumhi cast one last look back at the building, blinking from the rain, and then shook himself and followed her as she moved onto the street.

It was midday, and they were in a mostly unpopulated part of Oldtown, so around them the city was quiet. Squat little buildings walled in bleached white plaster were crammed tight together along the wet, pale street. Here and there the harsh odor of dung or urine marked a dwelling, but both Mhumhi and Sacha did not bother to give it more than a cursory sniff or two.

They stopped to get out of the rain for a moment under the plastic roof of a bus stop, panting, breath steaming. Sacha shook herself, and then again, snorting at the wetness. Mhumhi sat down and half-heartedly scratched at his shoulder with his hind claws.

The building across from them had a half-open door, and Mhumhi saw something peep out at it to look at them: a small face, as small as Sacha's, with grey-and-black markings. It vanished as quickly as it had come.

"Gray fox," said Sacha. Her tone was dismissive.

The gray fox reappeared in the doorway, and beside it, another one poked its head out. This one yapped across the street at them.

"Are you police?"

Mhumhi raised his head, tail wagging slightly against the concrete, but Sacha shot him a look.

"No, he is not!"

This seemed to bewilder the foxes, and they put their heads together and conferred for a moment before the male spoke again.

"But have you heard, about the West Big Park meat dispensary…?"

"We have not!" said Sacha. "Go away!" She uttered a fierce whine. This seemed to startle the foxes so much that they vanished entirely, and the door snapped shut.

"You're so mean," said Mhumhi, rising to his feet and stretching a little. "What do you think they heard? About the dispensary?"

"Rumors," said Sacha. "Like always. Somebody or some pack of somebodies is spreading them around. Stupid."

"Rumors like the dispensary doesn't give out meat anymore?"

"Stupid," Sacha repeated. "Trying to make dogs get upset. It's only mealy little foxes who'll get worked up about it, I think. The dispensaries won't stop giving out meat. We'd starve."

Mhumhi thought this statement over. He decided not to point out that their hunger might not be what caused the dispensaries to run or not; Sacha did not like being corrected.

"The rain's lighter," she said, peering out. "Let's go."

Together they trotted through the crammed-in dwellings of Oldtown, gradually reaching more populated areas. Other dogs wandered listlessly around in the wet; most of them were foxes, or the size of foxes. They watched lanky Mhumhi pass with a certain wary focus, but the vast majority of them knew of him already, and if they didn't they'd notice how meekly he followed the diminutive Sacha. He was not like other painted dogs.

They came to a sort of groove in the street with a metal rail running through it- a track for a trolley. Sacha sniffed at it warily and then hopped over it.

"I don't think it'll sting today," she told Mhumhi, "but don't touch it anyway. I don't trust it."

Mhumhi made a show of stepping over it, posturing with his longer legs. She snorted at him and then turned to continue walking, stub tail up and rigid.

They had arrived on their home street, and Mhumhi let his tongue hang out when he saw their house. It was one of those same packed-in buildings, visibly indistinguishable from the others, but the mingled scent of his small family made him feel warm in the chilly rain.

Sacha ran up to the front wall and backed up against it, nearly doing a handstand on her front paws, to mark it with urine.

"Liduma won't like that," said Mhumhi, waving his tail.

"If the police ever come here, they can tell me how much they don't like it," replied Sacha, and she ran to the door and nosed it open. Mhumhi followed after her, joining in her whining and yowling when he crossed the threshold with his own chirps and twittering.

They heard yapping from the second floor, and clattering down the narrow stairs came a medium-sized, cinnamon-colored dog, smaller than Mhumhi but still dwarfing little Sacha. Her black brush of a tail was wagging furiously and she ran to try and lick under

Sacha's chin. Mhumhi bounded in place once or twice and then joined her, bathing poor Sacha, who twisted and growled at them.

"Enough!" she finally barked. "Stop that!"

The cinnamon dog- which was called a dhole- parted her teeth in a smile, her tongue hanging out. Mhumhi panted happily in response and gave her a few licks around her jowls. She put a paw on his shoulder, pushing him away, and sniffed around his forehead and ears.

"Did you go to the subway again?" she asked.

Sacha spoke before she could answer. "Kutta, where's Kebero?"

"Oh, upstairs, he was sleeping," the dhole- Kutta- said, not seeming very interested in the topic. "Mhumhi, did you catch any sign of her?"

"I smelled her, but…" Mhumhi glanced at Sacha. "I don't know how old the scent was. It wasn't strong."

"Well, that's good- that's a start-" Kutta said, eyes bright, but Sacha interrupted her.

"He's not going back. And neither are you." She caught Kutta's gaze in a hard stare until she lowered her head and wagged her tail between her legs.

"I wasn't really planning on it- it's so dark and strange down there- but surely, Sacha, if Mhumhi smelled her, we should keep-"

"Take Mhumhi upstairs," said Sacha. "If he has any meat left in him, he needs to give it up."

"All right," Kutta said, looking away. Mhumhi's tail lowered too, though it was more related to the thing about the meat.

Sacha left them to go lap up some water from the sink embedded in the counter. Kutta nudged Mhumhi with her shoulder and led him up the stairs.

"How old do you think the scent was? Was it urine, or-"

"It was," said Mhumhi, "but…" He hesitated. "Sacha is right, isn't she?"

"That we shouldn't go looking for her?"

"That- that she might have left on purpose."

Kutta swung her head around to stare at him, but before she could reply a puppy burst out at the top of the stairs and began yapping shrilly.

"Oh go away, Kebero, let us through," Kutta said, shoving at his chest with her nose, and he backed off, ears back and rump wagging against the ground. He was sandy-colored, with a white underbelly and a narrow, foxy face: a Simien wolf. He was half-grown, not quite all the way weaned; but Sacha and Kutta could not produce milk for him, so meat was what he got.

Now he danced around Mhumhi's front paws, all a-wag.

"Auuwhooo," he said, his jaws working. "Auu- oo- hun-hungry!"

"Don't try and talk right now, Kebero," said Kutta, turning an ear back. To Mhumhi she added, more softly, "He's been doing this all day. I'm going mad."

Kebero shut his mouth and licked Mhumhi's chin. Mhumhi swallowed hard and leaned away.

"I ate so long ago, I think it's all gone," he said.

Kutta walked over and poked him hard with her nose in the corner of his mouth. With a surprised gag he opened his mouth and regurgitated a small pile of meat onto the floor. Kebero was on it at once, enthusiasm making up for his lack of skill at chewing.

"You puppy, Mhumhi," said Kutta, "hoarding from your brother."

Mhumhi wanted to whine. Until Kebero had gotten there he HAD been the puppy of the family, and hadn't had to give up any of his meat at all.

They left Kebero to his clumsy eating and leapt up together onto the moldy-smelling bed. Kutta started licking the subway dust and rain out of his fur.

"Did Sacha really say Mother left us?" she said, eventually.

"Not just like that," said Mhumhi. "She kind of implied it."

"Sacha always picks on her, you know that," said Kutta. "Mother didn't leave us. I mean- it would be better if she did, I suppose, because it would mean she wasn't hurt badly or- you know. But I know she wouldn't just abandon us like that."

Mhumhi, chin resting on the well-worn coverlet, rotated his ears forward and back, thinking of how Sacha had put it earlier. *Mother may not be dead.*

"Don't listen to Sacha," said Kutta said, more firmly, perhaps guessing at his thoughts, and nudged her head against his. "We're Mother's children. You know, I still think that- that any day she'll come back with..."

She stopped herself, raising her head to look at Kebero, who was sitting on the floor next to the remains of Mhumhi's meat. He was watching them, head tilted. At Kutta's look he licked his lips and gave his ropy tail a tiny wag.

It made Mhumhi recall the day their mother had shown up with him in her mouth, a tiny thing with round eyes and fur that was still dusted dark brown.

"He is Kebero, your new brother," she'd told them. Mhumhi, a year younger then, had not understood at the time the look that Kutta and Sacha exchanged, or why Sacha got up and left whenever their mother entered a room for several days afterward.

"Come up, Kebero," he said now, wagging his tail a little, and Kebero bounded eagerly to his feet and made a clumsy go of jumping up on the bed, sliding halfway back down before he managed to get on top. He situated himself, wagging, in a small space between the longer backs of his siblings.

Kutta made a little sound, not entirely pleased, but rolled over to give Kebero a few licks between the ears.

The three of them dozed together for a while, Kebero occasionally squirming and kicking, listening to the loud patter of rain on the metal roof above them. The acrid smell of it grew stronger, as did the strong scent in the room coming from Mhumhi's wet body. He licked his broad paws, trying to tease it out of his fur, but it was a halfhearted effort at best.

Sacha came up the stairs, hopping over each one, glanced at them, and went left. She disappeared into the other upstairs room.

Mhumhi rolled over with a sigh and stretched, eyes closed, feeling the warm little knot that was Kebero behind him. He indulged himself in a fuzzy half-daydream: his mother had been small, too, smaller than him when he reached his full size, though at one point in his life she was the biggest thing he had ever seen… He could imagine that she was still there, behind him, smelling of milk and warmth and home.

Then the daydream started going sour, because he was reminded of the morning he had woken up to find the spot beside him empty. No- think of other things- think of her voice, he told himself, firmly. She had a strange voice, not like other dogs, with a liquid sibilance to it, but she did not speak very often…

Abruptly he jerked up, out of his half-doze, for from outside there had come a loud howl, a sort of bay of rage, then a volley of fierce barking.

Kutta and Kebero woke up as well, Kebero whining wordlessly, but Mhumhi had already jumped to his feet and was running down the stairs. The barking had not come from a wild dog, but a domestic one- he had just been thinking about his mother's voice-

He nearly bowled over Sacha on his way to the door, and heard her give a startled utterance of some sort, but he paid it no mind and shoved his way through the door and outside onto the wet street.

Outside it was chaos, pure chaos- there was yelping and snarling and blood running through the cracks in the asphalt. And a mass of dogs, most of them small, two of them big and struggling with one another. Mhumhi tripped over a dark-colored fox that was lying very still, and suppressed a frightened shudder, pushing his way through. He was hoping to see a dog with a dirty white coat and a curled tail, smelling of milk and warmth, but when he saw the fighters he fell still.

One was a golden jackal, yapping and snarling, the other was a massive domestic dog, solid and broad, all dense rusty fur. His muzzle was streaming with blood, and when he turned his head all Mhumhi could see was the meat clenched between his teeth and his brilliant blue eyes filled with fear.

2

A Show Of Aggression

The crowd of yapping foxes started to clear rapidly from around the fight once Mhumhi appeared, his size and painted coat enough of a deterrent. The golden jackal backed up a few steps as well, licking her muzzle and growling. The domestic dog stood stock-still, though his tail was tucked. He still had the meat tightly clenched in his bleeding jaws.

"Are you police?" said the golden jackal, glaring at Mhumhi.

"Yes," said Mhumhi, trying to raise his tail a bit to look more important. "What're you fighting over? Has someone stolen that meat?"

The jackal looked him over, her lips still drawn back from her teeth. She was half the size of the big domestic, but easily twice as fierce, especially as Mhumhi could see the teats hanging swollen from her belly.

"That *domestic*," she spat, "is a filthy killer. He's killed before and he'll do it again. You should arrest him."

Mhumhi glanced at the domestic, uneasy now at the size and muscle of him- he was shorter than Mhumhi at the shoulder, but far broader and heavier-looking. The domestic did not move, though, just clutched his meat and stared at Mhumhi with those unnerving blue eyes.

"Who did he kill?"

The jackal gave a loud snarl. "Are you really police? You should know who he's killed. He's a domestic, anyway!"

Her last statement came out high-pitched and confused, and she stared at Mhumhi with an expression of consternation.

There was a yap, and a diminutive little fennec fox ran up to Mhumhi's front paws. "Hey, police, I saw everything that happened!"

Mhumhi glanced down at the fox, who lived in the storm drain down the street, and who definitely knew he was not a member of the police.

"Then what happened?"

"Nothing," said the fox. "He didn't do a thing- he was just walking. She jumped out at him along Food Strip Street and chased him down here. He never even nipped her, and look how she's torn him up!"

"You little rat," growled the jackal, and the fox ducked behind Mhumhi's front legs.

"The way I see it," he continued, from his safer vantage point, "she's just picking on him 'cause he's a domestic and she wants his meat!"

This brought out a great deal of yapping and whining from the foxes that still lingered in the area. Domestic dogs were not well-liked, but they were liked far better than meat thieves. The golden jackal trembled a little as she growled.

"Well, then," said Mhumhi, glancing at the domestic dog. He did seem a little pitiable, such a big fellow, and as the fox had said it was he who was marked all over, not she. "I think you should leave, jackal."

"What?!"

"I'll let you go," said Mhumhi, "but you'd better leave this dog alone from now on. And count yourself lucky he hasn't fought back today."

The jackal seemed shocked by his statement, and glared at him another moment in confusion. The domestic also gazed at him.

Someone in the crowd yapped, and the jackal jumped, and snapped angrily at the air.

"You're not police!" she cried. "I know what you are- you're one of the orphans of that wretched pup thief!"

Mhumhi went stiff with anger at her words, but his tail tucked as she advanced on him, fur bristling.

"You've got no authority here! You're as much as a domestic yourself, you coward!" She snapped her jaws again, threatening, and Mhumhi had to scramble a few steps backwards, ears back, and nearly tripped over the fennec fox as it darted out from underneath him and into the storm drain.

With an angry squeal, suddenly Sacha ran in front of him, all twelve pounds of her, and confronted the jackal with a terrible snarl.

"Get out of here," she spat, as Kutta came to touch shoulders with Mhumhi, wagging her tail against him reassuringly. "Leave my little brother alone!"

"Your little brother," the jackal snorted, but she seemed a bit too nervous to step forward again in the face of Sacha's wrath. "They call you the pack of orphans! You all know that your mother's a filthy kidnapper!"

"Leave!" cried Sacha, and lunged forward, and the jackal leapt and twisted in midair to get away. Kutta added her whistle, and darted forward and snapped at the jackal, who was forced to back up even further.

"I'll tell the real police about this!" she snarled, but she knew she had lost the encounter pretty badly. She ran from the scene with her head and tail very low, and disappeared around a block of houses.

At once Sacha and Kutta turned around and ran to Mhumhi together. "That vicious little thief!" Kutta said, licking his right ear, and Sacha, who was standing up against his shoulder to lick his neck, growled, "You could have taken her, you dumb brute."

Mhumhi shut his eyes, quite overwhelmed, then opened them again. The domestic was slinking away in the opposite direction that the jackal had gone in.

"Wait!" Mhumhi said, struggling to break free of his sisters' affection. "Don't go yet!"

The domestic looked back at him and tucked his rump and ran in a sideways, frightened scuttle. Mhumhi chased him, catching up easily with his lanky legs, wagging his tail.

"I won't hurt you! I just want to ask you- since you're a domestic-"

He caught a flash of the dog's vivid eyes as he looked back again. The meat- not more than a few mouthfuls, covered in blood and drool- swung from his teeth.

"I won't steal your meat!" Mhumhi cried, running to bound along directly beside him, so that he cringed away into a doorway and had to stop.

"It's all right," Mhumhi emphasized, wagging harder- he could hear Kutta and Sacha coming up behind at a more sedate pace, and he wanted to get the domestic to talk before Sacha bared her teeth at him. "I won't steal it- just speak to me."

The domestic either believed him or recognized he had no choice in the matter, for he slowly put down his meat. Mhumhi wagged harder and licked at the blood caking his muzzle as the dog flinched away.

"Tell me," he said, encouragingly, "have you seen any other domestics around this area? Any female domestics?"

"No," said the domestic. His voice was rough and blunt.

"I'm looking for a white female," Mhumhi pressed on, "who's kind of stout, with a curled tail and folded ears- are you sure?"

The domestic hesitated, his jaws open, his lower canines just grazing his upper lip. His thick pointed ears were laid flat against his skull.

"Maybe," he said.

"Maybe!" cried Mhumhi, bouncing on his forepaws. "When? Where?"

The domestic had shrunk back from his excitement, and flinched as Sacha and Kutta came up to flank him.

"Where what?" said Sacha. "You didn't-"

"He says he's seen Mother!" said Mhumhi, eyes alight. "He's seen her, Kutta!"

"Where!" said Kutta at once, leaning towards the domestic. "Where, where did you see her? How recently?"

Mhumhi had to glance at Sacha, but she was standing still, her small eyes devoid of expression.

"Not…" The domestic licked his lips. "Not recently. And only maybe. I saw her… I saw a white dog… She was running towards Big Park."

"Big Park?" said Kutta, exchanging a confused look with Mhumhi. "What would she do there? That's…"

"Domestic!" barked Sacha, making them all jump. "How many days ago did you see her? What did she look like?"

"I don't know," said the domestic, shrinking back. "I don't know how many days ago it was… many… She was white, but her belly was black with dirt… small…"

"Was she carrying milk?"

"I don't know… the dirt was on her."

"And was she hurt?"

"No, not that I saw…"

Sacha let out a small huff. "I see."

Mhumhi and Kutta looked at one another, Mhumhi's tail wagging hard, Kutta's waving more slowly.

"Tell me," said Sacha, pacing a bit before the cringing behemoth, "where are you going with that meat? Who are you taking it to?"

Mhumhi glanced at Kutta again, though she was focused on Sacha now. Domestics did not regurgitate for pups the way they did, which was likely why the domestic had been forced to carry the meat in his jaws, a moving target in the city full of dogs.

He seemed loathe to answer Sacha, glancing furtively from side to side, but a stern whine brought his attention back to her.

"My sister," he said, finally. "She's… she's sick, she cannot feed herself."

"Another domestic?"

"Yes…"

"Too weak to even walk to the dispensary?"

The domestic flashed his pale eyes at her. "It is a long walk… and she will not eat the meat. I must tell her it is from somewhere else."

"Won't eat the meat?" exclaimed Kutta. "Why not? What's the matter with her?"

The domestic gave her a frightened look. "She- she thinks it made her sick. She is childish. I can help her. But I must get her this meat, or she will die."

"And where do you tell her the meat comes from?"

"Where… a… a rat?"

"Is she stupid? She believes meat like that comes from a rat?" Sacha was growling softly now. "You know, that jackal was right about something- there have been dogs that have disappeared lately."

"Sacha!" cried Kutta. Mhumhi felt stunned.

"You and your *sister* don't know anything about the disappearances, do you?"

The domestic whined, a thin sound. "No! I would not- I could not kill a dog! I would not!"

"Sacha, smell the meat!" said Kutta. "It smells like ordinary meat, come on, he's speaking the truth. No one would- I mean, no dog would eat another dog, that's ridiculous!"

"Domestics don't think they're dogs," growled Sacha, but she sniffed at the meat, then took a few steps back. "Fine. Go on and take your meat to your stupid sister. But I don't want to see you near our house again!"

With a final whine, the domestic snatched up his meat and leapt straight over her, pushing roughly between Kutta and Mhumhi to dash pell-mell down the street.

"Sacha," Kutta said, sounding weary.

"He's lying, and I have a feeling I know what he's hiding," said Sacha. She swung her head around to look at Mhumhi. "And you- you'd better not believe a word he said about Mother, you know very well he was only telling you what he thought you wanted to hear!"

"But Sacha!" exclaimed Mhumhi. "He said he saw her near Big Park, that's not so far, maybe we could search-"

"Big Park! You think for a minute she'd go to Big Park?" Sacha whuffed with scornful laughter. "That's the hunting grounds of the police pack! You know they chase down hulkers there- why would Mother dare set foot into that place?"

Mhumhi was quiet for a moment, head turned away, and then he said, "She found me, didn't she?"

Sacha seemed to tense, and Kutta drew nervously away from the two of them.

"*Found* you?" she spat. "Found you? She stole you, Mhumhi, right out from under your real mother! And you!" She glared for a moment at Kutta, who now had her tail tucked. "Don't you dare forget that! Don't you dare forget what she's done to all of us!"

"So… so what?" said Mhumhi, though his voice sounded feeble even to his own ears. "We grew up together… it's never made any difference…"

"It makes *all* the difference!" Sacha gave an angry little shudder. "It's good riddance she left- and didn't you notice when she did it, just as soon as Kebero started eating solid-"

"Stop it, Sacha!" Kutta was quivering too. "That's enough!"

Sacha gave both of them a furious look and ran down across the road, back towards their home.

"Mhumhi, I'm sorry," said Kutta, licking at his ears, but he was still watching Sacha run away, looking tinier and tinier.

"Should we stop looking for Mother?"

Kutta seemed surprised by the question. "Of course not. Maybe we shouldn't tell Sacha about it, though."

Mhumhi let out a soft whine. "I want her to come back, but is that bad?"

"No, no," said Kutta, pressing against his side. "Of course not. She's our mother. Don't think about what Sacha says about her. You're right that it doesn't matter."

Mhumhi did not respond, head low: despite what Kutta might say, he never could stop thinking about Sacha's words.

"Let's go home now," Kutta said. "She'll work herself out of it. She always does. Just don't cross her for a bit."

"All right," said Mhumhi, but he was feeling very hollow now. The words that the blue-eyed dog had said should have filled him with hope, but now he could only doubt them. Where they true? And if they were, what *was* their small, domestic mother doing going towards the park where the massive pack of painted dogs hunted for hot meat?

3
Wounded Fox

Mhumhi trailed behind Kutta as they walked slowly back to their home. In the late afternoon the city was starting to come alive again. More of the little dogs were emerging from their dwellings, mingling with their neighbors. The street was growing crowded again.

At their doorway Mhumhi hesitated, and said, "I'll stay out here awhile."

Kutta gave him a light, understanding nudge. Sacha's scent was still pungent and strong on the wall outside.

After his sister had slipped around the door, Mhumhi trotted down the sidewalk, stepping gingerly over the smaller foxes when he came across them. Many of them were congregating to go to the Oldtown dispensary for their daily meat, making Mhumhi think wistfully of the stuff he'd given Kebero. There'd be no more given to him until the next day. He sighed, and stumbled over the back of a startled island fox.

He cut through an alley and found himself on a new street, not lined with houses but with storefronts and open stalls. As the shadows lengthened a few of the neon lights were flickering with a semblance of life, but it was a poor display. Little electricity still lived on in Oldtown.

They called it 'Food Strip Street' but Mhumhi had never seen any food there at all. He supposed the kiosks with their transparent shelves and clear-fronted refrigerators had once held food, for in places you could still catch a lingering essence of it, but they were brutally clean now, perfectly so, licked that way by a thousand starving tongues. Now, not being a suitable place to make a home in, the street was practically deserted. But the fennec fox had mentioned that this had been the place where he'd first spotted the domestic, and Mhumhi had half a mind to investigate. At least cursorily.

Most of the storefronts were dark, but here and there along the narrow street there would be one that flickered and flashed its bright white interior as the lights sputtered in and out of life. Mhumhi trailed along the gutter, sniffing at the sidewalk. Curious puppies had explored the area earlier that day and splashed some urine onto a metal signpost, but he couldn't catch a whiff of the blue-eyed domestic.

Even as he thought that he looked up across the street to one of the flickering storefronts and saw a small dark figure watching him. At the next moment the lights failed and the figure disappeared.

The lights flashed up again a moment later, and he flinched, blinking. There it was. A little fox, sitting on top of the gleaming counter, looking at him with dark eyes. It had enormous ears which seemed nearly too heavy for its little head, for they sagged forward and wrinkled the little brow.

Mhumhi recalled that it was a bat-eared fox, this thing, as it leapt off the countertop and came out of the store towards him. It was limping.

"Hello," it said.

Mhumhi was a bit surprised the little thing was talking to him. He supposed he was being mistaken for police again.

"Hello," he responded, trying to be polite, and tentatively sniffed noses with the fox. It was an older male, he gathered, and in poor health at the moment.

"I saw you earlier," said the bat-eared fox, once they had got the measure of each other. "With the domestic and that jackal."

"Oh, you did," said Mhumhi, somewhat feebly, for as far as he remembered he'd given a poor show.

"Is it true, that you're from the orphan pack?"

Mhumhi stiffened.

"I'm not trying to offend you," the fox said, swinging his ears down and back. "I'm just curious. The one who took you is gone now, isn't she? The white dog?"

"How do you know she's white?" asked Mhumhi, still stiff-legged, trying to ignore the word 'took.'

"I spoke with her once," said the fox. "It was a long time ago. She was taking care of one little puppy then. The bush dog."

Mhumhi's own ears swung forward. Sacha... that would have been Sacha as a puppy. The thought of it made him smile, letting his tongue hang out. Had she been cross as a puppy, or had she grown into it gradually? How had his mother ever managed, poor thing?

"Are there still more puppies?"

The question caught him off-guard. "What? What do you mean?"

"I haven't seen any, but you're keeping at least one in the house, aren't you?" the fox persisted, blinking his black button eyes. "I thought I could smell it."

"What do you care?" said Mhumhi, though he was now beginning to feel a bit nervous. Kebero was something that needed to be fairly secret, until he grew to a respectable size, at least. A Simien wolf puppy traveling with any one of them would raise suspicions, and Sacha was keen not to have the police over, hunting for pup-thieves.

"I'd like to help you," said the fox.

"Help us?" Mhumhi looked at the little thing, which must have been all of seven pounds. "How?"

The fox sneezed, which seemed to be his way of laughing. "With the puppy," he said. "I've long lost my own. I've lost everything, you see, and in that fight earlier I even got my leg injured. I thought you saw me, but…"

Mhumhi suddenly remembered the little body he'd nearly stepped on.

"I thought you were dead!"

The fox laughed again. "I thought so, as well, but I crawled out of there somehow. But you see, I'm in a bit of trouble. I was wondering if you would let me stay with your family for a while. In return, I'll help you look after the puppy."

"Stay with…?" Mhumhi put his ears back. He'd never heard such a bizarre request. He doubted either of his sisters would like it very much. "We don't need any help with him, though."

"I don't mean just looking after him," said the fox. "I'm sure you've had trouble getting enough meat for him. It isn't much, but I'll add my daily portion to yours. I don't use it anyway."

"You don't use it? Then what-"

"I've found that it doesn't agree with me," said the fox, flicking his brushy tail. "There's better food elsewhere, if you can scratch it out. It wouldn't satisfy a big fellow like you, of course, but I don't need much."

"What food?" Mhumhi asked. He glanced around at the flickering storefronts. "There's something here still?"

"No," admitted the fox. "I was too weary to go to my normal hunting grounds, so I thought I might nose around here a bit... but there's not so much as a crumb left here to attract any insects."

"Insects!"

"Yes." The fox's button eyes twinkled up at him. "I told you, it wouldn't satisfy you."

Mhumhi wrinkled his nose, drawing back his lips slightly at the thought. "Where are your normal hunting grounds?"

"Usually I hunt around the sewers, around the dispensary drainage. But I didn't want to risk putting this leg in that muck." The fox glanced back at himself, and Mhumhi suddenly realized how he was holding his left back leg slightly raised, as if it were painful. The fur around his heel was coarse and matted with dried blood.

"Oh, that looks awful!" exclaimed Mhumhi, suddenly full of sympathy for the poor old thing. "Let me see to it!"

"No, it's been too tender-" the fox had started to say, but Mhumhi planted one big paw over his back so he could lean down and sniff at the wound. The fox squeaked.

It didn't seem very deep, but it cut all the way down to part of the pad. Mhumhi licked at it, pulling at the matted fur with his tongue, and the fox flinched mightily, but did not make another sound.

"How did you cut it like this?" Mhumhi asked, as he worked.

The fox's response sounded pained. "I'm not sure- I think I stumbled over something sharp when I was trying to get out of the fighting."

Mhumhi gave a disapproving little twitter at the thought, but he had managed to pull most of the matting and crusted blood away with his tongue, and exposed the wound, which bled a little.

"That should feel better," he said, drawing away. "It smelled a bit like it was going infected, but you're all right."

The fox turned back and sniffed his foot, giving it a few licks with his own small tongue. "Thank you."

"You should come back with me," said Mhumhi, who was starting to feel warmly paternal, the fact that the fox was likely many years older than him notwithstanding. "There are soft places you can sleep, and you'll be out of the wet weather."

"I will if you'll have me," said the fox, raising his brush tail slightly. "My name is Bii."

"I'm Mhumhi," said Mhumhi, wagging his own tail, and took a moment to sniff around Bii's hindquarters and tail, getting accustomed to his scent. Bii took it patiently, leaning against him and raising his injured paw gingerly.

"I have an idea," said Mhumhi, drawing back from his inspection. He smiled a little, teeth showing. "Why don't I carry you? It'll keep you off that foot."

"*Carry me*," repeated Bii, turning his large ears back. "I think I'd rather walk."

"No, no, you'll feel much better off your feet, and anyway the walk isn't long," said Mhumhi, still smiling, and leaned down and caught the fox's scruff in his teeth. Bii gave a single, undignified yap, then curled in his paws resignedly as Mhumhi turned and trotted back down the street, tail still wagging.

He got more than a few alarmed looks, coming back down his home street with the bat-eared fox swinging morosely from his jaws. Mhumhi kept his white-flagged tail high, feeling in a much better mood than before. If Bii's meat went to Kerbero, it would mean less regurgitation duty for him.

He hopped up onto the curb in front of the house. Bii tucked his tail in tighter as it brushed the concrete.

"Mhumhi!"

Sacha rushed out of the house with a whine. "You better not have been sniffing around Big Park- what is *that*?"

Mhumhi put Bii down. The fox seemed shaky on his feet, and wobbled as Mhumhi licked the top of his head. "Let's let him stay with us, Sacha! He says he'll help us with Keb-"

"Don't talk about it out here!" said Sacha, looking around in an alarmed way, then raised a lip at Bii. "Come in, but don't take it as a permanent invitation."

They went inside, and Sacha hopped up to depress the door handle with her paws and pull it shut.

"You better have a good explanation, M-" She stopped, jerking her head back, for Mhumhi was whining and trying to lick her chin again, very relieved that she didn't seem to be furious with him anymore.

Eventually Mhumhi managed to get out the trade Bii had proposed, or some of it, though he was less eloquent about it than the fox had been. In the middle they were interrupted by Kutta running down the stairs to greet them and exclaim over Bii, and Mhumhi had to start over again. By the time he got through it, Sacha looked mightily skeptical.

"You just went and told him about Kebero, Mhumhi?"

Mhumhi licked his lips and wagged his tail between his legs. "I didn't tell him exactly-"

"And you opened his wound out there on the street!" said Sacha, trotting over to Bii. The fox gave her a startled growl, which she returned in full before bowling him over with her heavy head and examining his foot herself.

"You'll be the one to give him an infection, Mhumhi," she said, licking at it. It didn't seem as though she was being particularly gentle about it, for Bii was flinching again, but she was more skilled than Mhumhi and soon had the fresh debris out of the wound. Kutta nudged Mhumhi, flashing him a grin.

"She likes having someone smaller than her around," she said softly, and Mhumhi snorted and whuffed.

"Mhumhi!" snapped Sacha, giving him a sharp look. "Take him upstairs and put him on the bed. Don't let him give you any lip."

Bii growled up at her from his prone position, but she ignored him, stub tail waving slightly as she got off him. Kutta gave Mhumhi a meaningful look and trotted up the stairs ahead of them.

"Come on, Bii, you still have to meet Kebero," said Mhumhi. Bii gave him a tired look and curled his tail securely between his back legs.

Mhumhi picked him up again and bounded up the stairs. In the upstairs bedroom Kutta was play-boxing with Kebero, but the puppy quickly broke off at the sight of Bii, tail wagging stiffly.

Mhumhi had been planning to deposit Bii directly onto the bed, but the fox suddenly squirmed in his jaws.

"Put me down," he said, a bit breathlessly. "I have to greet him."

Mhumhi obliged, and the fox tottered a bit before getting his bearings again. Kebero whined and looked at Kutta for some direction.

Bii struck a peculiar pose, arching his back and tail, and hopped sideways towards Kebero. The motion was unfamiliar, but the intent seemed clear, and Kebero tensed for an instant before bowing on his front legs with his rump wagging in the air.

At once Bii hopped at him with his front paws raised, surprisingly spry even with his injured foot, and Kebero gave a puppyish growl and raised up to box with him, tumbling him at once- even Kebero was bigger than him. Bii took it well and rolled on his back and pushed at his muzzle with all four paws, tail wagging against the floor.

"They're getting along," said Kutta, glancing at Mhumhi, but he'd gone into a play bow instinctively at the sight of Kebero's and now bounded up to shove at her shoulder, wagging his tail.

"Oh, come on," said Kutta, but he batted at her shoulder with his front paw and she twisted and boxed back at him, waving tail betraying her.

The four of them play-fought for a little while, panting and laughing, until Kutta noticed Bii, who was pinned under Mhumhi's forearm, wincing and bleeding.

"Come on, stop, stop," she cried, nipping Mhumhi sharply on the flank so that he jumped away, and picked up Bii herself to lay him on the bed. "I'm sorry, Bii, I forgot you were injured."

Bii didn't respond, looking weary, and turned to gingerly lick at his foot. Kebero jumped up beside him, ears back, and licked under his chin.

"He likes, him, right?" Kutta said softly to Mhumhi. "That's good- no, stop it, Mhumhi, we're done playing now."

Mhumhi had been poking at her again, but he slowly put his paw down.

Kebero cuddled next to Bii, and the fox turned to lick the top of his head with his tiny tongue.

“Can you speak yet, little one?”

Kebero raised his head and gave a long whimper that turned into a word. “Auuuuuuuwoh- woh- yes.”

“Wonderful,” said Bii, drawing his lips back into a smile, as Kutta shuddered. “You’re doing very well. Can you tell me-“

“Wohhh,” moaned Kebero, and then he began to twitch strangely. “Wh- wh- wh-“ He bobbed his head, licking his lips convulsively. “Wh-“

“Kebero, stop it,” said Kutta. “Come on-”

“Let him work it out,” said Bii, suddenly somewhat sharp. “Kebero, it’s all right.”

Kebero's mouth worked, and he twitched and shuddered. Mhumhi was fairly sure Bii's words weren't reaching him anyway; his little eyes were focused on something beyond their vision. Eventually he stilled, his jaws slack and his tongue hanging out.

"If he talks too much, that always happens," said Kutta, her eyes rather thin as she looked at Bii. "It's not good for him."

"It's not good to stop him from speaking," retorted Bii. "You're hindering his growth, that's why he's having these difficulties. Didn't your mother teach you how to care for puppies?"

Kutta stiffened, her tail bristling, and Mhumhi licked his lips; but then she seemed to relax and ducked her head.

"Mother hasn't been around for a while. And Keb came to us when he was- well, when he was a little too old."

"I see," said Bii, rather softly. "It's all right. He'll be just fine." He turned to lick Kebero again, and Kebero blinked, coming out of his odd stupor. Mhumhi averted his gaze, feeling a bit ashamed. When Kebero's speech-convulsions had started he himself had been repulsed, and rather afraid of them, though his mother had assured him they were normal for a young dog learning to speak. Sacha had been indifferent, even cold; but that was no real surprise. She had taken some time to warm up to Mhumhi himself. Kutta had spent most of the time out of all of them with Kebero, but even she often went off with their mother.

Kebero had spent quite a bit of time upstairs alone.

"Come with me, Mhumhi," said Kutta, shouldering him out of the bedroom and away from his thoughts. She pawed open the door to the room at the end of the short hallway. It was a bathroom, with a knocked-over toilet revealing a gaping hole in the floor. Mhumhi hopped up to the sink, batting at the encrusted gray knob until a thin stream of water reluctantly came forth. It tasted like alkali as he lapped at it.

When he had finished he fell back on all fours, licking his lips, and Kutta hopped up to push the knob back down.

"Honestly, Mhumhi, you need to remember to turn it off, else it'll crust shut like the one in the kitchen!"

Mhumhi smiled and blinked at her.

"Listen to me now," said Kutta, mouthing his ear. "If we have Bii, this means none of us'll have stay behind and watch Keb anymore."

"But Bii's so little," Mhumhi pointed out, wagging his tail.

"So what? Keb likes him already, and you can tell he knows what he's doing. I wonder what happened to his puppies?" Kutta's brow wrinkled.

"I wonder why Sacha agreed to let him stay?" Mhumhi offered, as long as they were posing questions they couldn't answer.

Kutta gave a dismissive huff. "She did, anyway. I hope she doesn't change her mind. With his extra meat, we should be able to…" She licked her lips. "Mhumhi, tomorrow, I want to show you something. But you must keep it a secret, all right?"

"Show me what secret?" Mhumhi asked, tilting his head.

"I mean it, you've got to keep it a secret- and- and I think it's better if I show you, rather than tell you."

Mhumhi put his ears forward, intrigued. "Does it have to do with Mother, Kutta?"

There was a strange look in her yellow eyes for a moment, then she said, "Well- yes- it does have something to do with her."

"Oh!" said Mhumhi, bouncing on his forepaws. "Are we going to go to Big Park to look for her?"

Kutta looked away, bushy tail curling slightly around her haunch. "No… not that. But I suppose we ought to go there, eventually."

"Of course we ought to! She might be hurt, and waiting for us!"

"Mhumhi…" Kutta seemed to decide against saying what she'd been about to say. "Yes, we'll go look there soon. But this is important too."

"Well, if it has to do with Mother," Mhumhi said happily, though he noticed that Kutta gave a kind of anxious twitch when he said it.

"Yes," she said, licking his forehead. "Tomorrow, we'll go together. But don't say a word to Sacha about it."

"I won't!" said Mhumhi, excited in spite of himself. Tomorrow he'd be one step closer to his mother. No- perhaps they would find her tomorrow, perhaps she'd be all right, and she'd come home and meet Bii! She'd like him, he knew it. And Kebero would be so happy to see her again… he'd been so melancholy lately… yes, if she came back, everything would be so much better, and he was sure even Sacha would be pleased.

With these thoughts cheering him, he followed Kutta back into the bedroom with a spring in his step. Bii and Kebero were asleep on the bed, Bii curled up with his nose tucked snugly in his tail, Kebero sprawled at his side, snoring softly. Sacha was there as well, using her forepaws to dig into one of the flat, ruined pillows. She glanced up when they approached and yawned hugely.

"Looking at them has made me tired," she said, rolling her eyes towards Bii and Kebero. "It's been a strange day."

Mhumhi could agree with that sentiment. He overtook Kutta and hopped up onto the bed himself, licking Sacha's cross bear's face before curling up on the edge of her pillow. Kebero opened his eyes and then jumped when Kutta joined them, squeezing beside Mhumhi so that her other side was solidly in contact with both of them.

There was a great deal of creaking as the four of them re-situated themselves, tucking in their limbs where they could. Mhumhi yawned and laid his head next to Kutta's, Sacha a warm knot against his shoulder blades.

Tomorrow, he thought again, tomorrow his mother might be here… He happened to glance left and saw that Bii was still awake, his button eyes shining slightly in the dim light, his ears trained forward. His injured leg made the scent of blood linger in the air of the room as the remaining daylight faded away.

4

To Market

"Why does Mhumhi have to go with Bii?"

That had been Kutta, prowling around in their little kitchen the next morning, claws clicking on the tiles. Displeasure was evident in the way her tail swished low around her hocks.

"Because," said Sacha, who had taken up her preferred vantage point up on the counter. "Mhumhi's got the biggest belly, and he can eat the most meat. He'll be eating both his and Bii's portions."

"But why can't Bii just-?"

"He's told me he can't regurgitate it, like a domestic," said Sacha, tone wry. Bii himself was lying on the floor near the door, forepaws lined up neatly parallel to each other. He was clearly eager to go.

Mhumhi gave his own sad little whine, as he had hoped to be exempt from the whole regurgitation business. He returned to ripping at the tattered fabric that remained on their couch to vent his frustration. Kutta looked at him, and he knew what she was thinking: they'd have to postpone their secret mission until they could figure out a way to sneak out alone together.

"I'll go with you later, Kutta," said Sacha. "We shouldn't be all together in a group… no need to attract too much attention."

Mhumhi wondered if Sacha hadn't somehow got wind of their plan- she was being so nefarious- but of course everything she was saying made perfect sense. The addition of Bii to their motley group would be very noticeable, especially once they left their neighborhood and the dogs that were familiar with them, and it had been drilled into them since they were puppies not to have a reason to make the police take interest in them.

Kutta huffed through her nose and trotted out of the kitchen and up the stairs. They heard her scratching around in the bathroom a moment later.

Sacha hopped from the counter down to the scratched old table, onto a chair, and down to the floor.

"I feel better keeping an eye on her," she told Mhumhi. "She's been wandering off lately, and she hasn't been giving Keb much meat, either. Doesn't it make you wonder?"

"Wonder what?" said Mhumhi, turning so that his front paws dangled off the edge of the couch.

"If she's met somebody," said Sacha. "If she's thinking of splitting off."

Mhumhi was shocked. "Sacha!"

"Well, I don't know what else would make her act this way," Sacha grumbled, furrowing her brow. Mhumhi looked at her a moment, then stepped down off the couch to nose at her shoulder.

"Kutta just likes to run around. Don't worry about her, she's not going to leave anytime soon."

"It would be *good* if she did," said Sacha, turning her nose up and away. "For her. To be with her own kind, I suppose."

Mhumhi licked her tiny ears, saying nothing. Now he was beginning to feel rather guilty.

"Mhumhi," called Bii, over by the door. "Let's go now. We don't want to have to wait in line too long."

Mhumhi looked over at Bii, who he was feeling somewhat less kindly towards today. He'd been woken up to the loud crunching sound of the fox sitting up next to him devouring a large cockroach. When pressed, he had admitted he'd pawed it out from the underside of the toilet hole.

Still, a dog had to eat, after all. Mhumhi tried to let go of his negative feelings as he trotted beside the fox down the street, where the morning crowd was amassing. He spotted his fennec neighbor sitting in his storm drain, yawning. Mhumhi gave his tail a friendly wave and the fox blinked at him a moment before vanishing back into the darkness.

Even though it was still early morning it was shimmering hot in the streets, the last of the previous day's rain vanishing into a haze above the hot asphalt. The dogs around Mhumhi were all trotting with ears back and tongues hanging out, a crowd of lean legs and small white teeth. There were a few growls as more and more dogs fed into the crowd, but it was too hot to really fight.

Mhumhi still stood out as the largest animal, though as they got towards the edge of Oldtown there were more and more larger ones. A family of rotund raccoon dogs trundled up to join the fray, and a pair of thin black-backed jackals were squabbling outside their door while a third panted on the sidewalk. Mhumhi smelled the sickly-sweet musk long before a maned wolf, leggy and ruffled-looking, stepped warily over several smaller dogs and into the crowd. She was taller than Mhumhi, but she cringed nervously away at the sight of him. He kept his white-flagged tail waving high.

Oldtown's crowded apartments and townhouses soon gave way to larger buildings, squat and flat like the one that had housed the subway station. Some of the dogs spilled through a gap in a chain-link fence surrounding a playground, startling a family of Rüppell's foxes that had taken refuge underneath the roundabout into furious, sleepy yapping. Mhumhi could see movement within the darkened and shuttered windows of the school beside it.

There were old cars here, too, scattered and parked permanently in different areas along the roadside. Some of them had their windows broken in and served as makeshift dens for the smaller and less lucky dogs, but mostly they served as vantage points, especially as the crowd continued to swell. Mhumhi broke away from Bii for a moment to bound on top of a sedan, paws thumping dully on the metal, adding dusty pawprints to the dozens that were already there.

Beyond he could see the line where Oldtown ended and the rest of the city began. Far off there were skyscrapers, some square, some spiraling. The rest of the city fell into a kind of dip and formed a vast basin of buildings and metal winking and shimmering in the sunlight. There seemed to be no end to it at all. Mhumhi looked out to his left, where far in the distance he could see a large flat patch of yellow and brown: that was Big Park.

"Come on," Bii called, putting his paws on the car's fender, and Mhumhi leapt down.

Their final destination was along the street they called Wide Street, for it was exceptionally wide compared to the single and two-lane streets that wound through Oldtown. Across the massive intersection a single traffic light lay on the ground like a dead thing, glass lights long shattered. The rest still hung on their tall wire, flicking through colors for the carless streets. A narrow lane of gleaming solar panels stretched high above them; Mhumhi caught a glimpse of a lone fox running across it.

The horde of dogs hit Wide Street and fanned out, filling it with their grumbles and yaps. On the other side of the road there was a massive building, its tall walls a clean and gleaming mismatch to the dirty, tired buildings of Oldtown. It had a base of blue and white, and above that rose black metal struts and tall windows of blackened glass. Narrow concrete booths protruded every few feet along the outer wall.

The dogs organized themselves into rough queues behind each of these booths. Many were growling now, as impatience mounted; puppies yapped and whined next to their parents. The tall maned wolf cringed more than ever as her much shorter neighbors jostled her on both sides.

Mhumhi, panting from the heat of the sun and the streets and the commingled dogs, helped guide Bii to a spot in one of the queues. He was relieved to see that it wasn't terribly far back from the booth.

A sharp scent pricked at him, and he turned to see a three large dogs sitting together atop a parked car, surveying the crowd. Painted dogs, police dogs. Mhumhi, standing out in the crowd of little dogs and foxes, tried to make himself look small and solid-colored. Liduma, the head police dog for Oldtown, sometimes liked to give him a hard time.

Abruptly a loud tone rang out, and from beyond the gleaming black glass, something hissed and ground to a start. Several dogs responded to it with eager whines and howls, and the line began to move.

Mhumhi had been to this meat dispensary a thousand times, though he had never really understood it. Somewhere behind that brick and featureless glass lay a vast store of meat. No dog had yet been able to penetrate one of the dispensaries, but they had little need to. The meat was delivered to them regularly, once a day, one portion per dog.

As each dog took its turn and stood inside the booth, the slider clicked and hissed out of the rubber lips in the wall, bearing a package wrapped in opaque white plastic. The air was soon filled with the sound of hissing and the smell of bloodless meat as each dog carried its package away in its jaws to devour in a more secluded area.

A fight broke out on one of the nearby scales- a coyote had snatched the meat from a little corsac fox, which was squealing furiously. Immediately one of the painted dogs bounded down from the car. At the sight of it the coyote dropped the meat and darted away. The painted dog wheeled around, scattering the crowd, and hopped back up onto the car.

Mhumhi was caught up staring, but Bii nipped his heel- it was his turn. Hastily he loped over into the booth, claws clicking. The bottom of the booth was a metal scale that depressed underneath him as he stepped onto it. He ducked down and pressed his nose against a black button set in the wall.

A metal slider hissed and emerged smoothly from the wall, bearing a painted dog-sized hank of meat in a plastic wrapper. Mhumhi tugged it loose from its hook and stood to one side as Bii hopped up on the scale and reared to brush his nose against the button. The slider retracted back into the wall and returned a moment later with a much smaller package.

"Let's get out of the crowd," he called to Mhumhi as he leapt up to snatch it.

They squeezed back through the crowd, earning hungry looks- the rest of the dogs in line had yet to eat, and more were still squeezing onto Wide Street. Bii flicked his tail and led Mhumhi underneath a ramp held up with round concrete columns. There were a smattering of other dogs lurking there already, and they were greeted with growls, but Mhumhi's appearance was enough to keep them unmolested.

Mhumhi found an empty spot in the shadows and tore through the plastic on his package. As always, the malleable stuff got stuck to his teeth and on the roof of his mouth. He curled his lips and scraped the roof of his mouth with his tongue.

Bii was having an easier time of it with his needle-sharp teeth. He sliced a neat line through his wrapper and tugged it fully back, exposing the pale, bloodless meat. Mhumhi started salivating at the sight, which didn't help him much in trying to get a grip on the slippery plastic.

"I can help you," Bii offered, watching him struggle, but Mhumhi warned him with a soft growl. He hooked his teeth onto one corner and stepped on the package to squeeze the squashy stuff out of the hole he'd made. He gobbled it as Bii watched.

"Don't you ever get tired of eating the same thing every day?"

Mhumhi swallowed his mouthful and licked his chops. "There's nothing else to eat."

That was not strictly true- if a dog was clever enough to bargain, he could gain access to fruit from the Great Glass Garden that sat above the center of the city. But Mhumhi rarely desired any of the stuff, and it was never quite so filling as meat.

Mhumhi finished his portion and went on to devour Bii's little packet as well. It felt like a negligible addition to his stomach, and he found himself rather cross at the prospect of having to give much of it up again.

He licked his chops again and sat down, fully intending to digest a moment, but Bii was waving his tail.

"Let's go, Mhumhi. We'll want to hurry back. Aren't you and Kutta going somewhere today?"

"What makes you think that?" Mhumhi said, springing back to his feet, though his full belly protested. "Were you-"

"Listening? Not intentionally." Bii laughed, and rotated his overlarge ears forward. "I'm afraid you'll have to go further than the next room for me not to hear you. I would have warned you, but I didn't know the house would have secret conferences."

Mhumhi wavered there nervously, one canine exposed, until Bii added, "I don't plan to do anything about it. I don't have any stake in what you and Kutta do, or in getting on your bad side."

"What about Sacha's bad side?" asked Mhumhi, relaxing a little.

"I think that's the only side she has," said Bii, briefly drawing his lips back in a tiny, devilish grin.

Mhumhi wagged his tail, reassured, though the thought tugged at him that what stakes Bii himself had were as mysterious as the inside of the meat dispensary.

They made their way back through to the heart of Oldtown. The streets were much quieter now, as the flood of dogs leaving had turned into a slow trickle of dogs returning. Mhumhi kept an eye on Bii, who was starting to limp worse, debating on whether or not he should offer to carry him again.

Quite suddenly Bii stopped dead in his tracks, and Mhumhi nearly tripped over him. The fox had led them on a short cut through a dim back alley filled with blue dumpsters on the way to Food Strip Street. Bii was fixated towards the sunny intersection ahead of them.

"What's the matter? Is it your leg?"

Bii did not respond right away, just stood there with his ears forward and the fur on his back rising.

"I don't know what it is," he said, "but it's coming towards us."

Mhumhi was puzzled. "What, it's a dog, isn't it? How big is it?"

"Very big," said Bii, quivering, and then he turned and squeezed into the tiny gap between the nearest dumpster and the brick wall.

"You should hide too," came his strained voice. "It's coming faster. Hurry, Mhumhi!"

Mhumhi, bewildered, turned and sniffed towards the street. All he could make out was dog… and meat… and a faint scent of blood. He quivered slightly. Ordinarily he would have thought nothing of the three together, but Bii's fear was catching. He ran around to the front of the dumpster, thinking he'd jump into it, but the heavy lid was shut tight. He dithered, plainly visible in the middle of the alley, and briefly considered abandoning Bii entirely for a sprint in the opposite direction.

He deliberated too long, and now *his* ears caught the sound of it, big and round as they were. He understood why it had frightened Bii. It was a slow, shuffling, scraping gait that sounded like no dog he'd ever heard. And it definitely came from a very large animal. Larger than him.

Mhumhi, tail tucked as far up against his belly as it would go, slunk to the other side of Bii's dumpster, shaking, and pressed himself against the juncture between the metal and brick. Maybe the thing would pass right by the alley, not go in.

The shuffle-scrape continued, growing closer, pausing… Mhumhi was drooling now, out of fright. It entered the alley.

He heard its footsteps, and swallowed convulsively, pressing himself as far back as he could into the shadow. It had such a heavy tread, its paws must have been huge- and that scraping sound, that must be something *dragging*- Mhumhi was suddenly able to visualize it: a massive dog, badly wounded, dragging its heavy back legs behind it as it staggered on its front paws. Now that it was closer, it smelled like death.

He squeezed his eyes shut as he heard it start to pass the dumpster. He hadn't any idea what state Bii was in now, jammed into that little crevice. He did not know why he was so frightened. A dog was only a dog, and it sounded injured at that, so what did he have to fear? Why was his heart hammering so rapidly?

It was so close now, so close, and its nose should be able to pick up Mhumhi's scent now- it was coming past the dumpster now- if it looked to the left it would see Mhumhi pressed there, helpless- he had to open his eyes.

It was not a dog.

For a moment that was all he understood, that it was not a dog, as it continued to make its sluggish progress, looking neither right nor left. He had nothing *but* dogs to compare it to, but it was not one. It was tall- very tall- much taller than the maned wolf or any other creature he'd ever seen. It only had two legs- no, that was wrong, it *stood* on two, the others dangled straight down, looking broken at the shoulder. It was covered up in- in wrapping, he thought hysterically, like the meat from the dispensary. What showed through the wrapping was hairless, glistening skin.

Mhumhi swallowed again, feeling the meat he'd just eaten roil in his stomach. It had not noticed him, just kept moving forward in its slow, dull way, lurching step by step. He tilted his head up- up to see its face-

Its face- there was something horribly wrong with it. It had no nose. It was as if the muzzle had been chopped off, leaving a weal of raw flesh. It had no ears at all, just more wrapping around its misshapen head. Its eyes were huge and bulging and the white was showing all around them. It was a face of madness.

It took another lurching step forward. Mhumhi suddenly realized what it was: it was a hulker, like the police pack chased, like his mother had told him about. Slow, dull, and meaty, the painted dogs always said, when questioned. Gentle, his mother had called it. Different-looking, but a dog like we are.

The hulker heaved itself forward, feet thumping, and there came the scraping. It had something with its front paw, dragging behind itself. Mhumhi couldn't help but crane his neck from the shadow to try and see around the edge of the dumpster.

Its paw was naked, split, skeletal, curled around like talons.

It was holding the back feet of a dead dog.

Drool dripped from Mhumhi's lips as he struggled against the urge to gasp and pant- the dog was a coyote, yes, he saw that now, maybe even the coyote he had seen just earlier stealing from a corsac fox- he did not know, he could not recognize it, as its face was smashed to a bloody pulp that wobbled as it dragged along the ground.

Mhumhi couldn't stop himself then, he gave an awful rasping gasp, and the hulker's raw mouth split open, showing square flat teeth, and it turned its head and looked directly at him.

5
Hulker

The hulker's eyes were on him, wide eyes with mad white edges. It dropped the back legs of the dead coyote and swung to face him where he was cringing, terror-struck, against the brick wall. In its other paw, which he hadn't seen, it held a long piece of wood.

In a quick motion it swung the wood at him. Mhumhi heard it whistle, the speed and strength of it belying the hulker's earlier slow movements. He leapt forward instinctively and hit the creature squarely in the chest. It was horrid and warm and he squealed with fear and thrashed in midair as it grabbed at him, sending it over backwards.

Mhumhi did not look back, he ran, dashing full-speed down the street, around the corner, and away, fear propelling him until the buildings of Oldtown whizzed by in a blur.

He only stopped when he ran straight into a low-slung, trundling tanuki and tripped fantastically, flipping over onto his back. The tanuki mewled furiously at him and waddled off.

He rolled back onto his elbows, panting, looking around. The few small dogs that had been out on the streets were staring at him as he lay there. He could not get the hulker's nightmarish visage out of his mind. And the dead coyote… He retched.

The bright sunlight and the sight and smell of dogs like himself gradually dispelled his fear, though, and he eventually got up, still shaking a bit, panting as though he'd run twice as far. A horrible thought was coming to him.

Bii was still in the alleyway with the hulker.

He hoped that the old fox hadn't been spotted from his hiding place behind the dumpster. If he had, Mhumhi didn't know what the hulker would do. Did it have the strength to shift it? Mhumhi had the sinking feeling that the answer was yes, thinking of the strength that the hulker had put into the blow it had aimed at him, at the way that coyote's skull had been smashed.

Mhumhi felt ill. He had to go back, to at least see if Bii was all right. At least now he felt certain that he could outrun the hulker… unless it had been startled, or distracted, and had chosen not to chase him…

Forcing himself to retrace his steps back to the alleyway was the most difficult thing Mhumhi had ever done, but he did it, dragging his feet and shaking, until he saw the brick alley and glimpsed the blue bins.

The smell of the hulker- which he now recognized, though it was strangely indistinct- was still fresh in the air, but Mhumhi did not think it was in the area anymore, for his swiveling ears weren't picking up any movement. He crept back into the alley, hugging the wall.

No one was there, no lurking hulker or bat-eared fox. There were only a few smears of blood on the concrete to suggest that anything had ever happened.

"Bii," he called softly.

For a moment there was no response, and then suddenly the fox's tiny head wiggled out from behind the dumpster, nose first and huge ears popping out after.

"It's gone?" he gasped.

"It's gone," said Mhumhi, and Bii came the rest of the way out, back arched and quivering.

"What was it? I heard you scream- I thought-"

"It was a hulker," Mhumhi told him. "I've never seen one before. Bii, it was carrying a dead- a dead dog!"

"Ah," said Bii. Mhumhi suddenly caught a whiff of urine- the fox had responded to fear in his own way behind the dumpster. "Let's get out of this place, Mhumhi."

Mhumhi had no argument with that, and they trotted quickly out of the alley, aiming for home. Bii kept close to Mhumhi's legs, and Mhumhi kept turning to lick him between the ears, to reassure himself.

"I've heard that," Bii said, once they were in the same bright place where Mhumhi had originally stopped, "I've heard that the hulkers'll kill you if they can. I hear they eat dogs."

Mhumhi suddenly had an awful vision of the creature hunched over a dog's corpse, digging those talons into the belly and tearing out meat with its flat teeth, and shuddered.

"My mother always said that they were our brothers," he said. "She said they were dogs."

Bii sneeze-laughed. "Of course she would say that! She's a domestic."

"What do you mean, she's a domestic?" asked Mhumhi, feeling his hackles rise. "What's wrong with that?"

"There's a reason they're not well-liked," Bii said. "They have some sort of relationship with the hulkers. Protect them, bring food to them, that sort of thing. Nobody knows why they do it."

"Ah!" said Mhumhi, suddenly recalling the blue-eyed domestic. It had said it was carrying meat to its sister, but Sacha had been so suspicious. Had she thought…?

He thought of that dog, cringing with its meat, and felt a surge of disgust.

"My mother never went near any hulker," he said. "I know that much."

"I didn't say she did," said Bii. "I don't think all domestics associate with them- there's just not enough of them left. The police drive them to Big Park whenever they find them, to hunt them down."

"Big Park," Mhumhi repeated, and then shut his jaws tight. Big Park was where his mother had been last seen.

"I hear they can even speak," said Bii, apparently not noticing how stiff Mhumhi had gotten. "Or at least, they can mimic speaking, make it sound as though some dog is calling for help, lure you out, and then…"

The fur on Mhumhi's back rose. "I'm glad there's not many of them left."

"Yes," said Bii. "I think the police want to eliminate them entirely."

They didn't say much else the rest of the way back, and Mhumhi felt a great deal of relief when they finally saw Sacha's little head poking around the door of their home.

"Come on, come in," she barked. "Kebero's hungry!"

Mhumhi bounded up to her, twittering and whining, frantically bathing her neck and chin.

"Oh, Sacha, let's not ever leave the house again," he said, rubbing his head against hers so that she was shoved along the floor, ignoring her raised lip.

"What's the matter with you?" Seeing that Mhumhi was in no state to answer, she addressed Bii. "What happened?"

"We met a hulker," said Bii, who had gone to lie down on a piece of fabric torn off the sofa. His tongue was hanging out and he looked weary. "It went after Mhumhi."

"Are you all right, Mhumhi?" exclaimed Sacha, standing up on her hind legs to brace on Mhumhi's shoulder so she could inspect him. "Are you hurt?"

"No," said Mhumhi, turning to try and keep licking her. Sacha butted him away with her head.

"A hulker, you said. I thought they were all gone from this area."

Mhumhi glanced at her small eyes and wondered if she was thinking of the domestic, for she had sounded pensive.

"It killed a coyote," he said. "It was *horrible*." Sacha turned to lick his neck again, and he wagged his tail.

"Mhumhi came back to help me," Bii said. "Brave of him. I thought I'd die behind that dumpster, waiting for the thing to go away."

"You did?" said Sacha, pricking her ears, and then she hopped and snapped at Mhumhi's chin. "Don't you dare do something like that again! What if it had gotten you!"

"But what if it was attacking Bii?" he said, and flinched when she snapped at him again.

"What were you going to do, you big dumb puppy? Cry at it? You see a hulker, you run away! Understand? There's nothing you can do for someone who gets caught."

"Yes, I understand," he whined, falling to the floor and rolling over, tail wagging against his belly. Sacha stood over him a moment, letting him lick her face, then snorted.

"Stop fishing for attention and go feed Kebero now."

Mhumhi gave a heavy sigh and rolled onto his feet. He looked back at her, eyes wistful.

"Oh shut up, Mhumhi, you're not a puppy anymore." She gave his a elbow good-natured shove with her head. "Go on now!"

Mhumhi went upstairs with his tail wagging, and when Kebero came up and jammed his nose in the corner of his mouth, even regurgitated for him without complaining.

Kutta, who was lying on the bed, got up and stretched. "What was all the fuss about downstairs?"

Mhumhi told her about the hulker while Kebero ate, expanding on all the gory details. When he had finished, Kutta furrowed her brow.

"It attacked you?"

"Yes," said Mhumhi, a little put out at her dull response. He'd been expecting to be fussed over again.

"Are you sure it killed that coyote?" she asked. "It sounded like it was just carrying it."

"Well, it was *dead*, Kutta," said Mhumhi. "I don't know what else would have smashed it up like that."

"Exactly, you don't know," said Kutta. "Maybe it was just taking the body away somewhere."

"Why're you so eager to defend it?" Mhumhi asked, feeling a bit irritated. "It was certainly aiming to smash my head in!"

"Mh-Mh-Mhumhi!"

They turned, for that had been Kebero, slinking towards them with his tail tucked. "Will the huoooooolker come here?"

"Oh, no, Kebero," said Kutta, springing at once to lick his ears. "No, no, it won't come."

"Wh-wh-what if it smashes my head? I'm sc-scaaaaaowed…"

"Oh, it won't, Kebero," she said, shooting Mhumhi a look over his ears, as if it were all his fault.

"You don't know that," Mhumhi said, feeling cross. "I bet it could get through the door even if it was pushed closed."

"Stop, Mhumhi! It's all right, Keb."

Kebero was whimpering and huddling against her forelegs, and she was having to bathe his neck and shoulders to soothe him.

"It's not going to come in, Mhumhi's lying," she told him. "Don't listen to him, he's just trying to scare us."

"I am not, you didn't see it, Kutta-"

"Be quiet, Mhumhi," she said, glaring at him, and he snapped his jaws shut.

Kutta managed to quiet Kebero down with much cajoling, and settled him on the bed with the promise that she would bring Bii up to play with him. She rounded on Mhumhi in the bathroom again.

"Why'd you have to scare him like that? Bii got him talking so well- he wasn't stuttering at all this morning-"

"Well, he should know about it anyway, that thing was dangerous!"

Kutta gave him one of her rare growls. "I know you're exaggerating, Mhumhi. Mother told us all about the hulkers, they're not *really* dangerous-"

"Mother was a domestic!" Mhumhi exclaimed. "Of course she'd say that!"

Kutta went stiff. "How *dare* you speak that way about our mother."

Mhumhi knew he'd gone two far, and licked his lips nervously. "I'm not saying she was, you know, working for one, but Bii told me-"

"Why would you listen to anything Bii would say about our mother? He didn't know her!"

"I know that, but he just said that-"

"Do you think our mother would lie to us, Mhumhi?" Kutta's tail was high and rigid. "Are you on Sacha's side now?"

"I'm not on her *side*," said Mhumhi sulkily, looking away.

"I hope not," Kutta said. "Honestly, I don't know why you've got to act so immature all the time, coming in here with a story like that- you were just trying to get Sacha to pay attention to you, weren't you?"

"You weren't there, you didn't see it," said Mhumhi, but now he was slinking around the bathroom. "It was trying to kill me."

"Maybe it was," said Kutta, "but I bet it was only frightened."

"But it was huge!"

"Well, that big domestic was frightened of us too," said Kutta, and Mhumhi eyed her, wondering if she really understood the difference between a bulky domestic and a massive, blood-smelling hulker.

"Anyway, Mhumhi," Kutta was saying, seeming keen to slide out from under his gaze, "do you still have any meat left in your belly?"

"Yes, but it's mine." Mhumhi resumed his slinking, circling around the smelly toilet hole. Kutta gave an exasperated snort.

"I was only asking. Do you want to go with me today or not?"

"Oh," said Mhumhi, who had nearly completely forgotten about Kutta's secret expedition. "I guess so…" Going outside was somewhat less appealing than it had been that morning.

"If you guess you do, then we have to go now," said Kutta. "It'll take a little while, and Sacha wants me to go out with her this evening to the dispensary. I don't want her coming to look for us."

"Fine," said Mhumhi, with little enthusiasm.

"So let's send Bii up to look after Keb," said Kutta impatiently. "Come on, Mhumhi."

Mhumhi put his ears back, recalling the conversation he'd had with the fox earlier that day. Bii's big ears had probably picked up their entire little discussion. Perhaps, he thought glumly, it would be better if Bii ratted them out to Sacha. Then she'd yowl at them and send them back upstairs and they wouldn't have to go.

But when they went downstairs Sacha was napping in the kitchen sink and Bii was still lying on the floor where Mhumhi had left him.

"Kebero wants to play with you," Kutta told him, and he got up slowly, wincing as he put weight on his back leg, and limped over to the stairs.

"Should we really let him play like that?" Mhumhi whispered to her, but she merely gave him a mordant look and pushed out the door.

"Come on," she said. "Sacha's sleeping. It's perfect."

Mhumhi sighed and followed her.

6

Kutta's Secret

Kutta took him in the opposite direction of the dispensary, which he was glad about, for it also took him away from where the hulker had been. Instead she trotted towards the subway, out towards the edge of Oldtown, until they came to a dusty, empty street.

Mhumhi put his nose down but smelled very little. No one, it seemed, had been by since the rain, or at least no one who'd bothered to leave a mark. Kutta's pawprints ahead of him were the only ones he could see.

The buildings here were older, and falling apart into dry, crumbling plaster; many didn't even have roofs. A slight wind was blowing some of the dust around into a gently spinning cyclone in one street corner. Mhumhi paused to observe it for a moment until Kutta turned back to nudge him on.

"Look," she said, trotting ahead. There was a small arched bridge, and below it flowed a small canal, cut away into the concrete and plaster skin of Oldtown. It smelled foul, and the water that flowed sluggishly through it was brown and sinister-looking.

Kutta paused to put her paws up over a metal guardrail, tail wagging, and then ducked underneath and vanished from view. Mhumhi bounded after her and saw that she had taken a narrow brick stair that led down to a grate underneath the bridge.

"Come on, Mhumhi," she called up to him, waving her brush-tail. Mhumhi followed reluctantly- the smell was no better up close. She nosed him encouragingly when he reached her at the bottom.

"We'll have to swim a bit," she said, and then leapt into the water with a splash.

Mhumhi flinched and let out a miserable whine when the fetid water hit him, but she was already paddling away. There was a gap in the huge grate under the bridge- a spot where the bars had rusted away to ugly corroded stumps above the water. Kutta swam through it.

"Kutta," Mhumhi whined, but she was already gone into the darkness beyond the grate. He dithered for a moment on the stairs before wrinkling his lips and leaping into the water.

It was cold and unpleasant-feeling, and Mhumhi regretted it at once. The smell was going to cling to him for days. He was also not much of a swimmer- no opportunities to practice, really- so it was with some difficulty that he made his way to the dark opening in the grate.

He passed underneath and felt the air immediately get cooler. It was dim inside, filled with the sounds of dripping and trickling. The sunlight streaming through the gate cast a bright cross-hatch on the water.

Kutta gave a little whistle of encouragement somewhere ahead of him, and he saw that there was a platform with more stairs that she'd climbed onto. He swam to it, claws scratching on the brick, and dragged himself out of the mucky water in a relieved bound.

"That's it, that's the only hard part," Kutta said, standing away as he shook himself. "Now it's just a short walk."

Mhumhi shook himself again for good measure, snorting. "What are we going to see down here anyway?"

"You'll see," said Kutta. Her tail was still wagging, damp and draggled as it was. She seemed to be getting into a better mood the closer they got to her secret.

The platform lead further on into the dark tunnel, and there were more stairs going down, and it got even darker. As his vision left him Mhumhi kept close to Kutta, listening to her footsteps click on the concrete. The sound of slowly trickling water was with them always, as was the awful stench.

Kutta stopped suddenly and he bumped into her damp, furry rear.

"Wait a moment," she said, and he heard her scratching around in the darkness. Suddenly there was a burst of light.

Mhumhi had to blink for a while to get his eyes adjusted, and what he saw when they were was not reassuring. They were in a wide tunnel with a very low ceiling. Below the platform they were standing on there still oozed a viscous, nasty-looking stream. It looked shallow enough to stand in but Mhumhi felt distinctly better up where they were.

"What did you do?" he asked, still blinking.

"There's a switch," said Kutta, indicating with her nose on the wall. Wires ran from the switch along the ceiling to little lights in wire boxes strung every few feet along the tunnel. There were a great number of pipes and other wires running in bundles along the walls that Mhumhi could not make head or tail of.

"Just a little further," said Kutta, and trotted forward. Mhumhi glanced down at the shallow sludge and spotted a flicker of movement. It was only a very large cockroach, but he still felt unnerved.

The cockroach made him think of Bii, and he wondered if this was the place Bii went to hunt when he was in better health. If the little fox went down here, it couldn't be so bad, could it?

He followed Kutta along the tunnel, which seemed to stretch on forever, light to light with short patches of darkness in between, until finally she led him down yet another set of stairs and through an arched entryway.

Mhumhi's senses told him that he was suddenly in a very *large* space. He went to the edge of the platform to look out and felt weak. The ground dropped away from them into a huge concrete cavern. Broad pillars held up the ceiling while dangling bulbs cast round disks of light on a pool far below. The sound of rushing water was loud all around here, and he could see it draining into the pool from high pipes set around the room.

Kutta took him down the platform, which ringed the room, until they finally came to another set of stairs, these ones blessedly going up. Kutta hesitated.

"Stay a little ways back, now," she told Mhumhi. "Try to be quiet, and stop when I do."

"What *is* it, Kutta?" he asked, loud over the sound of the water, but she merely whisked her tail in his face and went up the stairs.

Here it was much quieter, as the concrete closed in on all sides again. There was no water here, and the tunnel was narrow and square. Suddenly they came to a door.

Kutta shot Mhumhi a look, warning him to stop, and then scratched on the door.

Behind the door, something moved. Mhumhi tensed.

Kutta rose up on her hind legs, tail wagging, and pushed the door slowly in. Beyond there was darkness, but through the overpowering sewer-stench something strangely familiar prickled at Mhumhi's nose.

Kutta trotted into the room, and Mhumhi followed. He could definitely hear soft movement nearby. It sounded like something small, low to the ground. Then it coughed. Mhumhi jumped.

"That's strange," Kutta said softly. "Just one…"

Just one *what*, Mhumhi wanted to scream, but his senses were on live-wire alert now. He crept forward after Kutta, sniffing. That scent… meat… dog…

Behind them, something screamed.

Mhumhi whirled around and felt Kutta do the same in the darkness nearby. There was a figure standing in the light of the doorway. Standing on two legs.

Mhumhi at once felt an overpowering desire to flee, his legs trembling, but in the unfamiliar darkness there was nowhere to go. The figure was small, but it was definitely a hulker, standing there on its thick legs, grimacing at them, its mad eyes bulging. It had wildly thick fur upon its head.

"Kutta, I think we can fight it off," said Mhumhi, attempting to sound braver than he felt. "It isn't as big as the other one."

"Don't even move, Mhumhi," Kutta said warningly. "Stay right where you are."

Mhumhi growled. The hulker seemed to flinch at this, and he felt a sudden touch of boldness. It was frightened of him. He opened his jaws in a snarl.

"Mhumhi!"

But the hulker had turned to run, and something seemed to snap on in Mhumhi's brain. He chased.

The hulker gave that awful, undoglike scream again, but it was slow and stumbling. Mhumhi could hear the thudding pulse in its neck, and he knew at once that it was *there* he had to go. He was salivating, drool dripping from his tongue as he ran, teeth aching for that pulse.

The hulker squealed and tripped, falling flat on the concrete. Mhumhi twittered his delight and bunched his muscles to spring-

-only to be unceremoniously bowled over.

"Kutta!" he cried, for she was on top of him, baring her teeth.

"I told you to stay put! Now look, you've ruined all my good work!"

Mhumhi, bewildered, tried to get back up, but she shoved him down with her chest and stood over him until he wagged his tail over his belly and licked her chin.

The hulker was still nearby, getting up slowly, and Mhumhi twisted underneath Kutta to growl at it. At once she bumped him with her chest, looming over him until he whined and put his ears back.

"They're not to be hurt, Mhumhi," she said.

"They?"

"Yes," said Kutta, turning her ears back in a sheepish way. "That hulker, and her brother."

"That..." Mhumhi repeated, unable to comprehend. "That... hulker?"

"Yes," said Kutta. "I suppose it would have been better if I told you ahead of time after all. They're hulker puppies, Mhumhi. Mother was taking care of them, and now I am."

7

Three Brothers, Three Sisters

"Hulker puppies," Mhumhi was still repeating, bewildered, a few minutes later. Kutta had told him sternly to wait by the door while she tried to coax the frightened female hulker back. From the dark room, there still came coughing, which Mhumhi supposed must be from the other one.

"Come here," Kutta kept saying, her tail wagging gently as she stepped towards the female. "No one will hurt you."

But every time she got too close, the little hulker would run further away.

"Don't go too far, Kutta!" Mhumhi called after her, feeling anxious for her. Kutta turned back to glare at him.

"Hush! You're frightening her more!"

Disgruntled, Mhumhi got up and looked into the darkened room. The coughing came again. He took a big sniff of air, but it told him next to nothing about whatever lay inside. Either it was the heavy reek of sewer muck or the hulkers' own mysterious scent preventing him from getting a lock on identifying them with his nose.

He stepped into the room, nosing around, feeling far more confident after his adventure chasing the little female. If it was a hulker *puppy*, it was really not so frightening at all.

Near the door he spotted a light switch like the one Kutta had hit in the tunnels and reared to jab it with his nose. Harsh electric light filled the room. Mhumhi blinked, and saw the second hulker, blinking as well.

It was lying in a nest of blankets, so that only the funny-shaped head protruded, and it was looking at him. It looked smaller than the other hulker, and less frightened. It sat up, coughing. Its movements were shaky and childish and it gave a kind of bleat.

Mhumhi felt that twitch again, as if a light switch had been turned on in his own head. He licked his lips. If he could only bear it back down to the ground- it looked so weak, he could just tear out the belly without bothering with the throat-

He was panting and drooling now. He tried to close his jaws and swallow. Kutta had said not to harm them- so he would not- but oh, how could she *stand* it!

The hulker was crawling towards him, and now it got up on its hind legs. Mhumhi shut his eyes painfully, unable even to look at the thing. It was bleating at him again, and he turned his ears back, trying not to hear it.

"Hello!" the hulker bleated.

He opened his eyes and put his ears forward. It was standing a few feet away from him, mouth open in what was almost a dog smile, paws curled near its chin. Again it spoke.

"Hello, dog!"

Its voice was eerie-sounding, not quite right, not quite *dog*. He backed up a few steps, feeling frightened, though-

It also reminded him a little bit of his mother's voice.

"Dog!" the little hulker bleated again, and took a tottering step towards him. Mhumhi's jaws opened of their own accord before he could stop himself, and he made an arrested lunge, jerking back halfway. The hulker stumbled back and let out a bleating fearful cry.

Mhumhi backed away further, shaking from his own forced self-control, and bumped into something behind himself that clattered and fell over loudly. The hulker gave out another startled wail. Mhumhi jumped forward and pulled himself back again with a yowl of frustration.

"You go away!" said the hulker, and Mhumhi felt another chill at the sheer *weirdness* of hearing it speak. It was retreating back to its little nest of blankets now, coughing and crying.

Mhumhi, panting, thought that going away was probably a good idea, and ran to the door and bumped into Kutta.

"Watch out, Mhumhi," she said, nudging him with her shoulder, and then spotted the crying hulker. "What happened to him?!"

"I didn't do anything!" said Mhumhi, running to the opposite corner of the room with his tail tucked. "I never touched him!"

Kutta trotted over to the crying hulker, which had curled up again, and licked its naked forehead.

"Don't cry," she said, pawing at it. "We've brought you food, don't cry!"

Mhumhi got a distinct sinking feeling when he heard these words, but was distracted at once by the reappearance of the other hulker, the larger one, in the doorway. Apparently Kutta had convinced it to come back after all, though it was staring at Mhumhi with those queer eyes. Mhumhi's lips wrinkled back.

"Stop that," said Kutta, spotting the motion. "Try to be nice, Mhumhi. They're only puppies."

"They're not puppies," Mhumhi muttered, but Kutta advanced on him, tail wagging, and started licking his chin.

"What- no!"

But he was too late; she had already jammed her nose into the corner of his mouth and up came more meat. Mhumhi tried to snatch some back up but Kutta shouldered him aside and picked up the lot, tail wagging.

Mhumhi paced back and forth in his little corner as she walked over to the coughing hulker and dropped it in front of him. He stopped crying at once and picked up the meat in his little fists.

"That's my meat," Mhumhi growled.

"Learn to share, Mhumhi," said Kutta. "I've been doing it since Mother left, now you can pick up some of the slack."

The mention of their mother gave Mhumhi pause, and with a nervous glance to the other hulker that was still standing in the doorway, he trotted closer to Kutta.

"Did you say that… that Mother was taking care of these?"

"Yes," said Kutta. "She showed them to me a little while… a little while before she left."

"You mean Mother and you were keeping secrets from us?" Mhumhi demanded. "For how long?"

"I don't know how long Mother was taking care of them! All I know is that she needed help, so she asked me to come down… She told me not to tell you or Sacha, so I didn't, but…"

"But what?" Mhumhi felt strange and miserable, thinking of his mother down here in the sewers with this horrible secret. He had just told Bii that his mother had never associated with any hulkers, and yet…

"I need help," Kutta said. "I can't take care of them alone anymore. The little one got sick."

Mhumhi glanced at the little one. It was still eating the meat, its fists sticky and black as it put them in its mouth.

"So leave them," he said. "They're not dogs."

"Don't say that," hissed Kutta, shooting a glance at the older one. "They *are*, Mother was right, they just look different. They can talk, and they've got names-"

"You *named* them?"

"They already had the names! Look, the little one is Tareq, and the big one is Maha. You should say hello."

Mhumhi felt that this didn't even warrant a response.

"Come on, Mhumhi," said Kutta, sounding a bit desperate. "Help me. They're Mother's children too… like Kebero… they're our brother and sister."

At the statement Mhumhi gave a low growl.

"If you and Mother were keeping this secret together," he said, "do you also know why she left?"

Kutta stepped back from him, then looked away.

"I… no, I don't. She just disappeared, Mhumhi. I think she must have gone looking for food or something… we were struggling to feed them so much then. I-"

She stared at Mhumhi then, her yellow eyes fearful.

"I'm afraid she might be gone."

Mhumhi tore away from her gaze with a kind of frantic whine.

"We don't know! We don't know that! What if she's really left, like Sacha said? What then? She obviously doesn't care- she's always just wanted puppies- any kind-" He looked angrily over at the standing hulker, which was still watching them. "Any kind she could steal."

"She didn't steal us," said the hulker.

Mhumhi jerked back with surprise, but the hulker was still talking.

"And *you're* not my brother. And she's not my sister."

Mhumhi could only growl softly, unsure really how to respond to this, but Kutta said, "Don't say that, Maha. We're here to take care of you."

"He doesn't want to take care of us," said the hulker- Maha- twisting her mealy lips downwards. "And you don't either. I know you're planning something. You want to get rid of us! Are you going to eat us?"

Mhumhi barked out a laugh. "Us eat them!" He glanced at Kutta, then addressed Maha directly.

"You'd eat a dog, if you had the chance, wouldn't you- little hulker?"

Maha seemed to tremble, and she pressed her lips together. "I- I *am* a dog!"

Mhumhi laughed again, at the bizarre little creature, hairless and shaking. "How did you trick my mother into taking care of you?"

Maha made a pained little noise, and Kutta said, "Mhumhi, be quiet. You think our mother- *our* mother- wouldn't want to take care of them?"

Mhumhi found himself regrettably unable to argue with this. He changed the subject. "You only brought me down here so you could give them my meat!"

"I brought you down here because I thought I could trust you," Kutta said. "I thought you'd understand. I thought you'd behave better than Sacha would, anyway. I guess I was wrong."

"That's not *fair*," Mhumhi said, tucking his tail, and Kutta continued.

"And I've been telling Tareq and Maha about the two of you for forever, too, and I told them all about how Sacha was the cross one but you were the sweet kind one, you know, and how you were the most fun to play with…"

"Come on, Kutta," Mhumhi whined.

"You haven't even met them, you just started going at them from the start, and all because you had *one* bad experience with a hulker. And now you think you know everything about them!"

"I don't think that," said Mhumhi. "I only thought- I-"

"And you're still willing to listen to that nasty old fox over our mother!"

"I thought you liked Bii!"

"Oh, he's all right," Kutta said, and then made her voice fiercer. "But he doesn't know what he's talking about. These little ones haven't done anything. And you just had to-"

"All right," said Mhumhi, "all right, shut up. Stop it. I'll help you. But no more meat. I'll give meat to Kebero, so you give all your meat to these things."

"Then let me have Bii's portion, since there's two of them!"

"Fine!" growled Mhumhi, who was starting to pace again. "I can't believe we've got even more puppies to take care of now!"

"We've had these," Kutta said. "It was just only me and Mother that were taking care of them. You never had to help."

Mhumhi wanted to raise his lip again, but she sounded so tired, and her words sparked a grudging little feeling of guilt in him.

"I'll help now," he said, though he had kind of a bad feeling in his stomach about the whole thing.

Kutta wagged her tail and came up to wash one of his ears.

"Good boy, Mhumhi," she said. "Come on, come meet them, I know you'll get to like them."

Mhumhi kept quiet about what he thought of *that*, but he let her tug on his ear and draw him towards the female.

"This is Maha," she told him. "She's the older one. She can find food for them sometimes down here, but she needs as much help as we can give her. Mother was giving them milk-"

"Mother was *what*?" Mhumhi interrupted.

"Hush. She was giving them milk, but obviously she can't anymore. That's when Tareq started getting sick, after she left. I think we've got to try giving them some fruit if we can get any."

"You're crazy," said Mhumhi, "absolutely... What are we supposed to trade for fruit? We're already running out of meat for everyone..."

"You're right," Kutta admitted. She glanced at Maha. "We'll talk more about it later. Now, go say hello."

Mhumhi wrinkled his nose at her, then went over to Maha. For a moment they gazed at one another, her from up high, him from below.

"Why don't you get down on all fours, like a proper dog?" he asked.

"A dog can stand on two legs if she wants," said Maha, clenching her little paws.

"If you want to greet me like an older brother," Mhumhi began, and she interrupted, "You're not my brother!"

"Maha," said Kutta, "listen to what Mhumhi says."

Maha pulled her lips down, blinking, and then squatted, touching her knuckles to the ground. Mhumhi raised his head and stepped over to gingerly sniff at her, nosing that thick hair of hers.

"Where are your ears, anyway?"

"They're right here," said Maha, taking her paw to pull her hair back. The movement startled him and he flinched away. She made a strange sound then. Tareq, behind them, made it too, putting his sticky little paws up to his mouth.

"What was that?" he asked suspiciously.

"I'm laughing at you," she said.

"Oh," said Mhumhi, rotating his ears forward and back, and then added, "Don't."

Maha stuck her fat tongue out at him, and he shuddered. "Don't do that either."

"Mhumhi, leave her alone," said Kutta. "Stop being such a puppy."

"Stop being such a puppy," said Maha, and she made that odd laughing sound again, though this time Mhumhi could pick up the derision in it. He laid his ears back.

"You haven't greeted me- you haven't sniffed, or anything."

"I don't need to sniff," said Maha, and Kutta said, "Mhumhi, the hulkers can't really smell anything."

"They can't-? Well, I suppose they can't, since they've got no noses."

Maha made a more bubbly version of her laugh. "My nose is right here!" She pointed to a protuberance on her flat face Mhumhi hadn't taken notice of before, because it looked very little like a normal nose. There were two holes in it, which he supposed were nostrils, but there were no side-slits, and it was the same color and texture as the rest of her dark skin.

"Kutta," he whined. It was getting too strange for him. She nudged him with her shoulder, then went over to Maha.

"Go and greet your brother properly."

Maha glanced at her, then crouch-crawled over to Mhumhi, who stiffened. The movement was so unnatural. Having her close reminded his mind of the frailty of her bare skin, as well; of the pulse he could hear beating in her neck. He licked his lips.

Maha put one of her front paws out to him and he jerked away.

"Let's not touch," he said. "That's enough."

"Fine," said Kutta. "Say hello to Tareq, and then we'd better leave. Sacha will probably be looking for us when we get back."

Mhumhi spared a thought for poor Sacha- though he was also rather jealous, with her being in the blissful state of ignorance he'd been in not too long ago.

He let Kutta lead him over to little Tareq, whom he dutifully sniffed as the little hulker lay and coughed and whimpered. Again he backed away when Tareq reached out to touch him.

Kutta seemed willing to accept this. "All right, Mhumhi. Let's get back. And you two-" She turned to where the two hulkers had come together, huddling in the nest of blankets. "I'll be back tonight with some more meat. Maha, you must eat some too."

"I'm not hungry," muttered Maha. Mhumhi focused his ears at her.

"If someone gives you meat, you eat it," he growled. "If you get too weak, I'll eat you myself."

Maha made a sort of disgruntled noise, though he was pleased to see her draw up closer against Tareq at his words. Kutta shot him a look but did not say anything until they had left the room to travel back down the narrow concrete tunnel.

"You really are beginning to sound more like Sacha."

"I am *not*," said Mhumhi sulkily, then switched his tail. Her words reminded him of something.

"By the way, she's getting suspicious about you disappearing so much."

"Oh?"

"She thinks you've got a sweetheart, or something."

Kutta laughed. "Oh, she does, does she? That's funny."

"It *is* funny, since it's you," said Mhumhi, and jumped away when she turned back to nip at him.

"If she thinks that, that's good," she said, resuming her trot and wagging her tail. "It gives me an excuse."

Mhumhi, loping behind, lowered his tail. "She is worried about you, though."

"I'm sure."

"I mean, she's worried that you'll leave."

"Well, why wouldn't she be," said Kutta, not looking back this time. "She's worried there'll be less meat for Keb, and that she might have to give some up once in a while."

"Don't say that, Kutta," said Mhumhi, furrowing his brow. "You know that's not true."

Kutta was quiet for a moment, then she said, "I know. I'm just very… I just get very tired of her sometimes. Don't you?"

Mhumhi couldn't say he did, so instead he squeezed up beside her and nuzzled at her neck.

"I'll help you now, Kutta. You won't have to do this all alone anymore, right?"

Kutta smiled at him. "I knew you'd come around. You're my favorite little brother, you know."

"Because I've got the biggest stomach."

Kutta laughed. "Yes, exactly!"

Mhumhi fell back behind her, noting the new spring in her step. He wished he could share it, but the thought of the two hideous hulker puppies that were now awaiting them weighed heavily on his mind.

8

The Horde of Hunger

Despite his concerns, Mhumhi did not have to see the two hulkers for a few days after that. The fuss Sacha kicked up about the way both of them smelled after they returned seemed to convince Kutta that it would be good to lie low for a while. She merely took Bii's portion of meat from Mhumhi every day before traveling to the sewer herself.

She also seemed to be encouraging the notion that she was visiting someone, something that Mhumhi himself was uncomfortable with. Every time Kutta dropped a casual hint, Sacha seemed to become more withdrawn. When he confronted her about it, though, Kutta seemed unrepentant.

"I'm not really going anywhere," she told him. "Sacha will come back around once she realizes."

Mhumhi didn't argue, though later he wished he had. He didn't like keeping secrets from his oldest sister, especially when he could see that it was hurting her. What exactly would Sacha do if they told her, anyway? He tried to think about it, but he really could not fathom what her response would be.

Sacha certainly knew something was going on with the two of them, but she did not know what, so she spent a great deal of time venting her frustration on the newest member of their household. If she spotted Bii she would go over to him and try to posture and get him to roll over and fawn over her, like Mhumhi and Kutta would. But it was not really in the fox's nature to do so, which tended to result in a great deal of bad-natured growling between the two of them. Bii ended up retreating mostly to the upstairs with Kebero while Sacha kept to the downstairs, and the two of them would not sleep touching one another.

It was frustrating for Mhumhi to see them at odds, especially Sacha, so he took to trying to spend a lot of time with her himself, wiggling and wagging like a puppy at every opportunity. He wasn't sure if this didn't just annoy her, though. It could be hard to tell.

One afternoon he tried to cheer himself up by playing with Kebero. The puppy, at least, seemed happier with the new family arrangement, since Bii spent nearly all of his time doting on him. He was bounding around the bedroom with frenetic energy, leaping clumsily on the bed and down again, coming to thrash and mock-bite at Mhumhi and away again. Mhumhi was hardly having to do a thing; he just sat back and watched Kebero tire himself out.

Bii was sitting on the bed, stretched out on his side. Whenever Kebero jumped on he would rise and lazily snap at him, which was enough to send the puppy out on another delighted romp around the room.

"Be careful, Keb," admonished Mhumhi, stopping the squirming puppy briefly with a leg over his back. "Watch for his leg."

"Oh it's all right, Mhumhi," said Bii, and he got up and stretched, yawning, showing them his tiny little teeth. "It's feeling much better these days."

"Is it? That's good." Mhumhi let Kebero thrash his way onto his back between his front legs, kicking and snapping, and opened his mouth and teased him for a moment.

"Yes," said Bii. "I think I'll be able to go back to the sewers soon and do some proper hunting."

Mhumhi's head came up. "Back to the sewers?"

Kebero squirmed around as well. "Bii, are you going awa- going away?"

"Of course not," the fox said, hopping off the bed so he could come and lick the top of Kebero's head. "I'll be here as long as your siblings let me stay."

Kebero wagged his tail. Mhumhi thought, wryly, that they wouldn't be making him leave anytime soon, not with the extra meat he was giving them. They needed every last bit they could get.

"What do you hunt down in the sewers, Bii?"

Bii gave him a surprised look. "The usual, I suppose… cockroaches, and things. There's always some meat and offal left over around the dispensary pipes, so you can get maggots there, too. I've seen some pretty large rats, but I don't care for them myself. I know a few foxes that do."

"Can I go there too, Bii?" asked Kebero. Bii gave him his impish little smile.

"Certainly you may. We'll make an insect-eater out of you yet, won't we?"

Kebero smiled and wagged his tail. Mhumhi tried to imagine what Sacha's thoughts would be on this: probably not positive.

"Do a lot of foxes go hunting down there?"

"Quite a few," said Bii. "We try to keep out of each others' way though. Too many spoil it for everyone."

"So I guess there are a lot of foxes who don't eat any meat?"

"I'm sure some are supplementing with it," said Bii, "but yes, I think it's fair to say that many don't use it. Why, are you thinking of getting a few more helpers like me?"

"Hm," replied Mhumhi, who had in fact been thinking of something along those lines. More meat would certainly help, even in small portions.

"Be careful about that, if that is what you're thinking," said Bii, looking at him with his black button eyes. "I'm not the only fox who trades, you know. Most of the ones that do aren't trading to the families from Oldtown, either."

"What do you mean- that they're trading to…?"

"The police, yes, and other better-off packs. A lot of them do it for access to fruit, some of them do it for protection, and some… well."

"Well what?" asked Mhumhi, intently curious. Bii glanced at Kebero, who was now lying down between Mhumhi's front paws.

"A lot of them will do it for access to hulker meat," he said. "A lump of cold flesh for a mouthful of warm. That's what I hear, anyway."

"Oh," said Mhumhi, feeling a weird tremor in his stomach. "Is it really that good?"

"I don't know," said Bii, flicking his tail at him. "I've always preferred the flesh that crunches, myself."

"I see," said Mhumhi. "Is that why you decided to come here, instead of to one of those better-off families?"

Bii sneeze-laughed. "I came here because I once knew your mother, and liked her all right. And because I'd rather give my meat to someone who needs it. And because, well, I like looking after puppies." He gave Kebero a fond little nuzzle.

"I'm happy you came, Bii," said Kebero, smiling at him.

"I am, too," said Bii. "You just wait, little wolf, I'll take you down to the sewers and make a rat-catcher out of you!"

"Yes, yes!" Kebero yapped, standing up and wriggling out of Mhumhi's grip. "I'll get all those rats! Eat 'em, down to their ta-tails!"

"Down to the tails?" Bii asked, amused. "Where did you learn to say such things?"

But Kebero was off again, whirling around the room, pouncing on a piece of the tattered bedspread and growling and tugging at it.

"Hey, Bii," Mhumhi said. "When you were down in the sewers, did you ever see a… a hulker?"

Bii pondered for a moment.

"No," he said, finally, "but I've heard of them being down there, creeping around to avoid the police. It's dark and strange down there- if you hear an odd noise, you run for a little tunnel and you don't look back. There can be strange smells, shapes… not just hulkers."

"Not just hulkers?" Mhumhi asked, intrigued.

"I've heard strange sounds," Bii said quietly, "and smelled a strange scent… darker and more powerful than anything I've ever smelled… heavy footsteps… a kind of moaning, from far away. Almost like the way a hulker sounds, but…" He hesitated. "It isn't a hulker. Or at least, I don't think it is. Maybe a different kind of hulker."

"A different kind of hulker?" Mhumhi repeated, feeling chilled.

"Yes," said Bii. "One with sharp teeth."

"Oh," said Mhumhi, trying to keep his tone light, "more like a proper dog, then."

"I suppose so," said Bii. "Still, I'd be careful. If you ever come across something like that down there, Mhumhi, don't stop to find out what it is. Dogs have been disappearing lately."

"I don't plan to be brave again," said Mhumhi, adding quickly, "and anyway, why would I be in the sewers?"

"Of course, why would you be?" said Bii, shooting him a look, and then trotted over to Kebero with his tail hanging in a playful arch.

Mhumhi, a bit shaken, wondered again exactly how much the fox's big ears were privy to.

He didn't have much time to think about it, though, because in the next minute Kutta came thumping up the stairs.

"Hey, Mhumhi," she said, and Mhumhi wagged his tail and went over to plant sloppy kisses on her chin.

"Why don't you go to the dispensary with me and Sacha today?" she asked, backing away a bit from his affection. "The three of us haven't been together much lately."

"We've been in the house," Mhumhi pointed out.

"Yes, but we haven't moved anywhere, really, and I think it would be good," said Kutta, giving him a kind of searching look. "I know you've already eaten yours, so you don't have to, but..."

"No, no, I'll go," said Mhumhi, bouncing on his front paws a bit at the prospect. Having the three of them out together *did* sound like fun, now that he thought of it. They hadn't gotten a chance to romp around outside together since their mother had left, since someone always had to be in the house for Kebero.

This made him think, as he tromped down the stairs after his sister, and he asked, "But will Sacha be all right with Kebero just staying with Bii?"

"Ask her yourself, she's the one that suggested it," said Kutta, stopping short, because Sacha was waiting for them at the foot of the stairs. Mhumhi pushed by Kutta at once and bounced over to go lick her, and she jerked away irritably.

"Come on, Mhumhi, we've been in the same house, we haven't even separated!"

"I missed you," said Mhumhi, pushing against her lovingly, so that she tottered on her short legs.

Kutta laughed. "Mhumhi says he wants to go, Sacha."

"Well, we should go, then," said Sacha, pushing back against Mhumhi. Mhumhi pretended he was being shoved back and her stub tail wagged. "All right, that's enough, let's not be stuck at the end of the line."

"Right!" Mhumhi cried, and bounded over to the doorway, falling into a play-bow from excitement. "Let's go, let's go!"

"Now he's all riled up, Sacha," Kutta told her older sister reprovingly, but Sacha's stub tail was still wagging and she gave a pleased little grunt as she passed Mhumhi on the way out.

They fell into their customary formation, single-file, with bear-faced little Sacha at the front, Kutta trotting behind, and Mhumhi loping and wagging at the rear. Sacha led them on a zig-zagging path, sniffing, brazenly ignoring the other little foxes that had to jump out of her way. Mhumhi was panting happily. There was a certain comfort and power from traveling in a group, even a group as small as three- when he was with his sisters, they filled him with confidence.

He entertained a lazy, happy vision of what it would be like when Kebero was big enough to join them, when he didn't look so much like a puppy anymore. Then they'd be four. Bii could even come, though Mhumhi felt more neutral on that point. Then they'd be five. And with his mother…

His wagging tail slowed. He hadn't spared much thought on his mother lately. It had been hard to, with the new, pressing worry of the two hulker children weighing on him, and the ever-present need for more meat. He had not tried to go to Big Park to look for her.

If she was even there, his mind added desperately. If she was not long dead…

That thought effectively obliterated the rest of his good mood. He trailed after Kutta, head low.

"What's going on?" Sacha growled suddenly, from up ahead. He raised his head again.

They had reached Wide Street, and had found it already very crowded with a mass of dogs. Mhumhi felt a strange chill. Many of these dogs were not little foxes. They were large ones, ones he knew he had never seen around Oldtown before. And when he looked around, he saw many, many more painted dogs than he was used to prowling on top of cars, overlooking the crowd.

The Oldtown dogs had noticed this, and there was a great deal of yapping and tail-puffing at the sight of these amassed interlopers. The little dogs had never been much for solidarity, and indeed fought more often than not, but the sight of strangers before their food supply united them. Loud growls reverberated all across the street. Mhumhi realized that Sacha was adding hers, and Kutta was showing her teeth. He put his ears back.

There came a short howl, and the fur on Mhumhi's back bristled. Standing on top of a large van prowled a massive dog. The biggest kind of all: a gray wolf, panting, yellow-eyed. She howled again, briefly.

Silence fell over the crowd of dogs as they looked up at her.

"Listen!" she barked, and then a painted dog bounded up beside her.

"Yes, listen," she said, voice clear in the new silence. It was Liduma, one of their local police. "Do not start fighting. These dogs have come from Zoo Park. Their dispensary is malfunctioning."

That set off a great deal of alarmed yapping and barking through the crowd, and the wolf howled again for silence.

"Don't worry!" said Liduma. Her eyes looked tired, and her belly hung low and heavy- she was far along in her latest pregnancy. "The dispensary will be fixed soon. We must be patient. In the meantime, you must allow these dogs- your brothers and sisters-"

There was an angry murmur in the crowd at this, and the gray wolf gave a warning snarl.

"These dogs will feed from the Oldtown dispensary until the Zoo Park dispensary is fixed," continued Liduma. "That is our final decision. Fighting will not be tolerated." She fixed a sharp eye on the crowd, and Mhumhi heard the other painted dogs give chirps and twitters of agreement from their vantage points on the cars.

"There is enough food for everyone," Liduma concluded. "Arrive early. Wait patiently. That is all." She turned and loped down from the van. The wolf remained, fixing her yellow eyes on the crowd.

"What a pile of scat!"

That had been Sacha, and she shot a glare at the wolf before turning around to face Mhumhi and Kutta. "You see what they've done? Zoo Park is a long walk from here, there's got to be dispensaries closer- but they've taken them all here, because these dogs are so little. They're counting on their fear stopping them from standing up for themselves!"

"You're probably right, but so what?" said Kutta. "What's the point of fighting? Liduma said it herself, there is enough meat for everyone. All we have to do is wait a little longer..."

"You don't understand," growled Sacha. "You know why the littlest dogs cluster here, in the worst part of the city? It's to get away from those big brutes, who bully them and steal their meat. And now they've brought them here. There'll be fighting, and the little fellows will be driven away... probably down to the sewers, to scrape up what they can, poor things..."

Kutta caught Mhumhi's eye in a worried way at this.

"What did she mean when she said the dispensary was malfunctioning, though?" asked Mhumhi. "Malfunctioning how? And how did she know it would be fixed soon?"

"I suppose she means it's not giving any meat," said Kutta. "Or something like that. I heard from the fennec fox that the East Big Park dispensary wasn't working either. I wonder where they've gone?"

"It shouldn't matter to them, they're off in Big Park eating hot meat and fruit from the Great Glass Garden until they can only roll around on their bellies," Sacha sneered. "What effect would one little dispensary not working have on them?"

"Well, if it's a police dispensary, maybe they do know how to fix it," said Kutta, furrowing her brow. "In the center of the city… they've got lots of things there, after all, that we haven't got…"

"You think they've been inside a dispensary?" Mhumhi found himself fantasizing again, about what that would be like. Rooms and rooms and rooms of meat…

Sacha snorted. "Not likely! I think they're lying, so as not to cause panic. No dog's been able to get inside one of those things, and it's no wonder they're starting to run out of meat. Every bitch in the city has been whelping where she squats, after all, and all those milksop puppies need more meat…"

She jerked her head meaningfully in the direction that Liduma had gone in.

"No, no," said Kutta, actually backing up a few steps in her anxiety. "The dispensaries can't just *run out*, that's impossible. Liduma was right, they're just not working properly."

"Hm," grunted Sacha, but she looked worried as well. Mhumhi looked between the two of them, his tail tucked. "There's no point in working ourselves up over it, you're right, Kutta. There's nothing we can do. Let's get in line before this rabble takes up all the good spots…"

She started moving away through the crowd again. Mhumhi noticed a swift fox and two Bengal foxes watching her, and when Kutta and Mhumhi started following behind her they hastened to run back and take up the rear. In fact, there were a few foxes around that seemed to have been paying attention to their little conversation, and they were all clustering behind them.

Kutta shot Mhumhi a nervous look, and Sacha let out a soft growl, but she kept moving, stumping forward on her short legs, leading their little train to a spot in line behind one of the booths.

They had ended up close to the front, near some of the strange dogs, because all of the little Oldtown foxes seemed more keen to stand in place behind them. Ahead of them was a Tibetan fox, small but heavy-headed, turning to give them a dour look with her narrow yellow eyes. Ahead of her was a little group of dholes.

Mhumhi looked at Kutta, to see what she thought of this, but she had her eyes steadfastly trained down on the asphalt beneath their paws. The stranger dholes were not looking back at them, anyway; they were wagging their tails and play-fighting, wrapped up in their own sense of warm packishness.

Mhumhi allowed himself a furtive glance around, but though he could see more dholes, and other large dogs like golden jackals and Simien wolves, he couldn't spot any groups of painted dogs lining up. He found himself rather relieved.

They got through the line without much trouble, thankfully. Mhumhi noted that most of the stranger dogs, despite Sacha's words, seemed more interested in getting their meat than anything else. When it was the dholes' turn they congratulated each member of the pack with whistles and screams as they took their turn. Their enthusiasm was infectious, and Mhumhi found himself smiling and waving his tail. Kutta still kept her head down.

When the Tibetan fox went to take her turn, Sacha looked back and gave a soft, warning whine. Mhumhi looked and realized that there were two painted dogs watching them from atop a nearby car, speaking softly to one another.

"Don't look at them," Sacha said, voice low. "We're attracting too much attention… keep together but don't touch each other. Don't talk to anyone."

Mhumhi and Kutta put their ears back and obeyed her, studiously looking at different parts of the asphalt, keeping their profiles low. Not for the first time, Mhumhi wished he didn't have such a distinct spattered coat.

Sacha and Kutta took their meat without incident, and the three of them managed to retreat to the concrete ramp that Mhumhi and Bii usually ate under. Sacha led them to the lowest and darkest part of it, growling to dislodge a trio of hoary foxes.

"We'll have to be more careful now," she said, voice low, after she had dropped her small packet of meat. "More police… they'll get more suspicious, and they're antsy anyway, looking for trouble. I might pass for a little fox, but you two they'll be suspicious about, especially if you look like you're together… We'd better stick to moving separately from now on." She let loose a heavy sigh through her nose.

Kutta gave Mhumhi an anxious look, and then said, "Well, the worst they can do is stop us, isn't it? Mixed packs aren't unheard of, after all. There's no reason for them to suspect us of- you know."

"No," said Sacha, "but lots of the little dogs around here know of our-" She stopped short.

Mhumhi looked behind himself. Three painted dogs were striding purposefully towards them. Liduma was one of them.

Sacha gave him a swift, meaningful look, but he could not decipher it, only stood there fearfully with his tail tucked and his head low. Kutta nudged him and turned to speak with them.

"Is something wrong? May we help you?"

The three painted dogs stopped a few feet away under the shadows of the overpass, white-flagged tails waving slowly.

"We have some questions we'd like you to answer," said one. Mhumhi noticed that Liduma was somewhat behind her, her head lowered; this strange dog must have been higher-ranking. The sight of pregnant Liduma acting so cowed gave him an uncomfortable feeling.

"Why?" asked Kutta. "Have we done something wrong?"

The lead dog smiled, but it wasn't in a very friendly way.

"We'd just like to learn a little more about all of you here. We're police from Zoo Park, and we've heard some interesting stories from the ones who patrol this area." Her gaze flicked to Liduma, who looked down at the ground.

"You know how little foxes like to gossip," said Kutta, smiling genially. "And I'm sure this place must be boring to patrol. I'm sure the stories will be much more interesting than the truth."

The dog beside Liduma whuffed, his lip rising, but the leader merely kept smiling.

"Tell me, how did the two of you- no, I should say the three of you-" She looked at Sacha, and her tail wagged slowly. "How did you come to be so close?"

"Dogs come together after bad times," said Sacha, her little head suddenly jerking up, meeting the painted dog's gaze. "We've all simply had bad times. Places we can't go back to."

The painted dog looked down at her, bemused. "I see. That's terribly unfortunate."

"Yes, well-" Kutta began, but the dog interrupted her, still looking down at Sacha.

"I have another question for you," she said. "Have you seen a domestic dog that is white, with a curled tail and folded ears? I believe she goes by the name of Pariah."

"Of course we have," said Sacha, much to Mhumhi's surprise. Her gaze was still steady. "She's well-known around these parts. She even stayed with us for a little while. But she's long gone now."

"Long gone?"

"Yes," said Sacha. "She left several weeks ago. I don't know where to, and frankly I was glad to be rid of her."

"I see," said the dog, again. Very suddenly she looked directly at Mhumhi. "And you, do you know where she's gone?"

"What?" said Mhumhi, shrinking away, pressing his ears back. "No, I- I don't know where she is."

"And did you know if she had any puppies?" The painted dog was stepping closer to him, her eyes intent on his.

"He wouldn't know anything," said Liduma. Her head was still low, and the lead dog ignored her.

"Did she have puppies or didn't she?"

"Puppies...? No, no, she didn't..." Mhumhi cringed, shutting his eyes against her gaze.

Kutta suddenly bounced up on her forepaws.

"Oh! This is about that absolutely vicious rumor, isn't it?"

"What rumor?" asked the lead dog, turning away from Mhumhi. He felt as if a searchlight had been snapped off of him.

"The one that Pariah stole puppies," said Kutta, very derisively. "Honestly, if I find the filthy fox that started that, I'll- I'll shake him! Dogs just have to go out of their way to be cruel to domestics, and I'll never understand why." She gave a sorrowful whine. "Pariah never harmed a soul in her life, and people had to say such terrible things about her… I don't doubt that that's why she left."

The painted dogs exchanged more looks. Liduma blinked a few times. The lead one said, "You three never saw her doing anything of the sort?"

"What, stealing puppies?" said Kutta, sounding appalled, but Sacha broke in with a growl.

"We don't know what she did before she lived with us."

"Oh, don't say that, it's really no wonder she left, with you in the house-"

The third dog finally spoke up, looking at Mhumhi. "And you, silent brother? What did you think of her?"

Mhumhi licked his lips, aware that everyone was now looking at him, Sacha and Kutta with a certain desperation in their eyes.

"I didn't… I didn't know her very well. Didn't speak to her much."

"Didn't speak to her much, hmm?" The dog flicked an ear towards Mhumhi, disbelieving. "Is that so? You're an awfully quiet one."

"Leave him alone," said Kutta, suddenly sharp-toned, and when they all turned to look back at her, added more quietly, "He's had a hard time."

The lead dog twitched her tail, and then suddenly the two of them seemed to converge on Kutta, coming from both sides, so that she backed up nervously against the concrete.

"Quick to bite, little whistle dog," said the lead dog.

"Quick to defend that pup-thief, too," said the other, tail wagging stiff and slow. He pressed closer to Kutta, who had gone into a kind of cringing crouch, jaws tightly shut and eyes fearful.

"Maybe the domestic isn't the one we're looking for," said the lead dog, pacing slightly in front of her. "Maybe it's a little whistle dog like you. You look like you could use some puppies." She laughed, letting her teeth show.

"Don't be ridiculous," said Sacha. Mhumhi saw that she was so stiff she was nearly trembling, and her eyes looked savage, but her tone somehow managed to be calm and dismissive. "She's no more a pup thief than I am. I'm certain you realize that."

"We're not certain of anything," said the lead dog. "But if you know where the domestic is..." She leaned close to Kutta, who shook. "We'd like to speak to her too."

Mhumhi saw Sacha's hackles rising, her small eyes narrowing, and felt petrified himself. The air was so charged there was certain to be a fight, and the police dogs would call more of their pack over, and that would be it for all of them, finished, then and there under the bridge...

There came a sharp whistle.

"Hey, spotty!"

The painted dogs all whirled around, their leader with a growl. The pack of dholes Mhumhi had seen earlier had come trotting under the ramp, seven or eight of them, waving their long black tails in the air. In their lead was a male, laughing with his tongue hanging out.

"Leave that poor whistle girl alone, police!"

The dogs behind him were laughing too, at least with their mouths, but Mhumhi noticed that they seemed to be fanning out, making a line of rusty fur and teeth.

The painted dogs drew close to one another, seeming to confer for a moment, and then their leader said, "What's your name?"

"My name's Rakshasa, ol' spot," said the lead dhole. "I guess you'll remember it, huh? I can tell you all the names of my brothers here, too. That one's Lal-"

"Quiet," said the painted dog, exposing a canine. "We will remember it." She flicked her tail at her companions, and they retreated, legs and tails stiff as they walked around the edge of the line of dholes. The dholes let loose derisive whistles and chirps as they passed, until Rakshasa stopped them with a look.

"That's enough," he said, and his brothers came and bunched up around him again, wagging and whining. The painted dogs were disappearing over the hill, Liduma dragging her dusty self with them.

"You clear off too, you dumb spotty," said one of the other dholes to Mhumhi.

"That's enough from *you*," said Sacha, shooting him a glare. "He's not police. What are all of you up to?"

"What're we up to?" exclaimed Rakshasa, letting his tongue hang out. "Hey, we can't let the police bully another whistle, can we?"

His brothers whistled and chirruped their agreement, and Mhumhi noticed Rakshasa looking hopefully at Kutta. Someone from the back called, "Have you got any sisters?"

Rakshasa laughed, and even Mhumhi smiled a little, feeling the tension ebb, but Sacha lifted her lip.

"I see what you're after. Well, you can plainly see she doesn't want anything to do with any of you. So go on! Move along!"

"Sure, sure, little war-dog," said Rakshasa, shooting one last wistful look at Kutta, who was still sitting pressed against the concrete, head turned away. "Come on, let's go, before we have our ankles bitten off, then."

Sacha growled at them, but they merely laughed and made their noisy way off again, over the hill in the direction the painted dogs had gone in. Mhumhi was almost sad to see them go- almost, until he saw how relieved Kutta looked. Sacha had already gone over to her and stood on her shoulder to lick her neck.

"You get yourself into trouble quick," she was saying, but there was nothing reproving to her tone. Mhumhi whined and went to roll over and lick under Kutta's chin as well.

"Let's eat our meat and go home," was all Kutta said, after a little while.

"Right," said Sacha, giving her one last lick, and then trundled over to her meat packet, where it lay untouched. She paused suddenly. Sitting curled up beside it was the little fennec fox.

"I thought you might need someone to get those police off your back," he said, wagging his tail against the ground.

"And get a little meat for yourself, as well?" said Sacha, looking displeased, but the fennec stood and they saw he'd been lying on top of his own tiny packet.

"For the little one," he said, and then bared his teeth in a grin. "I mean Bii, of course."

Sacha sniffed at the meat suspiciously. "What's this all about?"

"Take it," said the fennec, getting up. "I bet we'll be seeing less of it soon, and I at least can catch mice. You big dogs should fill up while you can."

"What do you mean by that?" Sacha's small eyes had gone flinty again. "What do you know?"

The fox merely blinked at her, and walked away, swishing his little tail. Sacha glared after him.

"You eat it, Kutta," she said.

"Me?" said Kutta, faintly.

"Yes, you, you're too skinny and tired." Sacha gave a little growl and batted at the tiny packet with her front paws. "Not that it'll make much of a difference, really."

Kutta did not respond to this, only glanced at Mhumhi and drew him to one side while Sacha tried to tear her packet open.

"You've got to go to visit the puppies tonight," she murmured. "I'll give you some of my meat…"

"What? Why now?"

"They haven't had enough today- Tareq is getting sicker- and Sacha's right." She exhaled softly. "I am too tired."

Mhumhi stepped back a little, staring at her, and was frightened to realize how tired she looked- how skinny she looked.

"You're giving up too much meat for them," he hissed.

"No," said Kutta. "Not enough…"

"Eat all your meat, Kutta," said Mhumhi. "I'll give them some of mine."

She looked at him, surprised. "But you haven't eaten since this morning-"

"Well, I mean, I'll take a little," he admitted. He'd sort of forgotten about that.

Kutta gave him a small smile, but it faded fast. "Mhumhi," she said softly, "what do you think the police will do if they discover…?"

"If they discover Kebero?"

They both jumped, for that had been Sacha, who had moved to sit down by their feet and glare up at them.

"You two and your little secrets," she growled. "Liduma wouldn't care, but if these upper city dogs discover Kebero, I don't expect them to show us any mercy."

"But we weren't the ones who…"

"Doesn't matter," said Sacha, and she cast her eyes over to the distant horde of dogs still waiting to receive their daily meat. "The fewer mouths there are to feed, the better."

9
Playing with the Puppies

Mhumhi navigated the sewers for the second time with some difficulty, only half-remembering the route Kutta had led him on before. She had left a few marks behind, but not many, likely worried about someone less sympathetic finding them and following them. Mhumhi had to wonder himself whether or not any hungry foxes ever wandered to that part of the sewer. If Sacha was right, they'd be down there even more soon, and hungrier.

After some backtracking and false starts, he managed to make his way to the massive cavern where the sewage fell from pipes. He couldn't help but take a whiff, wondering, perversely, if the commingled waste from his own house fell in there as well. It had been a long time since the police had put in place the rule that toilets must be used, to keep the waste off the streets. Oldtown citizens tended to be a bit lax about it, but he'd heard that it was rigidly enforced in other districts.

That made him wonder where, exactly, this massive cavern was located aboveground. He had no way of knowing. He might not even be in Oldtown anymore. It was a curious thought, but Mhumhi shrugged it off, steeling himself instead for the unpleasant task he had to perform.

He made his way down the little side-tunnel and finally to the door. It was a few inches ajar, and light was spilling into the corridor.

Give them the food, then leave, he promised himself, and nudged it open with his nose.

At once something came flying down with a *whap* and clipped the end of his nose. He yelped and jumped back.

"Go away!"

Mhumhi growled, and seeing that someone was shutting the door, threw his whole weight on it and shoved it open. There was a shrill hulker scream, and something *whapped* him hard on the head.

"Stop that!" he shouted, whirling around, and snapped at the thing. It turned out to be a wooden plank, which splintered under his teeth as he yanked it out of Maha's hand. She gave a startled cry of pain and fell back.

"Dog!"

That was Tareq, sitting up in his little nest as Mhumhi growled and vented his frustration on the board by tearing it into splinters.

"Oh!" said Maha, who had caught herself with one paw against the wall. "Oh, it's Mhumhi."

Her voice was a little uncertain, as if she was unsure if in fact this was an improvement. Mhumhi spat out bits of wood.

"Of course it's me! Who else would come down this stinking place to feed stinking hulkers!"

"Well, Kutta always scratches to let us know it's her," Maha said defensively, drifting back over to Tareq.

That was actually a decent point, so Mhumhi decided to drop it. His nose was still smarting.

"Come over here and get the food from me, so I can leave."

They both stared at him with their weird hulker eyes. Mhumhi scratched the concrete floor impatiently with one paw.

"If you two are puppies, come and act like it!"

Maha gave Tareq a light pat on his bony shoulder and then stood up on two legs. Mhumhi put his ears back and rumbled.

Maha bit her lip and crouched down and came towards him in that horrible half-crawl. When she got close enough she reached out her paw…

"What are you doing with your paw?" Mhumhi demanded.

"It's not a paw, it's a *hand*," said Maha. "And these are my fingers." She wriggled her weird little talons at him, as if Mhumhi hadn't been uncomfortable enough.

"You haven't answered my question."

"I'm coming to take the meat," she said, tilting her head at him.

Mhumhi stared at her. "Are you planning to bat it out of me?"

Tareq gave his bubbly little hulker laugh. Maha reached for him again, and he jerked away, raising a lip. She scooted closer along the floor and reached for him again. He growled, shaking from the urge to move away from the horrible talons, and forced himself to hold still.

She took her fingers and stroked him along the chin. It was a bizarre sensation, very different from something like Kebero licking him- more pressure, less dampness- and he did not think he liked it, but it had the desired effect. He turned his head away and up came Kutta's meat.

Maha snatched the goopy handful of it at once and backed away, as Mhumhi licked his lips and gulped. He was becoming a regurgitation machine lately.

He saw Maha moving to hand it all to Tareq, who was reaching his little paws- hands- out eagerly, and snapped, "No! You both eat."

"I ate this morning," said Maha.

"Don't lie to me," said Mhumhi, stepping forward threateningly, tail raised. "Your older sister gave up that meat for you, now *eat* it."

Maha stiffened her shoulders, but she took the meat and divided it into two not-quite-equal halves. Mhumhi noticed that she took the smaller portion for herself. He stepped closer to the two of them.

Tareq cringed away with a whimper, but Mhumhi was slightly distracted, sniffing at the nest of blankets. They smelled like old urine, though a kind of pale, watery hulker urine that he did not approve of.

"Where do you drink from?" he asked, hoping that the answer wasn't in the sewage.

"There's a tap right there," said Maha, raising her arm with one talon extended. He stared at it uncomprehendingly.

"*That* way," Maha repeated, and looked to his left. He followed her gaze and saw that there was a tiny little side room attached to the one they were in, with a sink and a little toilet. He supposed at least the waste didn't have far to travel.

"Doesn't the little one know how to use the toilet?"

"He does," said Maha, "he's just sick now."

Mhumhi gave Tareq another sniff-over as the little boy cringed. He wished that he'd stop whimpering like that, because it was making Mhumhi salivate again.

He did smell a kind of rubbery sickness on the puppy, evident in the urine and in the snot dripping from his nose.

"He'll make himself worse if he sits in it like that."

"We don't have any other blankets," said Maha. "He's too cold."

Mhumhi licked his lips. It was indeed very cold in the sewers; he would not fancy spending a night down here even while healthy and covered in fur.

"What about those wrappings you have on you?"

Maha seemed surprised, and looked down at herself. She plucked at the front of her wrapping.

"You mean clothes?"

Mhumhi gave her a blank look.

"I could get more, but I'm afraid," said Maha. "Mother brought us these from outside a long time ago, but the way she used isn't any good anymore."

"Isn't any good?" asked Mhumhi, distracted by the notion of his mother carrying wrappings to the little hulkers.

"Something uses it now," Maha told him.

"What uses it?"

"Something," Maha informed him, pulling the corners of her lips down.

Mhumhi thought of what Bii had been telling him about the things that lurked in the darkness of the sewers, and decided not to press the issue.

"Are there any other ways to the outside around here?"

Maha looked up, and Mhumhi followed her gaze. In the concrete ceiling was carved a circular tunnel going straight up, with iron rungs every foot or so.

"So there isn't," he said.

"I can climb up there!" said Maha. "You couldn't, but I could. I used to, but then more dogs came here, and I was too scared."

Mhumhi craned his neck up, trying to fathom how anyone would be able to make it up there. "Where does it let out?"

"On a big street," Maha told him. "Lots of tall buildings. Lots of stores. You could get clothes and candles and everything."

"What's a candle?"

"It's made of waxy stuff," said Maha, wiggling her hands around, "and you can light it with a match, and it gets warm and makes light."

"Like a lightbulb?" Mhumhi asked, puzzled.

"No, not a lightbulb, 'cause there's no glass. And it hurts if you touch the fire."

Mhumhi put his ears back- he knew what fire was, as he'd once seen a house- electrical wires laid bare by excessive chewing- go up in flames and take out half an Oldtown block before it wore itself out. It had indeed been warm, if demonic.

"It's just a little fire," Maha said. "This big." She moved her hands about again.

Beside her, Tareq, looking furtively at Mhumhi, tugged at her wrappings and gabbled something.

"What's he doing?"

"He wants more meat," said Maha. "I could've given him the rest of mine."

Mhumhi gave her a warning look, and she subsided.

"Why doesn't he talk more?"

"Cause he's little, and he also doesn't understand much Dog."

"Much... dog?" Mhumhi repeated. "What do you mean?"

"I mean, there's what we speak, and that's Dog," said Maha, scratching her forehead with her blunt nails. "And then there's what the hulkers speak, and that's- I don't know the word for it. Hulker language."

Mhumhi thought it over, wrinkling his brow. It had not occurred to him that the language he spoke might not be shared by all. "If there's a hulker language, why don't you speak it?"

"Cause I'm not a hulker, I'm a *dog*," she explained, as if he were stupid. "My first and third mamas were dogs."

Mhumhi gazed at her, and she sighed. "Our mother was my third mama. My first one, I was in a family of domestics and they took care of me and some others. I think- I think my..."

She paused for a moment, then used a word Mhumhi did not know. "My *human* mother got killed, so they took care of me and some other puppies, but then the police got them and they killed all of them but not me. I got into a little pipe like that one where they couldn't get me." She grinned, baring her square teeth. "They tried and one fell in and died. So they left me alone."

Mhumhi looked nervously up the long tunnel in the ceiling again. It would be a terrifying fall down onto the concrete below.

"Then I went and found Tareq and his mama," said Maha, putting her hand on little Tareq's head. He was coughing and whimpering again, his face somehow streaming wetness. It made him smell even sicker, and Mhumhi leaned away from him.

"That was my only hulker mama," Maha said. "I didn't like her. She tried to make me learn hulker language and everything and wouldn't give me meat. But she didn't last long. She never came back one day. Same as your mother."

Mhumhi stiffened a little. "And how long were you with… my mother?"

"I don't know," said Maha. "A little while. I thought we'd be able to stay with her. Or at least me. Tareq cried all the time."

Tareq sniffled loudly at this, seeming to recognize his name.

"And now she's gone too," said Maha, and she looked upwards for a moment, perhaps at the long tunnel, perhaps at nothing. "And now all we have is you wild dogs. I bet you'll eat us."

Mhumhi decided the option was still on the table. "What do you mean, wild dogs?"

"I mean not domestic, right? Mean dogs that kill people. Domestic dogs don't do that."

Mhumhi felt a little slighted. "We don't just go around killing people!"

Maha gave him a flat stare. "They killed and ate up all the hulkers I knew."

"Well, hulkers aren't *dogs*."

"Yeah they are!" Maha aimed a kick at him with one of her hind legs, which he sidestepped easily. "You wild dogs eat your own kind! You wanted to eat me, didn't you! I *know* you did!"

Mhumhi raised a lip, suddenly very angry in spite of himself, because he did, in fact, still have that desperate urge. He thought bitterly that it would leave a great deal more meat for the rest of them, especially Kutta.

"I'm not going to eat you," he said, "so shut up about it. Be glad I even came down here to feed you."

"I bet it's just because Kutta said!"

"I said shut up!" Mhumhi growled, and stepped close to her, letting her see his teeth, making her cringe down and whimper.

Tareq said, "Bad dog!" and Mhumhi shot him a look that made him clamp his mouth shut.

"You're meaner than Kutta said you were," muttered Maha.

"I'm not mean!"

"We're puppies, and you're mean to us!"

"You don't even act like real puppies!" Mhumhi said, a tad desperately.

"You don't even act like a real dog!"

"Oh!" said Mhumhi, and gave a little thrash of frustration. "If I was a *real* dog, I guess I would have eaten you already!"

Maha opened her mouth, then shut it again, her lips trembling.

"Now I have one more thing to ask," he told her, pacing a little in the small room. "Listen carefully. Tomorrow, if I scratch on top of that hole, will you move the top?"

"Why?" she asked, her voice oddly quavery.

"If I know where it is aboveground, I won't have to drag things through the sewer," said Mhumhi, thinking that it should be fairly obvious. "You need blankets, and those candle things, don't you? If I find the top, I can drop them down." He paced a little in the small room, pondering. "You should climb up there and put something strong-smelling at the top. That will help me find it."

Maha was staring at him. "You're going to get us candles and blankets?"

"Yes," said Mhumhi. "Unless you don't think they'll help him get better."

"No, they will," said Maha, wide-eyed. "If you get the really smelly candles, it makes it smell better down here."

"I still have to figure out what a candle is," said Mhumhi. "Is there anything else?"

Maha said, slowly, "Kutta said fruit…"

"It's too hard to get," said Mhumhi. "Nothing to trade for it."

"Oh," said Maha, downcast. "Then no. Nothing else."

"All right," said Mhumhi, shooting another dubious look at the hole. "Remember to make it smell really strongly. If you could mark it, that would be the best, but…"

"I can," said Maha. "I think I know what to do."

"Then do that," Mhumhi said. He was feeling weary from all the excitement of the day, and from growling and being mean. "I'm going to leave now."

"All right," said Maha, her eyes still big, and reached her hand out- his head gave an arrested jerk- and scratched him under the chin. "Goodbye, Mhumhi."

The sensation was still bizarre to him, and he stayed still for a moment, not sure if he liked it or not. It felt strangely intimate.

"Goodbye," he said, and turned around. "Close the door."

He heard Maha getting up behind him, on her two legs, and gave a little shudder. He was glad when he was out in the concrete hall and away again. It was all so strange… too strange.

The hulkers left in him an unease that he had never felt before, the kind of unease that came when something that looked so un-dog talked and acted like it had feelings like a dog, thoughts like a dog… He shuddered again, still feeling the hulker's touch on his chin.

If they were dogs, why did his every instinct tell him to bear them down, bite them silent? He had never felt the urge to kill before he had stepped into that room. It was as if there were parts of himself he did not even know. Or… two parts of himself, separated, coming back together again for the first time.

He did not like it. He found himself wishing passionately that the hulkers did not exist, for it was their fault… they had brought out this strange bloodlust in him.

His thoughts were dark as he trotted back into the large drainage chamber, but then he had to pause. An odd scent had come to him. It was nothing like the queer pale scent of the hulkers- rather, it was heady and strong, certainly strong enough to come to him over the odor of all the sewage. He took a deeper whiff. It was certainly a living thing, perhaps a dog- he sniffed harder- perhaps not a dog, for he had never smelled anything like it.

Again his thoughts turned uneasily to what Bii had said about there being other things in the sewers, and he glanced back behind him, at the stairs leading up to the narrow concrete tunnel. He almost wanted to go back, just to check… But no, that was pointless, the scent was not even coming from that direction.

Mhumhi licked his lips. If he could utilize the round tunnel in the ceiling, he wouldn't even have to come down this way again, which had been his intent. Now he felt slightly more urgent about it. That scent provoked a strange feeling of foreboding in him.

As if to confirm it, there suddenly came a strange cry. Mhumhi went stock-still.

It was muffled from the sound of rushing water all around him, but when it came again he was certain he had not imagined it: a low, lonely cry, like a moan, echoing all around the chamber. It seemed to be a question, or an inquiry: a sort of where-are-you?

Mhumhi almost found himself wanting to answer, to whine and invite the stranger over for a greeting, but no, that would be quite a bad idea. He went to the wire railing and put his paws over it, pricking his ears, but the cry did not come again, and he saw nothing but murky sewage underneath the spotlights cast far below.

The unknown scent was fading away, too, as deeply as he inhaled. He found himself strangely disappointed. Whatever it was, it seemed more familiar and more friendly than a hulker.

10

The Store

The next morning, while he was giving Kutta his excess meat, he informed her of his idea.

"I told the little hulker girl to mark the entrance at the top," he said, "and we can go and search for it aboveground and drop things down in there for them."

Kutta finished gobbling up the last of the meat, licking her lips, digesting his words. Mhumhi had led her outside, out of paranoia of being overheard by Bii, and they were standing behind the house on the sidewalk in the bright sunlight. It looked to be another warm, sunny day, and if Mhumhi had his way, he'd be outside to enjoy it.

"I never thought about that," she said, at length. "It's a good idea. But I'd have no idea where to start looking."

"We start by the entrance, and trace our steps underground," Mhumhi explained. "If we go roughly in the same directions, I bet we'll be able to smell it out."

Kutta tilted her head. "Maybe we would."

"You don't seem very interested in it," said Mhumhi, his tail drooping a bit. "Don't you think it'll help them?"

"Oh, I do, Mhumhi, it's just…" Kutta hesitated, rotating her ears, and leaned closer. "I have to tell you something."

"Don't tell me you've adopted more puppies! What are they this time, fly maggots? I'll feed them to Bii!"

Kutta laughed, her teeth flashing. "No! No, it's just something I've been wanting to do. It's sort of the reason I told you about them."

Mhumhi had a feeling he wasn't going to like what she was about to say. "Well, what is it?"

"You know the little one is sick," said Kutta. "And it's bad down there… bad water, bad air, no sunlight… I know they'll die if they stay down there much longer, Mhumhi, I know it. They'll get sicker and sicker." She paused to cough herself, perhaps in sympathy. "I want to move them."

"*Move* them?" Mhumhi gave her a wide-eyed look. "Move then where? How? Where is there that they can even go? And why should we risk getting caught, anyway?"

"Because Sacha's right, I think, that there'll be more dogs down in the sewers soon," said Kutta. "And anyway, if the police go in there and kill them, they're sure to smell us, too, and then what will happen? You think they won't go investigating?"

Mhumhi hadn't thought of that, and put his ears back.

"If I can figure out a safe place to take them, I think we can do it," said Kutta. "I just haven't figured out a safe spot yet. But Mhumhi, you'll like this part-"

"Will I?"

"Yes, because it means we won't have to see them again. If we can find an adult hulker that'll take them in."

Mhumhi blinked. "An adult hulker? If we can find one? How will we get it to take them in, even?"

"Well, I suppose we'd ask it…"

"Ask it!" Mhumhi laughed, incredulous. "Of course, we'll ask it!"

Kutta shouldered him. "I haven't got any other ideas. And the meat really is getting too low. I don't know how much farther we can stretch it out. I don't think we have a choice."

Mhumhi made a disgruntled sound- there seemed, to him, to be an easy choice.

"Well, I don't think we'll be moving them today," he said. "So let's go and see if we can give them more blankets. And candles. Whatever those are."

Kutta wagged her tail and came over to wash his ears. "What a strong, smart big brother you are," she cooed, until he went to nip her and she boxed him back, laughing. They fell to rolling and mock-biting there in the street for a few minutes, until Mhumhi was panting and laughing.

"Come on, come on then!" he said, bounding on his front paws. "Let's search it out, let's go have a race!"

Kutta gave a sharp whistle of agreement, and Mhumhi pressed his ears back and ran, using his lanky legs to their full effort. Behind him Kutta scrambled to catch up, her spine arcing. Together they dashed down the warm streets, leaping over startled foxes, turning tight corners in clouds of scrabbling paws and dust. Mhumhi's longer legs gave him greater speed, and he quickly outstripped his sister, but whenever he paused to wait for her she would give an extra sprint and leap right over him, whistling and laughing.

It seemed merely seconds before they reached the bridge, and Mhumhi skidded to a stop and was bowled over by his sister. This sparked another fierce bout of mock-fighting until he whimpered and wagged and licked her, conceding his defeat. She sprang off of him and he twisted to his feet, panting, smiling broadly.

"We go that way, then?" He trotted to the top of the bridge, peering down at the water flowing inwards through the grate. "Follow the water?"

"I think so," said Kutta, also panting, rather heavier than he was. She came by the bridge and gave a deep sniff. "Perhaps we shouldn't have done that right after eating."

"Come on, Kutta, don't get lazy," said Mhumhi, wagging his tail. "If it's this way, let's go this way!" He came off the bridge and galloped onward, nose to the ground. Kutta followed him at a more sedate pace until he slowed down enough for her to catch up.

"Look," she said, nudging him. There was a storm drain embedded in the sidewalk, like the one the fennec fox liked to hide in. "That leads down to the sewer, I bet. We must be going the right way."

"'Course we are," said Mhumhi, trotting over to sniff loudly at the drain. "Smells like scat."

"Well, I hope it's the right scat, and we haven't missed the turn or anything."

"Oh," said Mhumhi, who had forgotten to consider that the sewer branched out. "Well, it doesn't feel like we should've turned yet, does it?"

Kutta made no response, just circled the storm drain briefly, sniffing, then looked straight ahead. "Let's keep going this way."

"All right," said Mhumhi, and they went on, down through the dusty lower streets, which were silent and empty now that it was approaching midday. Mhumhi felt like he was starting to recognize some of the old buildings.

"Isn't this near where the subway entrance is?"

"Oh," said Kutta, glancing up briefly. "I guess so."

She returned her nose to the ground, sniffing, but Mhumhi looked up a moment, tongue hanging out. A place where he had smelled his mother… The subway was underground, too, like the sewers. Perhaps he had found Maha's 'other entrance.'

"Mhumhi," Kutta called. He shook himself, breaking away from his thoughts, and followed her.

They went up past where the subway had been, towards the northernmost part of Oldtown. Here they hit the broad edge of Wide Street where it swung in a curve before separating into branches and high concrete ramps. Streetlights swung slowly here too. Mhumhi looked up at them, as the light blinked from the topmost to the bottom slot, signaling for nothing.

The dispensary was a long ways down Wide Street from here, and on the other side they could see more buildings, much taller than those in Oldtown, with many blocks of stories. There was a large parking garage just alongside the concrete ramp, and Mhumhi and Kutta trotted over to it, sniffing curiously as they entered its shaded interior. It was full of empty cars, parked neatly side-by-side.

Mhumhi could tell that many dogs had come and left their marks here, perhaps for years, as the place stank strongly of urine. He wrinkled his nose.

Kutta hopped over a low concrete barrier and out of the parking garage. There was a little kiosk with a lowered wooden barrier, striped yellow and black, and she leapt over it playfully, kicking out her hind legs.

"I think we're getting closer," she called. Mhumhi could hear the excitement and nervousness in her voice. He felt it too. Past Wide Street and the parking garage, they were leaving Oldtown.

There were no strict rules about dogs leaving their districts, of course, as there'd be no way to enforce it, but dogs still rarely left their places of birth, unless it was to look for a new pack to make a family with. Mhumhi knew most of the types of foxes in Oldtown *only* lived in Oldtown, anyway, so they had no reason to leave.

He himself had never thought of seeking out a new pack or a mate. He did not think Kutta had either, for all her pretending. He couldn't imagine Sacha leaving; with his mother gone she was their lynchpin, the source of their strength.

"Let's go," said Kutta, whistling encouragingly, and Mhumhi followed her up the concrete ramp and into a new part of the city.

Here quite suddenly it took on a shift in mood, like a living thing. From Oldtown's pale apartments it went to stretch upwards, blocks and blocks of windows, dark glass, high metal struts, building after building after building. The street ahead of them seemed to narrow off into the distance, buildings growing closer on either side, though never touching. The skyline was jagged.

They trotted across the sidewalk here, as Kutta sniffed out the next storm drain, and then a metal manhole cover on one side of the street. There was a little fenced-in set of chairs and tables here in front of a building with a glass-fronted door. Most of them had been blown over by the wind, but Mhumhi could see a couple of them standing, with bright blue umbrellas tilted but not overtaken just yet.

"Here," said Kutta suddenly, and turned and took them down a street where the bottoms of the buildings were marked with awnings and tall black markings; "Here," she said again, and took him on another turn, where they ran across tattered plastic siding flapping over an unfinished building that was just a mass of metal struts; "This way," she said, and they ran across a broad intersection, gaping and empty, marked with white and yellow lines. She stopped here to sniff at another manhole.

Mhumhi looked up, and gave a jerk of shock. Suspended on the building above him was a huge rectangular board, and printed upon it was a lifelike image of a hulker's face, only magnified a thousand times its size. It stared down at him with its pale mad eyes, hundred-foot smile stretching white and menacing.

Mhumhi knew it could not be alive, that it was flat, and yet he tucked his tail. How could an image of a hulker be there like that, grinning down at the city? It was too unnerving, as if a hulker had taken his pale, watery urine and pissed a high mark for all to smell.

"Kutta, look at this," he called.

"Wait, Mhumhi," she said, and he could hear her sniffing deeply. "I think… I think that this is it!" She laughed, letting her tongue hang out. "Look, come over here, look at this!"

He turned nervously away from the mocking image and joined her at the manhole. By one edge something dirty-white stuck out. When he sniffed it he got a strong whiff of Tareq- Tareq's urine, to be exact.

"This must be it!" he exclaimed, excited in spite of himself. They had done it- they had found the other entrance!

Kutta began scratching at the manhole in excitement. "Maha!" she whistled. "Tareq!"

Mhumhi glanced around a bit nervously, but the street was completely deserted. "Don't be too loud," he warned her anyway.

Kutta twitched her ears but otherwise ignored him, concentrating on scratching away at the cover of the manhole, scraping all of its strange ridges. Finally it seemed to twitch underneath her, and she leapt off.

The manhole cover hissed and made a grinding noise as it slid over, pulled by some invisible electronic mechanism. Maha's small fingers curled over the edge.

"Look, Maha, we found you!" said Kutta, falling into a play-bow, as if it had all been a wonderful game. "Come up!"

Maha waited for the manhole cover to grind the rest of the way over before poking her head out. Her eyes rolled nervously from side to side.

"Come out, come out," said Kutta, raising one foot to paw eagerly at the air. "There's no one around!"

"That's not a good idea, Kutta," Mhumhi warned her, glancing around furtively. The street may have been empty, but that giant picture of the hulker's face still made him rather anxious.

"Oh come on, Mhumhi, she can come out for a little bit," said Kutta, wagging, but Maha looked around and shook her head silently. Mhumhi could smell how frightened she was. He licked his lips.

"Let's leave her be. We found where the hole is, now we can find the things to put into it."

"All right," said Kutta, sounding disappointed, and went over and licked at Maha's dense hair. "Take the meat now then, little puppy."

Maha did so, stroking Kutta's chin as she had done Mhumhi's, still queerly silent the whole time. She put the handful of meat in her mouth so she could use both hands to crawl back down the ladder. There must have been some mechanism to trigger the manhole cover closed again, for it hissed back to life and started laboriously shifting itself back into place.

"We'll be back soon," Kutta said, but Maha said nothing as the cover bumped and rattled its way back closed.

Kutta wrinkled her brow, looking at Mhumhi. "What do you think is the matter with her?"

Mhumhi was surprised. "She's frightened, isn't she? Of being on the outside? A dog could catch her here."

"But there's no one around," Kutta protested, almost childishly. Mhumhi gave her an odd look, and she sighed through her nose.

"You're right, of course. Let's look around these shops for some clothes and things. I think I know what a candle smells like, so I can tell you what it is if we see one."

Mhumhi agreed, glad to be leaving the giant grinning face behind. They wandered up and down the street for a bit, poking at doors, but none of them looked to be enterable, aside from the food shops, which had broken windows and long-emptied shelves.

Finally Kutta turned the corner and came across a building with a large set of wide clear windows, through which they could see tall shelves stretching gray and endless. As they passed the doors, they slid open like magic. Mhumhi jumped, and Kutta laughed.

"Let's look in here, there are a lot of things," she said, sniffing eagerly.

Mhumhi followed her, warily, jumping again when the doors slid shut again behind them. It felt like a seal had closed, for the air in the store was very still and silent.

Both Mhumhi and Kutta began sniffing at once, for at some point or another there had been dogs in this place.

"Probably just exploring," said Kutta, tone falsely bright. Mhumhi knew why she was nervous- the dogs smelled strong and large. "Let's start down there, where there's light."

Mhumhi followed her, feeling uneasy again. The store's artificial light had sputtered out in some places, so that there were patches of abrupt darkness amongst the shelves; in other places, the lights sputtered and flickered like they did on Food Strip Street.

The shelves Kutta took them along were lined with strange objects: coiled black hoses, small carts with wheels, large cans of strong-smelling stuff, and a whole bank of yellow clay pots. Some had been knocked over and smashed on the linoleum. Mhumhi stepped gingerly around the fragments.

"What do you think?" he asked. Kutta glanced back at him.

"Not here, probably," she said. "I think the things are arranged in some kind of pattern. There must be an area for bedding. We could split up and search for it."

Mhumhi trotted around the edge of a shelf to look down another aisle, where a few feet away the lights cut off, leaving it in darkness.

"All right," he said, as his tail tucked down.

"Are you frightened, Mhumhi?" Kutta asked. "We don't have to."

Mhumhi glanced back at her, said, rather sulkily, "It *will* be faster," and slunk down the aisle.

He stepped through the dark part, hearing Kutta's nails clicking away in the other direction behind him. Here it smelled strange, artificial, though it had gotten hard to discern shapes in the dimness. He gingerly nosed what was on the bottom shelves. His nose bumped against something smooth and yielding- cardboard. It just seemed to be a shelf full of cardboard boxes.

Mhumhi went on a little further, nosing every few feet, and discovered something smooth and metallic. When he put his head in it it tipped off the self and landed on its side with a deafening clang. Mhumhi froze instinctively.

From somewhere far in the distance he heard Kutta give an inquiring whistle, and breathed a slow sigh of relief. He gave a little chirp to let her know he was all right.

He sniffed whatever he'd knocked over- it seemed to be a large metal pot. He left it where it was on the ground.

The aisle he was in was yielding little in the way of bedding, so he broke into a brief run and circled around to the next one. At least here there was more light, though it showed him nothing, as the shelves were empty. Only bits of cardboard and plastic remained. Mhumhi surmised that they had once held food.

He went on to the next aisle, skipped it when it held much the same thing, and went trotting down the next. This one looked more promising- it widened out, and there were metal racks with cloth hanging on them. It looked like the same sort of cloth wrappings the hulkers wore. Mhumhi couldn't recall the name Maha had used for them.

They looked too small to be used as blankets, though Mhumhi supposed if you were to drag a whole bunch of them you could make a nice nest for a den. Indeed it looked as if some dogs had done just that, for there were plastic and wire hangers scattered on the floor in places where they'd been torn off the racks. The smell of large dog was stronger here. Mhumhi sniffed it in a worried way. It smelled as if whatever had been here had been here quite recently. There was new scent layered over old scent.

He trotted on and found another shelf full of cardboard boxes. The smell intrigued him, so he reared up and dug at one with his paws until it tipped off the shelf, spilling out… something. Something oblong made of rubber. He sniffed on it, gnawed briefly, and decided to leave it.

At the end of this aisle there was an open little corridor. Mhumhi went in curiously and found that it branched into two. On one side there was a carpeted floor and what looked like several empty stalls; on the other, a half-open door from which came the unmistakable smell of toilets.

Mhumhi went towards the toilet side, thinking he might be able to get a drink of water. Where there were toilets, there were sinks, after all.

He squeezed through the door and found that the bathroom was quite dark, with only one or two lights above the row of sinks still working. He leapt up onto the counter and got the shock of his life-there was a *huge dog standing right there beside him-*

No, it was only his reflection. Mhumhi let his tongue hang out in relief. He'd seen mirrors before, but none so big as these. He admired himself for a moment, winking his eyes and tilting his head, before lowering his head so he could use one of his paws to nudge a tap for some water.

He looked at himself while he lapped, twitching his ears, putting them up and down. In the dimness behind him one of the stall doors moved slightly.

Mhumhi blinked. The door moved again. There came a loud flushing noise, so loud he jumped, paws sliding on the smooth porcelain, one of his back feet slipping completely over the edge.

He was eye to eye with his reflection in this pose, so he had a good view of behind himself when the stall door opened all the way and something huge with yellow eyes leapt down from the toilet.

11

Consumer Wolves

Mhumhi fell completely off of the counter in his surprise, coming to a hard rest on the sticky tiled floor below. He twisted to his feet, paws scrabbling.

The yellow-eyed thing stepped into the light, and Mhumhi's heart sank. It was a massive male gray wolf, and it was baring its teeth.

"What're you doing coming here alone, you little spotted bastard?" it said.

Mhumhi tucked his tail and backed away, back towards the door. Gray wolves were the only wild dogs that were bigger than painted dogs.

"I'm leaving," he told the wolf, perhaps more hopefully than he should have, for it snarled, "No you aren't," and lunged at him.

Mhumhi squealed and scrambled back through the door, bumping through it. With a creak it began to slide shut, catching the wolf around the middle as he burst through. He yelped. Mhumhi didn't stick around to see if he was all right.

He dashed pell-mell down the aisle with the cardboard boxes, twittering and calling for Kutta. Behind him he heard the wolf snarl and give a short, sharp howl. That did not bode well. Especially not when it was answered with other howls.

"Kutta!" Mhumhi yelled, dashing around the next aisle, but instead he found a wolf, a female this time, snarling and advancing on him with her tail raised. Mhumhi scrambled to do an about-face, sliding on the linoleum, and actually ran into her. Her teeth caught him in the flank before he got his feet underneath him enough to run away.

He heard other nails clicking on the linoleum on the other side of the shelves on both sides. In a desperate move he crouched and leapt, barely catching himself with his front paws at the top of the shelves, and wormed his way over. The female wolf leapt after him but fell back.

Mhumhi ran along the top of the shelf a ways, then leapt to the next over, then the next, panting. Each aisle seemed to hold more wolves than the last, and they were leaping and growling at him. Panting, heart pounding, he wheeled around and leapt over the end of the shelves to a low-hanging wooden sign, suspended from the ceiling by wires. It swung wildly as he hit it, and his paws could not get enough grip on the narrow surface and he fell back and down.

His landing hurt a lot less than it should have- rather than a hard floor, he landed on something soft that yielded to his weight with the sound of crumpling plastic and a great *poof.* He scrambled to his feet, unsteady on the sinking surface. He seemed to have landed in a bin filled with plastic-covered quilts.

His first, dizzy thought was that he was incredibly lucky, but when he put his nose over the edge he changed his mind. The bin was now surrounded by three wolves, all of them showing their teeth. Somewhere in the distance he heard snarls, and Kutta yelping and shrieking.

A wolf came trotting up and said, "We got the other one. Should we kill 'em?"

"Wait," growled one of Mhumhi's captors, whom he recognized as the big male from the bathroom. "If this one's police, we don't want them sniffing around for the body. We'll have to make him disappear."

Mhumhi made a bold choice then, likely not one he would have made if he'd had his wits about him at the time.

"I'm not police!" he shouted. "Honest, I swear, I'm not! We only came in here looking for blankets!"

This prompted a great deal of surprise and growling from the wolves.

"Not police?" growled the lead male. "A great painted brute like you?"

"I'm not, really!" cried Mhumhi. "Ask her- ask my sister- don't hurt her!"

"Sister?" said the lead wolf, then turned to one of the others and barked, "I thought you said it was a whistle dog!"

"It is!" said the other. "He's lying to save his spotted hide!"

"She's my sister, she is, we're a mixed pack," Mhumhi babbled, frantic, seeing the tide turning away again. "Please, we'll leave, we won't say a word, please don't kill us…"

"He doesn't sound like police," said another wolf, the female that had lunged at Mhumhi in the aisle.

Just then two more wolves ran up, one dragging Kutta by the ear. She was whining, her paws slipping as she struggled to keep up.

"Hi, whistle dog," said the female wolf. "Who's this fellow?"

"That's my little brother," cried Kutta, whimpering.

The wolf released her and she crouched low on the floor, trembling. Mhumhi saw that her ear was bleeding badly.

"The stories match up," said the female. The big male raised his lip.

"Mixed pack," he growled. "I don't like mixed packs. They're full of puppy thieves, aren't they?"

This set the other wolves to rumbling amongst themselves. Mhumhi cringed into the quilt, making the plastic rustle loudly.

"We're not puppy thieves," Kutta gasped. "How could we? From you…"

"We had a puppy thief before," said the lead male. "Or- an *attempt.*" He licked his chops, and the other wolves exchanged looks. "Just one attempt."

"Please," said Kutta, "we didn't even know anyone was in here. We're not from this part of the city. We were just…"

"Why do you want blankets?" asked the female wolf. "Has someone in your pack got pups?"

Mhumhi and Kutta exchanged a frantic look, and then Kutta said, "Yes, and we only wanted more bedding, and there wasn't any around where we live…"

The female wolf turned to the male and said, "I don't think they're going to be doing any thieving. Let's let them go."

"Let them go?" growled the male, not seeming to like the idea. "What if they have the police on us?"

The female looked back at Mhumhi, her yellow eyes sharp. "Do they look as though they can go to the police?"

The male hesitated, then put his ears back.

"Go on and take your bedding," he said, roughly. "You've got a warning, this time."

Mhumhi sank into the quilt with relief, plastic crinkling. Kutta got to her feet again, still trembling. The female wolf came over and licked her bleeding ear.

"I know who you are," she said. "I've heard of you. The orphan pack."

Kutta said nothing, just kept her head and tail low and bore the licking like it was a punishment.

"Sorry for all the fuss," the wolf continued. "It's just that we make our den here, and most of the dogs in these parts know it and leave us alone. As we like it." She laughed softly, her yellow eyes gleaming.

"A few weeks ago, someone came after one of my puppies. I'm afraid our backs have been up ever since."

"That's horrible," said Kutta, squeezing her eyes shut.

"Yes, terrible," said the wolf, her tail waving slowly. "I caught her, though. It was just an old white domestic- quite fat and stout- filthy smelling. I'm afraid I nearly ripped her leg off."

Kutta flinched. The plastic on Mhumhi's quilt rustled loudly.

"I thought she'd get away from me, but my lover Amaguk there came and caught her," the wolf continued. "He caught her round the neck, made her scream. But that didn't last long. They're made of weak stuff, these domestics. It was over in a second."

Kutta opened her eyes and looked at Mhumhi. Mhumhi himself was frozen.

"You killed her?" he hard himself say.

"Yes," said the large male, Amaguk. "She was stealing my puppy, my daughter. She tried to tear her away from her mother in the night. I killed her."

"So you see," said the female, "that's the reason why we're all so on edge. I apologize for the rough treatment."

Neither Mhumhi nor Kutta said anything. The female wolf tilted her head and swished her tail, and the rest of her pack converged around her and the walked away, vanishing between the aisles once more.

After a long moment, Kutta looked up again.

"Mhumhi..."

Mhumhi stood, staggering on the yielding surface of the quilt, and hopped clumsily out of the bin.

"We'll kill them."

"Mhumhi, no!" said Kutta, putting her ears back, as he tottered closer to her.

"We'll kill them, won't we, Kutta?"

"Don't be stupid," said Kutta, and Mhumhi heard an edge of raw misery creeping into her voice. "We're not going to kill anyone. They don't deserve it."

"They don't-!"

She ran over and pushed against him, stopping him in mid-word.

"Please, Mhumhi, don't make this worse. Don't make it harder. Please, let's get what we came for, then we can leave… we don't have to come back…"

Mhumhi was stiff against her pressure for a few moments more, then he slowly yielded, all his legs going weak against the floor, like he was a puppy again, just learning to walk, with no strength in him, no strength built up… He felt like there was a bald, open wound in his chest, stinging, empty.

He got to his feet and turned around and took the quilt- the whole, heavy, plastic-wrapped thing- and dragged it loudly and roughly out of the bin. It was awkward to carry, and he bit down on it hard, plastic and then fabric and then feathers filling up his mouth.

Kutta came up on the other side and helped him drag it for a little while, and then, as they passed an aisle, she let go and ran down it and picked something up from the floor.

Mhumhi hadn't the mind to ask her what it was, so he kept dragging the quilt along as she came up behind him with something long and cylinder-shaped in her teeth.

He barely remembered what it was like to leave the store, then to drag the stupid heavy quilt all the way back down the street, around the corner, back to the striped intersection with that grinning, mocking hulker face leering down at him. He dropped the quilt and watched Kutta scratch the manhole cover again.

It seemed to take a very long time for Maha to respond, and while they waited Mhumhi stared hatefully up at the giant face.

Kutta put the thing she'd been carrying down on the ground and said, "Sacha and Kebero…"

"Let's not tell them," said Mhumhi, the words rattling out of him. Kutta looked at him, her eyes soft.

"We must tell them, Mhumhi. At least Sacha. She'll want to know what-"

"Sacha doesn't care!"

Kutta didn't say anything back after he spat the words out, just stood there in front of the manhole. Her ear still bled sluggishly, black blood crusting in her fur.

"She'll just say she deserved it," said Mhumhi, more softly.

Kutta might have said something, but the manhole cover jerked and shifted, and Maha put her fingers over the edge, peering shyly out. Her eyes brightened when she saw the white mass of the quilt.

Mhumhi was looking away, so Kutta walked around and caught it in her teeth to drag over closer. Maha looked around in a furtive way and pulled herself all the way out of the manhole.

She walked on two legs around Mhumhi, and looked at him, wide-eyed, but he continued to ignore her. She looked at Kutta, but Kutta said nothing as well, just listlessly tugged on the quilt.

Maha put her forelegs around the poofy mass and started to shove it down the manhole, finally sitting down and kicking at it until it dropped all the way down.

"Here, Maha," said Kutta, and she picked up the cylindrical thing to show to her. "I found you a candle."

Maha's face brightened with a real smile. "You really found one," she said. She looked at Mhumhi. "I thought you were lying to us."

Mhumhi glanced up at her, then away again.

"Mhumhi," asked Maha, "what's wrong?"

She moved closer to him. He leaned away, tensing, opening his jaws.

"Maha, don't," said Kutta. "He's- we're not doing well."

"Oh," said Maha. "But you're bleeding!"

She was pointing not to Kutta, but to Mhumhi's flank. He realized that it had been bleeding the whole time; he just hadn't noticed.

"Did someone hurt you?" asked Maha, and then she put her arms around Mhumhi's neck.

Mhumhi went completely stiff, rigid, even rising on his hind legs slightly against her grip. His mouth was open, his teeth bared. Kutta seemed frozen as well, eyes wide and staring.

Maha kept hugging him, blissfully, even, her arms and fingers hot against his fur, her strange bare hulker flesh pressing up against his, at once all too intimate and too close- he could hear her heart beat, her pulse. He thought of his teeth cutting her skin, of what her hot blood would taste like, pumping out into his mouth, of the way her flesh would fill his belly, of the way she would die, and he would steal her death for himself while he ate her.

It was strange, but even while these thoughts crossed his mind, he relaxed. He relaxed into the arms of the hulker girl, felt her touch become part of him, warming him, his neck to his own beating heart.

"That's enough, Maha!" said Kutta, her tone very, very worried, and Maha let Mhumhi go. His neck felt cold and bare.

"I'm sorry," said Maha, and crouched there, her eyes downcast. Mhumhi realized his mouth was still open. He closed it.

"You'd better go back," said Kutta, walking closer, shooting looks at Mhumhi as she did. Maha picked up the candle in one hand.

"Wait," said Mhumhi. She turned to look at him. He stepped over and gently licked her forehead, and then pressed his own against it.

12
Broken Glass

Mhumhi curled up with Kebero that night.

He let Kutta speak to Sacha, far downstairs, when she demanded to know why they had gotten back so late. In his cowardly way, he had slunk right by and up the stairs as Kutta started to talk, mixing the lies with the new truth that they had learned.

He hadn't said a word to Kebero, he'd just gotten on the bed and curled up around the sleepy puppy. Kebero had seemed groggy but happy about it.

Bii was in the corner, hunting a cockroach. He hadn't spared Mhumhi more than a glance since he came up. He was crouched by a little crack in the floorboards, big ears trained downwards, full of furious predatory intensity.

Mhumhi watched him with a strange curiosity. He had not thought about it, but Bii was a killer. Even the little bugs had lives, after all. Bii consumed those lives. And the rats and mice that other dogs ate were alive too, and even had blood.

He licked Kebero's head, thinking. Kebero had a pulse, and blood, and underneath his skin there was meat. Just like the little hulker children. But Mhumhi had never considered eating Kebero. He licked him again, to apologize for even thinking about it.

Mhumhi had always known, in a vague way, that the meat he ate had been something alive once. He could not remember that it had actually been explained or described to him, but it must have, mustn't it?

What living creatures had all that meat come from?

So much meat- meat to feed a hundred hundred thousand dogs- where had it all come from?

Bii suddenly lunged forward and stuck his nose in the little crack. A second later he drew away, squirming cockroach caught in his jaws, and crunched downwards.

Mhumhi watched him eat it, the evident pleasure he took in consuming it, even as the cockroach's legs still slowly rotated as he did so.

Kutta came dashing up the stairs and threw herself on the bed.

"What, what is it?" Mhumhi said, startled, as she crawled up next to him, whimpering. He licked her ear, feeling the dried blood encrusted on it.

"Sacha just went outside," she said. "I don't know where she went, I don't know what she's going to do… I thought she wouldn't be upset!"

Mhumhi pressed close to her, whining softly, trying to comfort her as she lay there and shuddered. Kebero twisted and pressed against his stomach.

"Where's Sacha going? Wh-wh-why did she leave?"

His voice went shriller, up to a puppyish yap.

"Is she leaving like Mo- like Mo- like Mother did?"

"No, Kebero, of course not," said Mhumhi, though the words sparked some alarm in him. Sacha could not leave, could she?

"She won't leave," said Kutta, or more moaned. "She has nowhere else to go."

Her words made Mhumhi swallow, and he turned back to pay more attention to her ear, gently picking at the dried blood with his tongue.

"She'll be back," he said, between his ministrations. "She needs her time. You know how she is. She'll be all right."

Kutta said nothing, just closed her eyes and let him tend to her ear. Mhumhi felt Bii's eyes on them from across the room.

"We have to tell her," he said.

Beside him Kutta went stiff.

"No… no, we can't…"

"We *have* to," he insisted. "We can't possibly go on keeping such a big secret from her, not if we want to… you know. She needs to be part of it. She's our family, Kutta."

Kutta was silent for a long while. Finally she said, "But she'll be so mean and- and *bossy* about it once she knows."

Mhumhi lifted his lips in a smile and nuzzled his sister, his cheek bumping against hers.

"It'll be better anyway. She'll know what to do. She always does, right?"

Kutta gave a soft sigh and leaned back against him. Their breath commingled. Mhumhi felt the close warmth of his sister, like the pressing weight of the hulker's arms around his neck, the strange and gentle effect of body against body.

He found himself worried, somewhat, for Kutta had not eaten anything that day for herself. They'd missed the second dispensary time since they had come back so late. Mhumhi hoped that Sacha at least had gone and eaten. None of them could really afford to skip a day right now, not with the meat being spread so thin.

He fell asleep with this sense of unease within him, curled with Kutta and Kebero. Sacha did not return to join them for the rest of the night. Nor, for that matter, did Bii.

The next morning he woke up abruptly, jerking his head up. There was a great deal of noise and barking coming from outside, and sunlight was filtering brightly through the curtains and onto the floor.

"What's going on?" Kutta asked sleepily, her eyes still tightly shut. "Is it another fight?"

Mhumhi recalled the fight that had occurred in the street a few days ago, with the golden jackal and the blue-eyed domestic. It seemed like an eternity had passed since then.

He got to his feet, gently dislodging a sleepy Kebero, and jumped off the bed. Behind him Kutta whined softly.

Mhumhi went downstairs and was startled to see Sacha there, standing by the door with her nose pressed to the crack and her short tail quivering. As he walked closer she spared him a brief glance.

"Something's going on outside," she said. "I think it's the police. It's got the foxes all riled up out there. I don't dare even open the door."

"Did you sleep down here last night?" Mhumhi asked, glancing at the tattered couch.

Sacha's response was somewhat clipped, as if she didn't approve of him broaching the subject. "Yes. I came back late. Didn't want to wake anyone up."

"Oh," said Mhumhi, and he went over to try and lick her chin. She tolerated it, he thought, better than usual.

They heard Kutta coming down the stairs behind them. Her footsteps faltered. "Sacha?"

"Hush, I'm trying to *listen*," said Sacha, very stiffly. Kutta came up and stood close beside Mhumhi, looking up at him.

"The police are outside," he murmured to her, and her ears went back.

"For who?" she asked. "For what?"

"Hush!" said Sacha, and then she suddenly jumped back from the door as someone scratched it loudly.

"This is the police!" the dog outside shouted. "You must open up! We're conducting a search!"

"A search for what?" Sacha growled, rearing up to balance her small weight on the door, as if that would be enough of a deterrent. "Who gives you the right, Liduma?"

"Open up," the voice repeated.

"Come on, Sacha, let's not cause trouble," said Kutta, swallowing nervously. Sacha growled and jumped up to tug down the door handle. Liduma pushed in at once.

"Is this everyone living here?" she asked, rudely shoving by them to prowl through their kitchen and living room.

"We've a fox upstairs, recovering from an injury," said Sacha. "Though I bet you woke him up with all that noise. What's going on? What's this about?"

"A fox?" Liduma flicked an ear at them, her nose twitching. "Typical." Her dusty pelt seemed to be hanging off her bones, her swollen teats sagging, and when she licked her nose, her tongue was pale.

"You don't look so well, Liduma," Kutta said, waving her tail down by her heels. Liduma wrinkled a lip.

"Where's Pariah? I haven't seen her recently. Is she here?"

"No, she is not," said Sacha.

Liduma looked down her nose at her. "Don't lie to me, Sacha. I could have this place searched-"

"Do it," growled Sacha, her stub tail quivering, "do it, scat-worm, you should smell we're not lying. Pariah left."

Liduma started to growl, but it turned into a surprised cough.

"Left?"

"Permanently. Why are you looking for her?"

"She wouldn't leave," said Liduma, sounding doubtful. She glanced at Mhumhi. "I thought-"

"She's really gone," Mhumhi confirmed. He kept his head low. Liduma could be a bit of a bully, but she'd never done anything more than harass them, and she'd never seemed interested in their mother before...

"Those upper-city police are biting into your territory, aren't they?" said Sacha. "You look like you haven't eaten in days."

Liduma gave another coughing growl. When she stepped forward Mhumhi saw a fresh, pale bite wound on her shoulder.

"The police are united," she said. "The painted dogs-"

She stopped short, shooting a glare at Mhumhi, and he tucked his tail.

"We have nothing to fight over. The one you have upstairs- it's not a domestic?"

"So are you looking for domestics?" asked Kutta.

"Answer the question!"

"I already said it was a fox. Use your nose," said Sacha. "What's going on with the domestics?"

Liduma drew a thin breath through her nose. "They're all to be arrested."

"*All* of the domestics?" cried Kutta. "On what grounds?"

"On the grounds that they are domestics!" snapped Liduma. "We have reason to believe that they are helping or harboring hulkers. So they're all to come in now."

Mhumhi raised his head, ignoring Kutta, who was trying to catch his eye. "Why go after them all of the sudden like this?"

Liduma gave a grunt and scuffed the dirty floor with her paw. "Some new information came in, up top. Somebody's been tampering with the dispensaries. Zoo Park, West Big Park, Center Road..."

"The Center Road dispensary's down?" exclaimed Kutta, and Liduma put her ears back.

"Never mind about Center Road. It's the hulkers' fault. And the domestics are helping the hulkers. Up top they've finally decided to do a sweep and wipe them out for good. There can't be more than a few dozen left, anyway." She coughed. "It's taken them long enough to get to it, if you ask me..."

"What are you doing with the domestic dogs that you catch?" That was Sacha, her gaze, as ever, very sharp.

"Question them," said Liduma. Her voice had dropped an octave. "You'd better not be protecting anybody."

"We're not."

"I mean it," growled Liduma. There was a wary edge to her tone. "Those above me, they asked for Pariah by name. If you're hiding her..."

"Tell them she's dead, then," said Sacha. Both Mhumhi and Kutta flinched.

"That's a lie," snorted Liduma.

"She died doing what she always did," said Sacha. "You know what I mean."

Liduma stared at her for a long moment.

"Well," she said, "if that's true- I suppose it was bound to catch up with her eventually."

"Like you and your pack never did," said Sacha. Now she was growling, high-pitched. "You sat and watched- you useless police brutes. You could have stopped her. It was your duty to stop her."

"Sacha," said Kutta, disbelievingly.

Liduma made no response to this. Her shoulder flexed, and again Mhumhi saw the shining bite mark.

"There's another announcement I've got to give you," she said.

"And what is it, then?"

"You're only to go to the dispensary in the afternoons from now on."

"What?!" exclaimed Sacha. "Are you saying our dispensary isn't working either?"

"It's working just fine." Real exhaustion was showing now in Liduma's voice. "We're splitting up the feeding times, that's all. The Zoo Park and the Center Road dogs go in the morning, and the Oldtown dogs go in the evening. It reduces fighting."

She cast her eyes over their stunned faces.

"If I were you," she said, "I'd find somewhere else to live. Soon."

Her gaze lingered for a long moment on Mhumhi, and then she turned around and stepped out of the house.

"I don't believe this," Sacha growled, as soon as her painted back had disappeared outside. "Splitting up the times! And they're expecting to feed even *more* dogs from our dispensary! I've already heard that some dogs waited so long they didn't get fed yesterday!"

"What are we going to do?" Kutta said. "We're already trying to keep a low profile, and now this... We have no choice but to go all together now."

"I know," said Sacha. "Though it may work in our favor if there's some confusion, at least. The police will be busy breaking up fights from the two different districts in the morning, I'll bet. They'll be tireder when it comes to us." Her eyes got small and crafty. "Perhaps... perhaps we could even sneak in Kebero."

"Really?" Mhumhi burst out, tail wagging. "We can start taking him?"

"He's not really big enough," said Sacha, "but at this rate no one'll be behind to watch him. He's small, he can pass for a big fox if the police are all as tired as Liduma is. There aren't many Simien wolves around anyway; I doubt they'll be that familiar with them."

"He'll be excited," said Kutta, smiling.

"Don't let him get too excited," Sacha replied, tail stiff. "If he acts like a puppy, he'll ruin it. Impress that upon him, would you?"

"I will do my best," said Kutta. "I bet he'll listen better if Bii tells him, though."

"Well, tell Bii," said Sacha. "Where is he, anyway? Hiding out upstairs?"

Mhumhi and Kutta exchanged a look, and Kutta said, in a worried way, "We haven't seen him since last night."

"He must be out hunting in the sewers, then," Sacha said. "He told me his leg was feeling all right again. Though why he'd choose this morning... We'll have to explain it to him when he gets back." Her eyes narrowed with annoyance. "If he's decided to take off..."

"I don't think he'd leave Kebero like that, you know he's fond of him," Mhumhi said quickly.

"True. Not that I'd be sorry to see the fluffy back of him." Sacha snorted. "You two had better not go running off on any more excursions today, by the way. The police are out in force. In fact, why don't the two of you come with me?" Her little eyes suddenly took on a glitter. "I've been investigating something around Oldtown anyway."

"What have you been investigating?" Mhumhi asked, wagging his tail a little. "Found any more sources of meat?"

"If only. No, I've been looking into our neighbors," said Sacha. "The little foxes have been muttering away, you know. They're less pleased about this whole situation than we are. They're the ones getting the chewed end of the stick, and they know it."

"It is strange how they took so many to eat down here," said Kutta. "It's a long walk from Center Road, isn't it? To go both ways in one day?"

"It is," said Sacha. "Which is exactly why they aren't doing it, or so I've heard. I wasn't sure until that dumb brute said it earlier, but the little foxes were saying last night that a dispensary had closed down and that the police were going to shift all of them here during the day."

"Shift them here?" Mhumhi repeated, dumbstruck.

"How?" demanded Kutta. "How many dogs is that…? Is it *all* of them? Where are they going to stay?"

"I don't know if they're splitting them up, like they did with the Zoo Park dogs- some of them did go to the other side, to the South Big Park dispensary, you know, so we don't have all of the stupid deadweights down here. But the foxes say that they're just going to evict everyone from the houses nearest the dispensary and just put them there."

"That's-!" Kutta seemed at a loss for words. "I can't believe they'd do that! How do they think they'll get away with it?"

"Center Street is a big, rough lot," said Sacha. "I imagine they'll do it quite easily. At least at first."

"What do you mean, at first?" Mhumhi asked. Sacha grunted.

"Let's go have a look. I'll show the two of you. Kutta, fetch Kebero."

"Now?!"

"He's going to go out tonight anyway, so we might as well take him for a practice stretch. It might be safer for him outside the house today." Sacha turned and put her nose against the crack underneath the door again. "We can sneak him out when no one's around."

Kutta gave Mhumhi a bewildered look, then trotted up the stairs. Sacha sat by the door and growled softly to herself.

"That stinking Bii had better be back by tonight…"

"Sacha," said Mhumhi, rather timidly, coming to stand next to her. "Kutta and I- we've got something we need to tell you."

Sacha sat down and turned her head back, giving him the full benefit of her little bear's face over her shoulder. "You're going to include me in your little secret now?"

"Well- I- we- yes," Mhumhi stammered, tucking his tail. "I'm sorry, Sacha."

"It's all right," said Sacha, turning back away. "I'm fairly certain it was mostly Kutta's fault."

Mhumhi felt that it might have been appropriate for him to jump to his sister's defense, but then again Sacha was absolutely correct.

"Can your secret wait until later?" Sacha glanced back at him today. "I'd rather pry it out of Kutta myself anyway, and I don't want to get into a squabble right now. Especially not in front of Kebero."

"I guess," said Mhumhi, feeling rather guilty for the eventual browbeating that Kutta was going to receive, and also wondering if he couldn't spirit himself away before it happened.

Kutta returned then, trotting down the stairs with Kebero in tow. He pushed ahead of her and fell into a play-bow, wagging eagerly.

"Are we going outside? Am I going too?"

"The only little puppies who get to come outside are the *quiet* ones," said Sacha. "The loud and disobedient ones go straight back inside. Understand?"

Kebero yapped and ran up to whine and lick under her chin. Mhumhi swooped in from the other side and did the same, nearly lifting Sacha off her feet with one overeager nudge of his nose. Kutta half-lunged as if she meant to do it too, but then pulled herself back, perhaps taking pity on her oldest and littlest sister, who was squalling and squirming in outrage.

They got themselves sorted out, finally, and Kebero positioned in the line between Sacha and Kutta so he could be under the sharpest scrutiny the whole time. Mhumhi was rather amused by this, as it meant that they had inadvertently organized themselves from smallest to largest. So much for not drawing attention to themselves; they'd make the strangest train Oldtown had ever seen.

"Come on," Sacha said, her nose pressed to the door. "There aren't any police just now. Follow me, and be quick."

She nudged the door open with her nose and paw and they did so, all single file. Kebero was a mess of floppy limbs and excitement, and Kutta kept having to gently tug his tail to keep him in line, but at least the only ones around were their neighbor foxes. They didn't spare them more than a glance or two. It seemed the mood of the neighborhood was rather low.

Sacha hugged the line of buildings, leading them through a narrow alley with cobblestones down onto Food Strip Street, and then down even farther south towards where the city started to get really faded and dusty. Mhumhi noticed that there were more foxes in the area than he was accustomed to seeing; perhaps Sacha was right, and they were already starting to be pushed out of their homes.

Sacha led them across the street to a large squat building with a faded blue awning. Mhumhi saw that the bottom pane of glass in the door had been broken. It smelled like there were a great number of dogs inside.

Sacha went purposefully towards the opening in the glass, but before she reached it a large red fox emerged from a turned-over trashcan that had been lying under the awning. Mhumhi could see more movement within.

The fox was walking towards them somewhat stiffly, but then she spotted Sacha and her bushy tail wagged.

"You brought your pack this time, did you?"

"I said I would," said Sacha. She glanced back at the rest of them. "This is Lisica. If you're polite to her, she may let us in."

"Oh, small-ears, I'd let you in anyway," said Lisica, and then she gave a huge yawn, showing all her teeth. "Pardon me. The rabble has kept me up all night with their barking and head-butting, I'm afraid."

"Is it about the Center Road dogs?" asked Kutta, and Lisica gave her a startled glance.

"Oh, some of it is," she said, with a short laugh. "But that's the shed fur of a much larger beast. Speaking of which…" She looked at Mhumhi, sniffing in his direction. "Better keep your head down in there, Dapples."

"You've got nothing to worry about with Mhumhi," Sacha said, stepping forward a little, as if she could shield him from view. "He's not police."

"I know that," said Lisica. "Just… don't talk in there, big fellow, all right? It'll be better off for you."

She went back into the trash can. Mhumhi could hear soft yipping and rustling from the darkened interior. A bright-eyed fox puppy peeped out at them for a moment before vanishing back inside.

Sacha redirected their attention with a grunt and carefully stepped through the broken glass into the shop. Kutta picked up Kebero by his scruff and squeezed after her, the puppy's dangling legs just brushing the lower edge. Mhumhi went last, sucking in his belly as he stepped through.

Inside the shop it was very dim and smelly, and crowded with growling, whining, yapping little dogs. There were a great number of booths and tables, as well as a long counter, and the dogs covered these and the floor in a confusing mass of shifting furry forms, leaping up and down from surfaces, getting into minor squabbles, searching for family members that had gotten separated into the mix.

Sacha lead them to a booth with dark leather seats. There was a pair of chillas already sitting on top of the table alongside a crab-eating fox, but they gave Mhumhi a startled look and hastily hopped down, one after the other. The crab-eating fox looked uncomfortable, but stayed, shifting aside to make room as Sacha hopped up onto the booth and then on the table. Kebero followed her, getting a bit of assistance from Kutta as his clumsy paws slipped on the leather.

Kutta hopped into the booth and placed her forepaws up on the table, tail wagging. Mhumhi jumped onto the table and bumped his head against a low-hanging lamp with a stained-glass shade. The thing swung wildly for a moment, casting colored shadows every which way. The noise faded in their little area as dozens of small faces turned around to stare. Mhumhi backed back into the booth and tried to make himself look like a fox.

The stares receded when Lisica entered, along with a male fox and three puppies. Mhumhi surmised that they'd all been crammed into the trash can together. Behind Lisica there walked a female golden jackal.

Sacha gave a soft growl of surprise and looked back at Mhumhi from her seat on the table. Mhumhi sunk further down into the leather seat, resting his chin on the wood. It was the jackal he'd stopped from fighting with the blue-eyed domestic.

The jackal herself was panting, flicking her gaze around the great mass of foxes; it did not seem to fall on their table in the back.

Lisica jumped up onto the high counter and then again to sit upon a derelict soda fountain, affording herself the highest vantage point, and gave a screaming bark for silence.

"I've brought Sundu here to speak to you tonight," she said, looking down at the jackal- a large space had cleared around her on the floor. "But first, I'll tell you the news: we've now got a few hundred squatters by the front of Oldtown. I'll tell you the streets…" She listed them, and the growling and muttering got louder with each name.

"Piss in their water supply!" shouted someone, and a heavy-headed short-eared dog leapt up onto the table alongside Sacha. "We ought to drive off the scum!"

The others around her roused in a brief rabble of yaps and growls of agreement until Lisica gave her chilling bark again.

"Be quiet for a minute. We still need to hear from Sundu. This relates to our primary concern." Lisica's sharp eyes scanned the crowd. Mhumhi thought they lingered on their table, but perhaps it was to admonish the short-eared dog, who was panting and smiling.

"I see that some of you haven't been here before," Lisica went on. "But I'm sure you've been hearing that there have been disappearances lately. Mostly puppies and young dogs."

The crowd got quieter at this. Mhumhi saw Lisica's mate nosing at their three pups.

"There's been no help from police, but of course, we're used to that," said Lisica, to the murmured agreement of the crowd. "But now we have evidence that these thieves and murderers aren't just attacking the smaller dogs and the foxes. Sundu, tell the others what you have to say, please."

Lisica jumped down from the soda fountain, and Sundu the golden jackal cast around a bit before leaping up onto a nearby table.

"I don't come from Oldtown," she growled. "I come from the far edge of Brick-and-Iron, which is on the other side of your dispensary here. That neighborhood's mostly jackals and coyotes and red wolves. We don't mix around with any of your fox business." She hesitated. "What I mean to say was, it was never any of my concern, or my partner's. I had heard a few rumors about disappearances, but never much cared for them- we had a litter of pups."

She paused a moment.

"I came back from the dispensary one morning, back to our home. The door was open and I could see my partner there. Well- I- I won't jump around it. She was dead. Not just dead. Most of her was gone. Just her- her head, bits of her pelt, some bones…"

Sundu trailed off. Mhumhi could smell the scent of fear rising in the room. He looked worriedly over at Kebero, but the puppy had fallen asleep curled up beside Sacha. He noticed that Sacha had put one paw on him.

"There was no other way to look at it," said Sundu. "There were toothmarks on her bones. Something had eaten her. She was a full-grown jackal, like me. Would take a large dog to pull her down like that..."

"A dog?" That was the short-eared dog again. "D'you know for sure it was a dog? What about one of them- you know- hulkers?"

"No," said Sundu. "No flat tooth made those marks. And a hulker always takes away what it kills. This... whatever it was... *who*ever it was... it ate her up right there."

"You said you had puppies," called someone else from the crowd. "What about them?"

Lisica spoke up. "Sundu has asked that we not discuss the puppies."

A brief blanket of silence fell over the crowd. Mhumhi saw all their staring eyes, wide and frightened, showing white.

"We have," Lisica said, after a moment, "what seems to be a dog- likely several dogs- that have been going around killing and eating other dogs. Again, the police do nothing. I know it's been put forth by several that the killers are in fact the police-"

"Muck-coated killers!" bawled out the short-eared dog. Lisica ignored her.

"-and there are some who think it's been done by the domestics. Which brings us to today. The police are hunting out all domestics in this part of the city. I don't know about others, but it seems likely that it'll start happening everywhere."

"Finally," growled Sundu. There were a few murmurs of agreement, though there were also several derisive hisses.

"Most of us have had our homes searched," said Lisica. "Not to mention that many of us and our families have now been displaced thanks to the Center Road dispensary getting shut down. It's obvious that the police are far from caring about what happens to us."

"Nor anyone else," said Sundu.

"But the rate of killing has been increasing," said Lisica. "We've been hearing about deaths every day- not just pups that are left alone-individuals leave to hunt in the subway and never come back. Dogs vanish down dark alleys. Big *and* small. If we want to protect our families, we've got to figure out who's responsible on our own."

"So what? Get to the point!" barked the short-eared dog, and now even Sacha shot her an irritated look.

"The point," said Lisica, "is that it's between the police, and the domestics. We know both are capable of killing. The police already hunt live hulkers in Big Park; it's no stretch to imagine they would turn on their fellow dogs. After all, the hulkers are running out."

Lisica stopped to glance at Sundu, then said, "But there are some that think it is the domestic dogs, taking meat to the hulkers that they serve. The evidence that supporters of this theory have pointed out is the half-breed cull."

This seemed to carry a lot of meaning throughout the shop; looks were exchanged, lips raised. Mhumhi poked Sacha with his nose.

"What's that?" he whispered.

"Hush!" said Sacha. "Remember what she said. Don't talk."

"Domestics are killers," snarled Sundu. "We've known that for a long time. They'd have the city cleared of dogs so that their precious hulkers are free to rut and breed again-"

"Sundu," said Lisica, and Sundu shut her jaws tightly, though her teeth still showed.

"We've got to take action," said Lisica, "but the problem is that we don't know who our real enemy is. Before we do anything, we've got to get more information on who's behind these killings. So if anybody has anything, now is the time to step forward."

With this she hopped down from the counter. At once the crowd burst into a frenzy of loud barking and yapping as all the other dogs tried to collaborate at once. The crab-eating fox at their table turned eagerly to the short-eared dog.

"The arrest of the domestics- it's a cover-up, isn't it? By the police? We know they're the ones *really* behind it."

"Of course they are," said the short-eared dog. "Domestics are too stupid to know a dog's throat from his asshole- half-breed cull, what rubbish-"

"I've heard enough," Sacha muttered to Kutta and Mhumhi, nudging the still-sleeping Kebero with her foot. "We won't be getting any more useful information out of this mess. Let's sneak out."

Mhumhi was fairly ready to go himself, and he slid down off the booth underneath the table, letting his rear legs come last. The chillas, which had apparently taken refuge down there, yipped in a startled way and huddled closer together. Mhumhi tried to give them a friendly tail wave and rattled the table.

In front of him Sacha hit the leather with a thud and then hopped down to the carpeted floor. Kutta followed her off the bench with a great deal more grace than Mhumhi had, especially considering she was carrying the heavy, groggy Kebero by the scruff.

The other dogs gave them a wide berth, many looking at Mhumhi's coat. They were almost to the door when Lisica stopped them.

"Do you know anything, Sacha?" she asked, suddenly materializing beside her. "You've been wandering lately, haven't you? And your mother-"

"Pariah's dead," said Sacha. "For weeks. We just got confirmation. So there's no need to pester us about her anymore."

In Kutta's jaws, Kebero gave a startled whimper. Mhumhi went to lick him, rather shocked himself by Sacha's harsh admission.

"I'm very sorry," said Lisica, though her tone was somewhat bland. "How...?"

"I don't believe it's your business," said Sacha. "But she's dead. So if you were hoping to get at her by inviting us to your little meeting- well, I'm sure that wasn't it, was it?"

Lisica drew back, the fur on her back rising a little. "That was never-"

"Don't listen to those domestic-sympathizers," said Sundu, pushing through the crowd to stand behind her. "I wouldn't be surprised if you were hiding her somewhere."

Sacha laughed, showing her teeth. "You're welcome to search for her, if you think that'll make your puppies come back to life."

Sundu gave a terrible snarl and lunged at her. Kutta dropped Kebero and leapt forward, arresting the golden jackal with a sharp bite on the muzzle. The two of them reared up, snapping, until Sacha gave a sharp squeal.

"Stop!"

Kutta backed off, giving Sundu a hard stare. Sundu still snarled.

"Sorry," said Sacha, looking up at Sundu. "Shouldn't have said that. I'm a bit tired of people ragging on my dead mother, that's all."

"Sundu, let it go," Lisica urged, from underneath a table- she'd darted there, out of the fray. "Sacha wouldn't lie."

"You're made of a lie," Sundu said, glaring at Sacha. "You suckled from the teats of a killer."

Sacha snorted. "Let me tell you something, jackal," she said. "Were some of your friends and family killed during the half-breed cull? Well, so were our mothers' puppies. Her *original* puppies."

"Your mother was barren," snarled Sundu. "A barren, filthy domestic thief!"

Sacha's eyes thinned, and for a tense moment it looked like she might start the fight up again, but then she looked back at Mhumhi and Kutta and said, "Let's go. I need to get the stench of scat out of my lungs."

Sundu rumbled, but the crowd of little dogs around her was starting to press in closer, many of them looking angry, and she seemed hesitant to make another move. Sacha turned, her short tail poking straight up, and hopped through the broken door. Kutta followed, shooting a final dark look at the jackal, and Mhumhi, his tail tucked tight under his belly, picked up Kebero and went last.

They retreated a good ways from the shop, turning several street corners, and then Kutta said, "Sacha, you owe us an explanation."

Mhumhi put down Kebero. The puppy was trembling and whining, and Mhumhi wasn't much better off himself, panting and drooling.

Sacha turned around to look at her. "I don't know that I do."

"You never told us about- about her puppies! And what's the half-breed cull? And how did you get *invited* to such a meeting? They were talking about going against the police!"

"Keep your voice down," said Sacha. "And as for the last one, that's easy. The little dogs have always thought of me as one of them. And Lisica- she wanted to use me, of course, for our connection to Pariah. I thought I made all of that clear in there."

"In there!" exclaimed Kutta, her tail rising in her anger. "Yes, in there, when you spoke about our mother being-" She stopped and looked at Kebero.

"Sorry," Sacha said. "I thought you two would've told him." Her tone was cool as she looked up at Kutta. "Apparently you did not. Well,." She turned to look at Kebero. "Our mother's dead."

Kebero whined and put his ears back. Kutta actually growled.

"*Sacha*!"

"He needed to be told," said Sacha. "He's told. I don't know how pretty and pleasant you wanted it to be, but her being dead isn't either. Let him cry for her. You should have let him cry for her a long time ago." She looked at Kutta again. "You should have let Mhumhi cry for her. You are the one who dragged this out. You are the one that lied, Kutta."

"I didn't lie!" said Kutta. "She could have been- she could have been alive!"

"She could have been," Sacha agreed. "She could have abandoned us. Those were your choices! Death, or abandonment! But you *lied* to our little brothers!"

"Sacha," Mhumhi whined, unable to keep quiet. She ignored him, advancing on the trembling Kutta.

"I know you've been hiding something from me," she said. "I know you've been putting Mhumhi in danger. For a mother you should have known didn't exist! You let him believe she might come back! Whatever it is you've been doing- I don't care what your excuses are- you *used* him. Your little brother. You should be protecting him!"

"I was protecting him!" Kutta snarled. "I was trying to-!"

"Don't you dare ever growl at me again," said Sacha.

It got deathly quiet. On the ground, Kebero shook, pressing himself against Mhumhi's forelegs.

"Sacha," said Mhumhi, "it isn't her-"

"It's very well her fault."

"No it isn't!" Mhumhi tensed, suddenly feeling a burst of anger. "You talk as if I would be too stupid to see on my own, that I wouldn't realize- I'm not a puppy! I believed what I wanted to believe!"

"Fine," said Sacha. "Fine! Then you should have known better too. Dragging this out for Kebero-"

"Don't you mean, dragging it out for you?" Mhumhi said. Sacha went stiff. He felt the urge to back off, to lie down for her, but he quelled it.

"Stop pretending she didn't mean anything to you."

Sacha stared at him a moment, then lowered her tail, and laughed.

"I will, when you stop pretending we meant anything to *her*."

"Sacha-!"

"Let's take Kebero home," she said, turning around. "He's had enough. We can talk more later."

Mhumhi opened his mouth to reply, but a sudden whine from Kutta stopped him. She was looking at Kebero, and with a glance at Mhumhi, went to pick him up by the scruff again.

Mhumhi had little choice but to follow his sisters back to the house. The walk was near-silent, aside from Kebero's occasional whimpers.

When they got to the doorway, Bii met them. The bat-eared fox was panting hard, blood dripping from his tongue.

"You're back!" he said. "I've been looking for you- the police keep coming by- I thought you'd all been dragged before the tribunal."

Kebero kicked and squirmed, twisting from Kutta's grip so that he dropped to the ground. He ran to huddle and lick at Bii, whining.

"What happened to you, Bii?" Kutta asked, licking her chops.

"What happened to him?" asked Bii, in a worried way, for Kebero was near-knocking him over in his attempts to get as close as he could. "Oh- and I only bit my tongue while I was running around."

"He needs some comforting," Sacha said. "Take care of him a minute, while I talk to my siblings. When we return, you can discuss where you were this morning."

"I was afraid to come back in with all the police!" Bii protested, putting his paws over Kebero's back. "I didn't know what to do, so I went to lie low somewhere else…"

"We'll discuss it," said Sacha, her eyes thinning. Bii pressed his jaws together, but seemed to take the hint. He got off Kebero and coaxed him into the house.

"Let's go," said Sacha, and Mhumhi and Kutta now exchanged a confused look.

"Where are we going?"

"Somewhere far away from his bat-ears," said Sacha. "I'll tell you what you want to know, though I expect it'll only make things worse."

"You were off on *me* for not being honest," muttered Kutta, falling in step behind her.

"I wasn't doing it to lead anybody through sewer muck," said Sacha coolly, and Kutta got quiet. Mhumhi put his ears back, though he was also somewhat impressed. He wondered how much they really had left to tell her.

There were a great number of new dogs- likely those that had been evicted from their homes- starting to wander along the normally deserted Food Strip Street, so Sacha had to lead them far to find a quiet area. Eventually she stopped in a quiet alley with nothing but a series of blue dumpsters.

Mhumhi was chilled, for he recognized the place, but there was no reason for him to feel frightened- he hoped- as there was no hulker here now.

Sacha sat down on the warm asphalt with a great sigh.

"All right. I'll tell you about our mother."

13

The Pariah Dog

"How can you know things about her that we don't?" Kutta said, almost jealously. "She never talked about herself..."

"She did to me," said Sacha. "When I was the only one. She never shut up, back then. She was still out of her mind."

"Out of her mind?" Kutta repeated, but Mhumhi thought he understood.

"From her... puppies."

"The half-breed cull," said Sacha. "It was a domestic thing. Before we were born. They were very concerned about it. Domestics can interbreed with a whole lot of the big dogs, you know, even though they don't do it now. The wolves... the coyotes... the jackals, too." Sacha paused to snort. "That golden jackal- I don't doubt she knew some half-jackals."

"Wait," Mhumhi said. "Half-breed cull- you don't mean to say that- that they killed...?"

Sacha looked at him. "Finish your thought, Mhumhi. Yes, there was a big group of domestics that decided to get rid of anybody who wasn't pure-blooded. It was done in two or three days, I think. They marked all the homes beforehand and then came in all at once in a gang and killed them."

"But why would they do that?" exclaimed Kutta.

"I don't know," said Sacha, glaring briefly at the ground. "Domestics have always had strange thoughts... when more than two of them get together they can come up with peculiar ideas... I think they were frightened that they'd be bred out, that's all. There were a lot of hybrids... they did very well. Maybe in a few generations there would've been no domestics left. And then who would've looked after their precious hulkers?"

"That's awful," said Kutta, "really awful- how could anybody have let that happen? How could it have gotten by the police?"

"That's a question a lot of dogs have asked themselves," said Sacha. "Mother always said that the domestics must have made a deal with the police. They must have worked with other ordinary dogs, too- a lot of those hybrids were no joke, in terms of size and strength, and there've never been terribly many pure-blooded domestics to begin with. I think they had grey wolves helping them."

Mhumhi thought of those great grey forms bursting into their home, yellow eyes flashing up the stairs, the way the teeth at his flank had felt- He shuddered.

"So what that means is," said Kutta, slowly, "what it means is- Mother's puppies were half-breeds."

"Yes," said Sacha. "I don't even know what they were half of. But someone tipped off the gang, and Mother's house was marked. She didn't know what the mark meant, even. No one did who wasn't in on the scheme. But they came in the next morning and killed all her puppies right there."

Neither Kutta nor Mhumhi said anything, and Sacha went on.

"She told me," she said, and Mhumhi thought he saw a strange flicker in her small eyes for a moment, "that she went a little mad then, and she went out and looked for them, because she didn't believe it. Stepped right over their bodies, went outside, around and around, street by street, calling for them. Came across a den of bush dogs. Saw the puppies. Started to take them."

"Then that was where she found you," said Mhumhi, and Sacha's eyes flashed brighter.

"She stole me, you mean. Yes. The adult bush dogs were attacking her. She fled with one. I don't remember being stolen, but she told me." Sacha gave a sharp laugh. "When I asked her why I didn't grow anymore. She told me. She was proud of it! She was mad, our mother, d'you realize that?"

"Sacha-"

"She told me she came to her senses, but she decided she'd have a puppy for each one she'd lost. That's what she said to me. As if it would make everything right. She came back with you, Kutta," Sacha said, suddenly looking hard at Kutta. "That's when she stopped speaking to me. She was done with me, you see. I'd served my purpose. I'd been a puppy, I'd suckled for her, loved her like a mother, and that was all she cared for."

"No, Sacha, no," said Kutta, her head very low. "No, that isn't true..."

"What happened when she came back with Mhumhi?" asked Sacha, and Kutta fell silent.

Mhumhi tucked his tail, for he, too, remembered a certain indifference in his mother's behavior after she had returned with Kebero one day.

"I think there's always been something wrong with the domestics," said Sacha. "Something wrong with their minds... it's like they've got to care for things, like they can't help it, like they- they *need* it. It's like our mother was the puppy, and we were the ones taking care of her... fulfilling her needs..."

"You can't just say that *all* domestics are like that, Sacha, you can't just say there's something wrong with all of them," said Kutta. "Our mother... I mean, anyway, what's wrong with being too... too loving?"

"You talk as if love is a nice thing," said Sacha.

"Well, of course it is! It's love!"

"Yes," said Sacha. "What d'you think those wolves were feeling, then, when they saw our mother with their puppy in her mouth? For what feeling do you think they murdered her?"

"You're twisting it all around," Kutta gasped.

"No. You don't understand it... it isn't nice. It's beautiful and terrible, but it isn't... nice." Sacha furrowed her brow, brooding. "I've lost the thread of what I was trying to say, anyway."

"I don't see how there's anything else left," said Mhumhi. He was feeling weary. Sacha was right, her words hadn't helped. His image of his mother was now murky, fouled. For what reason had he been taken? To serve a purpose? She had always whispered... she had always whispered in his ear that she had *found* him, chosen him specially. That he was her beloved. That she was his mother.

He had not thought of it before, but had there been another mother, one who had loved him before?

"Mhumhi," said Sacha- she was looking at him, coming over to him with her ears back. "Don't think about her."

Which her, thought Mhumhi, was she referring to- He stopped thinking, then. Sacha had pressed herself up against his front legs. He leaned down to lick at her muzzle and cheeks.

"I don't believe it…" Kutta said. "I don't believe how any of it… could have happened… how could we never have heard about any of that? The half-breed cull? How could it have just… gone *quiet*?"

She looked at Mhumhi and Sacha pressing against one another, a bit of desperation in her gaze.

"If that was really true about Mother- if she was just picking out one after the other- what about those two in the sewers, Mhumhi? Why did she start looking after them?"

"In the sewers!" exclaimed Sacha, jumping away from Mhumhi. "I knew it, I knew that's what you two were hiding- she *did* steal more puppies, didn't she? And you've been looking after them and keeping them secret!"

Kutta and Mhumhi exchanged a look. Mhumhi said, "Sacha, you're right mostly, but it's not just that they're… puppies."

"Well, what about them?" said Sacha. "I tell you, it's a wonder we've even been able to feed Kebero- I don't know what you two were thinking, trying to look after two more- but you'll have to take me to meet them, and then we can take them home."

"Sacha-"

"I can't believe you'd just let them stay down there in that muck! It's so cold- they must be getting sick-"

"Sacha," said Kutta. "They're hulker puppies."

Sacha paused for a long moment.

"What?"

"They're hulker puppies," said Mhumhi, wagging his tail just slightly.

"Hulker puppies, Sacha," Kutta put in.

Sacha sat down again.

"Hulker puppies?"

"Hulker puppies," Mhumhi confirmed.

"Just… baby hulkers," said Sacha. "In the sewers. And you've been talking care of them."

"They're not really *babies* anymore, but yes," said Kutta. "They really don't eat as much as you might think."

"And how many did you say there were?"

"Two. A boy and a girl."

Sacha let out a long, slow sigh through her nose.

"Hulker puppies," she said, again. "Well, you can't fault our mother for her choice of a parting gift."

Kutta winced, but Mhumhi had to stifle a laugh.

"Will you meet them, Sacha?"

"I don't see that I have any choice," said Sacha. "I'm assuming they're tame?"

"Very tame, though one isn't fully housebroken," said Mhumhi.

"Oh, he is when he isn't sick," said Kutta, in an exasperated way. "Yes, Sacha, they're very tame, and they can be very sweet- you should have seen the little girl and Mhumhi the other day-"

"All right, we don't have to get into the details," Mhumhi said loudly. Kutta shot him a wicked look.

"I'll look at the little things today, then, I suppose," said Sacha, rising to her feet. "After we get our meat. Though I don't know what we'll do with them in the long run... They'll make things quite dangerous for us, you know."

"I know," said Kutta. "But it isn't their fault."

Sacha snorted. "It is, in fact, their fault. If they were puppies, we could move them to the house, but I won't risk having hulkers around, even if they are tame."

"Oh," said Mhumhi, "you should tell her your plan, Kutta, about what you want to do with them."

Kutta gave him a look that was both annoyed and alarmed, but Sacha had turned her gaze expectantly upon her. She coughed.

"Well- I was only thinking- since we're having such a hard time taking care of them, we could find an adult hulker, and- and pass them on."

"I think that's an excellent idea," said Sacha at once. Mhumhi stared at her in surprise, but Kutta's furry ears pricked.

"Yes, and they'd be-"

"Gotten rid of," said Sacha, as Kutta said, "Taken care of properly."

Mhumhi's tail was quivering with suppressed laughter at the look the two of them exchanged after this.

"Anyway," said Sacha, "I know exactly where we can put them."

"You do?" Kutta took an eager step forward, her tail swishing lightly. "You know where a hulker lives?"

"Don't broadcast it," said Sacha, casting a furtive glance at the entrance to the alley. "Yes, I do. The foxes weren't the only things I was investigating while you two were off chasing wolves and adopting hulkers. I followed that domestic we saw the other day."

"The one with blue eyes?" said Mhumhi, and Sacha grunted in agreement.

"The pale-eyed one, yes. I followed him all the way to where he dens. You'd be surprised."

"But did you see a *hulker*?" Kutta asked, impatient. "You know not every domestic has one around…"

"No, but I'm quite certain that's who he's been bringing the meat to. His *sister*, no doubt." Sacha gave another grunt. "I suppose Mother wanted you to call those two little things in the sewer our brother and sister, too."

Kutta looked a bit guilty.

"Anyway, we should go get our meat, it's almost time," said Sacha, wagging her tail slightly. "I can show you were they live on the way."

"It's on the way?"

"Yes," said Sacha. "We pass it every day. Stupidly obvious. It's in that squat brick building- what did Mother call it-" She furrowed her brow a moment. "The school."

14

Teeth, Hand, Wire, Laughter

They were quite glad that Sacha had directed them to go early that day when they saw the lines already forming when they got there. Mhumhi had spared a wistful thought for the extra meat having Kebero might have gotten him, but there was certainly no way the puppy would have been recovered from his earlier distress; certainly no way he'd be prepared to face such a mass of strangers.

Mhumhi felt a bit down, thinking of what Kebero must have been feeling, and wished that they hadn't argued in front of him, but Sacha had been right. He'd have had to find out about their mother sooner or later, maybe it would help him get some closure and sleep through the night again.

He resolved, anyway, to pay Kebero some special attention when they got back.

When they finally got their meat Mhumhi was still thinking of Kebero, but Kutta's mind was clearly on the school.

"I still can't believe we passed it *every day*," she muttered to herself, snapping up her meat rather savagely. They were under the concrete overpass again, in the darkened corner. "Right there...! If I had known that, I could have tried to move them a long time ago..."

"Better you didn't," said Sacha. "Not without us there. You'd have been caught and had your throat ripped out then and there, I expect."

"Don't ease her into it, Sacha," said Mhumhi. "Really tell her what you think would've happened."

Sacha wagged her stub of a tail.

"Can we try to go in today?" asked Kutta.

"No, we'll have a look at the two little things first," said Sacha. "See how feasible it is in the first place. If they're unmanageable, it won't be worth it."

Mhumhi wondered if they ought to tell Sacha the hulkers could talk, but she was probably already suspending her disbelief enough for them. Best let it be a surprise.

"Oh!" said Kutta. "I've just thought of something that should make it a lot easier. They can come up through those metal lids- manholes, I think they're called. If we can find one near the school, we can just take them underground and have them pop out closer."

"There's lots of dogs in the sewers, though," Mhumhi reminded her.

"It's got merit," said Sacha. "It's probably still safer than overland. Though how can they move those metal things…?"

"You'll see it," said Mhumhi. "It's really strange. They use their front paws like- well- it's very hard to describe. They've got these talons-"

"Hands and fingers, Mhumhi," Kutta reminded him.

"Yes, well, they pick up everything in their front paws and walk around on their hind ones," said Mhumhi. "I've never seen then use their mouth to do anything but eat with. And they don't lick-"

"Don't lick?"

"I always thought that was strange," Kutta admitted. "They have never even tried to lick me or mother, they just use their pa- their hands all the time instead. But they've got funny fat tongues, so I suppose it's harder for them."

"Stop talking about them," Sacha said. "It's not making me more eager to welcome them to the family."

"Oh but you will like them, Sacha," said Kutta, wagging her tail earnestly. "I'm telling you, they are very sweet."

"Hmph," said Sacha. "It doesn't matter if I do or don't. With any luck we'll be rid of them in the next day or so. Then we can begin bringing Kebero with us and…" She gave a slow sigh. "We'll be able to have enough food again, finally."

"Oh," said Kutta. They were all quiet for a moment. Mhumhi could tell Kutta had mixed thoughts about it, but he liked the sound of that. They wouldn't have to hide anything anymore… They'd be able to eat *all* their meat. Kutta would probably be less tired and thin-looking, too.

As for the little hulkers… perhaps he'd miss them a little. Maha had been starting to grow on him, really. But it was for the best. They'd be better off with their own kind.

Sacha licked her chops, having finished all of her small portion of meat, and stepped around Mhumhi to peer out at the mass of dogs still waiting in line.

"We're lucky we don't live near the edge," she said. "I don't know what we would've done if the police had evicted us."

"Let's not think about it," said Mhumhi, going to stand beside her and rub his head against her back. "Anyway, we could take them on together."

"Get off, Mhumhi," said Sacha, who was being pushed off her feet again. "Like you could take anyone on! You big, useless-"

"But I have you," whined Mhumhi, wagging his tail. "You're always there to protect me, right, big sister?"

Sacha raised her lip at him. "I'll put some holes in your big stupid ears if I hear another word, Mhumhi-"

"Sacha," said Kutta, coming up on the other side. She put one of her forepaws over Sacha's back, smiling slightly. "Don't pick on our little brother so much."

Sacha squirmed and hopped at her with a snap of her jaws. Kutta fell into a play-bow, her black brush-tail waving gleefully. Mhumhi jumped sideways and gave Sacha a playful thump of his own so that she whirled around and snapped at him.

"You little brats," she growled. "I licked your behinds when you were puppies and I can do it again."

Mhumhi's tail was wagging furiously, for this was the playful side of Sacha- not more than a shade different from her angry side, perhaps, but to be savored as a rare treat. Kutta caught his eye, grinning, and he knelt down and bowled Sacha over with his snout.

Kutta took off first, laughing, and he jumped over his furiously squealing sister to follow her. Sacha twisted to her feet and gave chase, as they dashed headlong through the crowd of dogs and back across Wide Street.

They had not played with Sacha like this for a long time, but Kutta and Mhumhi were well-familiar with the game- they slowed down just enough to let Sacha's short legs catch them up, then turned back and nipped at her with whistles and twitters of glee. Sacha briefly became a furious little spitfire of yowling and snapping, and Mhumhi let himself be knocked over so she could hop on top of his side and tug on his ear. Kutta twisted and bounced back into a bow beside them, tail whisking from side to side.

They wrestled gently with her for a short time, making slow progress through the streets but getting quite out of breath. Sacha herself was panting the most, her bright tongue hanging out far over her teeth, but her tail was up and wagging.

"Alright!" she barked, flopping down on her side. "Alright, alright, enough!"

Mhumhi bounced towards her but Kutta pushed at him with her shoulder.

"Let her be," she said, and so Mhumhi flopped over himself at her feet, poking at her chin with his paws, trying to be a hulker.

"If we don't want the sun to go down before we get there, we'd better go," said Sacha, though she showed no sign of wanting to get up yet. "No more playing."

Mhumhi pushed at Kutta's chest while she snapped at him, wagging his tail. "No one's playing. It's serious practice-" He broke off with a yelp, as Kutta had given him a sharp nip on the ankle.

"Come on, you two," said Sacha, and with a grunt she pulled herself to her feet. "Let's meet these wonderful little things. Save your energy for all the muck in the sewers."

Sacha broke off tussling with Mhumhi to cough, perhaps at the thought of it. "All right, she's right, Mhumhi."

Mhumhi would've liked to point out that Kutta was in no position to tell him to get less frisky, but he kept his mouth shut and pushed himself back onto his feet. "It's this way, Sacha," he said, wagging his tail, and pointed himself down an alleyway.

Sacha ran up beside him with Kutta following her close behind. She was sniffing the air.

"Do you smell that?"

"Smell what?" Mhumhi took a few quick whiffs. "What, the urine? Smells a bit like that crab-eating fox-"

"No, not that," said Sacha, and she trotted a little ways ahead of him. "Smells a bit like… hm. I don't quite know how to describe it."

Kutta darted up to her other side and put her nose to the ground as well, and for a moment the three of them sniffed together.

"It smells like something big," said Sacha. "Though…"

"I remember this!" exclaimed Mhumhi. "I smelled it in the sewers once, Kutta, and I forgot to tell you- I think it made a noise, too, whatever it was-"

"Oh, you smell strange things down there all the time, Mhumhi, the muck will play tricks on your nose," said Kutta, though she sounded a bit nervous. Sacha pricked up her ears and rounded on her.

"You're not keeping secrets again, are you?"

"No, no! I'm really not!" yelped Kutta, half-laughing. "I really don't know what it could be! Mother just said that to me about the sewers, that's all."

"Hm," said Sacha, making Mhumhi think that the mention of their mother was ill-timed. "Well, we can't stop and investigate it now. Let's get going and get this over with, please."

"Right," said Mhumhi, bouncing a bit in spite of himself. "Then it's this way, this way-"

He sprinted up ahead, rounding the corner out onto the sidewalk.

"Mhumhi, wait!" called Kutta, chasing after him. "Wait for Sacha-"

Mhumhi turned around mid-stride, hopping sideways with impatience. The street was very open here, and deserted and dusty. There was a lone streetlamp with a bank of solar panels on top sticking up a few feet ahead of him.

Kutta whistled behind him, catching up, and he turned to dash towards the streetlamp and then he was jerked to the ground by one of his back legs.

He got up at once with a whine, leaping away and then was twisted back over. Something sharp was tight around his left hind leg, digging in painfully.

Kutta ran over to him.

"What's the matter, did you trip?" she asked, tongue still hanging out. "I told you not to go so fast-" She jumped when Mhumhi twisted and squealed.

"It hurts, Kutta, it hurts- get it off!"

Kutta put her ears back and whined, looking down across Mhumhi's back leg, which was sticking out at an unnatural angle where he was lying on the sidewalk.

"There's a- there's a wire or something you've got stuck on, Mhumhi," she said, sniffing at it. "It's attached to this pole. Let me see if I can bite through it-"

"Hurry, hurry," gasped Mhumhi, twisting again. "Hurry, Kutta, it hurts-" He thought he might go mad with the pain, it was so sharp, and his leg felt stretched and twisted-

Sacha came running up. "Mhumhi, quit moving! You're making it worse. Kutta, move away!"

Kutta did so, tucking her tail, and Sacha sniffed around Mhumhi while he quivered and tried to stay still.

"Mhumhi, you've got to come closer to the pole," she said. "If you can move a bit backwards, that should relieve some of the tension."

Mhumhi tried to do what she had said, though his leg hurt terribly when he tried to roll over. Kutta gave an anxious whine, dancing on the sidelines.

"It hurts too much," Mhumhi whined, falling back on his side. "I can't-"

Sacha growled and bit the wire- Mhumhi flinched, feeling the sudden movement go through his leg.

"I don't think it can be bitten through," said Sacha. "Kutta, see if you can work it off his leg with your tongue-"

Kutta came over and licked at the area where the wire had caught, making Mhumhi flinch and scrape his claws on the concrete. Sacha went around to the other side of the pole, her lip raised.

"I don't like this," she said. "It's got a funny- it's all got a funny scent-"

"Are you getting it, Kutta?" Mhumhi asked, raising his head to try and look. His sister gave him a worried glance and did not respond, just kept licking. Sacha came back around the pole.

"It's wrapped around here," she said. "We might have a better chance at it if we can find the end of it- come with me, Kutta, let's look."

"Wait," whined Mhumhi, raising his head again as Kutta backed away from his leg. "Wait, where are you going?"

"We're right here, Mhumhi," Kutta said, tone soothing. Mhumhi saw her rear up and bite at something high up on the pole.

"No, don't bite it, *pull* it," Sacha growled. Kutta tugged, and Mhumhi saw a bit of the wire coming forward in her mouth.

"It's wrapped," said Sacha, pacing and directing from the ground. "Come around again from this side- pull it here."

Kutta came back down on all fours for a moment, panting. "Oh, Sacha, I smell it too-"

"Shut up," said Sacha. "Come around- focus on your brother-"

Kutta reared up again to tug at the wire. Mhumhi had to put his head back down again to rest his neck then. He shut his eyes and panted, tongue lolling against the hot concrete. His every instinct was jangling at him to struggle and fight it, to twist away from the thing that had his foot gripped so tightly-

"Don't move," said Sacha's voice near his head, almost as if she'd heard his thoughts. "You'll break your leg. Don't think of panicking, Mhumhi."

Mhumhi opened his eyes and looked up at her. Her small eyes, buried as they were in her bear's face, were hard and expressionless. Mhumhi still found it comforting.

"Take me home?" he said, trying to draw his dry tongue back into his mouth. "Lick it better for me?"

"Once we get you out," said Sacha, and she leaned close and gave him a swift lick on the forehead. "Though it's nice having you down at my level, little brother."

Mhumhi gave a strained little laugh. Behind him, Kutta said, "I think I've got it, Sacha!"

Sacha went around and grabbed the end of the wire, which Kutta had managed to partially unravel. Together, tugging it in a circle, his sisters unwound the last bit of it, and suddenly all the tension on Mhumhi's leg eased off.

"Oh!" he said, rolling over, but when he got up he was jerked back again, his back leg sticking out straight.

"Wait, it's caught on something," said Sacha, rearing up to sniff. "I think it's just one last bit."

"Someone's coming," said Kutta.

Mhumhi looked up, and Sacha fell back on all fours. There was indeed a figure approaching them from far down the broad street. It was obscured a little by the shimmering heat rising from the asphalt.

"It's a dog, isn't it?" said Sacha. "Maybe he can help."

The figure kept moving towards them. Mhumhi thought it looked like it was limping.

"Maybe he's been caught in a wire too," he said, wagging his tail at his own attempt at a joke. Kutta gave him a concerned look.

"Just a moment, Mhumhi, we'll get you off of this," she said, biting and tugging at the wire. Sacha walked around her to trot towards the figure.

"Help us!" she called. "We could use…"

She trailed off. The figure limped closer.

It was huge. Mhumhi put his ears back. It was bigger than the biggest gray wolf he'd seem. It was not like any dog he'd ever seen before, in fact. It was a mass of dirty gray spotted fur, humped shoulders, a wide mouth, a face-

"It's got a face a little like yours, Mhumhi," Kutta observed, and Mhumhi had to agree, reluctantly, that it did share characteristics with a painted dog; the darkened muzzle and eye area, the rounded ears. It had a short tail, which it curled upwards over its heavy hindquarters.

"Hello!" barked Sacha. "What sort of dog are you? Will you say something?"

The dog opened its mouth and gave a strange kind of chattering noise. Mhumhi felt a strange chill, because it sounded rather like- He glanced at Kutta, and saw the startled look on her face, and knew she heard it too. Rather like hulker laughter.

Sacha, of course, picked nothing up of it, and trotted the rest of the way to the strange dog and gave an authoritative squeal. "Why don't you say something?"

The strange hulking thing seemed to cringe away from her, which Mhumhi found rather amusing- she was a fraction of its size.

"Oh!" said Sacha, a rare exclamation of surprise, and jumped back. Mhumhi hopped forward a little, tugging on the wire, trying to see what had startled her.

Now that it was closer, they saw why the dog had been limping. There was something wrong with one of its front paws- no, it would have been better to say that the wrong thing *was* its front paw. Instead of a blunt dog paw it had a dark, perfectly formed hulker hand.

Mhumhi had to blink hard to believe what he was seeing. Yes- it was certainly a hulker hand- the dog held its leg up and crooked so as not to step on it, and Mhumhi could see the individual fingers twitching as the hand dangled downwards.

"What's the matter with you!" Sacha shouted, angry in her confusion, and stepped back a little. The strange dog lowered its head and made a strange noise, a long moan, going higher like a question: a calling noise. Mhumhi recognized it; he'd heard it in the sewers.

"Stop that!" barked Sacha, moving to snap at the stranger, and he cringed away again, and then he snapped back. His jaws caught her around her small head, and he lifted her off the ground.

Mhumhi stared a the image a moment, not comprehending- Sacha's body dangling like that in his teeth, by the head- he could see her short legs kicking and whirling.

Kutta gave a scream and dashed over, baring her teeth; the stranger dropped Sacha on the ground and ran away a few limping steps, squatting low and cringing. Sacha did not move on the ground. Mhumhi's heart was hammering. He could smell her blood.

With a furious twist he jerked free of the pole, the wire finally dragging loose behind him, and ran limping towards Kutta. She was snarling and biting at the flanks of the stranger, which was having a hard time getting away with its one malformed paw; it squatted and cringed again, snapping at her, its heavy jaws just missing her head. It gave that awful chattering laugh again.

Mhumhi put on a burst of speed, his injured leg stinging as the wire caught and dragged on the street, and lunged at the thing. His teeth caught it in the shoulder and it wailed and whirled around to snap at him. He fell back, stumbling, but before it could really focus on him Kutta bit at it on the other side, so it whirled again, and again, squatting and wailing from their combined assault.

"Come on!" barked Mhumhi, his blood rising, a hot kind of rage filling him- he could see Sacha raising her bloody head from the ground- good, good, she was all right, just like he'd thought- but the thing had better pay for hurting her- he dug his teeth in again and caught skin, twisting, feeling it rip, and the thing shrieked.

It whirled, and he jumped back, waiting for Kutta to bite it from the other side- but then he felt a jolt of fear. Behind Kutta, who was now tearing at the thing's flank, was a second one- a second creature, loping fast towards them, and this one had all four legs working properly.

"Kutta!" he shouted. "Behind you!"

Kutta turned around and leaped sideways, but the second creature bowled her over and she screamed- Mhumhi slammed past the first one and bit the second on the nose, tugging him, feeling its blood fill his mouth as he dragged it around off of Kutta- then he squealed as well, because the first had started to move towards him, only it'd tripped over the wire still trailing from Mhumhi's leg- it was getting tangled in its blundering, dragging Mhumhi backward-

Kutta whirled to her feet, one shoulder an open maw, and drove at the second creature, driving it back with its nose still dripping blood. She staggered towards Mhumhi. The first creature was moaning and thrashing, getting more and more caught in Mhumhi's wire, inadvertently pulling him closer. Mhumhi realized that he was now tied to the abomination.

Kutta whined, and Mhumhi felt sick, looking at the mess that was her shoulder. She came close against him, panting, looking fearfully at the creature as it thrashed and tugged Mhumhi closer.

"Gat away now," Mhumhi gasped, fighting to stay standing. "I'm stuck- I can't get loose- you've got to run and take Sacha-"

Kutta whined louder and then lunged at the thing, raising her lips in a snarl. The second one lurched back towards them again as its compatriot squealed from the assault. Suddenly Kutta was trapped between them. Mhumhi's heart gave a horrible seize and he twisted around, trying to break in himself-

For a moment it was all a mass of thrashing limbs and teeth, the silver wire flashing in the sunlight, the smell of blood thick and strong in the air as it splattered on the street.

Abruptly Mhumhi rolled free from the fray. The wire on his leg had been snipped short- one of the strange things' jaws had closed on it and severed it in an instant.

"Kutta!" Mhumhi screamed, because he could not see her between the two thrashing gray bodies. He could not even hear her screaming anymore-

Then she suddenly came towards him, leaping high over their heads. The larger one tried to rear and snap at her but fell over, its own hind legs now tangled in the wire as well.

"Come on, come on," she gasped, tongue dripping blood, and together they limped and ran forward.

"Sacha-" cried Mhumhi, and turned to dart towards her small form.

"No!" screamed Kutta, and she grabbed his ear in her teeth, dragging him away, "Leave her!"

Mhumhi was stunned. "How can you-!"

The two things were twisting- the malformed one was still caught, but the second was freed, and it was loping towards them purposefully, ripped up nose shining like a dark badge. Mhumhi tried to limp towards Sacha but Kutta dragged him back. The thing looked, too, following their gaze, and changed direction towards where Sacha was lying still on the ground.

"Sacha!" cried Mhumhi, but Kutta was shoving him back and back, and he could not understand why. "Let me go! Why are you doing this!"

"Mhumhi!" said Kutta, and there was something in her voice, something he knew he did not want to hear her say- He pushed at her with his shoulder, willing her to let go, and she did, and she spoke.

"Mhumhi, stop! She's dead already! She's dead!"

Mhumhi screamed at her then, shoved her aside, but Kutta caught him by the tail before he could go any further towards the creature, which was now dipping its nose over Sacha's body.

"Let go-!" Mhumhi thrashed, struggling, and Kutta fell down hard on her side. The creature raised its head and looked at them.

"Mhumhi," gasped Kutta, rising up- Mhumhi looked away, back at Sacha-

"Mhumhi, we have to go, we have to run, now, while they're distracted," Kutta gasped.

It was opening its jaws over Sacha's body.

"No," said Mhumhi. No, he had seen her- he had seen her lifting her head- he had seen her-

"Mhumhi," said Kutta.

He turned and ran, ran behind her, ran away.

15

Stain on the Couch

They limped and staggered together through the streets. Kutta's breathing was a harsh rasp beside him. He could hardly hear it over the sound of his own hammering heart.

The sun was beginning to go down, coloring the pale white plaster of the houses around them a sickly yellow-orange. Mhumhi could still hear and smell the little dogs returning around them from the dispensary, their low noises of greeting and warning to one another, their reaffirmation of their old, illegal scent-marks.

For some reason he could not see any of them. He felt strange and blind. All the could really see were dark shapes- teeth- Sacha's legs kicking-

Beside him Kutta coughed and fell down on her side.

He stopped, trembling, and limped back over to her. The wire was still clasped around his back leg, and it had started to go numb.

Kutta breathed in a frothy way, lying there on the ground with her eyes closed and her tongue hanging out, and there came that terrible feeling in him again, seeing her weakness- he jerked and snarled, opening his mouth over her wounded shoulder.

But it wasn't just that, there was anger, there was rage in him-

"Why did you make me leave her?" he shouted. "You made us leave! We could have- she could have been still alive!"

Kutta whined and did not respond. There were bubbles around her tongue and lips as she panted. Another terrible snarl came out of Mhumhi, and he convulsed and snapped his jaws over her.

"It's your fault! You killed her! You didn't go with her at first- you left her afterwards! Now she's-" He was seized by another sudden convulsion, but this one took him away from his sister, pointing back towards the way they had come. "We must go back! We've got to go back and get her!"

His mind seized on this sickening point of hope. Yes, yes, they could go back, there was still time, she was still lying there, waiting

for them, and the terrible creatures would vanish like ghosts or bad dreams-

"She's dead, Mhumhi," said Kutta, without opening her eyes.

Mhumhi whirled around and roared at her. "STOP SAYING THAT!"

Kutta did open her eyes now, and she pushed herself up slightly to look at him. "You know… you heard… you heard what they were doing to her…"

Mhumhi growled and shook his head, his heart hammering and thudding, because he did not want to think about it, not about the hideous sounds of tearing and crunching and wet sucking they had heard behind them, with their sharp canine ears, as they had run away.

"She's gone," said Kutta. "She gave us our last chance… she distracted them for us…"

"STOP!" screamed Mhumhi, and he fell on her and bit her muzzle shut, snarling.

Kutta whimpered, and he felt her blood and saliva in his mouth, and he was so full of rage that she would dare even *whimper* that he thought he might kill her then and there-

He opened his mouth and backed away, stumbling on his injured leg, panting and drooling on himself.

Kutta, panting, was still looking at him, and he wanted to cringe away from her yellow gaze. He could see the marks his teeth had inflicted on her muzzle, more wounds to add to all the ones she had already acquired. His tail was tucked tight underneath his rump, and he was shaking, and now he did look away, shutting his eyes tight.

"Mhumhi," said Kutta, "help me… I don't know if I- I don't know if I can walk- we've got to get home- we have to meet Kebero and Bii- and we've left a blood trail, Mhumhi, what if they follow us, help me, *help me*-"

Mhumhi whined and shut his eyes tighter for a moment, then he went around to her other side, crouching to push at her shoulder. His sister got up, shuddering, the sticky fur on her shoulder warm and wet against his. She leaned against him heavily, panting hard, and then together they limped forward.

They were able to pass through several more dusty streets this way, panting into each other. Mhumhi felt the eyes of smaller dogs on them, smelled their fear at the awful sight of the pair of them, but again he could not really see them. He was seeing Sacha's body, the distorted shape of her head and the jaws opening over her, Kutta's yellow eyes staring at him…

They reached their house. Mhumhi could barely remember how they had gotten there. Kutta slid against him, gasping, and he pushed back, muttering at her, "We're almost there… almost there, Kutta, then you can rest… we've got to go through the door."

They limped to the door, and Mhumhi pawed it open. The interior of the house was dark and still, but there was something harsh and unfamiliar about the scent. Mhumhi felt sick.

"Kebero!" he barked.

Beside him, Kutta slid from his shoulder and onto the floor. She was coughing again. He spared a fearful look for her, then left her and limped up the stairs, his paws slipping and scraping for purchase on the wood.

"Kebero! Bii!"

The bedroom was dark and empty. He put his nose down and sniffed- he could catch their scents, they had been there not long ago, but they were not there now.

He went to look in the bathroom. It was empty, the toilet hole a yawning pit- not even a fly or a cockroach, since Bii had come.

He dragged himself back down the stairs. Kutta was still lying near the open door, and suddenly the sight of it frightened him. He limped over to catch the handle in his teeth to pull it shut.

The harsh smell was strong downstairs, and he followed it, unwillingly, to the couch, where there was a giant fresh piss-stain on a ruined cushion. The scent told him what he needed to know: it had been made by a member of the police. Their home was marked.

What had Liduma said, just earlier that day?

"*They're asking for Pariah by name.*"

"*If I were you, I would find a new home. Soon.*"

He looked at Kutta, but she seemed to have fallen into an uneasy doze, her breath rasping, and he did not want to disturb her. Rather, he was almost frightened to go near her. He limped into the kitchen, where in the dim light he could see all the open cabinets gaping blackly at him, mocking him. He had to investigate every one, knowing that he would find them completely empty, that each confirmation would drive the stabbing pain deeper into his chest…

The kitchen smelled like Sacha. Of course it did, it had been her favorite place in the house. There were things she could climb on, with her short legs; she could stand on top of the counter and be taller than all of them. He reared up painfully, his one good leg trembling, to sniff it. The sink was bathed in her scent. She liked to lie there. She had liked to lie there.

He felt a whine rising in his throat, and quelled it. He wanted to call for her, to cry. But he did not want to wake up Kutta. He got back down on three legs and limped beside her, intending to lie down, but almost as soon as he did he got back up, shaking, because he knew if he closed his eyes he would see Sacha's legs kicking, the jaws opening. He began to pace and limp around the empty house.

His head was drooping low, and a shaft of moonlight was coming through the window and dazzling his eyes, when he heard Kutta speak.

"Mhumhi."

He looked at her. She had rolled up from her side and her head was up. Her breath still rasped when she panted.

"Where's Kebero and Bii?"

Mhumhi looked at her, then away; he did not know what to say to her.

"They're not here?" she said. "They're gone?"

"They're not here," said Mhumhi. He looked at the couch. "The police were here."

Kutta looked towards the couch too, sniffing the air. For a moment she shifted and tried to get up, her feet slipping and sliding on the smooth wood floor, but she fell back down and started coughing. Mhumhi stared at her.

"Kutta..."

"I'm all right," she said, when she had got her breath back. "I'm just very tired... The police either arrested them, or they ran away. We can track them when I've got some strength back. You should sleep, Mhumhi..."

Mhumhi gave a little whine.

"What if the police come back here to arrest us? What if-" He stopped himself, but he knew she mirrored his thoughts, for her ears had gone back. What if those creatures came and tried to get in?

"We can't go anywhere- at least I can't," she said. "I'm worried about your foot, Mhumhi, it looks bad. I wonder if Maha could get the rest of the wire off of it."

"We didn't feed them tonight," Mhumhi pointed out. Another worry to add to the pile.

"They'll be fine. Maha catches rats sometimes, and I know they've eaten insects… they can eat about anything. They've got that new blanket, too, so they'll be warm down there."

Mhumhi thought back to the day before, when they had dragged the blanket out of the wolves' den. It seemed like so long ago. How frightening the wolves had seemed back then! How fierce their teeth! And yet, they had barely marked either of them. He looked at his sister, at her bleeding shoulder.

"Those things… those dogs… what was wrong with them?"

Kutta gave a little tremor from her spot on the floor, and he felt immediately bad for bringing it up.

"They weren't dogs, Mhumhi," she said. "That's all I know, that they weren't dogs. They didn't talk- they *couldn't* talk, I don't think- you saw the way they acted, mindless- it was like they weren't intelligent, like rats, like *animals*."

"Monsters," muttered Mhumhi, limping through the moonlight.

"The hulkers look more different from us than they did, but the hulkers are really dogs, Mhumhi, they can talk and think and smile- those things, those things were not *dogs*."

"Hulkers," said Mhumhi, slowly. "Kutta, you saw it, didn't you? One of those things- the first one- it had a, a hand. A hulker hand. Why? If it wasn't a dog, and it wasn't a hulker, why did it have a *hand*?"

"It couldn't have," said Kutta, though she looked and sounded unsure, her ears back and her eyes wide. "It couldn't have been a hand, Mhumhi, it must have just had mange or something, some deformity, because otherwise that doesn't make *sense*. We didn't see it correctly."

"Sacha saw it," said Mhumhi, and he saw Kutta tense, over on the floor, and then flinch as she disturbed her wounds.

"Either way," she said, "either way, we know- we know what must be killing and eating other dogs. It's not the police, nor the hulkers. It's those monsters."

Mhumhi agreed with her, though he thought there were things that didn't make sense. "What was that wire?" he asked, staring down at the mess that was his leg. Bald skin was showing around the area the wire had constricted. "I don't understand how I got so caught in it!"

He felt a sudden burst of guilt, for if he had not been caught, they would never have lingered in the area, so long, smelling like blood. They would have been safe down in the sewers, all three of them, safe and sound with the hulker puppies...

"I've heard of things like that," said Kutta. "Wires or metal jaws you can get trapped in... I've never heard that there were any in this part of Oldtown, though, I thought it was more of a mid-city hazard."

"But where did it even come from?"

"Oh, it must have been something that rusted, or fell down and got tangled," said Kutta, laying her head down on her paws. "I don't know."

"It wasn't there before," said Mhumhi, pacing through the moonlight again. "I've walked by that pole a hundred times... marked it, even. The wire was never there before."

"I don't know, Mhumhi."

Mhumhi glanced at Kutta, at her muzzle with dried blood in the fur, and felt a second surge of guilt.

"We mustn't stay here too long," he said. "The house... I bet it's being watched now. The police will come back. We've got to find a safe place somewhere else."

"Yes," said Kutta, softly. "Down in the sewers... If we could get down there, hide with the puppies, we might be better off. But swimming through the muck with these wounds- Mhumhi, it'll kill us."

Mhumhi thought of the sickening scent and the sewage, and shuddered. She was right. And he could not think of anywhere else- and even if they could find a safe place to lie low and lick themselves, they would leave a trail behind them, clear as day, with the smell of their blood and exhaustion.

He looked at the heavy-smelling stain on the couch again, wondering if it would be really so bad if they were caught by the police. Especially if it was just Liduma and her cronies. But Sacha's words returned to him, with another pang: they were always looking for ways to have fewer mouths to feed.

"Kutta," he said, feeling a strange idea come to him, unbidden, as he thought of the crowd that day at the dispensary. "Kutta, I know where you can go. If we find that pack of dholes again- the leader, what was his name, Rakshasa- I know he'll take you in. They can protect you."

"No," said Kutta, at once.

"Come on, Kutta- you'll be safe, they're your own kind."

"My kind!" Kutta cried, and she actually bared her teeth at him. "They're not my kind! Since when was I a dhole? I'm not a dhole, I don't know how to *be* a dhole- I'm a- I'm whatever our pack is, Mhumhi, I'm *you*, and I'm not a dhole! And don't you *dare* try to abandon me!"

In her distress, she was struggling to get to her feet again, slipping and sliding, until finally she did it, and staggered over to him with her teeth still showing.

"Kutta, be careful, your wounds-" he started to say, but she cut him off.

"What would you do if I left?" she said, coming up close to him, getting in his space so that he cringed. "Where would you go? To join the police? They'd kill you! How could you even think that I could leave you!"

Mhumhi whined, and fell trembling to the floor, wagging his tail over his belly. Kutta stood over him for a moment, shaking a little, then collapsed on top of him.

"Sleep," she said. "We're going to sleep- you're going to shut up, and not come up with any more ideas. Then we'll decide what to do."

She had fallen with her foreleg and head over his back, heavy and warm. Mhumhi twisted a little to lick her injured shoulder. She flinched.

"No… go to sleep."

He ignored her, focused on licking the area clean. She did not protest, only coughed again, her body rattling with it.

He must have fallen asleep for a time after tending to her, for the next time he woke up it was pitch black. The moon had gone down, and all was still and silent. Kutta's body was still over him, though he could no longer hear the rasp of her breath. She was a limp deadweight.

Mhumhi's leg was aching terribly, and he found he could not go back to sleep. He shifted painfully.

"Kutta, wake up," he whispered.

Kutta did not stir. In the darkness Mhumhi squirmed for a moment and managed to drag himself from underneath her.

"Kutta!"

He nosed her. She was still warm, but her sides did not move. He whined and pawed at her, fear rising in his breast.

"*Kutta*!"

Suddenly she gave a huge bray of a cough.

"It's so dark," she murmured. "What's the matter?"

"Oh," said Mhumhi, and stepped back, panting.

"What is it?" He heard her shifting around in the darkness, claws scratching the floor. "Are you all right?"

"I'm fine," said Mhumhi, which was a fantastic lie.

"I feel a little better," said Kutta, and he felt her warm form get closer before her nose brushed his cheek. "I think the bleeding in my shoulder has stopped, too. We should run away now."

"Yes," said Mhumhi, feeling lost. "Where, though?"

"At first I thought about trying to go to Lisica," murmured Kutta. "We could tell her what's really been killing other dogs."

"We don't even know that those things were doing all the killing," Mhumhi pointed out. "We don't even have proof they existed. And I don't like that golden jackal."

"That's a moot point," said Kutta, but he heard the faint amusement in her tone. "But I don't think we should go to them anyway. I don't trust them not to just turn us in if they hear the police are looking for us. I don't think they felt very strong allegiance towards us… we're not like them."

"So there's nowhere we can go," said Mhumhi. He found himself thinking of the pack of dholes again. If he convinced Kutta that he'd go with her, maybe…

"No," said Kutta. "There is one way we could go. Back down to the sewers, without swimming. There's a way there through the subway."

"Through the subway?" Mhumhi took a moment to revel in the fact that his guess had been correct. "Was that the other way you and Mother used to take? Wasn't there something wrong with it?"

"Yes," said Kutta, sounding uncomfortable, "but I think that if we're quick and quiet we should be able to get through all right."

"Quick and quiet?" Mhumhi glanced down at his injured leg. "Why must we be quick and quiet? What sort of thing will stop us from being loud and merry down there, exactly?"

"There's nothing really down there, not exactly," said Kutta. "Not that Mother or I ever saw… but there was a cave-in, and it- er- opened up a new way."

"A new way to where?"

"I don't really know," Kutta admitted. "But Mother was very frightened of it when she smelled the air. She said that way wasn't safe anymore and wouldn't use it. But if we've got no other choice, I think if we run straight through it we ought to be alright."

"Well," said Mhumhi, who has getting an extremely bad feeling about all of it, "that's very encouraging. But there's another problem with that, Kutta."

"What problem?"

Mhumhi gave a short, desperate laugh. "To get to the subway we've got to go back past that part of the city- back to where those things were."

16

The Tunnel

It was nearly dawn, and very little starlight remained to illuminate their way, but outside their house there were still working streetlights on a few corners, pooling soft yellow light. Mhumhi and Kutta avoided them, sticking to the shadows. Mhumhi was really beginning to feel the helplessness of their situation. Limping, smelling like blood, trying to pant softly… If another one of those awful creatures found them, there would be no way that they would survive.

They had both agreed that it would be best to cut a wide angle around the light post where Mhumhi had gotten caught in the wire. Not that Mhumhi really thought it would help, in the end- why would the creatures stay there? As he limped along, he suppressed a shudder.

Part of him wanted to go back, just to see, to look- to see if anything was left there.

He had to quell such thoughts. He had held them about his mother, the thoughts that held aloft that strange and horrible hope, and they had gotten him nowhere. Sacha… had been right, it was not good to hold on to them.

As he panted and pushed himself along on three legs behind Kutta, skirting another pool of golden light, he felt a raw longing. She would have known what to do. She would have known the safest course- she would have been able to find Kebero and Bii- she would have kept the pack together, where it had dwindled to only two-

He whined, the noise unbidden.

"Hush," whispered Kutta, glancing back at him. "I know your leg is hurting… we're almost there…"

Mhumhi licked his lips and followed her without saying a word.

They moved slowly through the sleeping city. Mhumhi thought he saw eyes gleaming in a storm drain once- it might have been a fennec fox- but they vanished at once. The warm night air lay heavily on them, wind mingling scents together. Mhumhi was certain he could smell traces of the musky scent of those *things*, but it could have been from earlier, it could have been from a different direction, he did not know. At least it did not seem that it had come from anywhere close by.

Before he would not have even taken notice of the smell; he'd have assumed it was just another dog, but now it was firmly ingrained in his psyche. There was that, at least. They wouldn't be caught unawares again by something that smelly.

"There's the subway," Kutta whispered to him. The pale white building was suddenly looming out of the darkness in front of them. Mhumhi saw the sheet metal that had been blocking the little entrance he'd found, though now it was lying on the ground.

Cutting through the darkness they suddenly heard a noise: a moaning call, rising up like a question.

"No," said Kutta, her tail tucking in fear.

"It came from far away," Mhumhi urged, even as they heard a second noise come from a different direction. "Hurry, let's go inside-"

They darted together into the little gap in the wall, into the total darkness of the subway.

"Oh, no," Kutta moaned, when they had both come through to the other side. Mhumhi's tail tucked too, in the darkness.

The interior of the subway reeked with monster. Mhumhi could smell its marks, its urine and feces, and the heavy musk of its markings. There had been more than two individuals in there- the smell was so strong that there was no telling if there were any in there even now.

"Come on," said Mhumhi, his heart thudding away, "come on- let's go as quickly as we can. We can't go back. We have to do it."

Kutta made no sound, but he heard her stumbling forward in the darkness, claws tapping on the tiled floor. He followed, vaguely remembering the layout from the time he had come there seeking his mother's scent. There were pillars- the trench of the track- the familiar rushing sound of air passing through long tunnels.

He nudged Kutta towards the way down, a pile of old debris piled up against one side of the deep track, and they slipped and stumbled down together. Their progress was very loud. If there was anything in the tunnel, it knew it wasn't alone now. Mhumhi hoped they were alone.

He kept his nose near Kutta's tail and followed her as she limped down the track, half-tripping over the metal rails as he came across them in the blackness. The smell of the beasts was not getting any lighter- they had been all along this area at some point, even far past the station where they had climbed in.

Both of them kept quiet, the sick feeling still rising in Mhumhi's chest.

"Here," whispered Kutta, and he heard her claws scratching. He nosed up beside her and felt his nose touch crumbling stone.

"It's the beginning of the cave-in," Kutta whispered. "There was an earthquake. We've got to climb over this part."

Mhumhi followed her over, his paws slipping on the loose shale. At the top he had to squeeze past a shattered part of the concrete ceiling, his back brushing up against it as he crouched. His injured leg dragged and caused him a burst of pain, and he had to stop for a moment, shuddering.

Kutta gave a soft whistle of encouragement, and Mhumhi went on, slipping down the other side, hearing rocks he had disturbed bounce and fall in the darkness.

When he reached the bottom, he felt a soft wind. He turned towards it, sniffing. The smell of the creatures was still very strong, but he also smelled something else, something he was not familiar with. There seemed to be a broad opening near him that the wind was blowing through. He turned towards it.

"Not that way!" Kutta hissed, nudging him. "That's the way that opened up. That's what Mother was afraid of."

"Really?" Mhumhi said, sniffing again. "I wonder where it leads…"

"Not now, Mhumhi," said Kutta. "Come over here. The way into the sewers is just past here, but we need to move some rubble out of the way first."

Mhumhi followed her over to another part of the pile and heard her begin scratching at it.

"You didn't say we'd have to dig!"

"Only a little," said Kutta. "I know it's narrow here- I can smell the sewers. Come on and help, Mhumhi, it's hard to use my leg like this…"

Mhumhi went to stand next to her, sniffing dubiously at the rubble. He could indeed catch a whiff of sewage. He began to help her dig, shifting the larger rocks with one paw, as it was hard to use both with only one good hind leg.

After a little while, his nose detected an influx of cold, smelly air. He thrust his head forward and was able to detect the beginning of large pipe, just barely big enough for a dog to get through.

"We have to go through here?"

"It's not that tight of a fit," Kutta replied, scratching away. "It's almost clear."

He heard more stones sliding from her efforts. He sneezed. The air was getting very dusty from all their efforts.

His sneeze echoed a bit, and then there was a response: a moaning whoop. He felt Kutta freeze next to him.

"Hurry," he said, and then they both began to dig, side by side. Behind them they heard paws thudding on metal and that eerie chattering laugh echoing.

"It's clear, it's clear," Kutta breathed, and she crouched and crawled inside. Mhumhi, panting, looked back in the darkness as he waited for her to squeeze inside. The sounds were coming in with the wind drifting from the large opening behind them. They were very close.

Kutta's tail brushed past his legs, and he squeezed in after her, gasping as his injured leg dragged uselessly across the metal bottom. Behind him there were grunting and snuffling noises- squeals- there was more than one-

The metal around them vibrated as claws scratched at the pipe. Mhumhi felt a nose bump his exposed rear. He tucked in his tail and heaved himself forward, heedless of the pain in his leg. He bumped into Kutta, who gave a frightened squeal.

"Hurry, hurry," he cried.

She moved forward, agonizingly slowly- he knew she must be in pain too from her shoulder, but there were *monsters* behind them. He felt the pipe shudder again from their pawing, and then with a nervous chattering laugh one shoved itself into the pipe.

Mhumhi felt its breath on his rear, heard it snuffling and sniffing blindly for his presence. He nipped Kutta's tail in his desperation to get away, and she jumped and dragged herself forward. Behind them the creature gave a squealing whine and made the pipe rattle as it withdrew.

"What's that, what's it doing," cried Kutta in front of him.

"Don't slow down, keep going," he urged her. "Keep going!"

She did, panting and gasping, and they squeezed forward through the narrow circular darkness. The chattering and moaning noises of the beasts faded away behind them.

It seemed like another eternity that they had to crawl together through that close pressing darkness, occasionally feeling the pipe shudder again from far away, and hearing the echoing sounds of moaning whoops.

Suddenly Kutta gave a little cry, and her warm presence vanished from in front of him.

"Kutta?" Mhumhi squirmed forward and suddenly his nose and forepaws encountered empty air. The remainder of his body followed, slithering out with a painful *thump* a foot or so down onto hard concrete.

"Are you all right?" said Kutta, coming to nose at him. He blinked, for he was beginning to be able to see again: there was dim light here. They had landed in a sort of concrete trench in an area where the sound of rushing water was very loud. He stood, shaking a bit, and looked through metal railing to a vast, murky pool of water, lit by a few dangling spotlights.

He recognized the place. It was the big reservoir in the sewers next to the corridor where the hulker children hid. Only they were at the bottom of it now.

"Come on, Mhumhi, it's just up some stairs," said Kutta, licking his face, and then turned to lead him on. "Do you think those things are following us?"

"No," said Mhumhi, panting slightly. "I don't think it could fit all the way into the pipe. I'm not sure, though."

"Oh, that would be wonderful," said Kutta, and coughed. "If they couldn't get through. I was afraid we'd have to try and move the puppies right away."

"I don't know how you thought we'd do that," muttered Mhumhi.

"And that's another good thing," said Kutta. "If the police try to track us, they're bound to run into some of those things down here. That'll distract them. Distract them to death, maybe."

"That's bloodthirsty, Kutta."

"I want to know what happened to Kebero and Bii," she replied, tone cool, and he had nothing to say to that.

They went up the spiraling stair, step by aching step, until they finally rejoined the path they took through the broken grate. Mhumhi thought the narrow concrete hallway looked like heaven, especially since the door was hanging partly open and golden light was spilling out.

"Maha!" called Kutta, breaking into a limping run. "Tareq!"

Mhumhi thought he'd never been more gratified to see anything than Maha's tangled head poking around the door.

Kutta tottered up to her, tail wagging, but Maha leaned back fearfully, her white-sided eyes wide.

"What's the matter?" Kutta asked, her tail slowing. Mhumhi limped up beside her.

"We're covered in blood," he pointed out, then addressed Maha. "Sorry, we don't have any food for you today."

Maha looked at him, her eyes flicking over him, and then her face screwed up and she gave a kind of wail. Mhumhi flattened his ears and actually took a step back. She was rubbing her face, which seemed to be getting damp and sticky, with her forepaws now.

"Don't cry, Maha," said Kutta, wagging her tail in an anxious way. "We'll get you some food soon. I hope you've been able to eat something."

"'M not hungry," said Maha, the words muffled through her hands as she continued to wipe at her face. Kutta gave Mhumhi a worried look, and Mhumhi limped closer so he could paw at her knee.

"Hey! Stop crying! We're all right, we're not too badly hurt-"

Maha gave another wail and knelt to grab him around the neck again. Mhumhi went stiff again as she buried her damp face in his fur

She was saying something, but it was too muffled to hear properly. Mhumhi looked back over at Kutta and saw that she was grinning at him.

"Maha," she said, coming over and licking her on her exposed shoulder. "Maha, let's go inside. I want you to help with Mhumhi's leg."

Maha mumbled something again, and Mhumhi said, "You'll see what's wrong with it when we go in, now get off."

She let him go, sitting back on her haunches to sniff and wipe at her eyes, and he breathed a long sigh through his nose.

From within the room they heard the sound of Tareq whimpering, rising to a crescendo. "Maha come back!"

Maha gave kind of watery giggle then, looking slightly guilty, and stood up. They walked into the room together.

17
Fever

The hulker puppies had made good use of the new quilt. It was big enough to spread out over the entire floor of the little room, making it soft and puffy, and there was still enough left over to wrap Tareq up in in the corner. Mhumhi almost felt sorry to bleed on it, but Maha didn't seem to care. She watched him lie down with that same sad, frightened look.

"It's here, Maha," said Kutta, limping over to nose Mhumhi's injury. "Do you see the wire?"

"Yes," said Maha, though she seemed hesitant to look that closely. Mhumhi didn't blame her- every time he looked at the swollen mess the area was it made it hurt even more.

"Try to get it off," Kutta said, swishing her tail gently, and walked over the lumpy fabric to stand by Mhumhi's head. "You're so clever with your hands, I know you can do it."

Maha did seem a little cheered by this compliment. She knelt down and tucked her tangled hair behind one of her rounded ears.

"It looks really tight," she said. "I can't see the other end…" She went to touch Mhumhi's leg and hesitated, looking over at him.

"It's all right," said Mhumhi, who was trying not to pant openly. Her nervousness was catching. "Just get it off."

Maha gingerly lifted up his leg so she could look at it more closely. Mhumhi gave a little grunt and licked his lips. Kutta licked his face and ear, soothing him.

"I see the other end!" Maha said triumphantly. "It's wrapped under, but I can unwrap it- I think-" She reached for the cut-off end and gave it an experimental tug. Mhumhi yelped, raising his head, as the wire pressed against his sore flesh.

"I'm sorry," said Maha, and she tried to move it again. Each movement brought fresh pain to Mhumhi, and he whined and shook. Kutta went to lay down with her head on his neck, trying to hold him still.

"It's not working," said Maha, dismayed. "It's hurting him too much- wait!" She suddenly bounced to her hind legs and ran around to one of the high shelves. She returned to Mhumhi's side with something skinny and black in her paw.

"What's that?" asked Mhumhi, trying to raise his head again, though Kutta was blocking him with her body. He could see flecks of his blood on Maha's hands.

"It's a clipper," said Maha. "I think it's little enough. i want to try."

She knelt down again and lifted his leg, and he put his head back down, mystified by what she had just tried to explain to him.

He felt a sharp pain, and tensed and whimpered, and she said, "I almost got it, Mhumhi!" and Kutta licked his ears more. The pain intensified, and he gave a sudden thrash and a wail.

"You must hold still, Mhumhi, you're making it worse!" Kutta urged, biting lightly on his ear, and he tried, though his whole body shuddered from the effort.

"I got it!" Maha suddenly crowed, and there was a very loud *snick* and suddenly the pressure around Mhumhi's leg was gone.

He whined and Kutta got off of him so he could sit up. Maha showed him the circular wire, covered in blood and fur and broken in the center.

"I cut it off," she said, sounding proud, and went to put it on the shelf up with the other things.

Mhumhi looked at his leg, which was aching, a pins-and-needles sensation filling his paw. The area where the wire had been was just a dark yellow gash, bleeding freely and almost too tender to lick, but he curled to do so anyway, whimpering with pain and relief. He could feel his paw again.

"Do you feel better, Mhumhi?" Maha had returned, and she went to sit next to him, looking shy. He looked up from his ministrations and licked her forehead, making her giggle. Kutta's tail was wagging madly.

"Oh, I'm so glad you're all right," she said, and went to give him a fierce nuzzle, nearly knocking him over. "I thought- I thought you'd lose the leg, or something!"

"Yes, well," said Mhumhi, not really wanting to think about his leg anymore, "how is your shoulder?"

"It's all right," said Kutta. "It's closing. It makes my whole leg hurt a little, though."

"And your- and your muzzle?"

"That never really hurt," said Kutta. "Don't worry about it."

Mhumhi hesitated a moment, then went back to licking his leg.

"Kutta," said Maha, "what happened? How did you both get so hurt?"

"Hm, well," said Kutta, looking away uneasily, "we just got in a fight with someone. Oh, and Mhumhi got his leg caught in a wire."

"Who did you fight with?" asked Maha.

"Just a big, mean dog," said Kutta.

"It wasn't a dog," Mhumhi. "It was a monster. Two of them. Actually, there are more than two."

"Mhumhi, I don't want to scare them!"

"They should know, so they don't try to- don't try to run up and talk to them," Mhumhi said, feeling a different sort of pain than that in his leg. "You have to stay away from them. Big gray monsters. Little tiny tails. They laugh like hulkers."

"Oh!" said Maha. "A hyena?"

"You know what it is?" said Mhumhi, startled. "What did you call it?"

"A hyena," said Maha, looking a bit abashed. "Tareq's mother told me about them. Big lumpy gray animals that laugh. She said if I saw one I should run away, same as if I saw a dog."

"Did she say anything else?"

"No," said Maha, and she shook her head from side to side. "Only that they were dumber than dogs. So it wasn't a big deal if one saw me, cause it wouldn't be able to tell anyone about it."

"Oh," said Kutta, and she and Mhumhi exchanged a look. "A hyena, was it? I think that's what they must have been. How come we haven't heard of them before?"

Maha had no answer for them; she merely blinked. In the corner Tareq snuffled.

"I'm hungry," he said.

"Sorry, little one, we have no food tonight," said Kutta. "But we'll sleep here with you."

"Why are you sleeping here?" asked Maha. "Why don't you have food?"

"We'll talk about it in the morning," said Kutta, and Maha pulled her lips down. "We will, really. Mhumhi and I just need to sleep now, understand? We're very tired."

Maha seemed displeased, but she nodded, and crawled over to pull half of the quilt up off the floor to drape over them. Mhumhi and Kutta ferreted their heads out over the edge, Mhumhi feeling a bit startled. Maha went over to the wall and flicked the light switch, blanketing them all in darkness.

"Goodnight," she said, which was a word Mhumhi wasn't familiar with. They heard her rustling around near Tareq.

In the dimness Mhumhi got up and felt Kutta do the same, the blanket sliding away from their backs. They walked together over to where the hulker puppies lay.

Maha sat up in the darkness when Mhumhi brushed her cheek with his cold nose.

"We're supposed to stay together, puppy," said Mhumhi. "Aren't you a dog? Don't you know the proper way to do things?"

He was teasing, but she sniffed a little and put her forelegs around his neck when he lay down. Mhumhi was suddenly glad for it. Her bare hulker skin radiated heat, and the cold of the sewer was starting to settle in his bones.

Kutta huddled on his other side, and Mhumhi felt unusually cozy, almost too warm, especially when Maha pulled the quilt over top of them. He heard Tareq shifting and whimpering on her other side for a little while before he finally went quiet with sleep.

Mhumhi did not know if it was really morning when they all woke up, as there were no windows in the sewer, but he did feel a great deal more rested. The pain in his leg had dulled to an aching soreness, certainly more manageable. Maha's arms were no longer around him- he could feel her hard back on one side and Kutta's paws on the other.

He was still debating whether he should wake Kutta or just let her sleep when Maha sat up, the quilt falling back as she did so.

"Mhumhi?" she whispered, in the darkness.

Mhumhi gave a little whuff of acknowledgement. Beside him Kutta coughed.

An answering cough came from Tareq, and he began to whimper himself into awakeness.

"I'm hungry, Maha..."

"Mhumhi, will you go get us meat today?" Maha asked, sounding hopeful. Mhumhi swallowed.

"I don't know," he said. "We might not be able to get to the dispensary."

He was feeling very nervous abut the whole thing; they might be more or less safe from the police at the moment, but going to the dispensary was a sure-fire way to get caught. They'd stick out in the Oldtown dogs like a sore thumb, and the police would be on alert for them. He turned and licked the side of Kutta's muzzle.

"Kutta, wake up!"

Kutta coughed again, and when she spoke, her voice sounded raspy. "What's the matter?"

"Nothing's the matter, only we should figure out what we're going to do," Mhumhi said to her, keeping his voice soft. "Should we go to get the meat, or…"

Kutta coughed again. It was a dry, hacking sound.

"I'm not sure, Mhumhi… I'm very tired. Perhaps we should rest some more."

"Come on, Kutta," said Mhumhi, impatient, and pulled out from under the quilt to shake himself. Maha got up too and he heard her fumbling around in the darkness.

"I don't know," said Kutta. She did not try to get up; Mhumhi only heard her slow breathing. "Meat… I don't know. They'll see us, surely, or we'll get tracked back here… and to get out, we'd have to go by those *things* again…"

It was unfortunate timing that it was then that Maha found the light switch and turned it on. Mhumhi jumped about a foot into the air. Maha giggled at him, and he gave her a dark look. He'd landed hard on his injured leg.

"That's true," he said to Kutta, and then stopped. In the light he could see that she looked absolutely wretched. Fluid was leaking from her eyes and black gunk had made trails down her scarred muzzle. Her nose, when he touched it to his, was bone-dry.

"Kutta, you're sick," he said, feeling stunned.

"I'm not sick," she said, but the words were feeble in and of themselves. Maha came running back over the blanket.

"She's sick? Like Tareq?"

Mhumhi looked over at the other little hulker, at *his* yellow-rimmed eyes, at the way he shrank back into his nest against his gaze. "Tareq got her sick!"

"No he didn't, it isn't his fault," said Kutta, trying to rise, but Mhumhi stood over her to stop her.

"Don't get up," he said. "Unless... are you thirsty?" He felt at an awful loss. If Kutta was sick, what then? What was he going to do? What if she died? What if... what if he was left all alone?

He got the shakes then, briefly, and Kutta whined and tried to tell him she wasn't sick again. He ignored her.

"You should drink some water," he said, latching on to the only suggestion he could think of. "Your nose is so dry... if you can stand, and get to the sink-"

"I can bring the water to her," said Maha, and she ran again up to one of the shelves and took a yellow plastic bowl from it. She padded on two legs over to the sink in the adjacent bathroom.

"She's bringing you the water, Kutta," said Mhumhi, just to have something to say, because he was really not sure how someone could carry water, unless hulkers could regurgitate it like dogs regurgitated meat. Except if they did that, how would one lap it up again?

"I'm not sick," said Kutta. Her head was lolling slightly to one side where it was laying on her paws, her eyes half-closed. Mhumhi whined and licked at the gunk on her face, trying to clean her.

Maha returned with the yellow bowl between her hands and knelt down in front of Kutta. Mhumhi realized it was full of water. So that was how she could do it.

"Kutta, lift up your head, there's water," he said, pawing at her shoulder until her eyes opened all the way.

Maha set the bowl down in front of her and she raised her head just enough to drink, sloppily, getting half the water on the quilt. Mhumhi found himself exchanging an anxious look with Maha, of all things, as Kutta lifted her dripping muzzle away from the bowl and laid it back down on her paws.

"I'll just rest now," she said, sounding groggy, licking her lips. "That's all I need, some rest."

"All right," said Mhumhi, licking around her ears. Maha picked up the bowl again and offered some to Mhumhi, who took a few mouthfuls before backing away. Maha raised it to her mouth and drank the rest herself, in a queer fashion, tilting it directly through her lips.

When she had finished and wiped her mouth with the back of her hand, Mhumhi rose from his sitting position and said, "Come with me a moment, Maha."

Maha looked surprised, the small hairy parts over her eyes rising up, but she stood to put the bowl on a shelf and followed Mhumhi just outside the door.

Outside in the cold concrete corridor, Mhumhi turned to face her, feeling very nervous, and not a little bit helpless. He was down to his last threads of hope now; if he could not keep this strange and fragmented pack together, he'd be entirely lost.

"I don't think I'll be able to get meat from our dispensary today," he told Maha. "The police are looking for us- we don't know why, exactly-"

Was it because of his mother? Or had they discovered Kebero? Either way, it was all wrong...

"And it's better for us not to be seen in this district. I think if I can make it to another district's dispensary, though, I might be able to blend in the crowd and at least get my meat. We can try to divide it between us."

He felt a bit hopeless as he said it, thinking of the meager portions it would yield, even if he saved none of it for himself.

"Kutta and Tareq should get most of it," said Maha. "They're sick."

Kutta should get *all* of it, thought Mhumhi, then chastened himself. He needed to start treating Tareq like he was part of the family.

"The problem is, I only know two ways out of this place," he told her. "And both of them are bad. If we were starving I would risk swimming through our old way, but..." His leg seemed to twinge at the thought. "The other way is surrounded by those hyena monsters. So I'm asking you- you've explored these tunnels, haven't you? Is there any other way out?"

"Oh yes," Maha said at once, then paused. "Oh. Maybe not."

"What do you mean?"

"I mean, I can get out in lots of places, but maybe not you. You can't climb ladders, right? Like the rungs going up to the manhole cover by our room?"

"Oh," said Mhumhi, thinking of the vertical climb. "I don't think I could do that, no."

"Then there's not many ways. There's lots of ways I can get out, but… I don't know how you'd do it." She chewed on her lip, which Mhumhi found weird and distracting. "There might be one way, but it leads to a scary district. Lots of police."

"That's perfect," said Mhumhi, and when she gave him a startled look, added, "The police around here know me, Maha, and have smelled my home, but the police in a big district like that won't have any idea who I am. And if they feed from the local dispensary, I'll blend right into the crowd."

He thought he sounded very confident, saying it, and wished he felt that sure in reality. Maha was paying rapt attention to his words.

"That's a good idea!" she said. "I didn't think of that. And the grate isn't very far from here."

"Grate?"

"Yes," she said, scratching her scalp with her blunt nails. "It's a storm drain. You have to crawl up through a little pipe, but the drain has a lot of trash and things in it, so you can climb out of it if you lift the grate."

"Lift the grate?" The sound of that made Mhumhi nervous, but he pressed on. "All right, then. All you should do is tell me how to get there, and I can be off." If he was lucky, it'd still be early enough for him to catch the morning distribution.

"Tell you how to get there?" She pulled her lips down. "I can show you, can't I?"

"No, Maha, it's too dangerous-"

"But hardly any dogs go down that way! And how will you lift the grate without me? I don't think you can get it up just by pushing on it yourself." She flashed her teeth at him in a swift grin.

Mhumhi's tail twitched in annoyance. "I can't risk bringing you with me-"

"I go down that way all the time without you," she cut in.

Mhumhi breathed a sharp sigh through his nose, but she had a point.

"Fine. But you'll stay behind me and keep quiet, understand?"

She bobbed her head up and down, which he couldn't make head or tail of, but her face looked pleased. He took it as an affirmative.

"I'll tell Kutta where we're going," he said, "and you can talk to Tareq, if you want. But we must be quick now."

She bobbed her head again and ran for the door, taking his words a little too literally, but she *was* a puppy. He followed her more sedately and went to nose Kutta.

"Kutta," he said, nosing her ear. She was asleep. He hated to wake her, but he more hated the thought of her waking up while they were gone and not knowing where they went.

Her eyelids fluttered open. "Sacha?"

He froze, a jolt going straight through his heart, and swallowed.

"It's Mhumhi," he said. She tilted her head to the side a little to look up at him blearily.

"Maha and I are going for a walk," he said. "We're going to get some meat. We'll be back in a little while. You understand? Don't you or Tareq leave this room."

She looked at him for a long moment, and he was afraid she was too delirious to comprehend, but then she said, "You are talking very rudely to your older sister."

He gave her a swift lick on the ear. "We'll be back soon."

"Mhumhi?"

He turned to look back at her, for he'd already been padding to the door. "What is it?"

"She's not really dead, is she?"

He was silent for a long moment, feeling like he was teetering on the brink of a terrible precipice, a terrible yawning chasm on each side.

"I keep falling asleep and waking up," said Kutta, "and sometimes she's dead, and sometimes she's alive. I don't know which one is real. I can never find her."

"She's…" Mhumhi struggled with his choice of words. "Right now, she's not here, Kutta. Go back to sleep. You'll feel better."

"All right," said Kutta, in the peaceable way of the delirious, and closed her eyes.

18
Rat Pups

Mhumhi led Maha out through the concrete hallway after instructing her to shut the door behind them, shutting Tareq and Kutta safely inside. Maha had brought with her something lumpy that she slung over her bony shoulder. When he questioned her about it, she explained that it was a bag.

"See, it's got all kinds of stuff in it that I can take with me," she said, reaching inside the lumpy sack and showing him the candle Kutta had found. He could still see her teeth marks in the soft wax.

"Why do you need to take anything with you?" Mhumhi asked, and Maha blinked.

"In case I need it, right?"

Mhumhi still didn't get it, but he let it slide. The bag wasn't costing him anything, anyway.

"Which way is it up ahead?" he asked. "This level, or the one below?"

"Below," said Maha, and so Mhumhi went in front, sniffing carefully for any other signs of life, and led her down the long, spiraling staircase through the large reservoir room.

Maha directed him down through another series of long concrete tunnels shuttling sewage, walking behind him on the narrow raised platforms. She sounded unsure of herself occasionally, and dithered at some corners, but for the most part she was a fairly good guide.

"Not that way!" she said, at one point, pressing back against the wall when Mhumhi nosed down a dark branch. "There's lots of dogs down that way. Rats, too, but lots of dogs."

"It smells a little bit like meat," said Mhumhi, trying to sort through all the scents that his nose was picking up. "And offal."

"It's where the pipes from the dispensary go out, I think," said Maha. "I went down there once or twice. There's stuff that leaks out sometimes that you can eat. But lots of little foxes. They get scared when they see me, usually." She broke into a brief, toothy grin.

"Aren't you afraid they'll go tell the police on you, though?" asked Mhumhi, and her grin faded.

"Well, let's go this way," he said, backing up to face the other fork. "And don't worry, I'm with you. I can fight off anything that comes after you."

Maha looked at him with her eyes shining a little, and again he wished he felt as confident as he sounded. Especially for a dog that still limped every third step on his aching back paw.

They went down the other fork, which sloped gradually upwards. Mhumhi liked that, though it meant it was sometimes slippery, especially for Maha on her two feet. It had not rained for several days, so in most pipes the sewage had slowed down to a sludgy trickle, a slick scum that Mhumhi did his best to avoid stepping in. Maha slopped through it, squashing it between her bare toes.

They came finally to a narrower tunnel entrance, an offshoot of the main line. It smelled somewhat cleaner.

"It's just up this way," Maha said, putting her forearm out over the metal railing on the concrete platform they were standing on. It looked as if it had not been completed: it was littered with metal things, round sections of pipe, coils of wire, flat sheeting. Across from them gaped the tunnel entrance.

Mhumhi could see a slight problem: the round opening was set up high, possibly higher than he could jump with his injury, and he would have to jump from down in the muck to get at it.

He poked his head under the railing and assessed: the entrance might have been reachable if he jumped from the platform without the railing in the way- though it was a fairly small target, and he was already not at his best. It looked as if his only choice was to have to get down into the muck.

"What's the matter?" asked Maha, watching him as he bobbed his head up and down under the railing.

"Nothing," said Mhumhi, withdrawing. "I didn't want to get my foot dirty, but it looks like I'll have to step down in there to jump up. Hopefully it won't get into my wound."

Maha squatted to look at his leg for a moment, brushing one hand down it, which made him stiffen.

"Don't do that!"

"I'm sorry," said Maha, backing away a bit. "But we don't have to walk through that part, Mhumhi! I'll show you, look, I'll make a bridge."

"A bridge?" Mhumhi asked. "How…?"

He was beginning to suspect that he'd have to learn to stop asking that question where hulkers were concerned. Maha smiled impishly at him and went to pick something up from the ground, a long, narrow plank of wood. She slid it forward, making Mhumhi jump sideways to get away, and out across the gap between the platform and the tunnel entrance.

"There," she said, puffing her little chest out. "A bridge!"

Mhumhi looked out across the narrow plank and felt impressed in spite of himself. It was a clever idea. He tested it with a paw, putting his full weight onto it. It wobbled slightly, but if he darted fast it ought to hold his weight.

Maha went behind him and slipped her hind legs out under the railing to dangle over the side of the platform in a kind of bizarre sitting position.

"Go across," she said. "Then I can climb up after you."

Mhumhi disapproved of the bossiness in her tone, but she'd built him a bridge, so he listened to her. He went across the plank in a cautious trot that turned into a run as the thing wobbled and bounced under his feet.

Maha gave a kind of hooting noise and slid down from the platform. Mhumhi was getting his bearings in the smaller concrete tunnel when she put her forelegs over the side, shoving away the board, and pulled herself up. Mhumhi backed up, half amused by the way her long legs kicked out into the air as she wormed her way inward.

"It's just up there," she said, when she had gotten into the tunnel far enough to kneel. One of her forelegs was scraped and bleeding, and Mhumhi went up to lick it without thinking.

Maha gave a little utterance of pain, flinching from his tongue. Mhumhi moved back and licked his lips nervously. Her blood tasted just the same as any dog's.

"Don't let that touch any sewage," he said, keeping his voice stern. "If you had proper fur, you'd be better protected from that kind of thing."

"What do you want me to do," asked Maha, "start growing it?"

"Can you do that?" Mhumhi put his ears forward with interest, and then back again at her peals of laughter.

"Come on," he said, as she covered her mouth with her hands to staunch her giggles. "We've got to hurry on, because even when I get out I'm going to have to find the dispensary, and then figure out what time it'll be open."

"Oh, it's just up that way," said Maha. "Don't be cranky."

Mhumhi gave a little huff and turned and trotted up the tunnel. Maha followed him at a much slower crawl, as the tunnel wasn't tall enough for her to stand up in.

He saw the larger chamber of the storm drain very quickly, and stopped abruptly. There was a mass of what looked like old paper and assorted wood near the bottom, and his ears were picking up all sorts of strange noises.

"Why'd you stop?" asked Maha, crawling up behind him.

"There's something in that pile," said Mhumhi, lowering his head with his ears trained forward. He was picking up rustling and high-pitched chittering. "And I think it's alive."

"Ooh!" said Maha, and she suddenly squeezed by him, shouldering him roughly out of the way. She was taking something out of her bag- a flat piece of wood- and to Mhumhi's amazement, she scrambled over to the pile and began beating it furiously.

There was more shrill squeaking, and something small shot out of the pile and passed Mhumhi, who snapped at it out of pure instinct. His jaws missed, and it vanished down the tunnel.

"Aw," said Maha, who had paused in her beating to wipe her forehead with a hand. "You let it get away!"

"It was *fast*," Mhumhi said, rather defensively. "You didn't get any!"

"Yes I did!" Maha hopped back off the pile and peeled back a particularly large piece of faded cardboard. Beneath protruded the limp gray body of a rat.

Mhumhi's ears pricked, and he helped her dig around the pile. They found another dead rat, and then something unexpected: a dying rat curled around a pile of pale yellow newborns.

When Mhumhi went to sniff the mother, whose back looked unpleasantly dented, she squealed and snapped at his nose from her prone position. He flinched away. Maha picked her up by the tail and bashed her on the ground, and she went still and limp.

Mhumhi stared at the dead rat in her hand, but Maha put it in her bag right away with the others and grabbed one of the blind, squirming newborns.

"These are the best!" she exclaimed, and bit off its head.

Mhumhi stared at her, eyes round, as she ate the rest of the body, which sounded crunchy. "You- it's only a baby!"

"Yeah, so you can eat the bones," Maha said, and reached for another one.

"But it's a *baby*!"

"So?" She drew up the hairy parts above her eyes. "That means they're better. And plus they can't get away." She bit through her second, and Mhumhi cringed. He looked back down at the remaining newborns, which were squeaking softly and beginning to crawl every which way.

"Do you want to try one?" Maha picked up one of them and held it out to him, flat on her palm.

Mhumhi stared at the tiny naked thing, its eyes still covered in skin, its soft little paws twisting as it tried to right itself. As horrible as it was, he could feel a sudden urge- that same urge he got when he watched sick Tareq whimper, when Maha fell down and he saw the back of her neck. He began to salivate.

"No," he said, licking his lips, and backed away.

Maha turned down her lips and moved her shoulders up and down, then ate the little thing herself.

"I'll have to bring one for Tareq," she said. "He likes these a lot… I found a nest in here before, but I didn't think any would come back after that…"

"What are they doing, having babies all the way up here?" asked Mhumhi, averting his eyes as she picked up yet another one. "Is there something to eat?"

"No, but I bet they were lookin' for a place those little dogs don't normally go," said Maha. "I mean, they *never* come up here. There's no reason to, cause when it rains it gets all flooded out. But it hasn't rained in a while."

"No, it hasn't," Mhumhi agreed. He could dimly remember the last time it had rained: the day Sacha had called him out of the subway. That had been the day that started everything- he'd seen the dogs fighting- he'd met Bii- and it was because of Bii that Kutta had felt it was safe to share her secret with him...

"Mhumhi, you can go up now," Maha was saying, and he blinked. She had stowed the remaining baby rats in her bag, and was now rearranging the pile of trash so they could climb up it. "I can move the grate. You have to hurry, right?"

"Yes," said Mhumhi, and watched as she clambered up the pile, teetering, and reached up for the rack of iron bars above. Sunlight was streaming through them, lighting her dark cheeks, and the shiny flecks of blood around her lips.

Mhumhi started up the pile, slipping on bits of loose cardboard, as she shifted the grate. It scraped very loudly. Maha gave a little grunt; apparently it was heavy.

"Have you got it?" he asked, bounding to stand next to her where she squatted at the top of the pile, straining with the bars. She did not answer, merely bared her teeth and squinted her eyes and forced the grate sideways. For a very frightening moment, as the edge cleared one side, it tilted diagonally and looked like it might fall in on them. But Maha caught it and was able to shove it the rest of the way to the side.

Mhumhi gave her bare shoulder a quick lick, feeling rather humbled. There would have been no way for him to do that himself.

She scrubbed at her forehead, panting a little, and then turned to give him an expectant look.

"You did very good," Mhumhi felt compelled to say, and she smiled and reached out to him. He moved back and away, paws sliding on the trash.

"I've got to go up now," he said. "Pull it back closed after me. I don't want any dogs catching you."

Maha's face fell a bit, but she bobbed her head in the affirmative.

"I don't know how long I'll be," he said. "I'll try to be quick... Stay here, understand? Don't go running in the sewers without me."

"But like I said, I do it all the time," Maha argued, but fell silent when he moved closer with his ears back.

"Do as I say. There are more dogs here than there used to be, and we don't want anyone to see you. When I get back, you need to be here to pull the grate off for me again, too."

Maha scrunched her whole face together at this, which Mhumhi found extremely off-putting.

"Eat the rest of your rats," he told her. "I'll be quick as I can, and I'll come back with proper meat."

"All right," she said. "Don't get hurt anymore, okay, Mhumhi?"

"I won't," he said, an easy lie, and then leapt through the opening above, out onto the street.

His paws touched asphalt and he felt his senses heighten, and he cast all around, sniffing. He could smell dogs, but not terribly nearby. It looked like the storm drain led out into some sort of alleyway, because there were very tall buildings on either side of him with banks of glossy black windows.

He turned back around and watched Maha pull the grate back over for a moment, grunting and straining.

"You should get out from where someone can see you if they look down," he told her. She stuck out her tongue.

Mhumhi decided it'd be prudent to leave her to it and trailed down the alleyway, limping a bit as the pain in his leg flared up again. The impassive rows of black windows seemed to go on forever on either side, and the street began to curve around. There wasn't a door in sight anywhere; Mhumhi wondered how anyone could possibly get inside. The way it looked reminded him a little bit of the dispensary, strangely enough.

He saw the corner, finally, and hastened around to it, hopping on three legs. He was not prepared for what he saw on the other side.

19

Dogs in the Field

Beyond the glittering black buildings that had surrounded Mhumhi in the alleyway, there was a vast field.

At least, he thought it was a field. He had never seen one before in his life. But it looked like a field should- it was flat and open, very dusty-looking, and covered with scrubby yellowed grass that waved gently in the wind.

Mhumhi had never seen grass before, either. He had to stare at it for a long time before he could really comprehend it. As he did, he suddenly realized where he was. This was a park- *the* park. Big Park.

As this realization slowly came to him, he suddenly heard a great deal of whining and twittering. Bounding high over the tall grass was a very large group of painted dogs, all sun-splashed pelts and white-flagged tails held high.

The one in front saw Mhumhi and stopped short.

"I found it!" he exclaimed. "I found what stinks! It's this fellow here!"

The others brought up a storm of twittering behind him, and suddenly Mhumhi found himself surrounded by them; at least ten, all sniffing and whining and nipping at him. Automatically he cringed, caught in the painted maelstrom, flattening his ears and wagging his tail down by his flanks.

"What pack are you from?" said one, sniffing closely at his ears. "Gosh, you stink! Did you fall down a sewer or something?"

"Ligwami, look at his leg!" said another, and suddenly the flurry of them were concentrating on that side of his body, all clucking and chirping sympathetically.

"What happened to you?" asked the one named Ligwami, licking at his ears. "That looks bad- what, did you get caught in an old snare?"

Mhumhi felt far too dizzy and overwhelmed to talk; he merely kept his head down and kept wagging his tail.

"Give him some room to breathe, back up, can't you see he's had a bad time?" said Ligwami, turning to scold the others. Mhumhi realized that more were still arriving, crowding at the edge of the field, leaping up in place to be able to see. He was very certain he'd be ripped to pieces any minute.

"It's all right," said another, coming to nuzzle gently at him. "Poor thing. Don't be frightened; you're out of danger now. You're just a puppy, aren't you?"

This was not strictly true, but Mhumhi decided to act the part, whimpering and crouching down in front of her. All the other dogs seemed very excited by this, and Mhumhi could hear things being passed back through the crowd: "He's escaped from a snare!" "He's just a puppy!" "He fell in the sewer!"

"He doesn't really look like a puppy; don't baby him, Nzui," said Ligwami, tail going a touch stiff, but the female named Nzui was leaning down to lick Mhumhi's forehead.

"Poor puppy, you've had a hard time, and now you're separated from your pack! Did they come for the hunt? We'll probably find them if we go back to the center track," she told Mhumhi. "Can you walk all right?"

Mhumhi opened his mouth, and all the dogs fell into a collective silence, staring at him with rapt attention. He had to close his mouth a moment, abashed, and then said, "I can walk all right."

The crowd seemed to ripple with excitement again: "He can walk all right!" "He can!" "He's fine." "What a brave boy!"

"Let's go back to the center track and look for your pack," said Nzui, nudging at him. Mhumhi swallowed.

"All right," he said, seemingly to the delight of the whole pack of them, for they cheered and twittered and ran around as he slowly got back to his feet and limped forward between Ligwami and Nzui.

Mhumhi's heart was beating at a fevered pace, but the painted dogs all seemed friendly, to a fault even, as each one of them tried to introduce himself to him all at once. Mhumhi let the names wash over him, hardly able to keep track as they bounded all around in the grass.

"And what's your name, pup?" asked Ligwami, when there was a long enough pause.

"My name is Mhumhi," said Mhumhi, without really thinking, then froze. How stupid of him! If the police were looking for him, it was probably through his name, and here he had said it into this massive pack of them…

"My name's Mhumhi too!" shouted one dog, bounding on Mhumhi's left, and behind him he heard another shout: "Mine too!"

"It's a very solid name," Nzui told him encouragingly, while on his other side he heard Ligwami distinctly mutter, "*Another* one."

Nzui trotted forward a bit to nip Ligwami's ear. "Wami and I are joining our packs for the running," she told Mhumhi, a touch of bashful pride in her tone. "I've been running about with my sisters, and him with his brothers, and we met- and, well."

She fell back to murmur in Mhumhi's ear. "Who knows what'll happen after the run?"

"What are you whispering to the puppy?" Ligwami said loudly.

"You said he wasn't a puppy," said Nzui, letting her tongue hang out in a smile. "Look, Mhumhi, we've reached the track. Do you see your pack anywhere?"

Mhumhi realized what they were indicating: ahead of them the field was cut apart by a circular track of white gravel, absolutely covered with at least a hundred different painted dogs that were making a ruckus of twittering and whining that filled the air with sound. In the center of it all was an ancient, rusted bus, the windows broken and the tires in shreds- Mhumhi saw two painted dogs playing tug-of-war with a thick piece of rubber nearby. Through one of the filthy, cracked windows he thought he glimpsed a flicker of movement.

He took his eyes away and pretended to scan the mass of dogs, all shifting and milling and twittering away with one another. He'd never seen such a gathering of large dogs before- he wondered if this was all the painted dogs in the entire city, massed up together.

"I don't see my family anywhere," he said, intentionally putting his ears back and tucking his tail.

"Oh," said Nzui, sympathetically, though Ligwami gave kind of an impatient huff.

"Well, you can look for them now, can't you? We've got to take positions… we're the first ones running today…"

"Don't be heartless, Wami, we can't just leave him."

"Well, we can't just *leave* the hunt, can we?"

Nzui gave her tail a stiff wag. "We won't leave you till you find your pack, Mhumhi."

"Nzui," said Ligwami, in an exasperated way, "come on, he doesn't really need it…" He trailed off under her gaze. "All right, fine! Then have him come on the hunt with us!"

"What? Are you trying to kill him?" Nzui's tail quivered. "And his stink will give us away!"

"Oh, now you're the one being heartless," said Ligwami, letting his tongue hang out in a brief smile. "You know the smell doesn't really matter. He can wait with the ambush. It'll be exciting for him! How many puppies get to be that close to a hunt?"

Nzui seemed swayed, and she turned to Mhumhi. "What do you think? Would you like to stay with us a bit longer? See the run? You won't have to participate, of course, not with that leg."

"I don't know," said Mhumhi, feeling a bit desperate. The hunt... they kept saying the hunt... They couldn't possibly mean...? He looked nervously over at the decaying bus, but there was nothing showing through the windows.

Maybe there were other ways he could use the kindness of these dogs to his advantage; maybe he could get them to take him to the dispensary instead. "I'm really hungry, actually-"

"Oh, then that settles it," said Ligwami, hopping a bit in place. "You can come with us. We'll let you have a mouthful of hot meat, eh? It'll perk you right up, make a bolder dog out of you."

Nzui pranced over and licked his ear. "Isn't this exciting, Mhumhi?"

Mhumhi said nothing, and luckily they didn't notice his tail tucking under, for they had gotten slightly distracted with one another, sniffing and half-nuzzling, stealing guilty glances towards their conjoined pack members.

Mhumhi looked at the vast swarm of painted dogs all around him and wondered how on earth he was going to get himself out of this. He spared a thought for poor Maha, waiting down for him under the grate; she might have to wait a very long time. If the sun went down and he hadn't returned, would she assume he'd been killed and leave? Would he, in fact, be killed?

He was working himself up into a decent amount of panic, so it was a good thing he didn't have much time to think about it. The yammering crowd was starting to get quieter, heads turning upwards.

Mhumhi followed their gazes and saw that two dogs had climbed up onto the top of the bus. Silence fell, and Mhumhi's ears, which had become accustomed to the din, felt oddly empty.

He couldn't make out the dogs very well, but he could make out the attitude that the others were affecting towards them. Ears were flat, tongues curled submissively, and the only sounds were faint whimpers.

One of the dogs, a male, gave a little prance atop the metal, his tail wagging high. The other, a female, seemed calmer, and laid down, crossing her forepaws. Mhumhi noticed that they both had notches in their left ears.

"Hello, all!" barked the male, commanding everyone's attention. "We all know why we're here, don't we?"

There was a rousing, cheery chorus of agreement; painted dogs were leaping and twisting with excitement all throughout the crowd.

"Then I won't waste your time!" he bawled, wagging his tail. Mhumhi saw his female companion sneak a discreet yawn.

"I can't believe she showed up today," he heard Nzui mutter to Ligwami.

"She has to show up sometimes, doesn't she?"

"She could at least pretend to be more interested," muttered Nzui. "All the young dogs that barely ever get to see her are going to be-"

"Hush," said Ligwami, licking her forehead. "Talking like that doesn't make anything better."

Nzui made a kind of grumbling noise and leaned into him. Mhumhi stared fixedly down at one of the little white stones near his forepaws.

"The first two teams are ready, correct?"

The male dog atop the bus was speaking again, and all at once dogs surged and jostled up around Mhumhi, hopping and twittering with excitement, rubbing up against each other, even mounting one another in their eagerness. Nzui got her head under Ligwami's stomach and thrust his hind legs up until he twisted away with a whuff.

"That's us!" she called to Mhumhi, her tongue hanging out.

"All right!" called the dog on the bus. "You all know the rules- let them get past the trees, then you can start. And that's all!"

He threw his head back, wolflike.

"Release the hulkers!"

At once there was a hissing, creaking sound, and Mhumhi took his eyes off the dog to realize that another had pulled the bus door open. He caught glimpses of the plastic seats inside, but nothing... No, there was something else. The bus shuddered with growls. Painted dogs were leaping inside through the broken windows near the back, their kicking legs disappearing into the gloom. Mhumhi heard a little cry that made him stiffen.

Shambling towards the open door came one, two... four hulkers. They were pressed together in a huddle, all bare dark skin; for they were wearing none of the coverings that Maha and Tareq wore, Mhumhi realized. They were naked.

Big Park. The hunt. And hulkers. There was no doubt, now, about what he had stumbled onto. A kind of shock and fear stabbed at his heart. Were they going to- and was he going to-?

There were dogs inside the bus trying to crowd the hulkers out, snapping and growling at their heels. The hulkers seemed reluctant to step outside. Mhumhi didn't blame them. Without their clothes they seemed horribly vulnerable with all that bare skin, like creatures half formed. Newborns. Like the baby rats Maha had killed. One of these hulkers looked rather young, and small, and female, just like her.

Maybe, Mhumhi thought, maybe if the hulkers didn't come out, the hunt would be called off, and they would be just left alone- just left by themselves, alive-

One of the dogs on the bus leapt up onto the back of the littlest one and she fell forward with a cry, hitting the stones hard. The rest of them howled out and surged forward- one grabbed the little one and pulled her to her feet- and then they scattered. The dogs parted to let them pass, ceasing their harassment. But their eyes- the way they looked at them- there was such terrible intention.

Mhumhi had never seen anything run like those hulkers, on their two long legs- muscles straining, limbs flying, they ran and scattered apart in the grass, though they left broad flattened trails as they did. They seemed to go in all different directions. Mhumhi saw Nzui and Ligwami putting their heads together, conferring; they seemed to be reaching a decision.

"First teams!" called the male dog on the bus. "Are you ready?"

Nzui and Ligwami wagged their tails, looking out across the field. Most of the hulkers had already vanished beyond the long grass, but perhaps they were visible from the top of the bus, because the female dog had raised her head to look intently at something in the grass.

"Mhumhi," said Nzui, turning to him, "you follow Umenzi, here, he's leading the ambush group. Stay right with him, understand?"

She did not wait for Mhumhi's reply; she turned back to Ligwami, quivering with excitement. The dog she'd named as Umenzi gave Mhumhi a friendly nudge.

"You may go!" cried the male dog on the bus, and Ligwami and Nzui burst together in a frenetic run, dashing forward across the gravel and into the grass. A good portion of the pack followed, ears slicked back for speed, and they vanished in an instant.

"Come on," said Umenzi, wagging his tail high, and trotted into the grass at a far more sedate pace. Mhumhi and the six other dogs left behind followed him.

The grass tickled against Mhumhi's chin and stomach as they moved, trotting silently. Some were sniffing a bit, but they didn't seem terribly concerned about it, their ears focused forward. Mhumhi was unsure of what he was supposed to do, so he merely followed them, exaggerating his limp. Umenzi drifted back towards him.

"I bet you're disappointed to have to be with the ambush and not the chasers," he said, in a genial way. "But don't worry, the ambush is better. They say it's for dodders and puppies, I know, but you really get the best crack at the hulker and you don't have to do all that running. Plus it takes a bit of skill knowing where to set it all up."

He paused, sniffing the air, then added, "I'm certain Ligwami and Nzui picked the biggest male, there's no point going first otherwise, right?" He laughed. "I really pity the ones who go last. They'll be left with that little female, and she'll probably have holed herself up somewhere small. Maddening work for less meat."

Mhumhi said nothing, but Umenzi didn't seem to need anyone else to hold up the other end of the conversation. He kept chatting away.

"Some of those big male hulkers can be real head-crackers when they get cornered, but don't worry. Ligwami can lose himself in a hunt, but Nzui's real sharp, and she always gets the dogs out of the way before the big stupid things can do anything."

"Hey, Umenzi," said one of the other dogs. "Let's let little Mhumhi have a nip at the belly! He can go back to his pack blood-faced! How will that be for an initiation?"

"Oh, I don't know," said Umenzi, but he looked very thoughtful. "It can be a bit rough, for a first timer- but then again, you're tough, aren't you, Mhumhi?"

The assembled dogs all exchanged looks, tongues hanging out and tails wagging. Umenzi nudged Mhumhi playfully in the shoulder.

"I bet you didn't think you were getting into anything like this when you woke up today!"

"No," Mhumhi said, very truthfully. The dogs around him whuffed with laughter.

Umenzi led them up a bit further, zigzagging briefly across one of the flattened trails the hulkers had left behind, and then stopped them beside some tall, blackened trees.

"Here's the spot," said Umenzi. His demeanor had changed, and his ears were flattened back against his skull, his head level with his shoulders. "Fan out, and keep quiet now. Listen for my signal."

The dogs did as he said, keeping their profiles low, spreading out in near-silence within the rustling grass. Mhumhi found himself suddenly isolated, the other dogs blocked from view.

He could leave now, he realized. He could run off and they'd probably be none the wiser- if they caught him at it he could just say he'd gotten turned around and lost in the confusing tall mess. He could even try to disrupt their hunt and make it look like an accident. There was no reason for him to witness what was about to happen.

Mhumhi thought this, and knew that he'd have to move, but he stayed still, stayed crouched low in the grass.

His mind was roving, thinking of Maha, her impish grin, those pale babies she'd crushed with her teeth; the little naked hulker girl, running, her two legs pumping; the hulker dragging the dead coyote with its head smashed in, and the vision of it crouching and glutting itself on its insides; the hyena lifting up Sacha's body by the head, her legs whirring; the crunch of the little rat's head disappearing between Maha's teeth.

There came a dull pounding noise from far away. Mhumhi wasn't sure if it wasn't his own heartbeat. He looked around himself at the shifting, whispering grasses, obscuring everything from view. There could be anything out there. Anything.

The pounding was definitely getting closer. It was not his heart. It was the sound of flat, heavy hulker paws crushing the grass.

He heard its heavy breathing, in the strange silence, the low breaths of the dogs around him, hidden from view, the very soft footfalls of the pack running towards them, driving the hulker- his breath came so *harsh*, so *desperate*- he knew what death was, he knew the stakes of this game-

Umenzi burst out of the grass beside Mhumhi, his companions following suit, as the hulker's footfalls got close- Mhumhi heard him slip, caught a glimpse of his naked back as he turned around- and suddenly they were all surrounding him.

The hulker was trampling the grass flat around itself as it spun and spun, looking for a way out, but the twenty or so dogs of Nzui's and Ligwami's combined packs were whirling all around him, bounding through the grass, twittering and cheering openly now. The hulker was caught.

Mhumhi saw his white-ringed eyes rolling, his flat teeth bared. The dogs ran around and around him, shifting between one another and changing direction like fluid, but none attacked him directly yet. He was holding a large branch with both hands, and he swung it wildly at the dogs each time they got too close.

Mhumhi had not joined in the circle- he merely stood back and away, watching. He could still run away, he knew. The hulker shook his branch and howled, his voice loud and booming. He swung the branch again, though it did not contact any of the dogs- they leapt away too quickly.

The hulker's roving eyes darted madly around the circle, and then suddenly they caught on Mhumhi. And they stayed. Mhumhi was petrified. The hulker *stared* at him, his mouth open, his chest heaving, clutching his branch to himself. Mhumhi could only stare back.

It seemed like longer, but it must have only been an instant, because the hulker yelled and swung his branch down again, turning. His calf was shining dark yellow and a dog was leaping back with blood on his tongue. The hulker screamed again a moment later- another dog had caught his leg on the other side, twisting viciously at a mouthful of skin. The hulker raised his branch but another two dogs grabbed the forked end of it in their mouths, holding it fast. A fourth dog ran to sink his teeth in the hulker's other leg.

The hulker screamed and screamed, tugging at his branch, his eyes wild- Mhumhi wanted to shut his ears, because the hulker was not angry, he was just scared, just scared now, so scared- A dog caught on his knee, and another on the inside of his thigh, as they swarmed up at him like ants, dragging him down- One caught him by his wrist and with a sob he fell.

They tugged him taut by his wrist and his legs, stretching him as he writhed and struggled with the branch still in his hand dragging against the grass. His chest and belly lay exposed and naked before them.

"Mhumhi," said a dog, and with a start Mhumhi realized it was Umenzi, leaping to him, smiling broadly with his tongue hanging out. He fell into a brief play-bow, wagging his tail.

"Nip at his belly, Mhumhi! Go on, open him up!"

Mhumhi said nothing- he could say nothing- and looked at the hulker's face. He was crying like Tareq, wetly, whimpered utterances coming from him as he cringed and turned his face away.

"Come on, Mhumhi," said Umenzi, his grin fading somewhat, and when Mhumhi stayed stock-still he glanced at his brethren in bewilderment.

"He's frightened," called one of them. "Hurry it up, Umenzi!"

"Come on, Mhumhi, he can't hurt you, look," said Umenzi, and he sprang forward and tore open the hulker's lower belly.

Mhumhi did not understand why the hulker did not scream then, for he was still alive. He stayed alive. The dogs ran forward, tearing at him, tearing at his skin and muscles and vital organs, all tugging in different directions- Nzui took a piece of skin at his flank and pulled too hard, exposing a stripe of white-yellow muscle, flaying him- and Umenzi was in the hulker's belly, his whole head, and Mhumhi caught the awful stench as the bowels ripped.

The hulker opened his eyes and looked at Mhumhi. His expression was dull and strange. His torso jerked as Umenzi leaned further inside and ripped away at something.

"Go on, go on," he was saying- the hulker- no, he had not spoken, it was a dog. Mhumhi recognized him as Ligwami after a moment, for his whole face was streaked with blood. He shoved Mhumhi forward. "Don't be frightened. You said you were hungry, take some of the meat. Go on."

And suddenly Mhumhi found himself headfirst in the hulker's chest cavity, jostling for space beside Umenzi and another dog as they tugged and ripped. It was drier than he had thought- there was merely exposed flesh everywhere, all around, coils of intestines in Umenzi's mouth, fat ugly globs, a dull thudding and thumping sound- Mhumhi bumped his head on something hard and turned it slightly. It was the hulker's ribcage. He could hear his beating heart.

Mhumhi seemed to lose himself for a moment. He did not lose his memory, nor his sanity; he merely lost his understanding. He opened his mouth and it filled with meat. It was like nothing he had eaten before, for it was hot, *alive*, pumping- it filled his mouth with softness and wetness and his mind with hunger.

He ate and ate, feeling the hulker's insides and the other dogs pressing all around him- he ate and ate and tore and ate.

At some point the hulker died. Mhumhi was not witness to when, but he knew it was before he had finished eating, for the hulker's heart was not beating when he swallowed it.

When he realized that, Mhumhi backed away from the crowd. More dogs jostled to fill the space he had left. They were all silent now, in contrast to their twitters and cheers before; the only noises were those of eating, of flesh tearing, of bones cracking.

Mhumhi's stomach felt warm and full, fuller than it had ever been. The hulker's heart was inside him. Mhumhi had seen him alive, and looked in his eyes, and his heart was inside him.

Mhumhi backed away further, turned, and ran through the tall grass, heedless of his injured leg and his heavy, swaying stomach.

The grass seemed endless. Mhumhi quickly got lost, but it did not matter. He just needed to be away. His paws thudded beneath him, his mouth open, panting- his heart was beating so fast- was it his heart, or the hulker's heart? Was the hulker's heart still beating inside him, thudding, like it had when Mhumhi had put his head inside his chest?

He nearly ran into a tree, but swerved just in time, skidding to a stop. There was something there, on the tree. Flies buzzing, a strange scent. He had no comprehension of what he saw for a moment, then he understood.

There was a hulker hanging from the tree by a cord, dead. The branch had cracked slightly, and her legs trailed against the ground. Mhumhi wondered how she had gotten up there. On the other side of the tree's base he could see another hulker- oh, he recognized her, it was the little hulker girl that had fallen out of the bus. She was dead too. Her neck was twisted to one side, as though it had been broken. Her eyes were closed, her face calm.

The old part of Mhumhi could tell they had not been killed by dogs. How had they both died out here alone?

The strange new part of Mhumhi thought, *Meat*.

Mhumhi turned and kept running, running and running, until he saw the curved black building rising in the distance through the grass. He ran towards it gratefully, out of the bloody grass, back onto the concrete, back into the world of metal and glass and processed, bloodless meat.

He found himself scratching at the metal grate before he really knew it, pawing at it with a kind of desperation.

Maha's face appeared beneath him, looking up.

"Mhumhi?"

He backed away from the grate, away and away. He heard her climbing up the pile of trash, saw her small fingers curling around the metal as she moved it aside for him.

"Mhumhi," she called, poking her head out, when he did not approach. "Mhumhi, what happened? Why's your face look like that? Did you get hurt?"

Mhumhi stared at her, not understanding, then slowly came into awareness: his face was coated with blood, his fur slicked back and darkened with it.

"Mhumhi, say something," said Maha. She sounded frightened.

"I'm not hurt," said Mhumhi. "It's not mine."

"Oh, that's good," said Maha. "Did you get into another fight? You won, didn't you?"

Mhumhi stared at her.

"Yes…"

"Did you get meat, then?"

"What?"

"I said, did you get meat, then?" She rubbed her round belly, and Mhumhi's eyes were drawn to the area. "I'm hungry again. I hope you got a lot."

Mhumhi stared. Maha furrowed her brow.

"Mhumhi! Why won't you answer me?"

"I got meat," he said. "I got some meat. It's for Kutta."

"What?" Maha drew back. "Why just for Kutta?"

"It's for Kutta," said Mhumhi. "Not for you. Not for Tareq. Feed him the other rats."

"Why?" Maha looked like she was going to cry. "Why?"

"Shut up," he said- near snarled. "Be quiet. We must go back now. Don't talk to me anymore."

Maha did start crying, sniffling, wiping her nose with her foreleg, and the sounds made him feel sick. He jumped into the storm drain, shoving her aside, and ran down the tunnel.

20
The New Monstrosity

Maha stopped crying after a little while as she trailed Mhumhi back to the corridor, sinking into a kind of sullen silence, her eyes raw and accusing. Mhumhi was relieved when they came to the reservoir room. The sound of rushing water seemed to help clear his head, block out the haunting sound of the beating heart. He thought he might stick his face in and clean it- even in the sewage, it might feel cleaner.

They came to the corridor and Mhumhi stopped short. Kutta was lying outside the door.

"Kutta!" he cried, dark thoughts about hulkers' hearts spinning out of his mind entirely as he ran to her. "Kutta, what are you doing, are you all right?"

Kutta opened her eyes slowly. There was gunk all over her face again. Mhumhi was suddenly aware of how cold the concrete under his paws was, and nudged at her urgently. "Kutta, go inside, you're sick-"

"I'm sick," said Kutta, slowly, and blinked at him. Her gaze seemed to slowly focus, and then she drew back a little. "Mhumhi, your face- what happened?"

"It's not my blood," said Mhumhi. "I'm fine. I have food for you."

She blinked at him again. Mhumhi looked back at Maha, who was standing a little ways away, staring at Kutta with wide eyes.

"Go in the room, Maha," he said. "Close the door behind you."

She brought her eyes up to him, and her gaze grew sullen again. "Why should I?"

"Do as I say!" Mhumhi snarled at her, open-mouthed. Maha put her hand up to her mouth and ran into the room and slammed the door.

"What was that about?" Kutta twisted her head back to stare at him, wavering slightly. "Why are you being cruel to her?"

"It's nothing," said Mhumhi. "Nothing… Take the meat, Kutta, there's enough of it."

Kutta seemed to accept that his tone brooked no argument, and slowly got to her feet. Mhumhi eyed her, her ribs and her bony hips.

"Where did you get the meat?" she asked. "Not our dispensary…"

"Another dispensary," he said.

Kutta licked at his muzzle, then the corner of his mouth, and his stomach gave that familiar heave. He hacked up meat into a pile on the floor. It was slippery and dark yellow-brown, different from the pale bloodless stuff they normally got, but Kutta said nothing. Perhaps she was too sick to notice. Mhumhi felt sick just watching her eat it. She did not know- he did not know if she would eat it if she did- he did not know how he himself had eaten it. He had looked into the hulker's eyes and eaten him.

"It's good," said Kutta, making him tense, but she merely raised her head to look up at him, licking her lips. "I feel better…"

"Good, then we should take you back inside, get you warmer," said Mhumhi, nosing up against her, but she drew away.

"Inside… no." Kutta backed away from him. "I can't go back inside, Mhumhi. I've done a terrible thing."

"What terrible thing?" asked Mhumhi, half-amused by the seriousness in her tone. "What could you possibly have done?"

Kutta did not answer, but she was shaking slightly. Mhumhi went up to her and pressed against her side.

"Come on, come back in, you can lie down where it's soft, and the puppies can snuggle with you-"

"No, no, it's that, it's them," gasped Kutta, pulling away from him. "It's Tareq, I've done something awful to him."

"What do you mean?" said Mhumhi, suddenly getting the worst feeling of apprehension. Kutta looked away from him.

"You must feel it," she said, "you must feel it, when he whimpers- when you see them stumble- that awful feeling, where you want to-" She hesitated. "Tell me I'm not the only one who feels it! Tell me I'm not the only one who wants to ki-"

"Keep your voice down," said Mhumhi, shooting a look towards the door. "No, Kutta, no… you're not the only one who feels it."

"Oh," said Kutta, shaking, and limped a little away from him. "And now I've done a terrible thing, poor Tareq, poor Tareq… I couldn't help myself."

"Kutta, tell me what happened," said Mhumhi, now truly alarmed, and looked nervously towards the door again. It had been very quiet.

"I was sleeping," said Kutta, "and I felt feverish, and he- reached towards me, to touch me, I don't know, and that terrible feeling came back again, and I- I- I couldn't help myself!"

Mhumhi drew away, feeling thick dread at the guilt in her eyes, and scratched at the door. "Maha? Maha! Let us in, now!"

"No!" came Maha's voice. "Go away!"

"Maha, please, let us in- we've got to see-" Mhumhi stopped himself, for he had been about to say "what's left of Tareq," but Kutta didn't look like she had eaten; had she left the body there? Was Maha inside with his lifeless body?

"Maha! Open the door!"

"No!" shouted Maha. "I'm not letting either of you in ever again! You're a bully and you don't share, and Kutta- she- she bit Tareq!"

"Bit him," Mhumhi repeated, slowly, then said again: "She bit him?"

"On the hand! He's bleeding! I hate both of you!"

Mhumhi put down his paw and looked at Kutta. She shuddered.

"It's true, I- I bit him! And then I ran out here. I'm a monster, Mhumhi."

"Kutta," said Mhumhi, "you only *bit* him. He probably deserved it."

"Don't you say that, he's just a puppy," Kutta moaned. "And I know why I bit him. I hate myself!"

"Stop that," said Mhumhi, coming close to lick her ears. "You're sick, and it's making you silly. Tareq is fine. You haven't done anything he won't recover from."

"Why do I feel this way, Mhumhi?" Kutta asked, leaning into him. "I don't want to… I hate it."

"You're sick," Mhumhi repeated, though his tone was more listless. He knew exactly what she meant.

He nosed Kutta and pawed at the door again. "Maha, let us in. Kutta and I are sorry. We've been mean to you."

There was no answer. He scratched with increasing urgency.

"Kutta is sick, and it's very cold out here. Let us in!"

Still she did not answer. Mhumhi growled, looking at his shivering sister.

"That little-"

"We'll have to wait for her to calm down," Kutta said. "She gets like this… angry…"

Mhumhi saw the sense in her words, but he was still annoyed. "But where will you go? You can't stay out here in this place when you're-"

"Sick, I know," said Kutta, weary-sounding. "There's a little alcove at the end of the tunnel that has some old paper and things…"

Mhumhi thought that sounded dubious, but he walked beside her and helped her limp to the end of the concrete hallway, where there was a closed door on one side and on the other side there was indeed a little alcove, just a few shelves and a pile of paper. Mhumhi, thinking of rats, nosed around in it a bit, but though he smelled a few dried droppings it appeared the paper had not been inhabited for some time. Perhaps Maha had something to do with that.

Kutta settled down on the paper with a sigh and put her head down, and Mhumhi curled up beside her, trying to share his warmth with her. The paper was a poor substitute for a blanket, but it was better than the bare floor.

Kutta was soon breathing evenly, if raspily. Mhumhi could not get to sleep himself. He did not want to get up and leave Kutta, but his mind ached for something to do to distract it from terrible visions of the day's events. He spent some time licking his injured leg. It seemed to be healing, though his paw still tingled oddly from time to time. The wound itself was closed and scabbed, so that was good.

He grew restless of tending to himself and nosed about in the papers. There were a great many of them stuck together, most faded down into whiteness. Some of the ones beneath the top layer, however, still had an odd glossiness to them. He pawed at them, enjoying the crinkling sound, and dragged a crumpled batch closer to himself.

On one page that still had a few dark colors he saw a strange image, and he had to blink at it a few times for it to make sense: it was a hulker.

He pushed the paper away from himself at once, alarmed. It reminded him of the eerie billboard with the smiling hulker face on it. The paper was attached to a bunch of others, though, and they crumpled open. More pictures of hulkers.

He was interested in spite of himself, and he pawed the thing back towards him and looked at the pictures. Hulkers standing, hulker faces… He licked a page with his tongue to turn it and found the taste awful and bitter. But there were still more hulkers… hulker after hulker… so many images of them. How did images like that get onto boards or paper, anyway? He thought that it might not be natural, but he did not know how anyone would put them there. And why? Who liked hulkers that much?

He turned the page again and was surprised to see not a hulker, but a dog. A domestic, by the look of it, for it had floppy ears. It was smiling, tongue hanging out. There were strange scribbles all around it.

At least there was some representation, Mhumhi thought, but it was somehow more eerie to see the dog there, smiling in that empty way at nothing, frozen in place. He pushed the papers away from himself, crumpling them loudly as he slid his paw.

"What are you doing?" asked Kutta, sounding groggy.

"Sorry, Kutta," he said. "I didn't mean to wake you. I'm only playing with these papers. There are pictures of hulkers on them, did you see?"

"Oh," said Kutta. "Yes… they're everywhere."

"I wonder," Mhumhi began, hesitating a bit, for the question sounded foolish to him. "Do you think… someone made these?"

"Made them?" Kutta was quiet for a moment. "Someone… who, though?"

"I know," said Mhumhi hastily, "that makes no sense. They just are, I suppose, like everything else."

"I don't know," said Kutta. "I don't know… Mhumhi, have you ever thought that the city felt like… like it wasn't made for us?"

"Sick-silly," said Mhumhi. "I shouldn't have said anything. The city, made? Who'd make it? The city is the whole world! Who could've built all this?"

Kutta did not respond, aside from a soft whine. He rolled over to nuzzle at her and felt her breathing start to slow again.

Mhumhi must have fallen asleep too, for the next thing he remembered was slowly waking up with a bad feeling. His eyes fluttered open. Kutta was still snoring softly beside him.

Something was making his stomach churn, though. He was not quite sure what- there was nothing he could see or hear, but- He raised his head and sniffed the air.

There *was* something strange. He could smell hulker, hulker he wasn't familiar with, and the scent seemed to *flicker*, somehow, like it was incorporeal, which didn't make any sense. The hairs on his back rose. He got up from Kutta's side, ignoring her sleepy murmur, and turned the corner.

There was a hulker crouching in front of the puppies' door. Mhumhi was startled by the sight of it- the scent hadn't smelled anywhere near that close, but there it was, touching the door with its hands and rocking back and forth in place. Mhumhi got the sense that something was wrong with it.

He was not sure what to do. The hulker had not seen him, and while it was an adult, it did not seem dangerous. It had nothing in its hands and it seemed fragile, the way it rocked. He thought it smelled like a female. Perhaps it had sniffed out the puppies and wanted to look after them…?

If that was the case, Mhumhi thought, it would be best for him to make himself scarce, not scare it off. But he stayed where he was, easily visible if the hulker should happen to turn her head. That bad feeling had not gone away.

The hulker raised a forepaw, crooked forward awkwardly. Beneath her dense coverings Mhumhi glimpsed a hairy wrist. She batted on the door.

There was a beat of silence, then Maha's voice came from the other side: "Go away! Bad dogs! You can't come in!"

The hulker paused, tilting her head slightly, then rose up on her hind legs. She looked unsteady, swaying for a moment, then batted on the door again.

There were a few scraping noises, and then Maha opened the door, her face tearstained. "I said you can't-"

She stuttered to a stop, staring up at the strange hulker, which still swayed as she looked down at her.

"Who are you?"

The hulker rocked wordlessly for another moment, tilting its head the other way, then grabbed Maha by the hair and dragged her out of the room.

Maha screamed, but Mhumhi was already running. He had not formed a plan or even had a coherent thought- his teeth merely hit the hulker's calf.

The hulker squealed and dropped Maha on the ground. It raised its hands and beat at his head, one, two, three blows that knocked him dizzy. He let go of its flesh to stagger back, tasting blood- his or the hulker's? How did it taste no different?

The hulker had not finished, though. While he was dazed it took one long leg and kicked him in the side. He staggered back with a yelp.

Maha was getting to her feet, one hand on her head pressing down her wiry hair. The hulker turned and lurched towards her. Mhumhi gave it a warning snarl and ran towards it, stopping short when it turned and swung its fist at him.

"Mhumhi!" Maha cried. The hulker turned to look at her, and Mhumhi threw himself forward, catching her elbow, bearing her down.

She squealed and kicked him away again, but he was faster this time and only caught a glancing blow. His injured leg wobbled.

On the ground the strange hulker pushed herself up on her hands and looked at Mhumhi. Her eyes showed no white. She opened her mouth and laughed, and all of Mhumhi's fur rose. It was not a hulker laugh. It was a hyena laugh.

Maha gave a little scream, and the hulker looked at her and crawled forward on all fours, grinning. Mhumhi lunged at her again, but this time he only caught the edge of the wrappings around her chest. She yowled and rolled, and Mhumhi let go, springing back. But this time he had gotten in front of Maha.

"Go!" he said to her, turning back to look at her. "Go back into the room and shut the door! I'll get rid of it!"

She merely stared at him and whimpered, both hands around her face.

The hulker gave that awful eerie laugh again. It had started to rock again on its hands and knees. Mhumhi got a sense of strange sickness from it. For once his instincts were not telling him to kill, but to flee- to flee as far and as fast as he could from this strange monstrosity.

The hulker giggled and crawled backwards. Through the hole he had ripped in its shirt, Mhumhi could see tufts of dirty gray hair growing on its scabbed ribs.

"Mhumhi!"

Mhumhi risked a glance back to see Kutta limping around the corner towards them. The strange hulker looked too, thrusting its chin forward, and then dragged itself to its feet. It broke into a shambling run away from them and disappeared around the corner out of the hall. Without thinking Mhumhi gave chase.

The hulker sprinted ahead of him out into the reservoir, loud with rushing water, and catapulted over the railing. Mhumhi skidded to a stop and stuck his head underneath just in time to see it land with a mighty splash in the filthy water far below.

For a moment there was no sign of it, just the water roiling from the impact. Mhumhi felt Kutta come up next to him by the rail, but he did not dare take his eyes away- there! The hulker's dark head had emerged near the edge of the pool, and it kicked and thrashed its way to the edge and climbed out.

"Should we go after it?" Kutta said, but Mhumhi did not answer. The hulker was climbing into a pipe- the very pipe he and Kutta had entered the reservoir through the night before. It wriggled inside, its flat feet the last things to disappear.

Mhumhi felt a chill at the sight. He glanced at Kutta, who was panting hard.

"It's not safe here anymore," she said.

They went back to the corridor. Maha was still crouched down on the concrete, hands clamped to her head, and without conferring Mhumhi and Kutta went on either side of her.

"Come on, puppy," said Mhumhi, and he licked her forehead. It tasted salty.

Maha put one hand on his neck, curling her fingers into the thick fur there. He winced but tolerated it. She rose and he led her back into the little room.

21

A Clean Face

"What was the matter with it?" Kutta asked, as soon as they were all safely inside, with the door shut tight. She had collapsed at once onto the quilt, looking weary, but more alert than she had been. The meat and the sleep, it seemed, had done her some good.

"You mean with the hulker?" said Mhumhi, who was pacing on three legs by the door. His bad leg was flaring up with pain again after the struggle.

"That wasn't a hulker," said Maha.

They both looked at her. She was sitting with her arms around Tareq, hugging him close. Tareq looked like he didn't have any idea what was going on, but he seemed pleased about the attention.

"No, it wasn't," Mhumhi agreed, after a moment. He thought Maha was reacting to her fright at the experience, but he also thought she was right. The thing had not moved, sounded, or smelled like any of the hulkers he had come across.

"Was it a new type of hulker?" asked Kutta. "One we haven't seen before?"

"Maybe," Mhumhi allowed. "But did you hear the sound it made? It sounded like a- like a hyena."

Kutta said nothing, but Mhumhi could sense her discomfort. He went over and licked the wound on her shoulder.

"Do you remember the first hyena we saw? The one with the hulker hand?"

"It couldn't have been a hand," said Kutta, her ears going back.

"It *was* a hand," Mhumhi insisted. He noticed Maha's eyes tracking him curiously. "It had a hulker hand instead of a paw on its foreleg. And this hulker- it laughed like a hyena, and it had fur."

"It didn't have fur," Kutta broke in.

"It did! Not everywhere, but I could see it in some places-"

"Adult hulkers have got more fur than the puppies," said Kutta.

"But did you look at her eyes? Do adult hulkers have dark eyes like that, Kutta?"

Kutta made no response to this, just favored Mhumhi with her own yellow-eyed stare.

"What are you trying to say, Mhumhi?" asked Maha.

"I don't know," Mhumhi admitted. "Only it seems like- it seems almost like-" He paused. The words he wanted to say would sound foolish, and he could picture what Kutta's scornful reaction would be. He glanced at Maha.

"It seemed like that hulker- like it was becoming a hyena."

"Mhumhi, don't be ridiculous," said Kutta at once.

"I thought so too!" said Maha, hugging Tareq to herself. Kutta glanced at her, then gave Mhumhi a fierce look.

"You're going to give the puppies nightmares!"

"It seemed like it, though," Mhumhi argued. "I know it makes no sense, but it would explain why that other hyena had a hulker hand."

"What, because the rest of it used to be a hulker? Are *you* sick-silly?" Kutta paused to cough. "Creatures don't just change into one another, Mhumhi."

"Well," said Mhumhi, looking away, "how would you explain it, then?"

"I don't know," said Kutta. "And I'm not going to try. Whatever that hulker was, it was just *bad.* And we should avoid it."

"It wasn't a hulker," said Maha, but quietly. Kutta did not seem to hear her, for she was putting her head down, looking weary. Mhumhi could tell she was tired, and beginning to be cross, so it would be better for her to be left alone. But he didn't think his idea had been *that* far-fetched.

He took himself to the bathroom to avoid being frustrated in front of her, and paced in front of the sink. There were so many strange things he did not understand… He allowed himself to utter a little whine. He and Kutta were always going to be at odds with each other, by themselves, and neither one of them really knew what was going on… they needed Sacha. Her head, her wit, her understanding of what to do and when to do it…

He whined again, thinking of her. He wished he had not. Every moment he was not thinking of her, it seemed like she was still there, still waiting somewhere… Every time he thought of her, he had to remind himself that she was dead.

Had the hyenas that had eaten her once been hulkers?

He reared up at the sink, his bad leg trembling, thinking he'd better get a drink of water. He happened to glance at himself in the mirror and got a shock.

His face was still coated in the blood of the hulker. Long since dried, it had left his fur coarse and saturated all around his muzzle and eyes. He looked wild and savage.

Frantically he pawed at the handle of the sink, clawing at it, but it was a smooth knob and his claws could not grip it. His bloodied face bobbed in front of him in the mirror, mocking. He uttered a whimper, scratching and scratching, but the handle would not turn.

"Mhumhi?"

He hesitated, then fell back on all fours. Maha was standing in the bathroom doorway.

"Yes?" he asked, keeping his voice even. Maha looked unusually timid.

"Are you trying to get some water? Are you thirsty?"

He did not answer. She crept past him and used her hand to turn on the water.

"There you go, there it is…"

He looked at his paws a moment, then reared up to lap at the little trickle, his leg shaking.

"Mhumhi?"

He paused, feeling impatient, as the cold water ran over his nose. "Yes?"

"Can I… can I wash your face?"

He let himself drop down again. She was sharp-witted, this little hulker, this puppy.

"All right."

To his surprise, Maha turned around and left the doorway, but she reappeared just a moment later with the yellow bowl and a rag. She filled the bowl with water again and then dipped the rag into it.

Mhumhi had assumed, perhaps naively, that by washing she had meant she was going to lick him, but of course she was a hulker and he'd never seen a hulker actually lick *anything*. He was still somewhat startled when she put the wet rag on his muzzle, and jerked away.

"It's cold!"

"Sorry," said Maha, and she reached out and stroked his forehead for a moment with her hand. "I'll be quick, okay?"

Mhumhi was having mixed feelings, as mollified as he was feeling by the gesture, but he held still and let her grip his lower jaw as she passed the rag over his face. Water dripped through his fur from the first few strokes. He blinked rapidly and winced- her scrubbing was becoming more enthusiastic as she went on. Between rubs he could see her little face wrinkled together, her brow furrowed down, her eyes focused on the task.

"That's better," she said, and dropped the rag in the bowl. "Look now, Mhumhi!"

With some misgivings, he rose up to the sink again and looked. To his surprise his face looked damp, but correctly colored again. He wagged his tail- it felt like the first time in a while.

When he got back down on all fours Maha was smiling at him.

"Were you grumpy because your face was dirty, Mhumhi? I hate that feeling too."

Something seemed to perceptibly soften inside of him at this. "That must have been it," he said. "I'm sorry I growled at you. I didn't mean it."

"It's all right," said Maha and she went and hugged him, a motion that was becoming all too familiar to Mhumhi now. It was almost pleasant, really. He wagged his tail again, though he stopped when he saw the bowl on the ground behind Maha. The rag was turning the water yellow-brown.

He gently pulled back from Maha's embrace, licking his lips.

"I was wondering," he began. She sat back on her haunches and looked at him with that particular wide-eyed expression, and he felt the need to turn away briefly to master his embarrassment.

"I was wondering," he began again, "if you could build another bridge for me. At another place."

"At another place?" Maha looked eager. "Where? With what?"

"I don't know with what," said Mhumhi, "but there's another way Kutta and I get into the sewers- the way we used to get in- under a bridge by a big, broken grate. I'm afraid to go that way now, though, because the water's so dirty and I'm wounded."

"Why's that a problem?" Maha interrupted.

"Because getting a wound dirty can make it worse," Mhumhi explained. "It can get infected, and that's real bad. Anyway, I think I'll have to go that way if I want to get meat tomorrow, so I was thinking-"

"Why can't you go the way you went today?" Maha interrupted, again, and Mhumhi cringed internally. He had been hoping she wouldn't ask that question. He entertained the macabre thought of what her reaction would be if he told her the truth: Maha, I watched a group of wild dogs kill a hulker like you, and then I put my head inside his chest and ate his heart.

"Because… because I got into that fight, so now I'll probably get into more trouble if I go back."

"Oh," said Maha. "Were there police?"

"A lot of police," Mhumhi confirmed. "I'm sure they'll recognize me if I go back. It's better to stay away for now."

"But will you be able to get meat from *this* dispensary? Won't they recognize you here?"

She was certainly asking all the right questions. "I think it's been long enough," Mhumhi lied. "I'm sure they'll be focused on other things. I'll be able to slip in and out quickly. But that all depends on whether or not you can make a bridge for me."

"I can do it!" Maha said, jerking her head. "I know that grate. I know how I can get you through it."

"Good, Maha!" said Mhumhi, wagging his tail vigorously. "Then we can go tomorrow!"

"Yes!" said Maha, smiling, but then her lips turned down. "Will you share the meat with me this time?"

"I promise I will," said Mhumhi.

They went together back into the main room and Maha left him to snuggle Tareq again. Mhumhi went to Kutta's side and hesitated. She was curled up, her nose tucked in her thick tail, and breathing deeply.

He wanted to confide in Kutta what his plan was, but now he was having misgivings. She might say it was too dangerous, or worse, she might refuse to cooperate with him. Mhumhi had instinctively held it back from Maha for the same reason.

But if he and Kutta were going to survive, they had to get rid of the hulkers.

He did not like the fact- considerably less so than he would have a week ago- but it was the truth. The longer that he and Kutta were bound down in the sewers, the more dangerous it became. Their hideaway had already been discovered by the strange hyena-laughing hulker, and he was afraid that she would return with reinforcements. The longer they stayed, the more his anxiety would mount. It was not *safe*.

And Kutta was sick. The cold and filthy surroundings would not help her.

And- there was yet something else- the longer they stayed hidden away, the less chance they had of ever finding Kebero and Bii again. He felt a little pang for Kebero especially. He had not allowed himself to entertain the idea that the little puppy was *dead*, but… where could he be?

He shook himself, trying to rid himself of terrible thoughts, and went and sat by the door, panting. Being attached to the hulker puppies was too dangerous. Tomorrow, if Maha could open a safe way for him back into Oldtown, he would seek out the only lead he had- the adult hulker in the school. And he would deliver the puppies into its care. And they would be free again.

22

Mhumhi Goes to School

The next day Mhumhi left Kutta with Tareq again and took Maha out to the giant grate.

He had only told Kutta he was going to get food again, not the where or why. She was in no state to make sense of it, anyway- her sickness had taken a turn for the worse, and she could only lay there, half-delirious, lapping weakly at the bowl of water Maha brought for her.

She had begged Mhumhi to take Tareq, too, for fear she would bite him again, but Mhumhi had not thought that there would be any trouble there. Tareq was staying as far away from her as he could now, pressing himself against the wall opposite where she was lying and keeping himself deeply buried in his nest of blankets.

"Look!" said Maha, bringing him back to the present. They were standing on the concrete platform next to the water rushing through the grate. Maha had put her hand up in a gesture Mhumhi was beginning to recognize as pointing, indicating a round circle on the ceiling. Affixed next to it was a gray plastic box.

"Is that a manhole?"

"Yes," said Maha. She went over to the wall and started climbing- there were metal rungs like there had been underneath the manhole in their room. Mhumhi watched her go up, nimble as a gray fox. His tail waved slowly.

"Are you saying *I'll* be able to get to that manhole? I don't think I can climb like that."

"You won't need to!" said Maha. She had gotten up the wall and was now moving, hesitantly, entirely upside down on the ceiling. Mhumhi licked his lips and couldn't stop himself from running back and forth underneath her, craning his neck back.

"You be careful, Maha!"

"I'm fine!" Maha replied, though there was a nervous quaver in her voice. She wrapped one elbow around a rung and reached out, fingertips trembling, for the plastic box. Mhumhi couldn't stop a nervous whimper bubbling up after she missed her first attempt and grabbed the rung again.

"Don't do that," Maha said. "You're making it worse."

Mhumhi tried to keep quiet, though he was still pacing in circles underneath her, staring up. She reached out again, and this time her fingers connected with the little clasp on the front of the box.

"Look out, Mhumhi!" she said, which was all the warning he got before the box fell open and a ladder clattered down loudly as it unfolded.

It was lucky he hadn't been standing more to the right, Mhumhi thought, tucking his tail, for the ladder had banged down on the floor there and partially folded back up from the force of it.

Maha now made her painstaking way back down, rung by rung, looking very relieved to be back on the ground again.

"There you go, Mhumhi," she said, wiping her dirty hands on her wrappings. "You can get up that ladder, right?"

Mhumhi went over and gave the thing a hesitant sniff. It was true that it was at much more of an angle than the metal rungs, but he did not like those huge gaps between the steps.

"I'll go open the manhole," said Maha, and she pushed in front of him to tug the ladder down the rest of the way, straightening it with a loud clang. He eyed the ease with which she scaled it rather enviously.

"Come on," she called, as she activated the hissing, rattling mechanism that moved the manhole. "Come- oh!"

"What, what is it?" Mhumhi asked, practically running circles around the ladder's base. She had stiffened suddenly.

"I think something saw me," she said. "It ran away…"

"Come down, Maha," Mhumhi urged, and she came quickly back down the ladder to go put her hands on his neck for reassurance.

"Will we have to go hide now?" she asked, fearfully. "What if it tells the police?"

"Don't worry about it," said Mhumhi, who was already thinking rapidly. "I have an idea. But you run back to the den right now, understand?"

"But… you don't want me to wait for you? What about the manhole?"

"Leave it open," said Mhumhi. "Dogs can get in here anyway by swimming; it makes no difference. You run back now and stay with Kutta and shut the door. You'll be safe."

"But..." Her eyes were wide. "What if that hyena hulker comes back?"

"Then don't open the door unless it's my voice," said Mhumhi, licking her hand, and then pulled out of her grip. "I've got to be quick now, and so do you. Hurry back!"

Maha went, her flat feet slapping loudly on the concrete, pausing only to give him a frightened glance over her shoulder. Mhumhi tried not to look at her, for his instinct had been to tense and want to chase her.

He was sorry to have to make her go back alone, but they had never seen another dog in that part of the sewer, and if the hyena hulker came back, well...

He forcibly put the image out of his mind. He had no time to envision horrors. He needed to chase down whoever had seen Maha, first of all.

He took the ladder at a run, which might not have been the best plan, for it rattled and shuddered unnervingly under his feet. At least his paws did not slip, and he was able to leap straight out of the manhole and onto thankfully solid concrete.

He put his nose to the ground at once. There was little scent in the area, and few pawprints had disturbed the layer of crumbling plaster dust. But there was a single, distinct splash of urine against a wall a few meters away. It smelled like fear. Mhumhi ran to it and inhaled deeply. It had been from a medium-sized animal, a male, and he had left a wet pawprint behind in his flight.

He was still sniffing with the intent to track it, but he needn't have bothered. The very same individual came back around the corner while Mhumhi's head was still down and froze at the sight of him.

It was a culpeo, a large fox, but nothing compared to Mhumhi's size. Mhumhi straightened and raised his chin very high.

"Fox, come here!"

The culpeo stared at him a moment, curling his luxuriant tail underneath his legs, and then slunk over to him.

"Yes, police?" he said, keeping his eyes down. Mhumhi was relieved; he'd been counting on the assumption.

"Did you see a hulker here just now, near the sewer?"

The culpeo squirmed a moment, the muscles around his lips tensing, perhaps trying to gauge the answer that would please Mhumhi the most.

"I think so- I think I saw one peeking out of the manhole on the bridge-"

"You think, or you *know*?" said Mhumhi, and the culpeo cringed.

"I- I think I know! I think it was a flat-headed hulker! It looked right at me!"

"Right," said Mhumhi. "Very good. You've helped me. Stand up straight, it's all right."

The culpeo backed a few steps away from him and looked up. "I've helped you?"

"Yes," said Mhumhi. "If you do one other thing, I'll be sure you get a mouthful of warm hulker meat in the next few days."

Now the culpeo's eyes were starting to look very bright and sharp.

"Other thing, what thing?"

"Don't mention it to anybody," said Mhumhi. "It's my prey; I don't want any other police taking a snap at it. You understand?"

"I understand," the culpeo said promptly. "I won't say a word!"

"Good," said Mhumhi. "Then get out of here at once. I'll be patrolling the area and I don't want you underfoot."

"I understand," the culpeo said again, backing away rapidly, then paused. "Don't you want my- my name? So you can give me the-"

"I'll find you again when I *need* to," said Mhumhi, letting his canines show slightly at the end, and the culpeo spun around and dashed down an alleyway at top speed.

Mhumhi allowed him a moment to gain some distance, then gave a little bound and a play-bow, tongue hanging out with laughter. *That* had been more fun than he'd thought. Maybe he should try to be intimidating more often!

He did not let himself get distracted for too long, though; he shook himself and trotted up the street, in the opposite direction towards Wide Street. It was a roundabout way to get to the school, but there was a certain area- a certain light post- that he wanted to avoid.

He made good time. The streets near Wide Street were emptied out for the morning dispensary run, but he could smell the aftermirage of hundreds of strange dogs, large and generally frustrated. They must have been the new squatters. He didn't see a hair of a fox anywhere; Sacha must have been right about how the balance of power would shift. He thought back to Lisica and wondered if she and the other foxes planned to act soon. Would they turn their anger against the police, or the domestics- or had they realized about the existence of the hyenas?

He was almost glad that he'd been confined to the sewers the past two days; if there was going to be fighting in the streets, he did not want any part of it.

He skirted round the part of Wide Street that aligned with the dispensary. There was a trickle of dogs leaving it, and a trickle of dogs arriving, but none gave Mhumhi more than a glance. As far as these strangers were concerned, he was a member of the police, and not someone to tangle with. Mhumhi had never felt so glad for his dappled coat before.

He was half-entertaining the idea of going straight up to the dispensary and getting his meat by the time he reached the school. He ducked through the gap in the fence around the playground, feeling the wood chips under his paws. What could the police do to him, really, if he said he was part of the crowd, just someone from another district…? Ah, but that would be so risky.

He nosed around the roundabout, but the family of Rüppell's foxes that had once lived underneath had moved, it seemed. He could see the dark space of the den they'd dug gaping empty. He got up on his hind legs and pushed the roundabout, for fun, hopping on his hind legs until it spun lazily.

He jumped up on it and sat a moment, tongue hanging out as he spun, before he remembered he was supposed to be police and anyone who happened to see him would think his behavior had been very un-police-like.

He hopped down, wobbling a bit from the ground staying still, and trotted nose-down over to the side of the school building. To get in, there had to be a door or hole somewhere around on the wall. He hoped it wasn't another bit of hulker trickery, like a smooth doorknob, but that big brute of a domestic had to get in as well, so there was some hope…

He hopped back over the playground fence, wincing a bit as he landed on his injured leg, and then hugged the wall, searching. He found several doors, all of which felt heavy and metal and did not yield to his pushing.

He was almost starting to get worried when he turned yet another corner and saw the ladder.

It was leaning up against the wall at a very steep angle, but up at the top he could just glimpse a window that looked open. Mhumhi's tail, which had been waving gaily, slowly went down. He did not like ladders at all- why did they keep coming into his life?

But there was nothing he could do. He braced himself and took the ladder at a run, as before. This turned out to be a terrible mistake- this ladder was not affixed to anything, and as his paws hit it bounced off the brick and wavered backwards. Mhumhi hooked his paws over and hung on for dear life, heart hammering, as the ladder eased back and thumped back against the wall.

He took it more carefully, though it hurt his leg a bit, step by step, feeling each wobble with trepidation. It was a relief when the open window finally came into view, just ahead of him. He put one paw on the windowsill.

The face of the blue-eyed domestic suddenly appeared before him, full-sized, and with a growl the dog reared up and shoved the ladder backwards.

Mhumhi gave a kind of shriek as the ladder pitched backwards, his paw scraping off the windowsill. More by instinct than anything else he pushed off the rungs and sailed through the window and on top of the domestic.

They were both very startled, and Mhumhi actually had a moment to sit there, on the other dog's thick furry side, catching his breath. Then the domestic growled and twisted out from underneath him.

He was quite different from when Mhumhi had last seen him- no longer was he cringing and whimpering, now he was giving quite a terrifying display of aggression, barking rapidly, his teeth gnashing. Mhumhi backed up against the wall, panting, and had to leap for it when the domestic lunged at him. He landed on a desk- there were a great number of them in the room- and jumped again when the domestic slammed his thick body on it, growling and snapping.

"Wait!" Mhumhi cried, putting his ears back and his tail down. "Wait! I'm not here to-"

The domestic leapt at him, slamming the desk so that it shrieked and slid against the linoleum, and Mhumhi fell off and hit his shoulder hard on the floor.

At once the domestic was on top of him, his teeth flashing for Mhumhi's throat, and Mhumhi shoved his head away with his forepaws and rolled and got to his feet, gasping. When the domestic whirled to lunge at him again he met him with a snap of his own, catching him by the nose and drawing blood.

The domestic backed up at this assault, panting, blood gleaming on his nose.

"Now listen to me for a moment," said Mhumhi. "I'm not here to fight with you or your hulker-"

"What hulker?" snarled the domestic dog, baring his teeth again. "There is no hulker here!"

"Well, if there was, I wouldn't be here to bother him," Mhumhi stressed. "I'm not police. Don't you- don't you remember me? You were in a fight with a golden jackal, and I came out and helped you..."

The domestic stared at him, his pale eyes uncomprehending, but at least he had stopped growling. Mhumhi decided to press on.

"I was with my sisters then- the dhole and the- and the bush dog- we asked you about our mother-"

"*You*," growled the domestic, putting his thick ears forward. "You- with the orphan pack."

"Yes, that's right," said Mhumhi, giving his tail a nervous wave. "So I'm not police- I'm not here to arrest you, or anything. It's the opposite, actually... I wanted to ask you something. Well, ask your hulker something."

Blood dripped onto the floor from the domestic's bleeding nose for a moment while he stared motionlessly at Mhumhi. Finally he said, "Very well. There's no way for you to get out, anyway, now that the ladder's down. I hope you realize that."

Mhumhi had not, in fact, thought of this; furthermore, now he was suddenly recalling his first sighting of a hulker, when it had been dragging around a dead coyote and had promptly tried to bash his brains in.

Perhaps this situation was not ideal, after all.

"I realize that," he said, trying to sound calmer than he felt. "Like I said, I just want to ask something."

"Then come," said the domestic, surprising Mhumhi, who had thought he might want to ask more questions. He pushed past him and out the open door of the room they were in, his curled tail vanishing from sight. It took Mhumhi a second to realize he was meant to follow him.

The inside of the school was filled with long hallways and rows of rooms. Mhumhi's nails clicked against scratched, dirty linoleum as he gazed around. He was not sure exactly what a school was- from the looks of it, it was a place where you stored chairs and desks.

The domestic led him down one of these long hallways, around the corner and down a set of stairs. Here there were strange papers on the walls, faded and tired, many only hanging by their corners. Mhumhi could not grasp what images were supposed to be on them- they just looked like random blobs of color, nothing like the almost-real images on the papers back in the sewers.

The domestic paused at a brown door and reared up to scratch it.

"Lamya," he called. "Wake up. We have a visitor."

There was silence behind the brown door, and the domestic scratched more insistently.

"*Lamya*."

"Leave me be," called a piteous, musical voice- Mhumhi started to realize it was a hulker's. "Why are you talking in Dog?" It went on to say something else that Mhumhi couldn't catch, in a strange, liquid tongue.

The domestic replied in kind, though in his mouth the words were more halting. He scratched on the door again, and after a moment the door opened.

Mhumhi was startled again, because two things happened very rapidly. He recognized the hulker as the one that had been dragging the coyote, and was promptly bashed on the head and knocked to the ground.

The domestic was laughing at him, he realized in a dazed way, as he struggled to get back to his feet. The hulker was swinging a broom around.

"How dare you bite my dog on the nose," she said. "I think I'll kill you and cook you."

"Wait!" said Mhumhi, still a bit groggy, as she raised the broom again. "Wait, please- there's puppies- hulker puppies- you have to help-"

The hulker hesitated, and exchanged a glance with the domestic.

"Hulker puppies?" she said. "What is a hulker, exactly, and why should I care if it has puppies?"

"He means human, Lamya," said the domestic, and the hulker's nose wrinkled.

"Ugh! You're not going to get into my good graces like that-" She paused, tilting her head. "Wait, hulker puppies- human puppies- you mean, *human children*?"

Mhumhi could only stare blankly, but the domestic said, "I think that's what he means." He was looking curiously at Mhumhi now. "Let him in, Lamya, let's hear what he has to say."

Lamya hesitated, swinging the broom a bit more between her hands, and then said, "All right, come in. We haven't had a real guest in a long time, anyway. I'll give him some tea."

Mhumhi looked at the domestic for some clue as to what that meant, but he had already risen to follow her inside the room. Mhumhi limped after him.

Inside the room there were several tired old couches, a long counter, a white refrigerator, and a shiny black microwave. The counter was covered with cardboard boxes, and unless Mhumhi was mistaken, the cabinets below were stuffed full as well. Mhumhi had to pause to sniff the air. There was a salty scent coming from the boxes that he was unfamiliar with.

The domestic went to jump up on one of the couches, and Mhumhi decided to follow suit on the other. It gave him a sudden pang of longing for his old home, where the couch had been ripped up to just the right level of comfort… this one was hard and scratchy.

The hulker did something to the microwave, which hummed, and then dragged a low table towards them.

"Lamya, you haven't even changed yet," said the domestic. "Have you even taken a bath?"

"I don't *need* a bath," said Lamya, crossly, and she put one of the cardboard boxes on the table. "Do you think he cares? Oh, ask him his name, we don't know it yet."

Mhumhi thought this was a bit rude, considering she was sitting right across from him. The domestic looked at him.

"What is your name?"

"My name is Mhumhi," he said.

"This is Lamya," said the domestic, rather formally.

"And your name…?" Mhumhi prompted.

"His name," said Lamya, tearing open the top of the box she was holding, "is Biscuit."

Biscuit gave his curled tail a grave wag.

"I see," said Mhumhi.

"Give him a cracker, Biscuit," said Lamya, thrusting the opened box at the domestic. He stuck his muzzle inside and dropped something on the table in front of Mhumhi.

"For you," he said. Lamya was grinning.

Mhumhi got to his feet on the couch and sniffed the thing- it smelled dry and tasteless, and was the color of old paper. He mouthed it cautiously and found it to be surprisingly salty.

"Aw, Biscuit, I forgot you were bleeding," said Lamya, looking into the box and wrinkling up her face. "Here, you two can have the rest."

She tossed the box on the table, and crackers spilled out. Neither Mhumhi nor Biscuit made a move to take one. Mhumhi was still working on getting the rest of his original cracker unstuck from the roof of his mouth.

"Lamya," said Biscuit, "you must eat proper food today. If you eat that meat I brought-"

"I told you not to embarrass me in front of Mhumhi," said Lamya, flicking her fingers at him. "Anyway, Mhumhi should tell me about those children he mentioned earlier. How many are there? How old are they? Were they tasty?"

"I haven't harmed them!" exclaimed Mhumhi, and Lamya laughed. He found he did not like her laugh- it sounded too close to a hyena's.

"Well, that's very nice of you," she said. "Biscuit said that you were one of the ones adopted by the pariah dog, is that true?"

"Yes," said Mhumhi, "or, well, my mother's name was Pariah-"

"She did not have a name," interrupted Biscuit. "A dog does not have a name until he is given one by a human, and she was never acting on behalf of any human. She called herself Pariah, but even that was a lie."

Mhumhi stared at him, both for the evident familiarity he seemed to have with his mother and the disdain in his voice when he spoke of her.

"Lighten up, Biscuit," said Lamya. "Mhumhi clearly loved his little mummy either way. I was only going to say that she probably taught you some proper respect for humans."

"You keep saying human," said Mhumhi. "Is that another word for hulker?"

Biscuit gave a soft growl. "It is the only *proper* word for humans," he said. "If you say 'hulker' again, I'll bite you."

"Clearly his mother didn't teach him everything," said Lamya.

"My mother taught me absolutely nothing about hul- about humans," said Mhumhi, who was starting to get a little annoyed. "We didn't even know she was taking care of the puppies until after she died."

"The proper word is children," said Biscuit.

"They're our puppies," said Mhumhi, and now he exposed a single fang as Biscuit began to growl.

"It's moot," said Lamya. "Biscuit, aren't all the domestic dogs supposed to know when somebody pairs up with a human?"

"Yes," said Biscuit, drawing back a little, shifting his broad paws on the couch. "It seems she took them in illegally. She probably kept them hidden because she knew we'd assign them to someone more responsible."

"Tricky little thing," said Lamya, reaching behind herself to grab another box. "And so, why have you come here? Have you got questions about changing their nappies? What is it?"

"I came here," said Mhumhi, steeling himself a bit, "to find someone who could take care of them. Someone who could do a better job than us."

Biscuit straightened up at this, staring at Mhumhi, but Lamya put her hand to her mouth and burst into peals of laughter.

"You want to abandon them! You really are a wild dog, aren't you?"

"I am not abandoning them!" snapped Mhumhi, because perhaps her words stung a little too much. "We cannot take care of them anymore, and if we die trying, it won't help them. I just need somewhere safe to take them. You seem like you have enough food-"

he cast a lingering glance over all the amassed boxes "-so it shouldn't trouble you at all!"

Lamya laughed again. "Food? Is that all it would take? What about a pair of screaming infants, disturbing my sleep?"

"They're not infants," said Mhumhi. "The older one, Maha, is already-"

"No, no, don't tell me their names," said Lamya, putting out a hand. "I don't want to know. I don't want them."

"But they're your kind!" exclaimed Mumhi, rising to his feet, ignoring Biscuit's warning growl. "And there are few enough of you left as it is! How can you be so selfish?"

"I'll tear out your filthy tongue, you-" Biscuit started to growl, but Lamya grabbed him by the scruff.

"Shut up, Biscuit. He's completely right. I am very selfish." She flashed her teeth at Mhumhi in what he was not sure was a smile. "But the reason any of us are left at all is because of that. Selfishness."

"What do you-"

"I tell you," said Lamya, leaning back, releasing her grip on Biscuit, who had gone completely cowed, ears back and tail under his belly. "I tell you, I watch you dogs every day and laugh. I'm waiting to see what will happen to you when the meat runs out. Will you all kill each other in the streets- or will you go the *kinder* route?"

"What are you talking about?" Mhumhi asked. "What do you mean, when the meat runs out?"

"Come on, doggy," said Lamya. "How much did you think there was? Did you think there was just a bottomless supply out there? Where did you even think it came from?"

Mhumhi felt a kind of fear, looking at the wrinkles in her furless face. "I don't know where it comes from, and I don't care," he said. "It's just meat. It's what we eat, and it's never run out, and it never *will* run out."

Lamya exchanged a glance with Biscuit, then snickered. "Well, good. Keep thinking that. That's what we're all counting on, you know?"

"Lamya," said Biscuit, his tone warning. She flapped a hand at him. Mhumhi wavered on the couch, wanting to question again what she had meant, but feeling certain he would rather not know the answer. In the midst of his thoughts there came a loud, shrill squeak that made him jump.

"The tea's ready," Lamya said, and pushed herself up from the couch and busied herself in front of the microwave. In her absence Biscuit seemed to recover completely from his cowering.

"You'd better be more careful about what you say," he told Mhumhi. Mhumhi found that he could use his pale eyes to good effect when he glared.

"Leave him alone," said Lamya, returning with things in her hands. "I'm enjoying myself- we never get anyone new to talk to. And here's your tea, Mhumhi." She put a mug down in front of Mhumhi. There was liquid in it that smelled bitter and steamed.

Mhumhi eyed it, wondering if she really expected to drink it. She had taken hers up to her face to start drinking in the hulker fashion, with the lips.

"We are lucky that some of the power still works," she commented. "Else I'd never be able to have hot drinks… my one remaining luxury. I suppose we're lucky we got overrun with dogs and not something like hyper-intelligent *birds*. The shit'd block up all the solar panels in a fortnight."

Mhumhi stared at her blankly, not even pretending comprehension.

"What's a bird?" asked Biscuit.

"Big feathery bug that flies," said Lamya. "And shits. I remember them- there used to be some in the Botanical Dome when I was little. Aren't there any left there?"

"Botanical Dome…?" Mhumhi repeated, wrinkling his brow.

"The Great Glass Garden," Biscuit translated.

"I don't know, I've never been inside," said Mhumhi. "I'm not police."

"That's right," said Lamya. "I forgot you were just a dirty little stray like the pariah dog." She laughed. "It's funny that you call them the police, isn't it?"

"Is it?" Mhumhi was starting to get weary of feeling like he was being ridiculed. He lay back down on the couch.

"Police dogs," said Lamya, and then she shook her head. "You wouldn't get it. They used to exist to protect us, you know."

"Protect who?"

"Humans, you stupid mutt, humans," said Lamya, aiming a halfhearted kick at him that brought him nervously back to his feet. "Dogs were meant to serve humans. Oh, don't look insulted, I don't mean wild dogs- you're just a freak side effect in the whole thing."

"What whole thing?" asked Mhumhi, the fur on his back rising. Lamya took another long drink of her tea.

"Where d'you think you got that brain from? There's no point to a dog being smart- it's just that some idiot thought he'd manufacture dogs that could talk like parrots and sell them."

"What's a parrot, Lamya?" Biscuit asked, his blue eyes wide.

"Shut up, Biscuit. Do you get it, Mhumhi? It's all genetics and stupidity. You're not supposed to exist, by nature. But you do, and I'll be damned if you haven't been very good at breeding."

"I haven't had any puppies," said Mhumhi, who was now thoroughly confused. Lamya sighed and let her head fall back.

"You're supposed to be intelligent, but you dogs are so *stupid.* I suppose I could spend all day explaining the whole thing to you, but I don't see the point. No, the point- the real point is that you mutts have been calling yourself police and all and strutting around this town like you own it. And you're just living off of our scraps! You're the dogs in the dustbin, Mhumhi!"

"Living off *your* scraps?" Mhumhi latched on to what little he could understand. "Haven't you got it backwards? There are only a handful of hulkers out there, and you're the ones eating *our* meat."

"Oh, my," said Lamya, though she looked somehow pleased. "Your meat, hmm? It's true that the dogs are everywhere in this city, and you have managed to kill a great number of us- have you ever killed a human, Mhumhi, by the way?"

"Killed a-? No, no I haven't," said Mhumhi, flicking his eyes away.

"You've wanted to, though, haven't you. Like the dog you are. I know about those hunts that take place up in the bloody park. D'you see this?" She raised her covering slightly, and Mhumhi glimpsed a cord around her smooth dark belly.

"What's that…? Were you caught in a snare?"

"Not a snare," said Lamya. "Though thank you for your kind concern. No, this is for if I ever get caught by those police of yours. Biscuit tells me they tear your clothes off, but I had a friend who told me about this trick. Keep the cord against your skin and they'll probably miss it."

"What's it for?" Mhumhi asked. Biscuit put his ears flat against his skull.

"I don't like the idea of being eaten alive," said Lamya, settling back into her chair.

Mhumhi still didn't get it, but there was a certain finality to her tone. "I'm not a part of those hunts," he told her. "And I- I don't like them. I don't think we should be eating hul- humans. They're dogs like us."

Biscuit gave a snort. "Dogs like us…? That's a filthy insult."

"Go back to the part where he doesn't think he should be eating humans," said Lamya, her eyes dark and glittering behind her bowl. "I think that's very funny."

Her scrutiny made Mhumhi have to pant. There was no way she could possibly know he'd participated in a hunt and eaten hulker meat, was there?

"Hey, Mhumhi," she said. "There used to be a whole lot of hulkers in this city. Millions of us. More hulkers than there are dogs."

Now Mhumhi snorted. "That's impossible."

"How many houses are there here in Oldtown, Mhumhi? How many apartments in the whole city? Did you know every one of them used to be filled with humans? My god, do you think this city was just shat out of the earth for the *dogs*?"

"If there were hulkers everywhere, where did the dogs live?" asked Mhumhi. "Did they just get along with the hul- humans?"

"*Your* kind was in zoos and cages," Lamya sneered. "I don't think that there were any left in the wild, even, not that I cared to check at the time… Anyway, we had proper dogs, but they acted like- well, like proper dogs did and lived with us. Like Biscuit here."

"You're saying too much, Lamya," said Biscuit. She ignored him.

"Anyway, when that group of idiots started selling IntelliDogs, they didn't realize the whole retro-thing was infectious. And it got into the conservation center, and nobody realized until it was too late. It only goes into effect on the second generation. So we had the smart talky pet dogs, but the wild dogs didn't care to be our pets, did they? So that was a real problem."

"So," said Mhumhi, who was doing his best to suspend his disbelief- and his best to keep up with what she was talking about.

"You're saying that these wild dogs drove out all the hulkers? Or- or killed them?"

"No," said Lamya. "Don't be stupid. There's no way a bunch of dogs could kill fourteen million humans, intelligent or not. You all were still stuck in the zoos and cages, anyway, you were nothing but freaks."

"So, what then?" Mhumhi said, feeling impatient. "Where'd all those humans go, then, if there were so many?"

"I just don't know, Mhumhi," said Lamya, and her cruel little smile returned. "You tell me."

23
Killing With Kindness

The heat in the little room was becoming oppressive. Biscuit was panting on the couch under his thick coat, and Lamya flapped her stomach covering a bit before rising to open a window. Mhumhi stared after her. He had sat in silence after her last words, trying to put them together.

"Where did all the humans go?"

Lamya did not answer him right away- she was leaning out the window.

"When are you going to find me that fan, Biscuit?"

"When it's safe to wander around the stores again," Biscuit replied, and licked his broad paws. "I told you, the police are hunting domestics right now. It isn't safe for me."

"What will you do if I die of heat stroke, you useless dog?"

"Please," said Mhumhi, "tell me. Tell me what happened." The heat was not affecting him, but he was panting anyway.

"You shouldn't be listening to her," Biscuit muttered.

"I heard that," said Lamya. She turned around in front of the window. "Mhumhi, use your expensive little brain. I don't think I've been very subtle about where they went. They're still in this city- well, what's left of them."

"No," said Mhumhi.

"And I suppose a great deal has been swept out through the sewers as dogshit, too. How much of it must there be for you to already be running out?" Lamya tapped her chin, then shook her head. "Whoever's left is still hanging in that big freezer underneath each dispensary, though. Bodies of man, woman, child, being ground up and prepared for your mouth-"

"No!" exclaimed Mhumhi. "No, that's impossible!"

"How do they taste, anyway? I've avoided having any, but-"

"The meat can't be hulker!" He had to leap off the couch, startling Biscuit to his feet, and paced on the carpeted floor. "Why would- I mean, who put all of them down there? The dogs?"

He was beginning to feel a dull horror, like the time Sacha had told them about the half-breed cull, only a thousand times worse.

"I told you, the dogs had nothing to do with it," said Lamya. "They put themselves down there."

"You mean, other hulkers-"

"No, I mean they put themselves down there, Mhumhi, how hard is that to get. There's no great secret. They all willingly became meat."

"That makes no sense!" exclaimed Mhumhi. "Why would anyone-?"

"The reason I am alive," said Lamya, "is because my parents asked themselves the same question. The selfless ones went and died, Mhumhi, and so it's only the savages like me that are left."

"But why-?"

"Because they needed meat," said Lamya. For a moment her face became slightly pinched, the first expression of discomfort Mhumhi had seen on her. "We were starving. There was a program. Advertisements everywhere. Celebrities volunteered to do it. Everybody was doing it, Mhumhi. Everybody wanted to save... everybody."

"But if everybody wanted to die-"

"That's right." She bared her teeth at him. "If everybody died for everyone else, they didn't die for anyone."

"I don't understand…"

"You're not human, Mhumhi." Lamya turned and gazed back out the window. "You don't feel that… oh, that special kind of compassion we feel. That altruism. You're just an animal. You wouldn't sacrifice yourself for anyone else; you've got instincts against that. Survival instincts."

Mhumhi was silent, and glanced at Biscuit. He was watching Lamya attentively.

"I suppose I'm like an animal too," she said. "Because I never wanted to die for anyone. Too scared, even though it was the right thing to do. I suppose that means that all the real humans are dead." She laughed. "We're an extinct species, Mhumhi."

"You're not extinct," said Biscuit. "Don't say that. When the time comes, you will be many again."

"When the time comes," Mhumhi repeated. "You mean, when the meat runs out, and there isn't enough left for all the dogs?"

Biscuit turned to glare at him.

"He's caught on," said Lamya. "Not that it matters." She turned to smile at Mhumhi. "You still have to eat, no matter what you think the meat is. You've got to feed those little kiddies, too, right? Kindness kills, doesn't it."

She stretched out her arms above her head for a moment, tilting her neck to and fro. "To tell you the truth, though, I really look forward to what you lot will do when it comes down to it. When the food runs out, like it did for us. If dogs start offering to die... well, I guess you've made it. You're an advanced species."

"*Advanced...*" Mhumhi shuddered. "You, you're mad, aren't you? If the meat runs out for the dogs, it runs out for you, doesn't it? What will the hulkers eat, then?"

"What do you mean, what will we eat?" asked Lamya, her eyes thin and sharp. "There'll be plenty of leftover meat, the kind I can stomach. Which reminds me..." She pushed herself up from against the window and went over to the white refrigerator. "You can join us for dinner, Mhumhi, if you want."

She opened the refrigerator. Mhumhi found himself backing away, bumping into the couch that Biscuit was sitting on. Draped over one shelf was the body of a red fox. Lisica. Mhumhi could see the snare wire still tangled around her neck.

"What's the matter?" Lamya asked.

"How... how can you..." He could not tear his eyes away from the indignity of her, the moisture beaded in her fur and the way her pale tongue hung out of her mouth.

"I don't understand what your issue is, doggy," said Lamya. "You don't want me to eat dogmeat? How many thousands of times have you eaten human meat, though?"

"I... it isn't..." Mhumhi found himself struck dumb, and Lamya grinned and swung the fridge shut again.

"I was lucky to get her," she said. "Someone's been picking the meat out of my snares lately. Someone who discriminates less than you, hmm? They seem to know just where my traps lie. I've had Biscuit try to track them, but-"

"Wait," said Mhumhi, turning, finding the big domestic staring down at him from his higher perch on the couch. "You… you help her?"

"Of course I help her," said Biscuit. He sat stiffly, his forelegs stretched out, his curled tail pressed tight against his back. "She must have good food. I am not a wild dog, I am a domestic."

"That's right," cooed Lamya, and she stepped forward to rub one of Biscuit's thick ears between her fingers. "And when all the wild dogs are dead, and you've fulfilled your role…"

She put two fingers against Biscuit's head. The large domestic did not move.

Mhumhi did not understand the gesture, but he felt a sort of sick chill all the same, looking at the two of them. There was something wrong… *terribly* wrong here… He should not have come.

He looked back towards the closed door, and both Lamya and Biscuit seemed to pick up on the motion, for Biscuit rose and Lamya flashed her square teeth.

"Ready to be off, Mhumhi? Sure you don't want any meat for your little kiddies?"

"No," said Mhumhi, taking a step back. Biscuit leapt heavily down from the couch and walked towards him, eyes thin.

"I hate to see you go, honestly," said Lamya. "I haven't been able to talk to anyone besides Biscuit for a long time.. it was nice. Especially as you're a terribly large animal. Hypothetically speaking, I'm not sure I could even fit you in the fridge."

Much to Mhumhi's surprise, Biscuit turned around, a few feet in front of him.

"Lamya," he said, "that is enough. We'll let him go."

Lamya pulled her eyes tight and the corners of her lips down.

"You were the one who said he was hearing too much!"

"That's your fault, not his," said Biscuit. "And I don't think it matters. He is already in too dangerous of a position to talk to the wrong dogs."

He glanced back at Mhumhi, who elected not to say anything. Lamya gave an elongated sigh and flopped back down on the couch.

"Fine, fine! Then tell him to come again. I'm lonely. Bring his sisters- not those children, though." She uttered a harsh laugh.

"Come," said Biscuit, tone cool, and he reared up and took the doorknob in his mouth to turn it. Mhumhi found he was still shaking a bit and said nothing, his tail tucked, as he left the room.

Biscuit led him back through the silent school until they came to a small room overlooking the playground. Here he again reared up and pushed a window pane with his paw, tilting it outwards with a soft creak.

"Through here," he said, and scrambled up on a desk, his claws scraping, and leapt out of it. Mhumhi followed somewhat more gracefully, though his injured paw clipped the sill and made him stumble on the landing.

When he regained his balance he saw that Biscuit was digging in the wood chips underneath a teeter-totter.

"Here," he said, as his paws made loose dirt fly. "I've got something for you… for the children."

Mhumhi went over cautiously and recoiled when he saw the domestic draw a long piece of tattered, dirty meat from the ground.

"I won't give them meat from a dog!"

"Don't be stupid," grunted Biscuit, dropping the stuff on the wood chips. "You can't afford to be picky right now. Besides, it isn't dog meat. It's my share from the dispensary. I hide it here to keep Lamya from suspecting what it is."

Mhumhi went up and sniffed the stuff warily. It did smell like dispensary meat, though the dirt had made the color unrecognizable. He found himself still rather reluctant to eat it, given what he had just heard.

"Listen," said Biscuit. "You must not pay any mind to the things Lamya told you in there. Being without other humans can- well, it can make a human act very strange. You must realize that she was trying to say the things that would shock you the most. And they simply aren't true."

Mhumhi raised his eyes up to meet Biscuit's. "The dispensary isn't stocked with hulker meat?"

"Of course it isn't," said Biscuit, licking his lips. "No… the meat is not human."

"Then where did all those hulkers go," said Mhumhi, "and where did all the meat come from?"

Biscuit hesitated for a long moment, wavering.

"The hulkers were killed and eaten by you wild dogs," he said. "You are the ones who ruined everything. You are."

"Then where did all the meat come from?"

"It must be dog meat," Biscuit insisted, licking his lips again. "Or rat meat. It does not matter. It is not *human*." His pale eyes seemed to fade even more. "This world was made by humans for their servants, the dogs. You are the ones who betrayed that. We must suffer the consequences... we must wait until the usurpers starve and eat themselves, like a string of rats eating their own tails, so that our proper masters can rise again..."

"You're the one who's gone mad," said Mhumhi, almost admirably. Biscuit's tone had taken on a strange fanaticism, his eyes staring somewhere beyond Mhumhi, but at his words he seemed to snap out of it with a snarl.

"Were you not taking care of the children, wild dog, you would be dead- remember that. You are lucky I can smell them on you." He prowled around Mhumhi, raising his lip, as if to remind him how very much larger he was. The hair on Mhumhi's back was rising again.

"But," said Biscuit, "you have done a good thing, and we cannot spare anyone else to look after them- not with the arrests- so you will be aided. I will try to bring you food, if you tell me where they are hidden."

Mhumhi hesitated for only a fraction of a second. "If you want to give them food, we can meet somewhere- but I won't tell you where they are."

This did not seem to please Biscuit, for he rumbled. Mhumhi managed to meet his gaze for a moment, and finally the large dog looked away.

"Fine! Then take this meat and go back to them. Count yourself lucky that you have the privilege to be near them."

Mhumhi said nothing to this, but he took the meat, in several quick, unhappy gulps. Perhaps it was the dirt smeared into it, but it was the worst he'd ever tasted.

24

His Hulker's Heart

When Mhumhi scratched on the door in the concrete hallway later that evening, he was met by a surprisingly enthusiastic greeting.

"Mhumhi!" he heard, as Maha yanked the door open. From behind her Kutta burst out, whining, licking Mhumhi on the chin and wagging, clearly very hungry. Even Tareq was up, toddling towards him with his hands outstretched, his mouth forming a crooked, gap-toothed smile.

"Have you got meat?" Kutta whined, still licking at him. Mhumhi was rather relieved to see that she looked much better than she had in the morning, but it was hard to keep the meat down with her going at him so enthusiastically.

"I'll give it to you *inside*," he managed to get out, and she relented very reluctantly.

"I'm glad you're back," Maha said to him, reaching to stroke his neck, and Tareq followed suit. Mhumhi tolerated it as best he could, pushing through the lot of them to get inside.

He gave up Biscuit's meat in the middle of the quilt. It looked much cleaner for having taken a turn inside of his stomach, and either way Kutta didn't seem to care much from the way she attacked it with gusto, tail wagging. Mhumhi had to push her out of the way to let Maha and Tareq grab handfuls, though he found himself not wanting to watch them eat it. He felt that sick feeling rising in him again.

"Is there more?" asked Maha, having already made her portion vanish. Tareq gave an affirmative whimper, sucking on two of his fingers.

"There's no more," said Mhumhi. There had been at least a whole portion and a half in the domestic's stash, but it did not go very far divided by four. Kutta gave a sigh and flopped back down onto the quilt.

"We've got to find a way to get more," she said, blinking her yellow eyes. "I'll go with you next time, Mhumhi, I'm feeling better today."

Mhumhi went over to lick beside her exposed ear. "Don't push yourself. I've got to talk to you about something…"

"What?" she asked, but he pressed his jaws together and flicked his eyes towards Maha and Tareq.

"Not now."

Kutta put her ears forward curiously, but laid her chin back down on the soft quilt. Maha, who was wiping Tareq's chin with her chest covering, was eyeing them.

"Mhumhi, I think I found more rats," she said. "Will you come with me and help me catch them?"

Mhumhi wrinkled his lips again- he had not found his last encounter with the creatures particularly pleasant- but then again, rats might be better than any other sort of meat right now.

"All right," he said, giving Kutta one last lick. "Is it far away?"

"No, no, it's just down the corridor…"

Tareq gave a little whine and reached his hands out to her, but she pushed them away. "Not now, Tareq. You stay here with big sister Kutta, all right?"

Tareq's eyes seemed to moisten. "Bad dog," he said. Mhumhi noticed Kutta's tail tucking even in her prone position.

"Let's go, Mhumhi," Maha said, rather hastily, backing towards the door. Mhumhi found he was inclined to agree with the sentiment.

Maha led him down the corridor to the little room he and Kutta had sheltered in the day before, with its pile of papers. He trotted forward and nosed around in them.

"I don't smell or hear any in here," he said.

"That's good, 'cause you would have scared them all away just now," Maha said wryly. She pointed up towards the empty shelves near the low ceiling. "I think there're some holes near the pipes up there. I hear them moving around, and you can see where the paper's been chewed on…"

Mhumhi could now see a few ragged edges in the pile, though he was feeling a tad sore from her admonishment.

"How will you catch them up there?"

"I have some old traps," said Maha, and she reached into her bag and drew something small and square out of it. "Only thing is that I don't have bait for them... but I figure if I put it right next to the hole..."

"And how will you get up to the hole?" Mhumhi asked, rearing up against the wall to try and see over the shelves. "There's no rungs here."

Maha put the trap in her teeth and used both hands to pull herself up onto the lowest shelf, her flat feet kicking. Mhumhi backed out of the way, watching the operation nervously.

"Be careful!"

Maha mumbled something unintelligible around the trap in her mouth, reaching up to the next shelf. Mhumhi's ears pricked- he'd heard the soft sound of tiny feet skittering behind the wall.

"I think you're right- I can hear them back there!"

"I told you!" Maha said, spitting the trap in her free hand. She tried to reach around the top shelf but suddenly wobbled dangerously.

"Maha!" Mhumhi cried, but it was too late. There was a loud *crack* and the shelf split and she fell down backwards.

Scraps of paper were flying- she'd landed in the middle of the pile. Mhumhi scrambled to her side, whining. She was lying there with her eyes shut and her face screwed up, but Mhumhi did not smell blood.

"Hush, you're all right," he said, licking at her coarse hair- she was lucky it was so thick; it must have protected her head. He could feel a bump forming with his tongue but nothing else.

"Ow," said Maha, in a shuddery way, and sniffed.

"You're just fine," Mhumhi said, pressing his muzzle against her warm cheek. "But no more climbing shelves."

"I have to get rats for Tareq," Maha protested. At that moment the trap, which had landed somewhere to their right, snapped loudly and spun itself in the air. Mhumhi jumped about a foot.

Maha sat up, giggling. Mhumhi put his ears back and used his shoulder to push her back over. She fell back laughing and squirming into the pile of papers.

Mhumhi looked at her for a moment, tongue hanging out in an unbidden smile. Then his eyes flicked to her stomach, her hairless skin exposed as her covering rode up, and his mouth closed. It reminded him of the glimpse he had seen of Lamya's stomach, of the cord around it- of her words about hulkers, about dogs, about meat- of the strange, fanatical raving of the pale-eyed domestic.

Maha's giggles slowed. "What's the matter, Mhumhi?"

"Nothing," he said, looking at her uncertainly, this deformed, hairless creature lying down in front of him.

Are you waiting for all of us to die, Maha?

"Mhumhi," she said, reaching her hand out, and he went forward and let her scratch under his chin.

"Puppy," he said. "Do you ever think about what it would be like if there were lots more hulkers?"

"Huh?" She rolled over on her side to look at him, rustling. "What do you mean?"

"I mean, if instead of lots of dogs and a few hulkers, there were a lot of hulkers and a few dogs."

"But hulkers are dogs," said Maha, blinking at him.

Mhumhi hesitated.

"Maha, do you know the word 'human'?"

At once Maha made a face.

"Tareq's mama taught me that word, and my first dog mama said it sometimes… But I don't like it. Tareq's mama tried to make me use it all the time."

"Why do you think that is?" asked Mhumhi, and he crept down to lie beside her. She put one arm over his back, running her fingers through the thick fur around his neck.

"I dunno… She thought hulkers were better than other dogs, I s'pose. But I think every kind of dog sort of thinks that anyway, right?"

Mhumhi was rather surprised by her insight. "I guess you're right."

"Tareq's mama said that too," Maha said, pulling her lips down and looking away from Mhumhi, so he could see the whiteness on one side of her eye. "Something like… there used to be a lot more hulkers. If that was true, maybe it would be nice… maybe the police'd stop killing and eating us, if there were a lot of us."

"Maybe," said Mhumhi, perhaps too darkly, for she turned back to look at him again.

"What's the matter? You seem like you've been upset since you got back."

"I'm only tired," said Mhumhi. "And as soon as I get back, a silly puppy wanted to take me out to catch rats, and I haven't seen a single one-"

"You said you heard them!" said Maha, kicking a flurry of papers at him, and he bounded out of the way and fell automatically into a play-bow.

Maha seemed to recognize the pose, for she pushed herself up with one foreleg, teeth bared in that impish hulker grin. Mhumhi went at her in a bound and knocked her back over, so she fell on her back, squirming and giggling again, pushing at his chin and chest as he mock-bit at her.

He found his play suddenly becoming more halfhearted, for it had made him think of Kebero, still missing. Maha seemed to sense his growing unhappiness and fell still against him.

"Mhumhi, look," she said, rustling around a bit in the papers. "Look, there's a picture of a dog here, see?"

She drew out a crumpled piece underneath her blunt claws. It was the same picture Mhumhi had seen the night before, or an identical copy: a smiling dog, blank-eyed, with strange dark scribbles all around it.

"Do you know what it says?" Maha asked, tracing a finger over the black lines.

"What it… says?"

"Tareq's mama said that paper talks if you know how to understand it," said Maha. "It's these things around the picture. She was trying to teach me."

"Paper talks, does it," said Mhumhi, humoring her.

"I'm serious! It's a silent language. You hear it in your head." She saw the look he was giving her and gave him a shove. "Like I *said*, Tareq's mama was teaching me, so I used to know when papers said 'dog.' Like this one- it's got to say it on here somewhere…" She furrowed her brow and ran her finger side-to-side along the paper, hunting. Mhumhi found himself entirely bewildered.

"Puppy, I hate to say this, but I think some hulkers are just-"

"Here it is!" said Maha, stabbing her finger down. "When you look at that it says 'dog!'"

Mhumhi couldn't stop himself from looking, trying to focus on the blurry lines and hear the magical head-voice, but all he felt was slightly dizzy.

"I don't hear anything," he said.

"You don't hear anything, you've got to- it's like the lines are a picture like this one, even though they don't look like it. You've just got to see a dog where there isn't one."

Mhumhi looked at Maha for a moment, her earnest wide eyes and all. He pawed at the pile of papers.

"I see a dog there."

Maha looked at what his paw was on: a glossy picture of a hulker's head.

"Of course that's a dog," she said, sounding exasperated. "But you've got to look at the word, Mhumhi, and see one, not a picture. If it's a picture it's not really talking to you."

"I hope not," said Mhumhi, leaning down to sniff gingerly at the hulker image. It really was lifelike, flattened as it was. "Why are the hulkers in the pictures always so pale?"

"I don't know, I guess they got faded," said Maha, putting her fingers over the face and wrinkling it slightly, so that it looked confused. "They're all old. No one makes pictures anymore."

Makes them, Mhumhi thought. So someone *did* make them. His thoughts veered uncomfortably back to his conversation with Lamya, and he shook himself.

"Let's go back to Kutta and Tareq now. I don't think we'll catch any rats here, they're too clever for us."

Maha pushed her lips together and out. "If I find a ladder…"

"No more ladders," Mhumhi said, very firmly. He went to the door, then paused. Maha was not following him.

"What's the matter?"

"Oh," said Maha. She was looking down, rifling through the papers. "I thought maybe I could find a picture of a hyena, but there aren't any."

"A hyena?" asked Mhumhi, feeling sour at the word. "Well, good."

"I wonder why," said Maha. For a moment there was a tremor in her voice, then she looked up at him.

"Mhumhi?"

"What, what now?"

"Will I turn into a hyena?"

He put his ears back, especially at her expression, at the vague horror in the suggestion, and went back over to her and licked her cheeks and forehead.

"You won't. Don't be silly."

"I had- I had a dream last night," she said. "About the hyena hulker. Chasing me. Except that when I looked down my- my arms were getting all hairy- and every time I wanted to scream I laughed-"

"That's just a dream," Mhumhi said, moving his head so that hers was tucked between his neck and shoulder. "Hulkers don't turn into hyenas. I mean, if they do, they've got to be a different sort, right? They're not dogs."

"Am I really a dog?"

"Of course you're a dog," said Mhumhi. "Well, you're only a little puppy. But you'll grow up into a nice big dog one day. If your arms ever start getting hairy, it'll just be because you've been eating a lot of good meat."

"In my dream," said Maha, her voice muffled in his fur, "I wished I turned into a painted dog instead of a hyena. Then I could go out in the city and run with you."

"That would be fun," said Mhumhi, imagining it: himself and his little-sister puppy, playing in the sunshine and on the warm asphalt, without the ever-lingering stench of sewage.

"Can I tell you a secret?" Maha asked.

"No," said Mhumhi, wagging his tail a little. "I'll tell everyone- everyone I know about it."

Maha tugged on his ear for that until he gently mouthed her hand.

"I'll tell you my secret, but you *can't* tell anyone," she said, pulling her lips very far down.

"Fine," said Mhumhi. "You're very mean to me, you know."

She ignored the statement. "You know when I said Tareq's mama used to say there were lots of hulkers? A million million of them? I always wondered where they went. Where they were hiding."

"Maha-" Mhumhi began, drawing away, his tail lowering.

"Shh! Let me finish! Tareq's mama would say they all ran away, or they all had a secret city, under this one, and they'd come back. But I think that's dumb. We've been all around these sewers and there's no secret anything. So I used to think- it was stupid, but we saw that hyena hulker, didn't we?" She swallowed, her eyes flickering. "I used to think that all the hulkers turned into dogs. I mean, four-legged dogs."

Mhumhi thought of the dispensary and the plastic-wrapped packages, emerging between rubber lips from the cold, darkened interior. Of the dangling hulker and the way his mind had thought: *Meat.*

"I don't think that's such a bad idea," he said. "You might be right. It's what makes the most sense, isn't it?"

"Right?" said Maha, her white-sided eyes lighting up. "Else where'd they go? They didn't go anywhere, right? They're all just dogs!"

"Right," said Mhumhi. "They're all still here." He felt the hulker's heart beating inside of him again. "They never left."

"Yeah," said Maha, and her face split into a broad grin. "So I want to be a painted dog like you, Mhumhi, when I grow up. Then we can go outside, okay?"

"I don't know about that," said Mhumhi. Maha's face fell.

"Why not?"

"Well, to be honest, you're a little smelly-"

"You're so mean!" she said, but she was laughing too, and she got up and started to chase him. He bounded down the hallway in front of her, wagging his tail and glancing back. His heart was pounding.

He felt strangely divided still, his happiness and a new, aching sadness to add to the sickening things he had learned that day. And yet- and yet- He thought of Lamya, of the way she had spoken, the way she had bared her teeth at him. What had Biscuit said about her? That she had been trying to upset him. She certainly seemed to take pleasure in it. No, no, perhaps Lamya was a so-called *human*, but she was nothing like his dear Maha, who was a dog, a dog in every sense of the word.

25

Kutta's Growl

It took Mhumhi some time to separate Kutta away from the puppies, as Maha had got into a playful, cuddly mood and kept trying to tease the both of them into roughhousing with her. She even tickled Tareq, who giggled between whimpers and then ran to hide in the bathroom.

While Maha was trying to extricate him from underneath the sink, Mhumhi managed to get Kutta to slip outside with him, first outside the room, then all the way back down the hall. He did not want Maha to hear what he was going to tell her.

"What's the matter, Mhumhi?" Kutta kept saying, unconsciously parroting Maha from earlier. Inside the little room, Mhumhi paced over the pile of paper, unsure of how he even wanted to begin. He glanced at Kutta. She looked weary, her eyelids drooping, but lucid. Now and again she would shiver a little from the cold.

Mhumhi went to stand against her, sharing his warmth, and licked the closed injury on her shoulder.

"How do you feel? I'm sorry for pulling you all the way out here."

"I feel fine," said Kutta, even as he felt a tremor go through her against himself. "I'm only tired. And worried. What are you so frightened of telling me?"

Mhumhi drew away from her a little. "I'm not frightened, exactly… Why do you say that?"

"You've seemed frightened," said Kutta, her voice rasping. "You've seemed frightened ever since you came back with that strange meat two days ago. It was so strange, too… where did you find it?" She drew her ears back against her skull. "To be honest, I keep thinking about it. It was so strange and… and dark."

Mhumhi licked his lips, and she took another step back from him.

"I'm frightened that you're frightened, Mhumhi," she said. "Where did it come from? Because I don't think it was from a dispensary- Mhumhi, you've got to tell me, please, I've got to know what I ate-"

"All right!" Mhumhi said, twisting around to pace by the wall with his tail tucked. "All right! I didn't get it from the dispensary. I- I got it from a hulker! A hulker hunt, in the long grass. I was there, and I- I-"

"A hulker?" said Kutta. "Oh."

"Oh?!" exclaimed Mhumhi, turning back around. "What do you mean, *oh*?"

"I mean, yes, it's awful," Kutta said, rather hastily, glancing at him. "It is… but I thought you were going to say you'd killed another dog and eaten him- Mhumhi, I'm sorry."

"You thought I'd- no! No! I didn't even kill the hulker, Kutta, I was just there when they brought it down, and they were eating it, and I-"

"Hush, hush," Kutta said hastily, and went to nuzzle against him. "You did what you had to do- the puppies had to eat- it's all right. You didn't harm anyone."

Mhumhi let her soothe him a moment, then drew back away. He could not help but think that the fragile distinction between 'dog' and 'hulker,' even for Kutta, was much stronger when they talked about meat.

"He was still alive when they were eating him," he found himself saying, the words all in a tumble. "And I- and he was still alive when *I* started eating him."

Kutta didn't say anything for a moment, staring at him for her yellow eyes, and then she finally said, "I suppose- I suppose it was painful…"

"I don't know," said Mhumhi. "He was crying out before they started tearing into him, but once they did he became very strange- very quiet-"

"Please," said Kutta. "Mhumhi, I don't want to hear any more, I don't want to think about it." She was swallowing convulsively, looking like she might be sick. "It was just the one time, and we really needed the meat. This time the meat came from- from a dispensary, right? Not from a hulker. It tasted like dispensary meat…"

"Kutta," said Mhumhi, resisting the urge to pace again. "That's what I've got to tell you. I've got to…" A wave of anxiety swelled over him, and he turned and started gnawing on his own haunch.

"Stop that!" said Kutta, springing forward, and she pushed him down on his side. "Calm down, Mhumhi, calm down. This is a bad time- we've been struggling, and we've seen terrible things and had to *do* terrible things- but you are still my brother, Mhumhi, and you can tell me."

"Yes," said Mhumhi, looking up at her scarred muzzle. He opened his mouth and started panting. "Yes, you're right. But it's not easy to say. I- well, first I should tell you that I went to look for the hulker. The adult hulker, to give the children to."

Kutta backed away from him, looking stunned. "You did…? On your own? Mhumhi…"

"It doesn't matter," said Mhumhi, rising to his feet again with some difficulty. "She won't take them in. They're as good as ours."

"Oh," said Kutta, glancing down at the floor. "Oh, I see."

Mhumhi thought she didn't look terribly disappointed. He scratched lightly at the papers with one paw, crumpling them.

"I've got to tell you what the hulker said to me, though, Kutta, while I was there. Listen…"

He began to speak, and found that it somehow got easier as he did, the words becoming dry and mechanical. Rather it was Kutta's reactions that expressed how he ought to feel: first curiosity, then unease, then outright disgust and fear.

"No," she said, after he told her Lamya's comment on where all the hulkers had gone. "No… Mhumhi that's awful, that doesn't make any sense, why would they… no…"

"There's more," he said, and he told her about Lisica's body being in the refrigerator.

"The red fox?" Kutta gasped. She trembled. "And you said there was a- a wire around her neck? Mhumhi, do you know what this means?"

"I suppose it means that the foxes haven't really got a leader anymore," he said. Kutta looked at him like he was mad.

"No, Mhumhi, it means that the hulker is the one who put out that wire that you were caught in!" She seemed hardly able to stop the snarl that bubbled up through her lips. "It's because of her that you were caught- and Sacha-"

Mhumhi had not even thought of this, but Kutta was completely right. His dislike for Lamya began to solidify into hatred.

"It was her- it had to have been! Her and that awful domestic! She said something's been stealing the dogs off her traps, too… I bet it's been the hyenas, drawn to the smell of blood… like that time…"

"She as good as *murdered* Sacha," snarled Kutta. "It's her fault! I'll tear that domestic apart the next time I see him!"

"Wait, Kutta," said Mhumhi, for she was getting very worked up, panting and slobbering and pacing the length of the room. "I'd like to rip him up too- believe me- but he's said he'll help us. He's offered to give us meat for the puppies. Children, he calls them."

"*He* could become the meat, for all I care," said Kutta, her yellow eyes shining evilly. Mhumhi swallowed.

"Ah… Kutta…"

She glanced at him, then seemed to deflate. "I'm sorry. I've just been… it does strange things to me, being sick and cooped up and hungry… And now you tell me this."

"Sorry," said Mhumhi. "Really."

"It isn't your fault," Kutta said. "And anyway tomorrow I'll be able to get outside again, if there's a way that doesn't involve getting wet. I can go with you- I can probably blend into the morning crowd at the dispensary, there're bound to be lots of dholes. And you can meet that stupid domestic and take all his meat."

Mhumhi had to laugh, his tongue lolling. "I guess I'll have to. I'm afraid you'd kill him on sight."

"I would!" said Kutta, and then she coughed. "It'd be better than sitting here.. waiting… Mhumhi, what are we going to do? I'm afraid that strange hulker will come back, or the hyenas, or the police… Did you check the house while you were aboveground?"

"No," said Mhumhi. "I didn't dare go near it- didn't want anyone to recognize me. A culpeo saw Maha peeking up, but I think I led him off our track."

"He saw her?"

"Yes, but I pretended to be police and told him to keep it secret- told him I'd give him hulker meat." He wagged his tail, but Kutta pulled her lips back.

"Oh, Mhumhi, that wasn't- when you don't give him anything, what do you think he's going to do? He'll go to the police looking for you, won't he? It'll all get out!"

"Well, I-" Mhumhi was appalled to realize she had a point. "Well, what would you have done, then?"

"I don't know… It must have all been lost anyway when someone spotted her, but to have you connected- Mhumhi, we need to hide somewhere else. Anywhere else. There're things coming at us from all sides, and I'm frightened for the puppies."

"But not for us?" Mhumhi asked, meaning it to sound light, but the way she looked at him seemed anything but.

"They're our puppies now, Mhumhi, and we've got to protect them no matter what."

Mhumhi was startled by the vehemence in her tone. "Kutta, I don't think-" He paused. He had not explained to her fully the nature of the domestic dog's ravings, nor the connections Lamya had made between kindness and the mass deaths of the hulkers. It had been too hard to wrap his own mind around.

"What, Mhumhi?"

"I don't think we should die for them, that's all," Mhumhi said.

Kutta gave him a strange look. "*Die* for them? In what way? In what situation would we die for them? If we die, so do they. I expect you to live for them."

"Oh," said Mhumhi. "Yes… I guess that's easy enough."

Kutta came over and licked his ear.

"I don't think we'll be able to move anywhere soon," she said. "We've got to hope everything holds out for another day or two. We can regain our strength with more meat, look around, see how things stand. Then we can figure out… figure out how and where we'll move them. Far away from here."

Mhumhi felt a little seize in his heart at the thought of their home, now standing empty. And Bii and Kebero…

"All right," he said. "A different part of the city, then. Maybe Zoo Park? We know it must be mostly emptied out now, and I hear there are lots of good dens and hiding places."

"Maybe," said Kutta. "It's a good thought. Though a little close to police for my taste… Mhumhi, I was thinking more- have you ever thought about what might be outside the city?"

"Outside the city?" Mhumhi repeated blankly. "What's out there?"

"Sand, I hear," said Kutta. "But I've heard other things, too… I want to find out more about it."

"What's sand?" asked Mhumhi, and then, seeing he wasn't going to get an answer, "Who will you ask about it? How do you even get outside the city? Does the city even *end*?"

"Of course it ends, Mhumhi, it can't just go on forever," said Kutta. "And I don't know who I'll ask. But I aim to find out."

Mhumhi was still trying to imagine what could be outside the city- what a not-city would even look like- but he was drawing a blank.

"Let's go back to the puppies now," said Kutta, licking his cheek again to draw him out of his thoughts. "Let's keep that door shut tight as much as we can for now."

"You're right," Mhumhi agreed, exiting the room and glancing furtively around the corner for any more lurking hyena-hulkers, but the hall was quiet and empty.

He and Kutta went back to the room and huddled down with the children that night, wrapped together in the fluffy quilt and the warmth of other bodies.

The next day he and Kutta left for the big grate. Maha wanted to go with them at least part of the way, but Mhumhi urged her to stay, to keep the door shut, thinking fearfully of monsters emerging from the dark pipes.

"You've made her cross again," Kutta said, once both of them had emerged cautiously from the manhole Maha had opened up the day before. "Shutting her up in that room'll make sure she stews on it all day, too."

"I don't care," said Mhumhi. "She's safe."

They parted ways soon after that, as they reached the end of the dusty, empty district near Wide Street. Kutta was going to brave the morning dispensary crowd, while Mhumhi thought he'd try to circle closer to their old home, at least to have a quick look at it, before going to find and meet Biscuit again to ask for more meat.

He managed to slip his way through to empty Food Strip Street, which smelled as thought it must have been less-empty of late- there were piss marks from what he surmised to be residents of Oldtown that had been evicted from their homes near Wide Street. Since they had been forbidden from going to the morning dispensary run, most of them seemed to be tucked in their homes, napping away the harsh morning sunlight. The few Mhumhi did see were not very familiar to him. He stayed tucked into the shadows and alleys where he could.

He finally managed to sneak into the alley with the blue dumpsters, where wild-eyed Lamya had once attacked him and Bii. He spared another thought for that poor dead coyote as he skirted the rusty stain on the concrete that still remained. It had not rained in the city for some time.

He slipped around the corner, past two more streets, and then-

He crouched, in the shadows of a narrow alley. A few yards across from him stood his own familiar home, the little townhouse.

He saw at once that the door was hanging open and that someone had shat in the doorway. It almost made him rise up and go over at once, both in justified indignation and to read what the scat would tell him, but he controlled himself. That would not have been a wise move.

He quickly realized how unwise it would have been when he rose to his feet to begin walking away, for he spotted a high flicker of movement out of the corner of his eye. There was a painted dog sitting on the roof of one of the townhouses in the same row. He had sat and extended his leg to lick his own genitals, but as Mhumhi watched he raised his head, licking his lips, and began scanning the street.

If that was not a sentry, Mhumhi was a fool. He possibly was a fool for getting so close anyway. He tried to make his retreat as silent and stealthy as he could, casting nervous glances at the roofs all around, but he could not spot any more watchers. It did not stop the fur on his back from rising and his tail tucking tightly underneath his belly. The police seemed to be very much still looking for them.

He cut a wide berth around their street, now twice as jumpy as before, heading for the school.

When he got close, however, he had to stop short. There were a pair of Sechuran foxes sitting on the roundabout, one yawning, one sniffing the metal curiously. Mhumhi stared at them from behind a dumpster across the street, heart pounding. What were they doing there? And how was he supposed to get near the school with them lounging about?

He had settled on the decision to try and bluff his way through as a member of the police again when a voice from behind him made him jump.

"Back for more meat, wild dog?"

He turned. Biscuit's head and forepaws were visible over the top of another dumpster, and now he jumped out and went to crouch next to Mhumhi in the shadows. Mhumhi was a bit startled by the sudden closeness and sidled a bit closer to the alley wall.

"You see them?" Biscuit said, pointing his nose towards the pair of foxes. "They've been there since yesterday- not just those two, but others, wandering around the school in shifts." He turned and fixed Mhumhi with a pale stare. "Do you know anything about them?"

"I have no idea," Mhumhi said, a tad sharply. "It's not as if I have any reason to want you in trouble. Like you said, I came here for meat for the puppies."

Biscuit exhaled softly. "I thought I should check," he said. "I thought the little dogs didn't like the police, so I've no idea what they're hoping to achieve by hanging around here."

"Hoping for a mouthful of hot meat, probably," said Mhumhi. "If they turn you in. I'm sure they've been feeling hungrier lately."

"They won't get any, if that's true," said Biscuit. "I'd kill them first, and give them to Lamya to eat."

His voice was grim, his blue eyes showing not the least bit of remorse for his words. Mhumhi got the urge to lean away from him again.

"So, the meat," he said instead, scratching the sidewalk with one forepaw.

"There's no meat," said Biscuit. "Sorry. I don't have any more cached, and I haven't been able to make it to the dispensary today. I doubt I'll make the evening run either."

Mhumhi put his ears back, wanting very much to snap, "Then what good *are* you?" He controlled himself.

"Fine. Then I'll come back tomorrow."

"I don't know that I'll be able to go to the dispensary tomorrow either," said Biscuit.

"Then I *won't* come back tomorrow," said Mhumhi, not bothering to hide his irritation this time. "Should I bother coming back at all?"

"Calm down," said Biscuit, peeping around the dumpster at the playground. "Don't draw attention to us. I said I had no meat, but I've got some other food here that you can give to them. And a proposition."

"A proposition?" Mhumhi turned around as Biscuit left his side to leap back into the dumpster behind them. He emerged with a cardboard box clutched in his teeth and dropped it on the ground with a loud smack.

Mhumhi flinched and peered over at the Sechuran foxes, but they had engaged one another in a playful wrestling match and had not appeared to notice.

Biscuit vanished and returned with a second box in his teeth as he leapt back out.

"Two should be all right for now," he said, after he had laid the second next to the first. "This stuff is no good if you regurgitate it, so you'll have to carry the box in your teeth."

"If that's true, I think I'll only be able to carry one," Mhumhi pointed out, coming over to sniff the box. It smelled a bit like the papery stuff Lamya had offered him, but with a much more interesting flavor.

"I can carry the other one, if you show me where to go," said Biscuit. Mhumhi's tail rose stiffly.

"I'll just take the one."

"I admire your protectiveness," said Biscuit, "but you're being foolish. If I know where the children are, I can provide you with more help. Others in our network could assist you. As long as you are helping humans, we are most certainly on the same side."

"I wasn't aware there were sides," said Mhumhi, tone cool. "And if there are, I'm not on the side of someone who kills other dogs."

Biscuit raised his head slowly. "I've never killed a dog."

"No- but you've helped that hulker set snares, and you've let the dogs here walk into them unknowingly-"

"Were you caught by one?" said Biscuit. "I noticed the injury to your foot. I am sorry; it looks painful. I thought about telling you where the others were set, but you see, I don't trust you not to warn the other dogs here. Lamya *must* eat meat occasionally, you know. This boxed food is not sufficient."

Mhumhi had felt a snarl growing in him the longer Biscuit talked, and now he took a step towards him, quivering with rage.

"Lives have been lost for your stupid hulker's health," Mhumhi snapped. "Don't you *care*? Dogs who can think and feel-"

"Do you attack the dogs who hunt down humans in Big Park the same way, Mhumhi?" Biscuit was raising his lip slightly. "You didn't seem to care when you mentioned it earlier- 'a mouthful of hot meat.' Doesn't it bother you where that comes from?"

"Of course it does!" said Mhumhi, backing away a step, feeling his heart suddenly thudding. "But I haven't murdered any hulkers-"

"And I haven't murdered any dogs," said Biscuit. "But I allow Lamya to exist, the same as you allow your police to do as they please."

"It isn't the same," Mhumhi insisted, though he had begun to tuck his tail.

"I suppose it doesn't matter," Biscuit said. "You are willing to accept my food, but no further help; does that assuage you of some guilt, somehow? If you take only food, those dead dogs will feel better, but if you let me know where the children are, you betray them?"

"That- that is- you've twisted it around," said Mhumhi. "I don't want you knowing where the puppies are because I don't trust you!"

"And why is that? You have some reason to think I'll hurt them?"

When Mhumhi was silent, he went on. "If you do not want me knowing where they are, that's fine. Take one box. But like I said before, I have a proposition for you."

"And what is that?" Mhumhi asked, somewhat through his teeth.

"Don't take this the wrong way," said Biscuit, "but I suspect that from the smell on you, you've been spending a lot of time in the sewers. You may not realize this, but it is a bad place to keep children. They can quickly get sick-"

"I'm not stupid, Biscuit," Mhumhi said. "We don't have a choice."

"That is my proposition," said Biscuit. "I know a safe place, where no other dogs should be able to get in, far from police. The children will be happy and healthy there."

Mhumhi did not speak for a moment, startled. It was almost as if Biscuit had somehow been listening in on the conversation he had had the night before with Kutta.

"It is very secure," Biscuit insisted. "I would have even moved Lamya there, but she is attached to our current home. It was going to be used by companions of mine, but with the recent police raids..." He paused, lowering his head. "They and their humans were caught trying to move in."

"Oh," said Mhumhi, not sure what the appropriate reaction to this would be. Biscuit seemed genuinely saddened by the memory. "That's... very unfortunate. Were the dogs part of your family?"

"No," said Biscuit. "A domestic dog's family are his humans. But to lose those four humans... we have very few left, you see."

"Well," said Mhumhi, "in that case I don't understand why you'd want me to move the puppies. Isn't it risky?"

"I've learned," said Biscuit. "It can be done much more safely, in the dead of night, by taking certain paths... There will always be some risk, of course, with humans out on the streets, but some chances you must take."

Mhumhi cast a wary eye on him. For all his talk of wanting to protect the remaining hulkers, he certainly seemed very eager to get Maha and Tareq moved- moved, Mhumhi suspected, somewhere where he could easily access them.

"You do not have to decide right away," said Biscuit, perhaps sensing his wavering. "I can take you there tonight to look at the place, and see for yourself."

"Tonight?"

"Yes," said Biscuit. "If you meet me at the south end of Wide Street after the moon has set, I'll guide you there. We shouldn't find any trouble at that time."

Mhumhi thought it over carefully. The offer seemed valid- there did not seem to be any obvious suspicious signs- but he was still uneasy.

"Fine," he said. "But I'll be bringing my sister."

Biscuit hesitated for only a fraction of a second. "Good. I want to meet her again anyway."

No, thought Mhumhi, amused in spite of himself, you might not.

26
The Caged Skull

"I still don't think we need him," Kutta growled.

She had said this a few times before, that night, but now she seemed to feel the need to say it particularly loudly, as Biscuit was slinking along ahead of her, rump tucked low. Mhumhi did not bother to contradict her. Rather, he walked beside her with his tail waving and his tongue hanging out.

He had got Kutta to agree to go with him with little difficulty, especially after she had learned that they would be traveling with the domestic; he suspected she'd been looking forward to an opportunity to vent some of her frustration. She had even suggested to Mhumhi that they go without any intention of moving the puppies at all and instead shove Biscuit into one of his master's snares. Mhumhi had not been entirely sure whether this was in jest or not.

Biscuit had responded to her aggression by reverting to the state in which they'd first seen him- the overly-humbled, pathetic creature that had been cowed by a golden jackal. Mhumhi had been thinking that it had all just been an act, but now he wondered if it was just a state that came naturally to him.

Regardless of it all he had to admit that Biscuit had been a great help to them. Maha and Tareq had reacted to the cardboard box with delight and had devoured its contents with gusto. The contents within appeared to be little crunchy bars formed with something sticky and sweet. Maha had offered one to Mhumhi, but it had just gotten stuck in his teeth.

Biscuit suddenly stopped short, and Mhumhi and Kutta froze. There was a streetlamp nearby and Mhumhi just caught a glimpse of a dark-furred tail as he heard the retreating sound of pattering paws.

"It's a Darwin's fox," muttered Kutta. "D'you think he saw us?"

"He saw me," said Biscuit. "But I think it's all right. If he dares to try and fetch anyone, we'll be well away by the time he gets back."

"They could track us," Mhumhi pointed out.

"Then don't pee on anything," said Biscuit. Kutta gave him a yellow-eyed stare for this and he resumed tucking his tail and slinking.

"You're going to scare him off," Mhumhi murmured to her. "I think we should look at the place, at least."

"I won't tell you what I'm thinking," Kutta replied, not bothering to keep her voice down.

They went on, slipping through the shadows and skirting streetlamps. Biscuit was leading them somewhat out of Oldtown, though by the opposite way that Mhumhi and Kutta had gone to encounter the wolves in the giant store. Mhumhi thought they might be getting close to Zoo Park, in his hazy mental map. He was glad his back leg had been feeling better, and Kutta seemed to be keeping up all right despite her cough. The journey was dredging up unpleasant memories of the night after Sacha had died.

The area they were traveling through was full of squat, featureless brick buildings, sort of like the school. Occasionally there were also shiner, more modern-looking buildings that put Mhumhi in mind of the dispensary. Biscuit had led them to leap over several short chain-link fences to enter the area, and now Mhumhi saw that there were numerous little kiosks with wooden partitions like the one he and Kutta had seen near the parking garage.

"Do you know what this place is called?" he asked Biscuit, trotting a little to catch up with him.

"They call the main street Silent Street," said Biscuit. "The buildings here are shut very tight and no one can get in them, so few dogs come here. Lamya told me it was 'high-security.'"

"Did she," said Kutta, in a clipped way. Mhumhi wagged his tail a tad nervously.

They came to another fence, this one very tall with barbed wire at the top. Biscuit sniffed along the length of it until they came to the gate, then rose and pushed it open with his weight. There was a cut padlock dangling from the clasp; Mhumhi glanced at it uncomprehendingly.

"It's this building," said Biscuit, and walked along the brick wall until they came to a little patch of dirt. Here he spent a good long while sniffing about until he suddenly began digging. Mhumhi and Kutta watched him blankly.

"Is he planning on digging his way inside?" Kutta asked.

Biscuit stuck his nose in the dirt and came out with something small in his teeth. He dropped it on the ground in front of himself- it was a small white card.

"This is important," he said. "This is how you get in. I'll show you."

He picked the card up again and led them back through the gate around to the front of the building, where there was a solid-looking door. Next to the door was nailed a featureless gray pad, and underneath that, a smaller blue pad with a white squiggle on it. Biscuit reared up next to the grey pad with the card in his mouth. Something beeped, and a light flashed. He glanced back at Mhumhi and Kutta significantly- they were both still entirely bewildered- and pushed on the blue pad with both paws.

Much to their surprise, the door swung open seamlessly.

Biscuit dropped the card to speak again.

"This unlocks the door, and then you must push a button," he said. "I think you understand how hard it would be for an ordinary wild dog to figure it out, and if you take the key, they still wouldn't be able to do it."

"'An ordinary wild dog,'" Kutta muttered.

Mhumhi asked, "What if we don't have the key?"

"Then you can't get in," said Biscuit. "Don't lose it. The humans that were with my companions had a difficult time finding it to begin with."

"Then how did you come across it?" asked Kutta.

"When the wild dogs took them, one of the humans dropped it," he told her. "They did not give it a second glance. After they were all gone, I came and got it and buried it here for safekeeping."

"Lucky for you."

"Lucky for us," Mhumhi said, nudging her with his shoulder.

The heavy metal door began to slowly swing closed, and Biscuit jumped to his feet.

"Come on," he said, snatching up the white card in his jaws again, and they followed him inside.

The door swung shut behind them, cutting off what little light there was from the streetlamps. Mhumhi blinked for a moment in the darkness. The only light came from faint stripes on the ground up ahead.

They heard the clatter of Biscuit dropping the card to talk again.

"There's a light switch somewhere around here, but I can't remember where it is. Step carefully- it's cluttered."

Mhumhi realized he was right when he immediately ran into something hard. It felt and smelled like a large, heavy cardboard box. There seemed to be stacks of them all around the room, creating a sort of maze; when Mhumhi tried to navigate it, the faint stripes of light completely disappeared.

The three of them bumped around for a minute. The place smelled strongly of paper, Mhumhi thought, and there was a kind of strange moistness in the air. He could hear water trickling somewhere nearby.

"I found the light," Biscuit called, and Mhumhi squeezed his eyes shut just in time before the place lit up in a dazzle of white.

"Mhumhi!" called Kutta, and he squinted in the brightness to see her teetering on top of a short stack of boxes. "There you are, I completely lost you."

She jumped down. One of the boxes followed her with a sloppy-sounding thud. Papers slid out of it in great piles.

"Be careful!" Biscuit snapped. "Those papers are very important to the humans-"

"I'll piss on them if you talk to me like that again," said Kutta, and he pressed his jaws shut. Mhumhi took the opportunity to nose at the papers, but he saw no pictures on any of them. Just more of the blurry black squiggles that Maha had said could talk to her.

"Come on, Mhumhi," Kutta called, leaping lightly over another box and spoiling the effect when she had to cough. "This way."

He followed her, scrambling and scratching over the boxes. Biscuit was walking through a doorway ahead of them that led into a long hallway with doors on either side. Down this way, the ever-present trickling seemed to get even louder. Mhumhi rotated his ears, trying to pinpoint it. It was coming from somewhere ahead and to their left.

As they left the room with boxes behind them it got dimmer again. They were passing windows with blinds over them, lit up by an outside security light; the source of the stripes of light on the floor. Mhumhi could see flickering shadows cast on the hallway wall, waving patterns. The air felt wet and heavy.

Biscuit led them around the corner and stopped. When Mhumhi followed him, he saw why: the room ahead of them was partially flooded, water just starting to slop over the doorstop. From the paneled ceiling above he could hear a faint trickling sound, and in several places there were dark spots that dripped.

Biscuit gave a soft whine. "A pipe must have burst! This was not here when I last came…"

"Not such a good hiding place anymore, then," said Kutta.

"A human's hands can easily fix this sort of thing," said Biscuit, though he kept his tail tucked. He stepped gingerly into the shallow water, which seemed to be no deeper than a puddle.

"Why are you going down there?" Mhumhi asked, eyeing the water doubtfully. It looked clean, but he was never in a hurry to get his paws wet.

"There's another thing I wanted to show you," Biscuit said. "Another reason it would be good for the children to stay here. It isn't far…"

Kutta exchanged a look with Mhumhi, but Mhumhi went ahead and stepped into the water. It was surprisingly cold.

They followed Biscuit through the room. It was a sort of odd room, with a lot of low counters and sinks. There were a great many wheeled chairs, several lying on their sides. They smelled like rotten fabric from the water, and Mhumhi saw that there was pale yellow moss growing on several of them, creeping upwards.

There were a lot of things on the counters that he could not identify- large plastic boxes, clear plastic tubes, paper tacked to the walls. Biscuit went to flick the light switch with his nose, but it appeared that the water had shorted it, for they only heard a crackling sound somewhere above. They were left in a peculiar wet gloom, the shuttered windows letting in thin bands of light, and the water casting flickering shadows on the walls.

There were several more doors leading out of the flooded room, and Mhumhi stopped short at one of them.

"Look, Kutta," he said, and she turned her head. The door opened to a room that held a rack of cages.

"Not that way," Biscuit said, coming back towards them, but Mhumhi went forward curiously, sniffing. There was water dripping in here, and drops were slithering down the metal, which was beginning to rust in spots. But it was not flooded- the floor had a drain in it.

Mhumhi stepped into one of the open cages, sniffing- it was quite large. There was a vague scent about it, not one he really recognized, more of a suggestion of history, of something that had been forgotten.

"Look, Mhumhi," Kutta called, and he stepped out of the cage and joined her in front of another. This one was shut, and there was a little plastic dish tacked on the outside, and a plate on the front that Mhumhi couldn't read.

Kutta was looking further in, where there was a small pile of bones.

"Something died in here," she said.

"It must have been a long time ago," said Mhumhi, peering at them- they were in the corner, and covered in what seemed to be a thick layer of dust.

"Those have always been here," said Biscuit, who had come up behind them. "At least, as far as I know. Must be from before…" He trailed off, seeming reluctant to say more, but Mhumhi thought he knew the event he was referring to.

"They must have come from a big dog," said Kutta, eyeing a long pale femur.

Mhumhi reared up to get a better look and was surprised to feel the metal front of the cage sliding under his paws.

"It's not even secured," he said, getting down, and used his nose to push it the rest of the way open.

"Be careful, Mhumhi," said Kutta, tail raising as he entered to sniff the bones. He did feel a brief pang of anxiety- what had led someone to die here, in an unlocked cage?

But the bones were quiet, calm even, gently nestled together, like their owner had been curled up. Mhumhi nosed through the dust and sneezed.

"It wasn't a dog," he said, and picked up the skull in his teeth to show them. It was domed, the muzzle flat.

"A hulker!" exclaimed Kutta. Biscuit said nothing, though he glanced away.

Mhumhi put the skull down, grimacing a bit from the dusty taste of it.

"If you're done," said Biscuit, "what I wanted to show you is back this way."

Mhumhi and Kutta exchanged another look, for the domestic's tone had been strange, but there were no obvious conclusions they could draw from it. They followed him together back out of the cage room, Kutta drawing her brushy tail along Mhumhi's side to comfort him, or perhaps to comfort herself.

What Biscuit wanted to show them seemed to be at the very back of the long room, on a wall upon which was suspended a strange rack of hanging metal frames. Each frame was cross-divided into a number of tiny sections, and there were masses of wires running from it in every direction, some lying in the water on the floor. Mhumhi gazed at it without comprehension.

"What is this?" he asked.

Biscuit pawed at one of the frames and it slid back slightly. "Doesn't it remind you of anything?"

Mhumhi tilted his head and looked at the wobbling frame more carefully. There was a clip at the top, and behind it, a narrow rubber chute.

"It- it looks like the things that give you the meat at the dispensary!"

That had been Kutta, who was now trotting and splashing along the length of the thing, eyes wide.

"Exactly," said Biscuit. "That's what the humans who wanted to live here said; that's why they went at such great lengths to try and get the key. It is my understanding that they knew how to activate it to give them meat, right here in this room."

"Really?" exclaimed Kutta. "But that would mean-"

"It would mean a lot of things," said Biscuit. "Safety, security from the outside. And this small dispensary would not be limited to the times the big ones are, and it would not limit the amount of meat one dog could get from it each day... I'm sure you understand how important this was."

Mhumhi gazed up at the silent racks. If they had had access to this sort of thing before, his entire family might still be together.

"Why didn't you tell us about this in the first place?" Kutta demanded.

"Because I did not think you would believe me. I thought it would be better to show you." Biscuit's curled tail wagged slightly.

Or because you thought it would be very dramatic, thought Mhumhi, eyeing him. And impressive.

"If I understand you," he said, "you mean to say that Maha and Tareq could activate this instead? But they're only puppies."

"It doesn't matter," said Biscuit. "Give a human enough time and space, and he can create anything with his hands. If you let those children toy with this, you will have as much meat as you could ever want."

"Really," said Kutta, who was beginning to sound very interested. Mhumhi glanced at her, then back at Biscuit.

"If that's true, why haven't you moved Lamya here to let her play with it?"

"I told you," said Biscuit. "Lamya will not move, and even if she would, she refuses to eat any meat she knows comes from a dispensary."

"Even so, doesn't she care about what might make your life easier? Surely she realizes that you'd be much safer eating from this place!"

Biscuit went slightly stiff.

"My needs are not important, not compared to hers."

"Isn't she your sister, though?" Kutta challenged. "Your pack? She should take care of you!"

Now Biscuit actually growled. "That is an insult to both of us," he said. "We are not brother and sister. We are human and dog. I am her loyal servant. My life belongs to her- I am her tool, her living shield, the one who carries her burdens. I am faithful. That is a dog's purpose. Faith!"

His jaw had gone slightly slack, his pale eyes wide. Mhumhi glanced nervously at Kutta and saw she had put her ears back.

"Don't say anything," he murmured.

"I've no idea what I would say..."

Biscuit wavered there for another moment, then suddenly seemed to snap back into focus. "So! You've seen the place I can offer you. What do you say? Will you let me help you move the children here?"

Mhumhi felt Kutta shifting uneasily beside him. He said, "Maybe- maybe we need some time to think on it."

"That's fine," said Biscuit. "But think quickly. They longer you leave them in one spot, the more danger can come find them." His blue eyes bored into them.

"We'll think," said Kutta. "Moving them is dangerous. And the little boy is sick."

"Then you should get them out of the sewers, quickly," Biscuit urged. "This place has things that can be used to heal; the humans know how to find them. It will be a safe place for him to recover. He cannot be allowed to die- especially if he is a male."

"Especially if he is a male?" Mhumhi questioned.

"There are only a handful of male humans left in the city," said Biscuit. "The police hunt them with more vigor, because they think they give more entertaining hunts. If the humans are to survive, we must protect the remaining males with our lives."

"You want to use Tareq in some sort of- some sort of breeding program?" Kutta wrinkled her lips.

"Not against his will!" Biscuit said. "But he will want to mate when he grows up, anyhow. It takes a long time for them to mature- then they only have one infant at a time. It is imperative that he grows up, starts boosting the population..."

"We aren't turning this place into some type of- some type of hulker breeding center!" Kutta snapped.

"Well," said Biscuit, "that doesn't really matter. As I said, they take a long time to mature. We may all be dead by them, and new generations of domestics will have taken over their care. You needn't worry."

Kutta seemed shocked into silence by the audacity of this. Mhumhi nudged her again.

"We'll think on it," he repeated.

"I hope you make the intelligent choice," said Biscuit.

27

Eyes in the Dark

Hulkers, Mhumhi had discovered, were surprisingly difficult to groom. He had spent a great deal of time licking the puff of coarse hair on Maha's head, trying to tease the natural oils out with his tongue, but there was no end to the stuff. And it didn't help that she kept wiggling and making little impatient noises during all his ministrations.

She had been lying on her stomach to let him reach, arms crossed underneath her chin, but now she rolled her head to one side and glared at him.

"Stop squirming," he said, putting one paw over her back, and stretched his neck to get at her hair again. She pushed herself up and out of her reach.

"Quit tugging on it! I'll just cut it with something. I don't care." Her lips were pulled down very far. Mhumhi sat back on his haunches and licked his lips.

"Don't talk that way to your older brother, Maha," said Kutta. She was lying on the quilt near the wall, with Tareq curled up against her belly. "He's trying to do something nice for you."

"Well it isn't nice and it hurts," said Maha, and she got up and slouched into the bathroom. Mhumhi watched her go, then sighed through his nose. She'd been cross and sulky for the past couple of days- he suspected it was from the prolonged confinement. He'd been loath to let her outside for fear of more hyena-hulkers appearing.

"Don't bother," said Kutta, seeing him about to get up. "Let her have her space-"

"I wasn't going to go near her," said Mhumhi, giving the bathroom door a dark look, and went over to sit beside Kutta. "Maybe a night in there would do her good."

Kutta laughed, in a kind of pale way. Against her belly Tareq stirred, small face furrowed, and put his thumb in his mouth.

"You've been having him sleep with you a lot like that," Mhumhi observed.

Kutta laughed again, this time almost guiltily. "It's stupid- I know it is- but I've almost been hoping that having him there at my belly would make me produce milk. I've even tried to get him to suckle once or twice."

"Kutta!" said Mhumhi, a bit appalled.

"Well, it would certainly help," said Kutta, raising her lip slightly at his tone. "We do need food..."

"We don't even have enough meat for you to produce milk from," Mhumhi pointed out, and she lapsed into silence.

He looked at his sister's ribs, wanting to laugh himself at the cruelty of their situation. They were getting less food than ever. Kutta had been able to get meat a few more times across the span of several days, and they had split what they could between themselves. Biscuit had been able to help some by providing them with boxes of things for the children, but Mhumhi thought he was right- it wasn't as good for them as the meat was, for it left them sickly-smelling and less robust.

"We'll have to take him up on his offer," he told Kutta. She looked up at him, and still said nothing. He understood her reluctance, but the food situation was not the only problem they were facing. The night before, when they had returned to the room, there had been a strange, ugly stench in the hallway, and a sort of thick paste smeared against the walls. It bore the reek of hyena.

"I hate that domestic," Kutta said. "And I don't trust him. He wants us to prostrate ourselves in front of these puppies..."

"He can't make us do anything," Mhumhi pointed out. "And he wants them to live. I don't like him either, but he is our ally right now."

"Yes, right now," Kutta muttered. "What happens when he finds more of his little domestic friends to help him out? We'll wake up in that place with teeth at our throats. Like Mother's puppies."

Mhumhi recoiled slightly at the memory, and she gave him an apologetic look.

"I'm sorry. But I still don't think we should be hanging around with someone who wants us and our kind dead so badly."

"No, but I don't think we have a choice," said Mhumhi. Kutta pulled her lips back in a tight smile.

"I thought you just said he couldn't *make* us do anything."

Before Mhumhi could respond, Maha reemerged from the bathroom. She'd put a great quantity of water from the sink on her hair, slicking it down somewhat, and now she stood and scowled at them, dripping.

"What're you two talking about...?"

Mhumhi flicked his eyes at Kutta, then said, "We're talking about moving somewhere else."

This seemed to surprise Maha a little, and they saw her struggle a moment to keep her face set and surly.

"Where?"

"A place a friend showed us in a different part of the city," said Mhumhi. "It might be safer there, with more food."

"Oh," said Maha. "Then- then why don't we go?"

Mhumhi had to laugh a little. "I guess we will, won't we, Kutta?"

Kutta looked up at him. She wasn't laughing.

The next morning he found Biscuit and told him their decision. The domestic dog seemed delighted, but not very surprised, to hear the news.

"We can move them tonight," he said, a bit breathlessly, "at the same time- the darkest time- and if we are quick and quiet enough, we shouldn't have any trouble. The three of us are enough to defend them from little foxes, and there shouldn't be many police out. Quick and quiet... then it'll all be over."

Mhumhi was not completely inclined to share his optimism, but it almost did seem possible that everything would be all right, the way he described it.

It was a harder sell to Maha, who had to be reminded about the part where they would have to walk aboveground.

"But why can't I just go out of a manhole?" she whined, for the umpteenth time.

"If you want to be eaten by a hyena, feel free," Mhumhi said, for he was beginning to slightly lose his patience. "And Biscuit tells me that there are a million little dogs down there too now. Feel like being part of a crowd?"

"Mhumhi," said Kutta, nudging him, and he closed his jaws. He knew Maha would be persuaded eventually- it was really little Tareq that might be the problem, with his tendency to whimper and cry.

"And why can't I bring the blankets?" Maha asked.

"We can come back and get them later," Kutta said. "We don't want to be weighed down tonight, so we can get there as quick as we can. Understand?"

"But how will Tareq be able to sleep at night? Does the new place have blankets?"

"Millions of blankets, loads of blankets," spouted Mhumhi, until Kutta caught his eye again.

It was a trial to get the puppies assembled that night. Maha dithered and deliberated over what to put in her bag, which Mhumhi insisted she pack light, sticking his head in to pull things back out until she got frustrated and tried to wrestle with him. Kutta kept running around trying to think of ways it might go wrong, and kept inadvertently waking up Tareq. Tareq did not seem sure what was going on- they had tried to get Maha to explain it to him, but even she admitted that he was being obtuse- but what he did seemed to get was that everyone was stressed, and cried so he could experience it with them.

Presently Mhumhi got fed up with the whole ordeal, his nerves on a knife's edge, and in a surly way announced that he was going ahead to scout out the tunnel to be sure the way was clear. Kutta gave him a dirty look around Tareq's arm- he was clinging to her and whimpering. Apparently he'd entirely forgotten the time she'd bitten him.

"I'll be back soon," said Mhumhi, and slipped out of the door.

He hadn't taken four steps when he stopped. The soft slap of bare feet came from behind him, and stopped as well.

"Maha," he said, turning. He could just make out her silhouette in the dim light.

"I'll scout with you," she said. He couldn't make out her expression, but he could imagine it, and he could smell her still-damp hair.

"Fine," he said. "Come up next to me, and be very quiet."

She did, and put a hand on his back. Together they padded wordlessly through the cold, dripping dimness.

"Are we really going to go to a house?" came Maha's tiny whisper.

"Not really a house," Mhumhi admitted. "But a building."

"Above the ground?"

"Oh, yes."

Maha said nothing for a bit, and Mhumhi's nose twitched in the fetid air.

"How long have you lived down here?"

"Forever," was her immediate reply, and then, "No... just since Tareq's mama died. I dunno how long ago that was. Maybe not that long, actually... I had to teach Tareq how to speak Dog so he could talk to our new mother when she came."

Mother, thought Mhumhi to himself. Aloud he said, "How did she find you?"

"After I ran away from those dogs and jumped down the manhole... she just showed up. At the door. And she was all calm and gentle, and she said 'Come on, I know a place where they can't get you,' and she took me to that room we stay in. Then I told her where Tareq was hiding and she brought him. It was so quick and simple I didn't even realize I started calling her Mother..."

"That was her way," murmured Mhumhi, and they lapsed into silence again. Mhumhi's mind was not quiet, though, as they continued to walk forward. A flicker of anxiety was growing in him: the thought of exposing the little hulkers to the dangers of the surface world twisted his stomach. He could not forget the fear Maha had shown the time she'd poked her head up out of the manhole.

But it was going to be just fine. This was Oldtown, anyway; normally worms in scat was one of the biggest worries here.

They came to a forked pipe, and Mhumhi scented both ways, and then said, "We should probably start back-"

Then he stopped, and lowered his nose.

"What d'you smell?" whispered Maha, clutching his fur.

"Shh," he murmured back. "Stay here for a moment."

"Why?"

Her voice rose a little, and he turned and licked her hand.

"Just a moment. I just need to check something..."

Reluctantly she crouched by the wall of the junction, and he moved forward, sniffing, his heart pounding loudly.

Such a familiar scent...

He wandered a few feet further into the tunnel, which was a branch away from the giant grate and the usual way they went out. Something squeaked, and his ear flicked. A rat?

He stayed completely still for a moment, barely even breathing, and then he saw something. Eyes. Brown eyes, watching him.

Mhumhi moved, just a slight shift of his weight on his paws, and the other dog turned and fled, scampering down through the dark tunnel and out of sight. Mhumhi jerked, then stopped, the knowledge of Maha crouching behind him holding him fast. He had thought... he had almost thought...

Had that been Kebero?

No... no, surely not; for one thing, it had seemed too large, and for another, he was certain that Kebero would have run towards him, not away.

His mind buzzing, he turned and went back to Maha. She clutched at his back at once.

"Did it see us?"

"I think he only saw me," said Mhumhi, "and he ran away. It's all right. We'll be gone even if he bothers to get someone."

Maha made a sound that did not make it seem as though she felt reassured, but she followed him quietly back to the little room.

Kutta still seemed rather irritated when Maha opened the door. Tareq had vanished, but there was a lump under the blanket.

"Well?" she asked. "Did you see anything?"

"Not really," Mhumhi dithered, unsure if he should even mention the other dog. A less frazzled version of his sister might have picked up on his uncertainty, but she only snorted, Sacha-like, and dug at the lump with her paws.

"Come on, Tareq, it's time to go... *Come* on..."

They had a bit of difficulty trying to get Tareq out of the room even when he emerged from his hiding place. He whimpered and clung to the doorway while Maha pushed him from behind. Finally Mhumhi yanked on the front of his shirt and he tumbled out.

"All right," said Mhumhi, panting, as Maha quickly shut the door to prevent any retreat. "All right, now let's practice being quiet while we walk to the exit."

Practice went better than Mhumhi had anticipated. Kutta took up the lead position, and Mhumhi the rear, keeping the puppies linked hand in hand between them. Once outside the room, Tareq seemed struck dumb with fear, incapable of doing anything aside from clutching Maha's hand in his. Maha held him grimly, her face set, and did not utter a word.

They made it through the sewers without incident, and Mhumhi wagged his tail when he saw the pale metallic shine of the ladder still extended underneath the manhole emerge ahead of them. It was just the easiest leg of their journey, but perhaps the rest might go just as smoothly. He could hope, anyway.

From the shadows behind the ladder emerged a large, rusty shape: Biscuit. Mhumhi saw his sister's hackles rising. He ran to her side.

"It's all right," he said. "I told him where to meet us."

Biscuit came forward, his curled tail wagging, and Kutta stepped into his path, stopping him.

"Let's go," she said. "You in front."

"I must greet the children," Biscuit said, peering around her at Maha and Tareq. "Then we can go."

Kutta seemed displeased by this, but with a glance at Mhumhi she stood aside. Mhumhi himself was less than thrilled as he watched Biscuit walk up to the puppies, wagging his tail low now, mouth open in a smile.

"Dog!" said Tareq, eyes wide, and he let go of Maha to toddle over and fist his small hands in Biscuit's thick fur. Biscuit turned and licked his chin and cheeks. Tareq giggled and curled his hands up by his chin.

Maha said, "Hello," and held out her hand, and Biscuit turned and licked her fingers. Her lips pulled back slightly in a small hulker smile, then a grin, and suddenly she was scratching and patting him all over, ruffling his fur, while he whined and licked her face.

Mhumhi, watching, felt confused. Biscuit had greeted the hulkers as if he was already familiar with them, a long-lost loved one, part of their family. And the puppies had responded in kind. It was as if no tension or introductions had to happen between them at all. He looked at Kutta and saw that she seemed uncomfortable, mirroring his own emotions, flicking her eyes to and away from the scene.

He had not spared much thought to the relationship between hulkers and domestics, much-touted by Biscuit as it was, but now for the first time he wondered if there was not some sort of merit to it.

There were no barriers between them at all from the start. Mhumhi, watching the three of them laughing together, felt queer- almost- almost jealous. Where did such unfettered affection come from?

But then, it did not come without a price, he reassured himself, for Biscuit was subjugating himself utterly, acting the puppy, and himself a grown dog-!

"All right!" barked Kutta suddenly. "That's enough playing. We need to go now, if we want to arrive before the sky starts getting lighter."

Biscuit separated easily from the children, mouth open in a smile, and Mhumhi thought he detected a certain self-satisfaction emanating from him.

"So be it," he said. "Then I'll go in front. Children, stay between the wild dogs."

"Dog!" said Tareq, reaching after him sadly as he trotted back to the ladder. Maha took the boy's hand, but her eyes were also tracking Biscuit. Mhumhi felt a sudden flash of annoyance and flicked her with his tail as he walked back behind them. She jumped.

"What was that for?"

"Nothing," said Mhumhi. "Just making sure you're paying attention to your surroundings."

She pulled her lips down in a frown at him.

Biscuit made his way up the ladder, rung by rung, then Kutta after him. Tareq followed her easily even though Maha had to let go of his hand- he was eager to get back near Biscuit. Mhumhi watched Maha disappear up through the hole before going up himself, wishing for the first time that he was not stationed at the back of their little train.

The upper world was cool and quiet, with that sort of liquid darkness that came after the stars had gone out. Mhumhi heard the faint scream of a vixen disturb the silence, but it was far off, and likely intended for other ears. Still, they all tensed, and Maha gripped Tareq's hand so hard he whimpered.

"Hush, Tareq!" said Kutta, who had not seen. Mhumhi went forward and nosed the back of Maha's thigh, making her jump again.

"Calm down," he said softly. "We're here to keep you safe."

Maha did not respond, and he did not see any of the tension evident in her form dissipate. She was scanning all around, her eyes wide and distracted.

Biscuit wagged his tail in what was likely meant to be a reassuring way and they all went off, Mhumhi nosing Maha again to get her to start moving. They had debated for some time about how to structure their journey, but had eventually settled on simply taking the fastest route that they could. It was likely they'd be seen by *someone*, anyway, and the best thing to do would be to have themselves in a safe place before repercussions rolled all the way to the police.

The puppies could not move near as swiftly as Mhumhi would have liked, but they strode as quickly as they could on their long legs while their three guardians stalked around them, focusing their eyes and ears on the silent darkness.

They reached Wide Street, the asphalt under Mhumhi's paws cool and wrinkled like the skin of some gigantic beast. Despite the evening chill in the air, Kutta was panting, her tongue hanging low as she zigzagged forward. She stopped to cough, flinching when the sound was loud in the silence.

Mhumhi would have liked to comfort her, but he felt he had to stay focused on the puppies. Tareq had been hovering delicately between quiet and noisy tears for some time- his rate of sniffing was steadily increasing- and if he started wailing, it was all over. Maha seemed to get this as well, for she kept directing increasingly frantic looks at him as they walked.

Ahead of them, Biscuit suddenly stopped in his tracks.

Kutta went up to him, turning her ears forward and swallowing in an effort to keep her breathing quiet. Mhumhi pressed close to Maha's side, and she suddenly reached out and dug her fingers in his fur.

Ahead of them was the line of stoplights that hung near the dispensary, blinking yellow at this time of night. It shed light on a dark object below: the stoplight that had fallen onto the street. Mhumhi was familiar with it, as a landmark that showed they were getting close to the dispensary. But it was not the fallen light that Biscuit was looking at; rather, it was the figure of the small fox sitting on top of it.

"He sees us," said Maha, in a kind of gasp-whisper

"He can't hurt us," said Mhumhi, leaning closer to her, but he felt sick all the same: they had been seen, and the fox was staring straight at them.

Kutta stepped forward beside Biscuit, blinking in time with the pulsing yellow light. Mhumhi heard her sniffing.

"Is that... is it Bii?"

"Bii?" Mhumhi repeated, his eyes widening.

The fox leapt lightly down from the stoplight, arcing his tail in a familiar way.

"It's been some time since we last met," he said.

"Bii!" said Mhumhi gladly, his tail wagging, and pulled out of Maha's grip to go greet him with an excited twitter. Kutta jumped at him and gave him a sharp nip on the shoulder.

"Shh! Not so loud!"

Mhumhi put his tail down and swallowed, stopping just short from licking Bii. The fox glanced between him and Kutta, then behind them.

"Interesting company you keep," he noted. "Especially this time of night."

Mhumhi opened his mouth to responded, but then Biscuit muscled his way between him and Kutta.

"You know this dog?" he asked, glaring down at Bii.

"Yes, so back off," said Kutta, raising her lip, though she barely reached Biscuit's shoulder. "And you- Bii- where have you been all this time? When we found the house empty we thought..."

"To make a long tale short," said Bii, "I heard the police approaching before they got to the house, and decided to slip myself and Kebero out through one of the back windows."

"Kebero? He's all right?" said Mhumhi, bouncing. Kutta shot him a look- he'd forgotten to be quiet again.

"Of course he is," said Bii, giving his tail a single wag. "Growing quite fat off of rats now, in fact. Quite a natural hunter. He will be glad to see you again."

"This is wonderful, Bii, I'm glad we met you," Kutta said. "But we can't really stop and talk now- we've got- we've got some business to take care of. You can come with us-"

"No, he may not," growled Biscuit. "How am I to know this creature is trustworthy? He cannot be allowed to know too much."

"He's perfectly trustworthy," Mhumhi snapped. "He's practically a member of the family!"

"If you'll allow it, I'd like to ask you about this business of yours," said Bii. He looked through Biscuit's legs to where the two hulkers were crouching together, behind their little conference. "I couldn't help but notice you've got hulkers with you. Are they in the care of this domestic?"

"Hold your tongue," growled Biscuit. "We shall not-"

"No," said Kutta. "No, Bii. It's hard to explain, but... they're like Kebero. They're our brother and sister now. I know it seems strange, but..."

"Like Kebero," said Bii, in a thoughtful way. "I see."

Mhumhi wasn't sure why, but a nervous feeling crawled up from his stomach just then.

"I would guess that your mother had something to do with this?" said Bii.

"Yes, but we really need to keep moving now," Kutta urged. "Once they're safe, we can talk all you like, and bring Kebero in too-"

"Where is Sacha?" interrupted Bii. "Did she not like these new family members?"

Kutta drew back a little, and Mhumhi answered. "Sacha is not... She never had a chance to meet them, Bii."

"Oh," said Bii. "Does that mean... no, I have another question. These small hulkers- what do they eat?"

"What?" Kutta snapped. "What kind of question is that? Bii, really, we've got to-"

Tareq screamed. They all whirled around.

Maha was pulling him to his feet- he seemed to have fallen over- and there was bright blood on his wrist. Mhumhi at once went to lick it, but Maha grabbed the fur on his back, gripping him tightly.

"Mhumhi," she whispered.

In the dark all around them, shining in the flickering yellow light, were countless pairs of eyes. And they were getting closer. Biscuit gave a tremulous growl.

Mhumhi himself was frightened and bewildered. The forms that were emerging around them up out of the darkness were small and sleek: little dogs, foxes, not a sign of the dappled coat of a police dog anywhere. Yet there were so many of them, and they were coming up so quietly and assuredly, with hard stares and heads lowered.

He could feel Maha trembling against him.

"It's all right," he murmured, though he felt that it was anything but.

Kutta backed up closer to them, leaving Biscuit trembling and growling in front of them all.

"What do you all want?" she said, letting her voice carry; the time for silence was very much over.

A dog leapt up onto the stoplight behind Bii- a large dog, a golden jackal: Sundu. Beside her came a culpeo, a culpeo Mhumhi recognized with a sinking feeling.

"Bii...?"

Bii said nothing, just sat and curled his tail around his paws. The nervous feeling crawled up to Mhumhi's mouth, and he began to pant.

"Hello, orphan pack," said Sundu. Her eyes flashed as the light above her head flickered. "I like not the company you keep these days."

Biscuit glanced back at them- apparently he'd recognized her too. His tail had tucked entirely underneath him again, and he started backing up closer to them. Mhumhi really wished he wouldn't.

"If you don't like it," said Kutta, raising her tail, "then stand aside and let us take it away with us."

"I think not," said Sundu, baring her teeth. "I'd rather have answers- answers about the disappearances, answers about what has eaten our families-"

"You think we have something to do with that?" snapped Kutta. "Don't be stupid!"

"You're working with this traitor domestic," said Sundu, jerking her head at Biscuit. "You've been conspiring with him, and now you're traveling with *live hulkers*. I'm sure we don't know what to think..."

"You've been spying on us!" cried Mhumhi, feeling it all click in his head. He looked again at Bii, and Bii tilted his head, and then flashed that implike little grin of his.

"Lisica's idea, not mine. You can understand our anxiety at having such large dogs in our midst when the rest of the city seemed so against us."

"Anxiety!" sputtered Kutta. "Come on, now, when have we ever-"

"Yet here you are," said Bii, "with this domestic, and those..." He glanced at Maha and Tareq again, and then seemed to decide not to say the word he'd been about to use. "It surprises me. You seemed genuinely frightened when I led you to the other hulker."

"I was!" said Mhumhi, still unable to quite believe the words that were coming out of Bii's mouth. "Bii- you- how could you spy on us? I thought-"

"What you thought is not important," said Sundu. "What is important is what is going to happen now. You can trust us to show you mercy if-"

"Trust you? After you've been *spying* on us?" cried Kutta, in a tremulous voice.

Sundu seemed to shrug this off with a flick of her ear. "You're moving these hulkers tonight to Silent Street for some plot, we know that much. You had better provide answers now, or we'll tear you apart."

Mhumhi laughed. It was a bold laugh. "Is that a serious threat? You think we're frightened of a bunch of foxes?"

He saw the assemblage around them flick their eyes at one another; some *did* look nervous. Sundu, however, flashed her teeth again.

"It may take longer to kill you this way, it is true. I don't mind."

Maha's fingers squeezed painfully into Mhumhi's fur.

"I'm sorry to let you down, but we aren't the ones behind the attacks," said Kutta. "You've wasted your time. Or did you think that these puppies could really harm you?"

Sundu opened her mouth in a snarl, and there were some fierce yaps from the crowd.

"That domestic dog was seen carrying Lisica's dead body in his mouth!"

"Then go ahead and kill *him*," said Kutta, bluntly. Biscuit whirled around to give her a shocked look as the crowd fell into barking and growling.

"Silence!" Sundu barked, and they quieted, though there was a sense of restlessness in the air all around them. "The bat-eared fox has made a deal for you. If you stand aside from the hulkers and the domestic, we'll take you into custody and let you live. If not-"

"Take the domestic," said Kutta. "But the hulkers are ours. If you wish it, we'll disappear from Oldtown with them, but you won't be killing them here tonight."

"Shame on you!" cried another voice- it was the little fennec, their one-time neighbor, emerging from the shadows. "I thought you all were all right, I thought you were on our side, but you've been feeding these monsters the flesh of other dogs-"

"We don't eat dogs!"

That had been Maha, her voice shrill with fear, and it made the crowd fall very silent. She shook with fear, looking all around, and licked her lips before she spoke again.

"We're dogs like you- really- and who would eat their own kind?"

There was another moment of complete silence. The stoplight cast flickering yellow across the raised fur on many backs.

"Kill all of them," said Sundu.

The crowd all rushed forward at once. Mhumhi saw Bii lay his ears back, his button eyes fearful, before he was suddenly overtaken by a pair of hissing cape foxes, darting forward to nip at Mhumhi's legs. Two snaps were all it took to send them back, but more were coming up on either side, snapping and lunging. Mhumhi kept his teeth bared and his body pressed against Maha, who was crying and clinging to him- Kutta had leapt around on the other side to defend Tareq, her eyes wide and her teeth bared. Ahead of them Biscuit whined and thrashed and spun around. Mhumhi smelled blood.

Sundu leapt down from the stoplight and ran directly at Mhumhi, mouth open, and Mhumhi barely had time to lay his ears back before Kutta leapt in front of him and engaged her, snarling, both rising to their hind legs in a flurry of snapping and yowling.

Mhumhi wanted to help her, feeling his heart pounding away with confusion and fear, but there were more sharp teeth in his injured leg, and with a yelp he whirled around and snapped at the dark-furred Pampas fox that was leaping away, catching her ear so that it tore through his teeth.

Tareq screamed. Mhumhi turned to see the little boy crouching with his arms over his head while the culpeo tore at the back of his neck.

Mhumhi reared up and caught the culpeo around the shoulders and tore him off, flinging him to the ground as the fox gave a surprised little scream. With an angry twitter Mhumhi lunged down at him again only to break off just as abruptly.

A sound had filled the air, a kind of moaning whoop.

The foxes either did not hear or did not understand the meaning; they continued surging forward, snapping and growling. In front of Mhumhi, Kutta and Sundu broke apart, the latter panting and bleeding profusely from the neck and muzzle- it seemed she'd come off the worse.

"What's that noise?" she asked. Kutta looked at Mhumhi, eyes wide.

Sundu yelped- Biscuit had come at her from behind, dragging her by the haunches with his huge jaws, and shoved her to the ground. There was blood covering his muzzle, and his pale eyes were sickeningly bright.

"Save the male!" he cried to Mhumhi. "Save the male, get him out of here, I'll cover your retreat! The female can be sacrificed-"

Maha gave a pained little cry- Mhumhi and Kutta exchanged a look and turned their backs on the domestic together, standing on either side of Maha and Tareq. Mhumhi pushed his shoulder against Maha.

"Do you think you can run?"

She bobbed her head, sniffling and sobbing- there were bite marks on her arms and legs. Mhumhi felt a warm fury building up inside of him, quashing his fear.

"Then when I give the word, you take Tareq's hand and head for the nearest house- we'll cover you-"

A fox screamed ahead of them. Mhumhi looked up and saw a hyena standing at the edge of the crowd with a limp body in its mouth.

"RUN, MAHA!"

Maha burst into a sprint, dragging Tareq behind her- the surprised foxes fell away, for most of them were staring at the hyena- the hyenas- more were coming out of the darkness, squealing, sniffing, dark eyes gleaming. The air was sodden with the scent of blood.

Kutta raced forward, catching them up- Mhumhi lunged after her with a snarl, shaking the culpeo's teeth out of his leg. They ran to the nearest building, a rack of apartments- Maha's hands fumbled at the door and she choked out a sob when the knob would not turn.

A few foxes had started to chase them, but many were scattering, whining and yelping with terror: the hyenas were moving through the crowd, almost leisurely, catching fox after fox in their teeth. Mhumhi did not dare stop long enough to count how many there were.

"Come on, Maha, down this way," he shouted, and Maha ran again, stumbling, dragging the howling Tareq as they turned together down an alleyway. Kutta leapt back and snapped at one of the sand foxes that was following them, making it spring away.

That seemed to be enough for the foxes, and they peeled away, tails tucked and panting fearfully. From behind them they could hear the sounds of the hyenas gibbering and laughing- ripping- tearing-

Kutta retched but did not stop moving, helping Mhumhi herd the terrified and sobbing children forward. They rounded the corner of the alley into a street lined with parked cars. Maha broke away from Tareq and ran to the nearest door to rattle the knob- it was locked.

"Come back!" shrieked Kutta, and Mhumhi whirled- a gray blur was streaking towards them around the opposite corner.

Mhumhi had a moment of frozen terror before he realized it could not be a hyena, for it was half his size- it was Sundu, snarling, bloody. From the streets behind her Mhumhi could hear heavy paws thudding on asphalt.

"Car, car!" Tareq shouted, and Mhumhi looked back at him for a split second, bewildered. But it seemed to spark something in Maha, for she turned around and grabbed at the door handle of the nearest car. The door opened.

"In here!" she shouted, and more shoved than helped Tareq inside. She climbed inside, then Kutta leapt after her, a cinnamon blur- Mhumhi was gaining, seeing Maha's reaching hand-

A hyena thumped loudly on the top of the car, squealing, and then launched itself at Mhumhi.

Mhumhi turned end over end with the heavy reeking body- he heard the car door slam and other hyenas gibbering behind him. The hyena had not yet bitten him, merely struggled against him and wafted its hot foul breath into his face and neck. He wrenched himself from underneath it and took off, trusting that somehow the car was secure, that he could lead the hyenas away-

I didn't want to die for them, he thought, heart pounding and thudding, and he knew anyway that his death here would be pointless,

it would not help them, yet he could not stop himself from running- *Follow me, follow me, don't hurt them-*

It had worked at least partially- heavy paws were thumping after him. He jumped as something again streaked by his side- Sundu. They exchanged a terrified glance, her with her eyes wide and fearful and blood smeared through her fur, certainly no longer enemies now, not when these monstrous beasts were chasing them.

They turned a corner, thumped over parked cars, scrambled through the gap between a lightpost and a brick wall-

Sundu suddenly gave an awful sound, a strangled choking gasp, and jerked backwards. Mhumhi could not stop himself from skidding to a halt, turning to fight the creature that had caught her- but there was nothing, nothing holding her- she was choking and thrashing against air-

The light from the lamp gleamed against the wire caught around her neck.

Mhumhi whimpered, because there came the hyenas, loping easily in their queer hunched posture, noses sniffing for Sundu's blood. Sundu had already stopped thrashing, her eyelids drooping. She slid downwards, trembling, held taut by the wire. Her eyes met Mhumhi's, wet and shining, and he realized that she had already given up.

There were two hyenas, grunting and yowling as they approached, sniffing and jerking back when she gave a straining twitch. One of them looked up and its black eyes met Mhumhi's.

Mhumhi turned and ran, wishing he could shut his ears, wishing for a hulker's dull hearing, wishing for anything, really, other than the reality that he was in.

He ran around the next corner and circled the block, heading back towards the car, now that the hyenas were no longer interested in following him.

When he returned he had to jerk to a stop, tongue hanging out as he gasped and panted. The car door was hanging open, the interior was empty, and he could smell blood.

Maha's distant scream made his sinking head fly up, eyes wide and ears pricked, and he ran in that direction, sprinting, muscles churning like they had never before.

He came down the street and saw her and Tareq being held by two hulkers, dragged by the arms, towards a large black car. In front of them there was a hyena, standing on top of Kutta's body.

Mhumhi gave a scream and lunged forward, catching the hyena's sloping flank with such force that they both spun around. The hyena squealed and giggled and ran a short distance away, head low and trembling. Mhumhi lowered his head over Kutta's, shaking.

Her head bumped painfully against his, for she had been trying to get up, and they both flinched.

"I'm all right- it couldn't bite me-"

He registered her words with both relief and confusion, and looked over at the hyena, which was cringing ahead of them. There was something solid covering its muzzle, rendering it biteless.

Someone spoke in an unfamiliar language, and Mhumhi realized it was one of the strange hulkers, the one gripping Maha around her chest. It raised an arm and pointed at him.

Maha was fighting her, thrashing and kicking and sobbing. "Let me go! Let me go! Mhumhi! Mhumhi!"

Mhumhi snarled as Kutta got to her feet beside him, and they advanced more slowly on the hulkers, hackles raised.

The one holding Tareq let him go and raised something- a metal thing Mhumhi had never seen before. Maha screamed and aimed a kick at her, shouting words in that strange liquid language. The metal thing went spinning away. The hulker cried out a string of sharp words and then grabbed something else- a sort of long pole that had been leaning against the wall.

Tareq had been huddling on the ground, eyes wide and fearful, but as the strange hulker raised the pole he rose and went in a stumbling dash towards Mhumhi and Kutta. Mhumhi ran forward at once, bracing himself to take the blow that now seemed to be aimed towards the puppy. He saw too late the shining loop hanging from the end of the pole.

Tareq's fingers touched him just as the loop tightened around his neck and he reared with a squeal, thrashing, accidentally knocking the Tareq over. Kutta cried out as Mhumhi continued to struggle, feeling terror rise up in him- the loop was tight around his neck, squeezing against his windpipe, and he had just seen Sundu die-

He was still connected to the hulker holding the pole, and he dragged it forward, making her stumble. He heard Kutta give a panicked cry, her head darting between everyone assembled- the hyena, the puppies, the strange hulkers, captive Mhumhi- before lunging at the hulker holding the pole.

The hulker aimed a kick at her and she fell back with a yelp. Mhumhi thrashed harder in response, struggling to move closer, but the pole held him away. He changed tack and bounced towards the other hulker, the one holding Maha; his captor shouted and dragged him backwards, upending him, making him fall on his back.

Maha was screaming now, alternating between two languages: "Stop it! Let him go! Let him go!"

The hulker holding her picked her up, even as she struggled, and threw her into the black car. She slammed the door and turned just in time to come face-to-face with Kutta, who had sprinted in a flash of teeth to leap at her throat.

The hulker got her arm in the way just in time, but it did not stop Kutta bearing her down with her weight. She shrieked.

The hyena, which everyone had mostly forgotten about, gave a whining squeal and bulled its bulk into Kutta, knocking her off the hulker, which whimpered and clutched at its bleeding arm.

The hulker holding Mhumhi at the end of the pole bellowed something and threw open the car door. The hyena leaped through it without hesitation, and Mhumhi, filled with brief terror for Maha, threw himself after it. He yanked the hulker forward as he entered the car, gasping through his constricted airway, claws scratching at the cloth seats. The hyena squealed and cringed away from him as far as it could.

There was a tremendously loud *slam* from behind him and Mhumhi turned, the pole now hanging unsupported from his neck, and realized he had been trapped.

"Mhumhi!" cried Maha, and he turned to see her curling her fingers through the links of a fencelike barrier that separated the two rows of seats. He and the hyena were on one side; she on the other.

The hyena was cringing and muzzled; no real danger, so he felt safe to turn and do his best to lick her fingers. The pole was braced against the door, preventing him from moving much further.

"Mhumhi, hurry, get closer," she was gasping. "I can pull it off- I can get it off-"

There were noises from outside, curiously muffled from within the enclosed car- he heard Kutta whistling and shrieking, the hulkers bellowing. He pressed his neck as close as he could against the fence so Maha could hook her fingers through the loop, then with a great tug pulled himself backwards and free of it.

The hyena uttered a little whine as he stumbled free, falling halfway down into the carpeted space below the seats, but did not move towards them.

Mhumhi leapt back up, sparing a brief sniff for the metal barrier separating himself and Maha- there looked to be no getting to her through it.

"The door, Mhumhi, open the door," Maha urged, crawling along alongside him as he moved. "The handle- you gotta lift it up."

He gave a wag of acknowledgement, glancing back towards the hyena to make sure it still hadn't moved. Then he bit at the thing that looked like a handle to him, sinking his teeth into the queer rubbery substance that coated it, and tugged backwards. It did not budge.

"No, Mhumhi, the plastic thing underneath that!"

"Oh," said Mhumhi, letting go. He saw what she meant- there was a handle in a little plastic square above the thing he'd been tugging on. He put his teeth to it, mashing his nose, but his teeth caught and the plastic handle started pulling forward.

It slipped out of his teeth, visibly marked, and snapped back into place without opening anything.

"Pull it harder!"

"What about *your* door?" he asked, pawing his sore nose.

"It's locked and it won't open," said Maha, clutching her fingers around the fence links, and he supposed that was a good enough excuse. With a growl he went back to the handle, pulling back and drooling from the effort. This time his teeth held, and there was a loud click.

"It's open!" cried Maha. Mhumhi reared to put his body weight on it, swinging it partially open. Through the window he saw a hulker whirl around, white eyes wide. It slammed itself back against the door, shutting it and sending him backwards into the hyena.

He twisted and the hyena squealed, squirming past him to press itself against the door. Mhumhi, seeing his opportunity, ran to the other side, where there were no hulkers. Maha crawled after him.

Before he could tamper with this door, though, the door on Maha's side of the fence opened and Tareq came tumbling inside, wailing loudly. Mhumhi spun around as the door slammed, and then the car creaked and wobbled- the other hulkers were getting inside in the very front.

Mhumhi felt a burst of fear, looking at Maha and Tareq unprotected in front of him. He reared and scratched at the fence, growling; he even bit it, but it was unyielding. The hulkers squeezed Maha and Tareq between them as they came in, the smaller of the two dragging Tareq onto her lap. The doors slammed shut again.

Maha was struggling between the two of them, but the one holding Tareq put a hand on her shoulder and said something in the hulker language, a long stream of incomprehensible syllables. Maha fell still.

"What did she say to you?" cried Mhumhi, slamming his paws against the chain-link. The strange hulkers both turned around to look at him, eyes wide.

"I don't know- I don't know-" Maha said, in half a sob. "She has such a strong accent- she says we'll all be hurt if we don't hold still!"

Mhumhi snarled and slammed against the barrier again; the hulkers exchanged a look. One of them did something to the car that suddenly made it growl back, the insides rumbling. Maha gave a little scream and covered her ears. Mhumhi fell back in surprise against the hyena again, which merely squirmed a little and looked up at him.

He pushed himself up, only to flinch- from outside there came a scratching and scrabbling at his window. Kutta, whining, was leaping and scratching at the glass from outside. He ran forward and put his paws against it, unable to suppress a whimper of his own. Then he stuck his head down to tug at the plastic handle again, growling from the effort, but through he pulled it back fully, the door would not open. The hulkers had done something to make it lock like the others.

Kutta whined and yelped, her voice muffled, and he gave a hoo-bark of his own. The car gave a jerk and he slammed forward into the barrier and fell down into the carpeted space again.

Kutta kept leaping at the window, whistling and whining, but by the time Mhumhi had got up again it was moving faster, the buildings outside crawling away with increasing speed. Kutta had to run to keep up, giving out guttural contact calls for him, even as he scratched at his window and whined for her.

Maha was squirming again, saying something in the liquid hulker language, but the hulkers did not respond, and the car moved faster and faster, and Kutta got further and further away behind them, and soon Mhumhi could not see her at all.

He turned and met Maha's eyes again, and they shared a moment of sheer terror: they were trapped in a vehicle with two strange hulkers and a live hyena, speeding towards the unknown.

END OF VOLUME ONE

About the Author

Lydia West is twenty-three and lives with three axolotls and a cat. She enjoys writing stories about mythology and the natural world, and spends a great deal of time researching animal behavior. The original serialized version of Darkeye, as well as other webnovels, short stories, and nonfiction articles on biology can be found at her website, koryoswrites.com.